DECALOG 2

LOST PROPERTY

TEN STORIES
SEVEN DOCTORS
NO FIXED ABODE

Edited by
Mark Stammers
&
Stephen James Walker

First published in Great Britain in 1995 by
Doctor Who Books
an imprint of Virgin Publishing Ltd
332 Ladbroke Grove
London W10 5AH

ISBN 0 426 20448 4

Cover illustration by Colin Howard

Typeset by Mark Stammers Design, SM5 4LY

Printed and bound in Great Britain by
Cox & Wyman Ltd, Reading Berks

CONTENTS

For David J. Howe
the third member of the
H.S.W. triumvirate

EDITORS' NOTE

Welcome to *Decalog 2* – our second collection of original *Doctor Who* short stories.

This is very much a case of 'back by popular demand'. The first *Decalog* has proved to be one of the biggest-selling titles in Virgin's extensive *Doctor Who* range, and has gained some extremely positive feedback from the general readership. Naturally this has been very gratifying for us personally. But more importantly it has also demonstrated the enormous appeal of the short story form, and the clear viability of a continuing series of *Decalog* collections.

In this second volume, we have departed slightly from the format of the first in that we have included no over-arching plot to link the ten stories together. Instead, we have chosen a common theme for the writers to explore: specifically, that of the various homes owned or otherwise acquired by the good Doctor during the course of his travels through time and space.

Decalog 2 does however resemble its predecessor in that each of the seven television Doctors is featured at least once, and that the ten stories cover a very wide range of different styles and genres. This emphasis on variety has been a conscious policy on our part, and one to which we have accorded a high priority. Not only does it serve as a reflection of the eclectic qualities of the TV series itself, but it also means that everyone who reads the book should find that it contains something that appeals to their own particular taste in fiction.

This is the last *Decalog* that we will be editing (at least for the time being), but we know that a number of other editors are keen to put together similar collections and feel it is only fair that they are given a chance to do so. We would like to take this opportunity to offer our thanks to everyone who has contributed to this book or to its predecessor – including those whose submissions, for one reason or another, we sadly weren't able to use – and also of course to Peter Darvill-Evans, Rebecca Levene and all their colleagues at Virgin.

Vortex of Fear

By Gareth Roberts

Brachinnen stirred. The sedative was wearing off. He sat up on the rumpled sheets of his bed, his joints aching, looked across the room – this infernal, unchanging room of his! – at the gilt-numbered clock over the mantel, and a nervous spasm rushed through his body.

The Doctor would arrive soon.

His head thick and aching unnaturally, his temples pounding, he leapt for the door. Ferrix had locked him in, as usual. Following a routine he had kept for what seemed an eternity, Brachinnen took a spare key from the top pocket of his pyjamas and unlocked the door. The click of the lock was a small reassurance. Opening the door was an event he had created, not a part of the original sequence. It was significant, proving that he at least retained a measure of independent will.

He stole out into the corridor, his bare feet taking comfort from the deep red carpet. A pair of voices rumbled from the upstairs apartments, the lounge. Kya and Leeth, it sounded like, going through their argument about the viability of land revenues in the Brere territories. Kya was winning. She did very little but win. There was another clock, tall and mirrored, before Brachinnen, showing him as gaunt, crop-haired and clean-shaven, his eyes bulging with terror, the picture of a lunatic. But the time was right, corresponding within a few minutes to the clock back in his room, so the shift was minimal at the moment.

At the moment. Brachinnen ran his tongue around his drug-dried mouth, thirsting for the certainty of the concept. At the moment.

He took his eyes off the clock face for an instant. When he looked back it had lost fifteen minutes. Damn, that meant–

'We all think it'd be much better if you stayed in bed.' Ferrix, the light from the chandelier shining on his shaking bald head, stood at the far end of the corridor. 'We've been talking, and we're all concerned.'

'I'm your friend and I've done you many favours in the past, and so you're particularly worried,' Brachinnen muttered bitterly, preparing to run. He knew the pattern.

Ferrix's brow twitched. 'Yes. That's what I mean to say. There's no need to take that tone.' He raised the sedative pad and came closer. 'Let's get you back to bed, yes?'

Brachinnen looked again at the clock. Fifteen minutes, swallowed back. There was no point in running now; the Doctor wasn't due for another hour. He shuddered. Sometimes (sometimes, another of those distinct and much-missed concepts) he wondered if the shift had intelligence and, more specifically, if it knew about him. Every now and again, it offered him a chance to get out, to escape, just a peek through the blue wooden door of the TARDIS. But it forever crushed him by keeping him back, pushing him away. Not letting him reach the Doctor. Slamming the door in his face. It worked in shadows, changing the clocks when unobserved. Memory was not as it was, more a splintered grey haze than anything now, but he seemed to recall sitting for hours once before one of the clocks, hardly daring to blink. The second he took his gaze away, the shift played its trick. Swallowed a minute. So, was his enemy a thinking thing? No. His real enemy was giving up.

'Let's get you back to bed,' Ferrix said again, advancing with the pad outstretched.

Brachinnen reviewed his options. Run, hide, resist. Or sleep. More beautiful sleep. The shift couldn't reach him in his dreams. Yes, the real enemy was giving up, but he was so tired.

'There we are.'

As Ferrix settled the bristled side of the pad on his forearm, and the sedative sent the corridor spinning, Brachinnen heard his own sobs, pathetic as a wounded puppy's

* * *

Kya removed the long cigarette holder from her lips and blew a funnel of blue smoke around the lounge. 'It's ridiculous to complain about disputed land rights if one of your own companies is buying development stocks.' She kept her voice level, although her heart was raging at the stupidity of the man. 'You either support independent arbitration of claims or you don't.'

Knightsir Leeth settled his brandy balloon on the bar and smoothed his iron-grey hair with one long finger. 'My dear,' he replied, in the patronizing tone of the gentry, 'that's precisely my point. In law as it stands, I'd lose my position as a major stockholder if I followed my own principles.'

'That means you're actively competing against several of your own interests.'

'What's the alternative?'

'Oh, there is one, but you're too stubborn to admit it. Stop buying up stocks in Brere, show a bit of moral indignation, get the House on your side.'

'I'd look a fool.'

Kya smiled. 'Better than a hypocrite, darling.' She sat back in the wing-backed chair nearest to the fire and stretched, indicating her unwillingness to continue on this subject. 'Oh, how long now?'

'Four hours exactly.' He sat opposite her, cradling his head in his hands. Fool or hypocrite? Fool, decided Kya. And in four hours he'd know just how much of a fool. 'Tell me,' he said, 'what'll be the first thing you do, when you get back?'

She had to bite her tongue. It would be very satisfying to tell him the truth, but there was only four hours in it. Much better to see his face on tomorrow's news bulletins. That was almost worth spending a year in suspension with him for. 'After I've complained to the Agency, I'll rush round to see my children. They are so important to me.'

'More important than your businesses?'

She glared at him. 'I trust my deputies. My businesses are in the safest hands.' Lies, naturally. She was itching to get back. Her eyes longed to settle on a set of accounts.

Ferrix entered the lounge, massaging his chin with worry. He nodded to Kya and addressed Leeth. 'I found Brachinnen wandering about.'

Leeth sighed. 'You were supposed to lock his door.'

'I did. I'm sure I did. But I've given him another dose and sent him back to bed.' He poured himself a drink. 'I really don't understand all this. First Kandol, now Brachinnen. It must be the effect of being shut up here, in this damned box. A good thing we're going back today.'

Kya stood and placed a hand on his trembling arm. 'You need to rest.'

He smiled weakly. 'How can I? We've been cut off for seven months. What am I going to find when we get back?'

Kya grimaced. They had been through this what felt to her like a thousand times. Ironically, she thought, Ferrix probably had the least to worry about on this score. 'A caffeine production empire valued at sixty-five billion, I'd say.' She tried to sound confident, for his sake. There was something about Ferrix she liked. He was absolutely no threat.

'But my deputy, Horril.' He took tiny sips of his drink. 'I've barely slept the last couple of nights. I can't help but wonder if the communicator failure is down to him. It'd give him the opportunity he's waited for. He's always wanted me out of the way, you see. Always tried to undermine me. Oh, there's been nothing you could point to, no hard evidence, but my instincts warn me. I can almost see him now, sitting behind my desk, giving orders to my secretary. Flirting with my wife, damn him.' He raised the glass to his thick lips with a shaking hand, trickles of gin running over his chin.

'Relax, old man,' said Leeth, pointing to one of the couches. 'In four hours you'll be back and nothing will have changed. We'll all be much the same, just a couple of billion wealthier.' Kya smirked inwardly at his words.

'A lot can happen in a year, you know,' Ferrix replied, settling down.

'Remember, this is my third time in suspension,' said Kya. 'I know how you feel, and the last few hours are always the worst. Whatever the circumstances.' She crossed to the door. 'It's getting quite stuffy in here, with one thing and another. I'm going to lie down in my room.'

It was in Zoe's nature to investigate, to understand and to catalogue things. Her curiosity was strictly scientific in its methods, and her previous post as astrophysicist-in-residence to a space station had lent a pleasing sense of order to her life. There was so much about the universe still to be discovered, and it had thrilled her to be literally right out on the frontier. Since joining the Doctor and Jamie aboard the TARDIS, and taking active part in a series of adventures that gave her little time to stop and think, that security had been overturned. It frustrated her that the Doctor, a man she had come to trust with her life, was so chronically vague. Here was somebody who knew the answers to most of the riddles of all time and space, as far as she could tell, but was totally disorganized. His approach to the problems he faced, from the erratic behaviour of the TARDIS to an invasion by Ice Warriors, was often blind panic, and it was very difficult to pin him down on anything. He was secretive to a fault. Now, as she watched him flicking hesitantly at levers and knobs on the overheated TARDIS console, his hand wrapped in one of his coat-tails, she decided that this was as good a time as any to clear up some of her worries.

She pointed to the panel he'd been working on. 'These controls are for space-time orientation, aren't they?'

'Eh?' He looked over briefly. 'No, no, Zoe. Those are the guidance regulators.'

'Last week you said they were space-time orientation controls.' She flicked one of the switches to get his attention. Nothing happened.

He scurried round the console and slapped her lightly on the wrist. 'Now, please don't touch, my dear. The TARDIS isn't safe in unskilled hands.'

Zoe bristled. 'I'm perfectly skilled, thank you, Doctor.' She waited a second, then asked, 'At the moment, we're travelling through the space-time dimension, aren't we?'

The Doctor hesitated before replying, forming his grubby, chemical-stained fingers into a steeple shape. 'Well, yes. Well, no. Well, not exactly. It doesn't have dimensions as such. It's more of a... Well, it's more of a vortex, really. It's all rather compli-oh.' He noticed a flashing light on the console and hurried to attend to it.

Zoe looked up at the scanner screen. When the TARDIS was in flight, the screen displayed a dizzying array of symmetrical blue patterns, the visual representation of this vortex through which they were flying. It fascinated Zoe, although both Jamie and the Doctor had advised her not to look at it for too long. A place, if indeed it was, that she could see with her eyes but couldn't begin to rationalize scientifically. It unnerved her. Sometimes she fancied she could almost see the Doctor's face being formed in the pattern. It prompted her to ask another question, in a roundabout sort of way. Fight vagueness with vagueness.

'Doctor. This space-time vortex. I suppose you might call it your home. I mean, you must have travelled though it so many times.'

He finished at the console and joined her beneath the screen. 'Not really, Zoe. The vortex is a most unfriendly place. It would be very foolish to make your home out there, I can tell you.'

As he spoke, Jamie entered the control room through the inner door, pulling a grey sweater over his head and yawning. 'The Doctor's right enough about that.' He pointed with his thumb to the large pair of exit doors. 'It's like the worst storm you can think of. It could tear you to pieces.'

Zoe gasped as she realized the implication of Jamie's words.

'The doors opened while the TARDIS was in flight?'

'Aye, well, it's a long story. But you can take it from me, Zoe, you don't want to go poking your wee nose out there.'

Zoe's curiosity remained unsated. 'Then how is the TARDIS protected?'

The Doctor busied himself with the controls, where the light had started to flash again. He spoke in that infuriatingly off-hand way of his. 'Well, it's really very simple. The TARDIS has shields to protect it from the time winds, Zoe.'

'Time winds? I assume that's scientific romanticism. How can time have winds?'

'If you'd felt them, lassie,' said Jamie, 'you wouldn't be asking.'

The Doctor waved an agitated hand in their direction. 'Hush, you two. I'm picking up some very odd readings. Vibrations? Surely not.'

Zoe and Jamie exchanged an anxious glance. The ever-present hum of the TARDIS's systems rose in pitch. 'What's the matter, Doctor?' asked Zoe.

The Doctor twisted a lever. 'The anti-collision control, it isn't working!' he howled childishly.

'Collision!' exclaimed Zoe. The TARDIS began to shake alarmingly from side to side.

The Doctor wrestled with the lever. 'The blessed thing's stuck! Hasn't been used in centuries!'

Jamie came closer. 'Give it a big pull, Doctor.'

'That's what I'm trying to do!' He shook with the effort, then stepped back, mopping his brow with his spotted hanky. 'It's no good. You try, Jamie.'

Zoe watched as Jamie, triceps bulging, struggled to turn the lever. The TARDIS lurched, throwing the Doctor to the floor.

The lever came off in Jamie's hand.

'Oh no!' cried the Doctor, clambering up. 'We'll crash for sure, unless I can. . .' He scratched his head. 'Unless. . . oh dear.'

Zoe lost her balance as the TARDIS rocked. 'Think of something, Doctor!'

He tapped his head, as if dislodging chunks of information. 'Oh flip! Of course! A materialization flip-flop!' He dashed back to the console and set to work.

'Aye, well why didn't you think of that sooner,' Jamie mumbled sarcastically, throwing away the lever.

The metallic clang as it struck the wooden chest in the corner was the last thing Zoe heard before she was overcome by the vibration.

She woke to find the Doctor slapping her cheek gently. 'Wake up, Zoe. You're quite safe. Everything's going to be all right.' Typically, he didn't sound at all confident.

'Oh, my head.' She reached up to find a painful lump on her brow. 'I must have fallen. What happened, Doctor?'

'It's quite fascinating, actually. The TARDIS was about to collide with. . . er, with something, but following emergency procedure, I was able to flip us inside.' He mimed an acrobat's loop with his index fingers.

Zoe sat up and gave him a look she hoped would fully express her worries. 'Inside what?'

'Er. . . something.'

'Not another TARDIS?'

It was Jamie who replied. 'Well, if it is, it's a sight dandier than this one.'

Zoe got to her feet and joined him below the scanner screen, which showed a landing in what looked like a house from an old country estate. Ornately framed pictures were tastefully arranged along the walls, there was a plush carpet all along the landing and a crystal chandelier clung to the ceiling like an upturned spider. The impression of opulence was almost too studied to be real. 'It must be some sort of an illusion.'

'Not according to the sensors,' the Doctor said. 'Whatever's out there is real enough. But no, it isn't another TARDIS. It's something far less sophisticated. In fact, I don't think it's designed to travel at all.' He chewed on a dirty thumbnail. 'It really shouldn't be here. It's appallingly primitive.'

There was a note of interest in his voice that Zoe recognized. 'Are we going to take a look?'

Jamie shook his head. 'Oh no. I say we clear off now. This thing has caused enough bother.'

'It could cause a great deal more,' the Doctor said worriedly. 'I think it'd be best to check. Open the doors, Zoe.'

The nearest of the ornately framed pictures depicted a crowded city street. Zoe was almost convinced of its authenticity until she noticed stress lines in the corners. 'This is a computerized image. Far more advanced than it looks, this place.'

'Hmm.' The Doctor stopped to examine a small wooden table positioned halfway along the hall. 'Second Empire, I'd say. All these frills, this sumptuousness. Decadence.'

'Which Second Empire?'

'Oh, a long way in your future, Zoe. A great civilization that flourished from a small Earth colony at the far edge of the galaxy.' He frowned and looked about. 'I had no idea that their technology had progressed to this level.'

Jamie, despite his earlier protests, was sneaking through a side door. 'Be careful, Jamie,' the Doctor called after him.

'I've noticed something strange, Doctor,' said Zoe. 'There are no windows.' She shivered. The silence around them was total. 'It feels very odd. Dead. Who could want to live here?'

Kya threw her book aside and slumped down into the cushioned comfort of her chair. She checked her watch. Only three hours now before the return. Her movements back on Dephys had been planned to the most minor detail. First, she would slip out from the vortex port, after registering her complaints; then a cab to her accountant's; lunch at Gruyère's on Whitborough Street, in perfect solitude; only then she'd call her children. They were grown now, but the pain of missing them still sat in her throat like an undissolved pill. It occurred to her that she might get back and find she was a grandparent! Thoughts danced through her mind, making it impossible for her to relax.

She went through into the communal food area to dial herself a snack and a coffee, and saw him. After so long, the sight of an unfamiliar face made her jump. Hastily she recovered. 'You've taken long enough!' she shrieked at him. 'We lost contact seven months ago.'

He stared back suspiciously. Kya was almost too angry to reason, but it occurred to her that there was something odd about the newcomer. He was not much more than a boy, twenty at most, and whereas most Agency employees were humble to the point of superciliousness, this fellow, who from his low brow and rough hands had to be a technician, stared at her with a friendly but uncivilized expression which was positively plebeian. Oddest of all were his clothes. He was wearing a kind of check-patterned skirt. The habits of the lower classes baffled Kya. In the main she tried not to notice them.

'The communicator failed,' she continued. 'It's part of our contract that a breach in the vortex can be made to replace or repair any faulty component. Do you realize what it's been like in here for the last seven months? Kandol went crazy, threw himself through the disposal chute. Brachinnen's out of his mind too. Leeth and Ferrix are halfway there.' The sentences poured out. 'We sent the emergency signal.' She found she was jabbing a finger at him. 'Where were you?'

He shrugged insolently. 'I'm sorry, but I don't know what you're talking about.'

'Oh, hell!' She pointed upstairs. 'When you're ready, we're up there. Get us a line-out and make it quick.' She pushed past him, taking satisfaction only from the prospect of the case she was going to bring against the Agency. She enjoyed legal battles, and enjoyed winning them even more.

Brachinnen stirred. The sedative was wearing off. He sat up on his rumpled sheets, his joints aching, and focused his blood-shot eyes on the gilt-numbered clock on the far wall of the room, this infernal and unchanging room of his.

Another chance. The Doctor would be here soon, might have arrived already.

He tried the door. Locked, of course. But Ferrix didn't know about the spare key.

Leeth poured himself a whisky. Alone in the lounge, he studied himself in the mirror. A wasted year. A calculated saving of two billion in liability for revenues. Was it worth a year in here, seven months of it in isolation? In the last few weeks he'd tried to remain calm, employing boardroom tactics to reassure the others. A strong leader encourages respect and confidence. The problem was Kya, who took every chance to undermine him. He thought he'd detected a secret smugness behind her smile, as if she was concealing something from him. It wasn't important. Even if she suspected him over Kandol, she couldn't have proof.

She came into the lounge. 'Where is Ferrix?'

Without turning he replied, 'He's with Brachinnen.' He pushed a finger backwards through his hair. 'We thought it best to lock Brachinnen in until the line-out opens. None of us can help him.'

'It should have been done days ago.' She took a cigarette from an open packet on the table, lit it and inserted it in her long marcasite holder. 'The Agency are squarely liable, of course. Brachinnen's people will clean them out.'

'Along with your people, and my people.'

'Exactly.' She sat. 'And when the dust of all that litigation has settled, I doubt if there'll be an Agency for anybody else to sue.'

'Although their equipment will remain intact. They'll probably be desperate enough to sell it off at a ridiculous price.'

Kya's heavily mascaraed eyelashes fluttered and she tapped

the ash from her cigarette. 'Do you know, darling, I hadn't thought of that.'

Leeth sat opposite her. 'But you're always thinking ahead. Your land in Brere–'

'Was acquired legally,' she said, raising her voice. 'Your moral objections to my developments there are based solely on malice and envy.'

Leeth tried to remain calm. 'That's nonsense.'

'Is it? Why the sudden scruples, then? And the most stupid thing of all is that you have plots in Brere yourself!'

'The market forced me to buy in Brere.'

Kya snorted. 'Oh, good God. We've been through this a hundred times, dear.'

The argument continued.

The Doctor rattled the handle of a door at the end of the landing, shrugged to Zoe and took the sonic screwdriver from his pocket. As he applied it to the lock, he told her, 'Now while this looks like an ordinary lock, it's actually activated by electronic means.'

Zoe had been examining an antique hat stand in a corner. She reached up and unhooked a jewelled headpiece plumed with feathers which could almost have been a crown. 'I wonder what happened to the people here? Whoever they were, they lived in luxury. These stones must be priceless.'

The Doctor nodded. 'Quite. Although I wonder if this place is as deserted as it appears.' An inner mechanism of the electronic lock clicked and the door swung open. 'There we are.'

'Zoe, Doctor!' Jamie's voice stopped them from going through. He stepped into the hallway from the other door, shaking his head. 'I've just seen somebody. A woman.'

'So there *are* people here,' said Zoe.

'Er, not necessarily,' said the Doctor, a worried look creasing his heavily lined features. Zoe got the impression that his vagueness in this instance was a cover for something he didn't care to reveal. 'Jamie, tell me exactly what you saw.'

'Well, like I said, a woman. More of a lady, really, all in finery. She was shouting at me, about something called the Agency.'

The Doctor tapped a grubby finger against his chin. 'And you're sure she saw you and talked directly to you?'

'Of course I'm sure. Hey!' He took the headpiece from Zoe's hands. 'She was wearing something just like this.'

'Really?' The Doctor looked past Zoe to the TARDIS and shook his head; a small but decisive movement. 'I suppose we'd better have a look round, just to be certain. But I really don't care for this place at all.' He stepped through the door he had opened.

'Do you know what he's talking about?' Jamie asked Zoe.

'I don't even think that he does,' she replied.

They followed the Doctor.

Avoiding Ferrix was easy, thought Brachinnen. Avoiding the shift was impossible. Twice on his journey from his room, he'd found himself back there and had to start again. The headache was getting worse. Painkillers, he knew, had little effect. The shift was everywhere, and just one jump forward or back could bring the agony surging back.

He heard Zoe's voice, chirpy and girlish, followed by a gruff reply that could have been only from Jamie. They were near. Just through the storage area.

Brachinnen raced through the landing of the rest quarters, slammed through the empty storage area, noted the broken lock of the far door, a victim of that special screwdriver the Doctor carried, and stepped through into the landing of the eastern annexe.

No TARDIS. A square indentation in the carpet where it had stood. The echo of its roaring engines all that remained. He'd missed them again. The shift had won again.

He collapsed weeping, pounding his fists frenziedly on the

sides of his head, whimpering, screaming for release, for death. Through gathering tears he caught a glimpse of blue.

The TARDIS was next to him. The shift had erred, given it back. Brachinnen staggered to his feet and pounded on the door. Perhaps this was earlier. Perhaps the Doctor, Jamie and Zoe were still inside. He called out their names in a cracked voice, begged them for mercy, closed his eyes – and he was back in bed. He stirred. The sedative was wearing off. He sat up on his rumpled sheets, still in that infernal, unchanging room of his, joints aching. He checked the gilt-numbered clock and fumbled for the spare key in the top pocket of his pyjamas.

Beyond the doorway was a large dark room. Stacks of crates were arranged in neat rows on either side. Zoe took a closer look at the nearest crate; its side was embossed with a line of serial numbers and a corporate design depicting a hunting bird in flight and a clock face. Jamie stepped forward and attempted to prise off the lid, but for the second time his strength failed him. 'It's no good, Doctor, you'll have to use your screwdriver.'

'Nonsense, Jamie.' Zoe pressed a button on the corner of the crate and the lid opened smoothly. Inside were stored plastic packets containing a powder of some kind. 'Concentrated foodstuffs, aren't they?'

The Doctor nodded, peeling open the corner of one of the packets. He gave the contents a suspicious sniff, as if he half-expected it to blow up in his face. 'Chicken korma,' he pronounced at last. 'Simply add water.'

Zoe had opened another crate and found it empty. 'There must be enough food in here to sustain, say, eight people for eight months. But who would want to spend that amount of time suspended in the space-time vortex?'

'The Agency?' Jamie suggested unhelpfully, wetting his finger and dabbing some of the food powder on his tongue. 'D'you know, this isn't half bad. Better than your food machine, eh, Doctor?'

'The Agency.' The Doctor pointed to the design embossed on the crates. 'This lady you saw, Jamie. You say she was shouting at you?'

'Aye. She said it'd been seven months since the communicator failed, and why had I taken so long, or something. She said that people were going mad, somebody had died.'

'Really? It's no wonder, I suppose.'

'Now, Doctor, if you know something about all this, it's only fair that you tell us.'

Zoe's attention was attracted by something that looked like an old- fashioned paper magazine lying open on top of one of the crates. She picked it up and flicked through the pages quickly, committing each to her memory. Her ability to memorize scrolls of data at incredible speeds was a legacy of her training at the Earth school of parapsychology. Some of her peers aboard the Wheel had disapproved of the school's methods, and Zoe felt sometimes that something in her had been damaged by the lengthy sessions of brain electro-stimulation.

'Doctor, Jamie. I think I can answer your questions now.' She held up the magazine. 'This is the Agency's brochure.'

The Doctor took it and studied the opening pages. 'Oh dear! This is exactly the sort of silly business I had feared.'

Zoe nodded. 'It doesn't seem very safe, does it?'

'Will one of you tell me what's going on?' asked Jamie. 'I'm not daft, but I wouldn't mind a few facts now and again.'

'This is a kind of hotel, Jamie,' said the Doctor. 'A luxury hotel for very rich people, who wish to spend a year away from home in the space-time vortex.'

Jamie scratched his head. 'But why? It's a gloomy place, for sure.'

'They come from the Earth colony on the planet Dephys 49,' Zoe explained patiently. 'The legal code on Dephys allows people to avoid paying revenues to the state only if they spend a twelve- month period outside legal jurisdiction. Before the law was tightened up, that meant they could spend a year in space, or outside the planet's influence.'

'But now,' the Doctor took up the story, reading from the brochure, ' "It is possible to avoid revenue collection only by spending a year in suspension in the space-time vortex. At our luxury seven-star auto-hotel." ' He closed the brochure and raised a hand to his troubled brow. 'They seem to have worked out how to get into the vortex, but not how to navigate it.' He looked about the room. 'This hotel of theirs is in a stable zone of the vortex, protected by shields similar to the TARDIS's, although far inferior.'

'If it's worse than the TARDIS,' grumbled Jamie, hooking his fingers into his belt, 'then we really should clear out straight away.'

But the Doctor was already working on the far door with the sonic screwdriver. 'Feel free to return to the TARDIS, both of you, if you want. But I must find someone here and explain the dangers. If necessary, I'll shut the whole thing down with my own hands. Mucking about with the vortex could lead to all sorts of trouble.'

'All right then,' said Jamie, turning back.

Zoe grabbed his arm. 'Don't be silly! Of course we'll come with you, Doctor.'

Leeth kept his eyes on his book, forcing down the temptation to look up at the clock. Each page was a struggle, as his mind was fixed on the time, estimating how long it would take before the line-out opened. He longed for the crowds of Whitborough Street: the smells from the commoners' market which drifted over the low crenellated rooftops of the elite quarter; the sound of masses of booted feet; the cries of traders. In just a couple of hours now he'd be there, away from Kya and her pettiness, away from Ferrix and his nervous twitches, away from Brachinnen's ramblings. Away from the memory of what he'd done to Kandol. The wonder of drawing breath from natural air, the simple marvel of a cold breeze brushing his face, eating a meal prepared by human hands. He would never take a pleasure for granted again. It would be winter on Dephys. Perhaps there'd even be snow, children skating in the town square.

Ferrix shifted position in the chair opposite, then sat upright. He moved to the door and pressed his ear to the frame. 'I can hear voices, from the stairwell.'

'Kya cursing me, I imagine.' Leeth turned a page he hadn't read, to demonstrate his self-control.

'No, I don't recognize them.' Ferrix's bald head glistened with perspiration. 'Men, two of them. It must be the team from the Agency: Mr Illifant and his junior. They've come!'

Leeth listened. 'I dare say.' He put his book to one side. 'There; I told you there was nothing whatever to worry about. The line-out's open, we're going home. Now, for goodness' sakes, man, sit back down. Don't let them know you're rattled.'

Ferrix smiled for the first time in months. 'You're right.' He returned to his seat. 'Although I won't feel safe until I set foot back on Dephys. Get back to my club. They're keeping my chair, you see.'

The voices came closer, the door opened.

Leeth leapt up at the sight of the newcomers. Whoever they were, they were not from the Agency. The first to step through was a small and shabby individual dressed in a dirty black coat of unfashionable cut and a pair of baggy checked trousers. His face was deeply lined and there was an aura of worried authority about him. Leeth felt he was in the presence of a small piece of destiny, as though this scruffy figure was actually somebody very important. The man's colleague was very different, though. A lad dressed in some kind of primitive tribal skirt.

'Ah, hello,' the small man said, waving hesitantly.

Ferrix slapped the palm of his hand on the table. He spoke confidently, the assurance that had built his caffeine production empire returning. 'At last! What the blazes have you been doing back there for the last seven months? You're liable, you realize?'

The lad stepped forward aggressively. 'Listen, I've already taken enough of your insults,' he said in a heavily accented voice. 'We're not from your blessed Agency.'

'What?'

The little man nodded. 'Yes, I'm afraid Jamie's right. You misunderstand. We are not from the Agency.'

Leeth instinctively felt that this was true. 'Then how the hell did you get in here? And who are you?'

The little stranger extended a hand politely. 'I'm the Doctor, my young friend here is Jamie. We're travellers in the space-time vortex.' He chuckled. 'Do you know, it's almost a relief to meet somebody who'll understand that. Yes, well, we were passing and we thought we'd take a look at your' – his eyes travelled around the room, not missing a detail – 'residence. I say, you do very well for yourselves, don't you?' He picked a fruit from the bowl and sniffed it.

Ferrix slumped back in his chair, his face turning a ghastly white. Leeth felt his own level of panic rising. 'How in God's name did you get in here? This place is protected, we were told.'

'I'll destroy the Agency for this,' said Ferrix. 'The incompetence. . .'

'I have my own craft,' the Doctor replied, taking a bite of the apple. 'Perhaps your protection isn't as good as you thought it was.'

The lad Jamie added, 'We just arrived, in the TARDIS. One box inside another.'

Leeth's mind was racing, but his motivating instinct triumphed. 'We were guaranteed that this place was totally secure.' He tapped his wristwatch. 'We're going back to Dephys in another hour. I want you to come with me. The scientists at my factories will be very interested in your craft. I'll make you a good offer.'

'I don't believe it.' Ferrix cradled his head in his hands.

'We're invaded, some fellow just walks in here, and you're thinking of money.' He got up and paced the lounge, wringing his hands. 'They must open the line soon, get me out of this madhouse. I have to get back to Dephys.' He looked between Leeth and the strangers and snarled. 'I wouldn't be surprised if this is all some plot.'

'It isn't,' the Doctor said firmly. He turned to face Leeth. 'Thank you for your offer, but I'm afraid that the TARDIS isn't for sale. And I wonder if you really are going back to Dephys, any of you.'

'What do you mean?'

Before the Doctor could reply, Kya entered the lounge. She froze at the sight of the strangers, then gave a tight little smile. 'Ah. You're here at last, then.' She cast her glance over the newcomers' clothing and general untidiness. 'My, the Agency's standards have slipped.'

Jamie sighed. 'Look, I've told you, we're not from your precious Agency.'

'You certainly haven't. I don't believe we've met.' She turned to Leeth. 'Aren't you going to introduce me, then?'

'But I spoke to you!' Jamie insisted.

'No, you didn't,' Kya, with an irritated frown, replied.

As soon as he and Jamie had entered the room at the top of the stairs and found it occupied, the Doctor had signalled to Zoe to keep out of sight. She had listened at the door for a few moments, until she had heard the sound of footsteps ascending the carpeted steps. Thinking quickly, she had concealed herself behind a large hook-nosed bust and watched the newcomer – obviously the woman encountered downstairs by Jamie – swagger by. She had remained in hiding until the woman had gone through into the room, then decided to return to the TARDIS and wait there for the Doctor and Jamie. Probably her safest bet.

One gift of augmentation that Zoe treasured was her sense

of direction. From the age of four, her memory had been tightened up in a series of rigorous daily tests at which she had excelled. As she had grown, she had become a little shy of demonstrating this power; it agitated people to be corrected all the time. Logically that made no sense. Any resource should be valued. But there was enough humanity left in Zoe to see how her attempts to help could be misconstrued, and since she had started travelling in the TARDIS her qualms on this score had lessened. Both the Doctor and Jamie were inclined to get themselves hopelessly lost, and her ability to retrace their route through corridors had been much appreciated.

With total confidence in herself, Zoe slipped quietly down the staircase, around the corner, along the hallway, through the door that led to the storeroom, and –

The storeroom wasn't there.

She hadn't made a mistake, she couldn't have made a mistake. The door at the end of the hallway at the foot of the stairs led to the storeroom, from which another door led to the downstairs landing and the TARDIS. It was simple enough, she couldn't have taken a wrong turning. But now, beyond the door that had led to the storeroom was another, unfamiliar, room, much darker and smaller than the others. Although decorated in the same opulent style, it also seemed somehow older and less frequented. Zoe felt that she was disturbing something, as if this was the room of an invisible man. Her eyes swivelled nervously, peering into every dark corner, checking the door through which she had entered, which was not the same one she had pushed open at the end of the hallway. She shivered, inwardly chastising herself for such illogical behaviour. Everything could be explained rationally. Perhaps there was a mechanism that switched the rooms around. That could make sense, and might account for the queasy feeling rising in her stomach. And of course, there was nobody here. There couldn't be. She was alone.

Alone in a dark, grey, silent room. Surely there had never

been such a silence, a stillness as dense.

The sound, when it came, made her jump. A high-pitched sound; distant, but surely on this floor; several doors away. There was something urgent about this sound, something desperate, scared. It was a cry, repeated again and again, the ghostly voice of a child, a crying child. The words were indistinct. The voice seemed to be familiar, to have something familiar about it, a familiar thing distorted.

She gasped.

It was her own voice, calling desperately.

'Doctor! Jamie! Oh, Doctor, Jamie, help me!'

Terrified, her stomach churning and her mouth dry, Zoe wrenched open the door and hurtled out of the small dark grey room. Outside was another unfamiliar area, a narrow grey tunnel with walls of metal. It was almost pitch black here. She turned to retreat, back to the other room, but the door had gone, swallowed up by the blackness, and her flailing arms scissored helplessly through empty air.

Silence again. The voice, her voice, had stopped calling. She shivered and rubbed her bare arms, feeling the goose bumps. She was starting to panic – the least sensible thing to do. She forced herself to take deep breaths and steadied herself against the nearest wall. There was no point in worrying. There had to be an answer.

The wall vibrated against her hand. So, behind the wall was some piece of machinery. Curiously, her eyes adjusting to the dark, Zoe inched forward, testing each step she took. Her foot nudged something. She crouched down, put out a hand to examine her find. She felt something soft, in tufted strands. A length of carpet, probably.

The tips of her fingers brushed something cold and round.

Her pulses thudded against her skull.

The cold thing was an ear.

She shrieked and leapt up. It was several seconds before she calmed herself. Her inquiring nature reasserted itself, and she crouched back down, cradled the head. Bristles and jowls, a faint whiff of alcohol. Crusted blood about the nose, a fist-sized bump on the back of the head. Killed only minutes before, she estimated.

So where was the killer?

As if in answer to the thought, footsteps sounded in the dark up ahead. Zoe backed away nimbly, thanking fortune for the soft- soled plimsolls she had taken to wearing.

The footsteps came closer, loud, booted. Somebody with no desire to conceal himself.

Zoe searched behind herself for some way out. There was none.

A small point of light glowed up ahead, the footsteps stopped. The glow from a lantern held in the hand of the newcomer revealed his face; fierce dark brown pupils, a mighty nose, iron-grey hair. Grunting to himself in the way people will if they believe themselves unobserved, he settled the lantern on a ledge and hooked his arms under those of the body. He hefted the lifeless thing around until its gruesomely lolling head faced the wall. The wall slid apart automatically, and Zoe heard machinery. A kind of grinding, chomping. A waste disposal unit.

The limp body was lifted up and pushed through, its sightless eyes flashing in the lantern's beam for a ghastly second before it tumbled out of sight. The grinding and chomping increased in ferocity for a few seconds, then returned to its usual level.

The killer listened, grunted his approval, and muttered, 'You'll not take up those leases, Kandol.'

He picked up the lantern and wiped away droplets of perspiration that glistened between his nose and mouth. Then he started walking forward.

Directly towards Zoe.

She flattened herself against the wall, closed her eyes as the measured tread of his booted feet came closer, each thud like a nail being hammered into a coffin lid, wished herself away;

anywhere but this, anywhere–

Without warning, the footsteps stopped. No, Zoe decided, that wasn't quite what had happened. The footsteps had disappeared, the sound clipped off abruptly as if silenced by a stop button on a disc player. Simultaneously, through her eyelids, she became aware of a change in light quality.

She opened her eyes, to find that she was back in the small, silent grey room, pressed up against the door. And she was alone.

Desperately, she turned and pulled at the door handle.

The door was locked.

A wave of nausea surged up from her stomach, filling her mouth with bile. Her head span, a knife-sharp pain jabbed repeatedly between her eyes. Her knees quivered and, losing control, she started to sob as she kicked and pummelled at the locked door like a spoilt child exiled to her room.

'Doctor! Jamie! Oh, Doctor, Jamie, help me!'

Jamie hadn't taken to the powdered, pomaded layabouts that inhabited this hotel place. They had the mark of the gentry on their smooth white hands and large paunches. It amused him to see the Doctor baffling them as he hopped from one foot to the other, his eyebrows folded down with customary worry.

'Now, really, I must have a look at the mechanisms you used to get yourselves here,' he said, addressing the alarmed nobles. 'Which one of you is the technician?' There was silence as the three dandies looked blankly at one another. The Doctor bit his upper lip. 'You do have a technician?'

'It's unnecessary.' The speaker was the older man, the one with the iron-grey hair and the fierce dark eyes. Jamie had gathered that his name was Leeth. 'The Agency didn't supply a technician.'

'All the equipment was checked before we set off,' said the woman, Kya.

'Ah. So where might I find your control unit?'

The three strangers couldn't answer. The younger man,

Ferrix, who had been nervously twisting a glass around in his hand, stood suddenly. 'I say, what the hell is going on here? You still haven't given any kind of account of yourself.'

'Do sit down, Ferrix,' said Kya, lighting another cigarette. 'You're only making yourself look silly.' She smiled up at the Doctor. 'We don't know anything about the workings of this place. The Agency take care of that. We're certainly paying them enough.'

Ferrix sat, putting his shaking bald head between his hands.

'Well then. If you'll allow me, I may be able to help.' The Doctor produced his sonic screwdriver and started to fiddle with the tiny switches on its side.

Jamie edged closer. 'What'll your wee gadget there do, then?'

The Doctor smiled briefly, and replied under his breath, 'I've converted it to sniff out the machines that are suspending this place in the vortex. Now then.' He switched on the device and held it at arm's length, then turned about slowly, as if surveying the room. The sonic vibrations increased their pitch as the screwdriver passed before Leeth.

'Ah.' The Doctor motioned to Leeth. 'If you wouldn't mind getting up?'

Leeth grunted. 'I don't suppose it'll make any difference.' He stood while Jamie pulled his chair away.

Ferrix caught his arm. 'Leeth, we don't know these people, we can't trust them!'

Leeth shook him away.

Jamie watched as the Doctor examined the section of wall to which he had been drawn. 'Shame to spoil this lovely wallpaper of yours,' he said. He held out a hand. 'Jamie, may I borrow your dirk?'

Jamie handed over the knife and watched as the Doctor scored a large oblong on the wall, removed the wallpaper and revealed a glittering array of electrical foolery. It looked even more of a complicated mess than the insides of the TARDIS, with little bits of wire tangled about a glass orb. A white flash pulsed through the globe every couple of seconds, making a noise like a gulping frog on a lily pad.

The Doctor's face fell. 'Oh my word.' He tutted and shook his head. 'Oh dear.'

'Would you mind telling us what you're doing?' asked Ferrix.

The Doctor poked at the tangles of wire. 'This is very bad, very bad indeed. A combination of crude time corridor technology and interface theory.' He looked around the room. 'And we all know what that means.'

'This system is perfectly safe. I've been in suspension twice before.' Kya remained seated, apparently unperturbed. 'Our current problem is just a communications failure, that's all.'

The Doctor crossed to the large mirror suspended above the fireplace, that dominated the room . 'This is your communications unit, I take it?'

Leeth nodded. 'It was working fine for the first five months. Then, suddenly, nothing. We were expecting somebody to repair it. But no-one ever came.'

With surprising ease, the Doctor unhooked the mirror from its place on the wall. Behind it was another box of electronics. A green light flashed at the centre of the box. 'No-one came to repair it, because it's in perfect working order.'

Ferrix stepped forward. 'What are you saying?'

The Doctor faced him calmly. 'Communications were broken off from the outside.'

'No, that's impossible!' Ferrix shook the Doctor by the shoulders. 'That's impossible!'

This was something Jamie could understand. He leapt forward and pulled Ferrix off. 'Leave the Doctor be!' He flung Ferrix back in his chair.

'Why would the Agency have broken contact?' asked Kya. 'It's nonsense. Unless there's been some great disaster back on Dephys.'

'I don't think so.' The Doctor returned to his examination of the control unit. 'I think we'll find the answer here.' He extended a hand and gently felt the surface of the globe. His expression grew graver and he closed his eyes. For a moment, Jamie thought he saw a look of great fear cross his face. Before the young Scot could comment on it, a sound came from outside the room.

Zoe's voice, calling his name. The lass sounded terrified. Jamie ran for the door.

Zoe had collapsed in the corner of the grey room, exhausted. Her throat was hoarse from screaming for the Doctor and Jamie. She rested her forehead against her knees and reviewed the confusing sequence of events that had taken place in the last few minutes. There was no pattern to them, nothing that made sense.

She heard voices, male voices, coming towards her. She looked up.

The grey room had gone – or she had – and she was back in the narrow metal tunnel, next to the waste disposal chute. The light from two lanterns shone at the far end of the tunnel. The lanterns were held by the two men descending a circular stairwell. One of them, the first down the steps, was carrying something else, a sack of refuse. He was a cheerful, smiling man, dressed in finery like the others, but with something likeable about his heavily jowled face. Zoe recognized him instantly as the dead man she had seen tipped into the chute not ten minutes earlier.

His companion was the killer.

'So I said, "Kya, I've beaten you," ' said the dead man. ' "You can't dispute the outcome. I've simply won the game." Her face was purple. I thought she was going to faint!' He came closer, to within a couple of feet of Zoe, and tipped the refuse into the chute.

The grinding blades chomped loudly for a couple of seconds. Zoe winced as she recalled what was about to happen.

The killer came closer, put his lantern aside. He raised his other hand, in which a viciously-spiked truncheon was gripped tightly.

'She said, "Kandol, you have got to realize that the result is a draw." I said that if I had more points than she did on the scorewheel, how could it be?'

The killer weighed the truncheon in his hand, droplets of perspiration forming between his nose and his mouth. He readied himself to strike.

Zoe leapt forward. 'Watch out!' she shrieked.

The dead man, Kandol, looked up, saw her.

His killer dropped the truncheon.

Zoe backed away.

Jamie felt as if he'd been kicked in the stomach. As he raced for the door, desperate to rescue Zoe, he was pushed back by a pressure that squeezed his insides. In agony, he turned to see the Doctor bent double and toppling over. As his own nose bumped the carpet, Jamie was vaguely aware that none of the other four in the room seemed to be affected.

Four?

Yes, four. Leeth, Ferrix, Kya and. . .

And?

The fourth man, a cheerful sort with a heavily jowled face, looking down with a concerned frown.

As the pain receded, Jamie felt the Doctor tugging at his shoulder. He opened one streaming eye and saw a crumpled paper bag. 'Take one of these,' he heard the Doctor say through a wave of fever. Jamie reached inside the bag and pulled out one of the Doctor's striped boiled sweets. Without stopping to question why, he put it in his mouth and sucked. His ears popped and he felt a lot better.

The Doctor winked and put away the bag. 'Very good for the side effects of time spillage, these.' He dusted himself down and pulled himself to his feet, then helped Jamie up. 'How are you feeling?'

'Terrible,' groaned Jamie.

'Good, good. Now then.' He pointed to the fourth man. 'Who might you be?'

'I'm Kandol,' the newcomer said simply, with a baffled shrug. 'Aren't you going to tell us what's wrong, Doctor? Or are you just going to roll about on the floor?'

Jamie was peeved that this Kandol fellow was acting as if he and the Doctor were the odd ones out. He tapped Kandol on the shoulder. 'Well, would you not mind first telling us where you've appeared from all of a sudden?'

'After all,' said the Doctor quietly, so that only Jamie could hear, 'you are supposed to be dead.'

'This is ridiculous.' Ferrix crossed to the fireplace, joining Leeth and Kya, and gestured towards the Doctor. 'Surely you must see that this man is some sort of an imposter, an enemy?'

Leeth pointed a fat finger at the Doctor. 'Doctor. You were saying.'

The Doctor held up one of his own fingers. 'First of all, may I ask you three a question? I think I may. How long has Kandol,' he indicated the newcomer, 'been standing in this room?'

'Whoever you are, you really are quite mad,' said Kya.

'Well? Answer the Doctor,' said Jamie.

'He's been here all the time, of course, since before you walked in.' Ferrix appeared close to tears. 'Now, for the last time, will somebody please do something about thi-'

The pain returned suddenly, and Jamie fell, knocked down by what felt like a storm wind. He felt the Doctor grab his hand. 'Hold on, Jamie! Hold on!'

Brachinnen raced through the kitchens and burst onto the upstairs landing, not giving the shift the time to work against him, keeping his eyes wide open and unblinking. The TARDIS had gone, but the landing wasn't empty. Huddled against the antique cabinet, her knees up to her chin, was Zoe.

He called her name, ran over.

Immediately she stood, backed away, her pretty blue eyes widening. 'Who are you? How do you know my name?'

Damn it, she was out of phase. It didn't matter. All that mattered was the TARDIS, his escape route, his line-out. He grabbed her by the shoulder, pointed to the square indentation on the carpet. 'Has it gone? The TARDIS? Did you see it go?'

She pushed him away with a deceptively gentle-looking flick of the elbow which he knew well, and he was knocked to the floor. 'Who told you about the TARDIS?'

Brachinnen stared up at the ceiling, the chandelier. Tears blurred his vision. This couldn't go on. Not again. He longed for anything to break the shift, any torture than this. 'You did,' he whispered. 'You did, Zoe.'

He felt the shift.

Opening his eyes, he saw that he was back in bed. Ferrix was pulling the door closed, shaking his head. 'You rest there a while. A few more hours and we'll be home.'

The door closed, and Brachinnen heard the key turn in the lock.

He screamed.

Jamie shook his head to clear away the fuzziness. His senses slowly realigned, the lounge spinning back into place around him. It was empty, apart from himself and the Doctor, who was standing before the section of wall he had opened up.

The wall was sealed again. There was no sign of the Doctor's earlier investigation. The striped wallpaper was unmarked. 'Ah, Jamie, may I borrow your dirk?'

'What? I've already given it you, Doctor.'

'I'm afraid that you haven't.'

'Yes, I gave it to you when you–' Jamie looked instinctively down at his sock, from which protruded the haft of his dirk. 'Hey, I gave it to you when you–' He pointed at the sealed wall. 'What's going on here? Have we gone back in time or something?'

'If only it were that simple, Jamie.' The Doctor took the dirk and scored out the same square in the wall as he had done earlier. He pulled away the wallpaper and revealed the control unit again. 'Here's the culprit.'

Jamie stood, scratching his head, which was aching to make some sense of his surroundings. On the table in the centre of the lounge was the bottle of whisky from which Leeth had been drinking. It was nearly full. Jamie glanced at the clock above the fireplace. It had lost four hours.

The Doctor removed a slim silver box from the tangle of wires around the control unit, and blew away some dust which had settled upon it. 'This is the device that governs the shields protecting this place from the time winds.' He held the box to Jamie's ear and shook it. Something loose inside rattled loudly. 'It's been tampered with. The people here have lost their protection against the vortex.' He shuddered. 'It's horrible, horrible. We must get away from here. Quickly now, back to the TARDIS.'

He hurried from the empty lounge. Jamie followed, but turned at the door for a last look, trying to answer the puzzle and put the Doctor's fears in place.

The lounge was occupied again.

The new man, Kandol, sat facing Kya over some sort of games board. Both were dressed differently from when he had last seen them. A variety of coloured tokens were scattered between them.

'I'm telling you, this is a draw,' Kya said smoothly.

'I have more tokens than you, darling. How can it be?' Kandol protested, smiling.

Jamie looked past them. The control unit was sealed up again. He looked down. The dirk was back in his sock.

He hurried after the Doctor before Kandol or Kya had a chance to notice him.

Zoe was overjoyed to see the Doctor and Jamie appear in the

hallway. She ran up to the Doctor, burying her face in his shoulder. 'Oh, Doctor, I thought you'd gone and left me here!'

He patted her awkwardly. 'There, there, my dear. Now why would I go and do a thing like that?'

She pointed behind her. 'Doctor, there was a man, some kind of lunatic. And I found a dead body, but then he came back to life. And the TARDIS. It's gone.'

'You're seeing things, girl,' she heard Jamie say. When she turned her tear-stained face from the Doctor's collar, she was perplexed yet relieved to find that he was right. The blue police box had returned to its position at the end of the hall. Jamie rested his hand against its sturdy side. 'I think we'd best be away from here.'

Zoe turned back to the Doctor. 'Oh, but Doctor, it wasn't there a moment ago.' She put a hand to her head. 'I think I'm going mad.'

'Not a bit of it.' The Doctor cradled her chin in his hand. 'Now, for once I agree with Jamie. It's time we put this awful place behind us. Definitely not somewhere I'd care to spend any length of time.' He took her hand and led her to the door of the TARDIS, through which Jamie had already passed. Zoe felt like collapsing in relief against the Doctor's side, but steadied herself.

'No! You can't leave me!'

The man she had seen earlier stumbled from the door at the end of the landing. He was wiry and dishevelled, and his deranged eyes rolled in their sockets. 'Doctor, please!'

'How does he know us?' Zoe asked the Doctor. 'I haven't met him.'

'You're about to.' The Doctor walked forward slowly. His eyes narrowed and his kind face creased with anxiety. He shook the stranger's hand. 'Mr . . ?'

'Brachinnen.' The stranger wrung his hands. 'Please, Doctor, take me with you. I've got to get out of this place. They think I'm mad. They locked me up.' He started to sob. 'But I can see it, Doctor. I can see it, as you can. Time, running about us, breaking in, changing things, moving us back and forth, crawling all over us like an infection.'

Zoe stepped forward. 'I can see it too, Doctor.'

'Of course you can. You and me and Jamie, we can all sense the effect of the time winds. We're frequent travellers, you see, and the TARDIS gives us a certain amount of protection. You might say that we exist outside of time, in a way.' He turned back to the stranger. 'Some people, like Mr Brachinnen, are naturally time- sensitive. But the others here are too much a part of the effect to be aware of it.' Zoe realized that he was edging slowly back towards the TARDIS door.

Brachinnen leapt forward. 'Please, Doctor. I've seen you leave before. You have the way out.'

'For myself and my companions only.' The Doctor shook his head sadly. 'You and your colleagues chose to suspend yourselves in the vortex. One of your enemies sabotaged the control unit, and removed your defence against the time winds. Somebody didn't want one of you, or any of you, back. The Agency must have realized what had happened, and abandoned you. After all, they had no way of bringing you back, once this,' – he gestured around himself – 'unit was breached.'

Zoe was staggered. 'That's appalling. These people here are lost in time, forever?'

'Forever doesn't come into it. Time means nothing in the vortex.'

Zoe regarded the weeping stranger, who had fallen to his knees before them. 'Then we must save this man, at least.'

'It's impossible, Zoe. The time winds will have eaten away at him and all the others here.' He lowered his voice to a whisper. 'They're less than shadows. If we took him aboard the TARDIS, he'd simply turn to dust. And it wouldn't change anything, because he's part of this place now. Until the vortex ends – if it ever can.'

Brachinnen moaned, clawing at the carpet. He gurgled, 'No,

no. . . I've tried for so long to reach you, to get here, to speak with you. . . You can't leave me!'

Gently, the Doctor pushed Zoe inside the TARDIS. The doors closed behind her, cutting off the hollow, drawn-out screams of Brachinnen.

As soon as the TARDIS was safely back in flight, the Doctor hurried from the control room, a haunted look on his face.

The TARDIS had materialized on an unspoilt, sandy beach beneath high cliffs. The sun blazed down from a cloudless sky, picking out every detail for miles out to sea. Through her sunglasses, Zoe saw a blizzard of fish jumping through the glittering water near to where Jamie was snoozing on a lilo that the Doctor had produced from somewhere deep within the TARDIS. It felt good to be back in the open. She yawned and pushed her fringe back over her forehead. Sunbathing was fine, but she missed intellectual stimulation. Her mind wandered back to recent events. There was something she'd been meaning to ask the Doctor. Perhaps now was a good time to try.

'Doctor?' She leant her head over the metre-wide hole in the sand which he had dug out over the last couple of days. 'I've been meaning to ask you something.'

He peered up, her face and the sky above reflected in his sunglasses, trousers rolled up to his knees, water up to his ankles. He shook his plastic bucket and spade. 'Look at these. Tremendous finds.' He waved a yellow bone up at her, expecting her to be impressed. 'Just think, a woolly mammoth once roamed this land. Fascinating.'

She refused to be diverted. 'Jamie told me that Kandol suddenly appeared in the lounge. Well, that must have been because I saved him.' The Doctor looked away and started digging again. 'Don't you see, Doctor? Something changed. I changed something. That must mean that we were as much a part of that time spillage as the others were.'

The Doctor's red plastic spade scooped up more sand at the

bottom of the hole. 'Well, time theory was never my strong point, Zoe. And the vortex breaks so many physical laws that there's really not much point thinking about it, it's so confusing. Just be thankful that the TARDIS is a lot more sophisticated than the system Brachinnen's lot were using.'

'Yes, we got away. But surely, if – once – we were there, a part of things, a part of that paradox, then the time we spent there must *still* be a part of that paradox. I mean, Brachinnen recognized us, he'd seen us before.'

Suddenly the Doctor yelped and clutched one of his bare feet. 'Oh no! Oh dear!'

'Doctor, what's the matter?'

'Oh, I've been stung, I think. A rotten old jellyfish or something.' He rubbed his toes and winced. 'Perhaps it's time we were moving on, eh?'

As he climbed from the hole, Zoe realised that she would never get an answer to her question. Perhaps the Doctor didn't want to alarm her by confirming her fear. Her fear that somewhere, somewhen, they were still in that place. Always had been, always would be. It hurt her head to think about it.

She waved to Jamie and, when she had his attention, pointed up the beach to where the Doctor, boots in his hand, was unlocking the door of the TARDIS.

Leeth followed Kandol down the stairs to the basement, the spiked truncheon gripped in one hand, a lantern in the other. The back of Kandol's head beckoned to him. Fermenting in that bog of a mind was a plan. Leeth's men had alerted him to Kandol's desires just before they'd gone into suspension. Kandol's people planned to buy up Leeth's land leases in Brere when they got back, using the savings accrued during the suspension period. Leeth would be left destitute.

He'd considered all his options, but this was really the only practical solution. He had to strike now: he might never have another opportunity. Kill Kandol, say that he'd gone insane, like Brachinnen, push him out through the disposal chute.

Kandol was babbling, about some game that he'd been playing with Kya, as he tipped the refuse away. Leeth set down his lantern, weighed the truncheon.

'And I said, "If I have more tokens on the scorewheel, how can it be a draw?" '

Time for the kill. The crucial moment.

'Watch out!'

A girl's voice, a cry, a glimpse of her in the glow from Kandol's lantern as he whipped around, and the moment was lost.

Then she was gone.

Kandol turned to Leeth. 'Did you hear something?'

In the lounge, Leeth took another sip of whisky and smiled. 'My land in Brere is quite secure.' He nodded to Kya. 'Only an hour now.'

Two hours and he'd be back at his desk, looking through the wide picture window at Pinchere Square. And Kandol? He'd hire a killer and have him disposed of before he could reach his people. Everything was going to be all right.

Kya smiled wickedly across at him and raised her own glass.

At the end of the downstairs landing, a blue beacon began to flash in mid-air. A few seconds later, to the accompaniment of a raucous groaning noise, the police-box shell of the TARDIS had solidified from transparency.

Zoe was the first to emerge.

'And I said, "How can it be a draw, then?" '

Leeth raised the truncheon.

In just an hour, thought Kya. She'd wave Leeth goodbye at the vortex port, climb into the cab, see Ferrix back to his beloved chair in that stuffy club of his. She really couldn't wait to get back and do a bit more winning. Waiting just wasn't her style.

'It's time,' said the Doctor, 'we got away from this awful place. Definitely not somewhere I'd care to spend any length of time.'

Brachinnen stirred. The sedative was wearing off. His joints ached and his head felt like it was going to split. He looked across the room – this infernal, unchanging room of his! – to the gilt-numbered clock.

The shift had taken him back. The Doctor would arrive soon.

He sank back, pushing his aching head into the pillow, gave up, and let the enemy take him.

Crimson Dawn

By Tim Robins

Figures in bedouin robes and army fatigues stole across the dusk-shrouded desert of Cydonia. Ahead of them, the ruins of Necropole, the city of the dead, were thrown into sharp relief by the cold light from the ascending moons, Phobos and Deimos. Moving beyond the city and the Great Pyramid to the west, the figures finally reached the base of the Martian Sphinx and quickly scaled its scaffold cage. When they reached its head, their cybernetic tools began peeling back its obsidian mask of carbon and volcanic ash. Soon the excavations of Redpeace gave birth to a Sphinx with the face of an Ice Warrior.

Morning on Mars saw the Doctor – hat, scarf, all teeth and curls – relaxing on board his houseboat, the *Dejah Thoris*. The vessel was built in the style of the narrowboats that had once plied Britain's canals: first as cargo-carrying homes to boatmen and women; then as chic leisure craft for the 1960s Chelsea set; and then as slum dwellings for home-counties refugees waiting in vain for the nation's transformation into a post-apocalyptic pastoral idyll. It was also crafted from traditional materials, with oak sides, an elm keel and iron ribs. A brightly painted cabin to the stern was adorned with bold, white letters which proclaimed the vessel's company and place of registration: I. M. Foreman (London).

The *Dejah Thoris* was being towed from a canal bank by a pair of sturdy equoth. The shaggy, six-legged creatures were of less traditional construction – a genetic splicing of shire horse and giant sloth. Despite their startling bloodline, the Doctor considered them to be graceful creatures. Although their pace was slow, they were taking him exactly where he wanted to go, which was nowhere at all. Inadvertently, the Time Lord caught

sight of two other creatures: Leela and K-9. Leela was tensed
on the prow as if preparing to defend herself from imminent
attack, and the Doctor saw a number of lethal janis thorns
patched beneath her leather bodice in blatant defiance of his
instructions. K-9 was sometimes next to Leela and sometimes
teetering at the cabin door. The robot dog seemed unable to
find its sea legs, despite numerous attempts to recalibrate its
stabilizers.

K-9, on request, was providing Leela with a pedantic litany
of facts, figures and fantasies about Mars. 'Mars: the fourth
planet in order of distance from the sun. Day (sidereal): 24 hours
37 minutes 22 seconds. Year: 687 days. Orbital eccentricity:
0.093. Mars: reduced form of Mavors; the Roman equivalent
of Ares, the god of war. Mars: flora and fauna: petrified remains suggest a prehistoric ecosystem viable for complex life
forms. Aboriginal species are believed to have included the
humanoid reptiles known as Ice Warriors.'

Leela stared towards the horizon and tried to look through
time. 'This is not a place of warriors. There is no honour here,
only death.'

Leela and K-9. The Doctor couldn't decide which of them
was the more difficult to train. He slid his hat over his eyes and
continued fishing, tugging on a length of catgut which ran
through a porthole and into the waters of the canal. A yellow,
three-eyed fish, stuffed and mounted in the manner of a sculp-
ture by Damian Hirst, stared impassively down at him from its
resting place on a small shelf next to the food cupboard. It was
a memento from the Doctor's villa overlooking the Lake of
Mutations on Skaro. At least on Skaro there had been plenty of
fish, thought the Time Lord, even if each catch had been a fight
to the death.

'The fish are dead,' said Leela.

The Doctor ignored her. He wondered why the *Dejah Thoris*
had stopped moving. Then Leela flopped a dead fish onto his
lap. 'The fish are dead.'

'Leela, I told you: no more janis thorns. You should throw the fish back alive.' The Doctor wondered how one fish could reek so much of death.

'The fish are dead,' said Leela emphatically. She grabbed the Doctor's scarf and used it to haul him up on deck.

The Doctor looked into the waters of the canal and saw to his astonishment that the *Dejah Thoris* was held fast by a thick red carpet of scum, scales and rotting flesh. Leela was right. The fish were dead. All of them. And on the towpath, the equoth clawed the earth in terror.

It had taken over a century to prove that the canals seen by Schiaparelli and Lowell did not exist; it had taken less than a decade for the Ares Corporation to make sure that they did. Terraforming Mars had been made easier by the Clean Earth Act of 2350 which had designated the planet a land fill site for waste products too dangerous to be left on Earth. Aerosols and cheap fridges had been dumped first in the high street stores of Europe, then across Utopia Planitia where leaking fluorocarbons had produced a 'greenhouse effect', releasing hydrogen, oxygen and carbon from the permafrost and the rapidly melting poles. For the first time in over a billion years water had swept down the canyon tributaries of Valles Marineris, turning chaotic terrains into lakelands and deserts into beaches.

From his pyramid penthouse on the moon Deimos, Paul Ares, vice-president of the Ares Corporation, looked upon the face of the waters and decided that Mars was good – but with plenty of opportunities for further development. Ares's mood was portentous, his aspect divine. He rubbed the inlaid ruby eyes of an enamelled money spider which nestled on the index finger of his left hand. An open sore beneath the ring was painful enough to remind him that he was not in heaven and all was not right with his world.

The Doctor held a fish in front of K-9. The dog sniffed it, analysed its chemical emissions, then extended a sensor probe to bombard the body with electrons. The autopsy complete, the computer delivered its verdict. 'Cause of death: oxygen starvation and lethal extra-cellular toxins. Electroscopic analysis reveals the presence of dinoflagellates of the genera Gymnodinium'.

'Red blooms,' said the Doctor. He threw the fish on a pile of shrimps, mackerel and tuna. Their over-ripened bodies were bloated with bacteria-blackened flesh. *Fruits de merde*.

'The fish were killed by flowers?' asked Leela. The Doctor had told her of planets ruled by carnivorous plant life.

'Planktonic algae,' replied the Doctor. 'Red blooms occur in marine and freshwater ecosystems, producing a red discoloration in rivers, ponds and oceans. They were the basis of biblical tales of rivers of blood. The algae produce specific toxins deadly to a range of fish, molluscs and mammals. Am I right K-9?'

'Correct, Master,' replied the Doctor's best friend. 'Gymnodinium Veneficum produces a water-soluble toxin of high molecular weight which kills by acting on the nervous system.'

The Doctor leapt into the cabin. 'Come on K-9, its bath time'.

'A bath is unnecessary, Master.' Leela thought she detected a hint of anxiety in the computer's metallic voice.

'An enzyme bath,' clarified the Doctor. 'I want you to extract genetic material from the algae.'

Ares greeted Shunro Oshikawa, president of the Tsunami terraforming conglomerate, across a mahogany table in a boardroom situated within the communications web spun between their respective worlds. The rival executives used image capturing and morphing techniques to appear to each other as sprites, computer generated to represent their respective corporate identities. Oshikawa took the form of Tsunami's iron-clad surfer robot, the Ultratetsuozoid®. The colossal robot had the head of a Tyrannosaurus Rex, the face of a delicate white porcelain doll and a body capable of transforming into a choice of jet-fighter insects, war reptiles or corporate skyscrapers.

'Shunro-san. This is an unexpected pleasure,' said Ares. He noticed that the robot had put on weight since Tsunami had acquired Venus. On screen, Ares himself resembled the Star Child from *2001: A Space Odyssey*; wide-eyed, with translucent embryonic skin and a voice capable of persuading any employee that being sacked was the ultimate destiny of the human race.

The Ultratetsuozoid® smiled, its plump, red, doll-lips parting just enough to reveal the serrated teeth of an ironclad carnivore. 'Paul, old chap. I have been monitoring your company's stock movements. I thought Tsunami could offer a hand in your hour of need. After all, that is what friends are for, what?'

Ares was irritated by Oshikawa's affected English accent, but his Star Child self simply smiled. 'You're too kind. And I, in turn, hope things are running more smoothly on your pleasure planet. I hear Waterworld went Jurassic. How much are the families suing you for?' The American knew that this information had been obtained from covert operations within the Inter-World Web, but his Star Child persona still radiated innocence.

The Ultratetsuozoid® took a step forward. 'At least Tsunami does not allow its customers to be mown down by terrorists.'

'Dream on, Oshikawa. The Crimson Dawn are under control. Unless you know different.'

'Are you suggesting that Tsunami consorts with terrorist organizations? This is an open line.' The Ultratetsuozoid® hungten towards a rising sun, but not before chewing up some of the boardroom furniture in a fit of pique. The Star Child exited through a doorway shaped like a black monolith.

Out of his Star Child character, Ares was worried. Oshikawa rarely phoned just to trade insults. During the last financial year, Tsunami were thought to have donated a billion dollars to the cause of Redpeace and their campaign to restore Martian land rights to the Ice Warriors. Ares knew that only he and his company stood in their way.

The *Dejah Thoris* was becalmed on the Century Steps, a series of one hundred locks designed to raise craft up to the level of the Grand Canal. The Doctor busied himself in the larger of the narrow boat's two cabins. It was considerably smaller on the inside than the outside, but he had managed to install navigation equipment and a small laboratory. He held up a scroll of paper marked with purple bands. 'What is this, K-9?'

'A chromosomal map displaying a binary code, Master.'

'Exactly. The algae's genes are imprinted with a registration number. The red bloom has been patented. I wonder who the patent holder is?'

'The killing flowers belong to somebody?' asked Leela. The warrior had been waiting out the houseboat's ascent in a lockside pub, the Jigger's Mate. The regulars had greeted her with furtive glances and whispered suspicions, but Leela had quickly won them over with her rude humour and ready violence and had returned to the narrow boat laden with flagons of ale – the spoils of several arm-wrestling competitions.

The Doctor explained the principles of terraforming. 'The aim is to manage the ecosystem of a planet and produce an environment capable of sustaining human life. On Mars, this must have included seeding the planet with microscopic organisms that would recycle carbon and oxygen. Every part of the terraforming process had to be controlled and standardized, so even the micro-organisms had to be manufactured.' Terraformers were a lot like the motorcar manufacturer Henry Ford, thought the Doctor. In the assembly-line world of planet production, no two snowflakes were unalike.

'The question is,' the Doctor continued, 'whose plan are the red blooms a part of? K-9, where can I access the Patents Database?'

The robot computer scanned the information it had

downloaded from Tourist Information. 'The Administry of Environmental Affairs in the Martian capital.'

'The city is many full moons from here,' said Leela.

'Not if the *Dejah Thoris* travels under her own steam,' grinned the Doctor. 'Leela, loose the equoth!'

This used to be the moon, but now it is Whitechapel. You used to look out across a crater filled with space shuttles resting nose to nose, wing tip to wing tip. To some, the craft were shameful reminders of the bankruptcies and liquidations that had marked the end of the second space race. But to you they were sleeping swans waiting to take flight again. And you woke them, with your money and ambition, and watched them flock between Earth and Mars. But now, in the memory of your personal computer, your thoughts have rebuilt the system's architecture in the manner of Victorian London, and you walk amidst the hansoms and the hackneys and choke on the brooding fog. Finally, you reach the Patents Office and pull registration documents, genetic blueprints and legal depositions from a rusting filing cabinet. You look at the family album of the Last Martian, then creep back through the fog to your office beyond.

The capital city of Mars was built on the southernmost foothills of Olympus Mons. It had been designed along the principles of laissez-faire socialism as a series of crescents radiating from the mountainside and demarcated by open parks, canals and bridges. These harmonious zones had then been handed over to the whims of the tourist industry, multinationals, theme-park developers and other eccentrics. The itinerant workforce shuttled from Earth had created a thriving shanty town of makeshift houses, lean-tos and market stalls. The result was a sprawl of architectures and lifestyles which gave the impression that 18th-century Venice, 19th-century Paris, 20th-century Amsterdam and 21st-century Euro Disney had all collided in time and space.

The Doctor, K-9 at heel, drifted towards the administrative heart of the city. Observing the phantasmagoria of crowds, cafes and department stores, the Time Lord imagined himself to be a *flâneur*, one of the gentlemen of leisure who took turtles for walks in the arcades of 1840s Paris, letting the creatures set the pace of their travels. Although *flâneurs* desired only to lose themselves in the luxury of shop windows, their travels inevitably brought them to the scene of a crime.

The Doctor was the most unwilling of all detectives and his mission to solve the mystery of the red blooms suffered frequent interruptions as he stopped to observe the urban jungle. His journey took him past coffee shops where smokers with limpid eyes and frozen-lipped smirks watched engine oil create impossible patterns in the waters of the canals. Crossing a bridge, he found himself in the red-light district formed from bordellos of the imagination. Here men and women, some of them human, composed themselves in neon-framed windows for little else than the gaze of tourists. But the Doctor's attention was caught by a department store displaying a range of merchandising based around a rubber cephalopod called the Last Martian. The Doctor decided to buy some of the action figures as souvenirs, but reached his credit limit before he could afford the play environments such as New Xanadu (a mansion on the moon Phobos) and the *Aelita* (an opulent cruise liner).

When he eventually arrived at the Administry of Environmental Affairs, the Doctor was greeted by a large group of demonstrators waving banners that read: *Mars for the Martians*. Some of the group were dressed in what appeared to be homemade Ice Warrior costumes consisting of green-painted corrugated cardboard torsos, strapped in place with lengths of string, and helmets cut from plastic buckets. The demonstrators were outnumbered three to one by Mars's private police force. As the Doctor entered the building a scuffle broke out and an earnest young man pressed a leaflet into his hand. The demonstrator managed to cry: 'No peace without Redpeace,' before being clubbed down by a police night stick.

Inside the Administry, the Doctor whispered in K-9's sensor array ears, then stalked off towards the information desk. He thrust a mackerel down in front of a robot receptionist. 'Hello. I'm the Doctor, this is K-9 and this is a dead fish.'

The receptionist, all chrome and indifference, ignored the fish. 'I am sorry but customer complaints are closed. You may leave a message or come back tomorrow. Have a nice day.'

The Doctor leant across the desk and stared into the receptionist's dead eyes. 'Tell him how the fish died, K-9.'

'Toxic shock from Gymnodinium Veneficum.'

'The administrator is aware of the situation,' said the receptionist, his metallic voice twanging with ill-concealed impatience. 'The administrator apologises for any inconvenience. This is the result of a temporary readjustment of the ecosystem. Rest assured that all fish served in restaurants approved by the Mars Tourist Board are fit to eat. Have a nice day.'

'These algae were manufactured,' pressed the Doctor. He had many regenerations' experience of jobsworths – human and robot. 'This isn't a temporary anything, this is an act of biotechnological warfare.'

The Doctor gave a prearranged signal to K-9 and the robot ground forward and extended its gun barrel. 'No! Don't do it K-9!' The Doctor held out his hands melodramatically, as if to ward off an attack from the pet computer, then turned to the receptionist and whispered, 'I think you're annoying K-9. K-9 doesn't like to be annoyed. Now why don't you do something before he gets really irritated?'

'I already have sir,' said the receptionist. At that, K-9 was enveloped in a stasis field, klaxons sounded and armed security guards ran onto the scene to subdue the Doctor.

Leela was lost.

The Doctor had instructed her to remain on the *Dejah Thoris*, but she had felt that he needed her protection and had followed

him along the labyrinth of *caletta* and baroque *palazzi* that
mapped out the Martian capital's Venetian-style waterfront. But
the warrior's tracking skills had failed her when the Doctor and
K-9 had entered the shopping zone and her senses were over-
whelmed by the kaleidoscopic chaos of the cavernous mall.

Unlike the waterfront, the shopping zone was assertively
modernist. Giant photomontage billboards publicized the future with icons from an avant-garde past, merging bodies and
machines with flocks of bowler hats, spiralling-eye marbles and
a necklace wrap of zeros and ones. Shoppers, riding ceaseless
escalators, gazed enviously at the latest creatures of fashion
only to find that these were their own images reflected back at
them across the mall's gleaming mirrored surfaces, so that the
objects of their desire were none other than themselves. All the
most exclusive brand names were here: Georgio Armani, Hugo
Boss, Happy Shopper. In this circle of desire, paradise was always postponed.

Leela experienced the zone as a series of sudden shocks. In
front of her, a naked man, bronzed muscles taut and rippling,
scaled a mountain face towards a young woman poised on a
ledge. Beads of perspiration rolled over the pores of the man's
body, sculpting pathways through the fine hairs of his back. He
reached the woman. The woman smiled and, in close up, began
to bathe the man's bronzed muscles in a fine spray from a tear-
dropped glass bottle. A husky voice whispered: '*Eau d'Aggedor;
the misty musk of mountain monsters.*'

Leela watched the advertisement, which was projected onto
a shop window. The man's hand tentatively touched the woman's right breast, then morphed into a clawed paw. The claws
left ribbons of blood across the breast. '*Eau d'Aggedor; brings
out the beast in your man.*' A final pack shot showed the bottle
of amber perfume resting amongst the hairs of the man's abdo-
men. The woman's hands caressed his torso. '*Eau d'Aggedor
from the House of Peladon. Parfum pour l'homme.*'

Leela knew nothing of the financial disaster that had forced the Pels to turn their monarchy into a toiletry franchise, nor of the slaughter of the planet's sacred beasts for their scent glands, but she had learnt all about the beast that lurks in men at her initiation into Sevateem adulthood. She imagined the man's hand clawing at her own breast and the pleasure she would feel as she drew her knife across his throat, severing his arteries and sending him to a grave of foaming blood.

The warrior smelt cooked meat, remembered how hungry she was and stalked towards an escalator which carried her up to a carousel of cafes. The smell led her to the Mars Bar. Entering the diner, she was confronted with a large mural entitled *Mars Snack Attacks*. It depicted salivating, bulging-brained mutants descending from flying saucers to feast on bewildered cows.

An anaemic waiter, his face liberally decorated with freckles, ushered her to a table and took her order. He wore a fluorescent green badge which read: *Kall me Kevin* and a green bandana holding in place two springing antennae which bobbed about every time he moved his head. 'Mars welcomes you to his palace of culinary delights. I, Kevin, am your champion against the forces of the snack attack. How can I battle on your behalf?'

Leela felt more disorientated than ever. 'I want food,' she ventured. 'But you do not have to fight on my behalf. I am a warrior of the Sevateem.'

Kevin grinned nervously and reeled off the menu. 'Your mouth-watering Martian menu for this morning is burgers, drumsticks, pizzas, fries, fillets, nuggets, nachos...'

Leela tried to interrupt the waiter's litany, failed and eventually shouted, 'That! I'll have that!' She was unaware that all she had ordered was a side salad.

'Mayonnaise, salad cream, pickles, chutney, ketchup?'

'Yes, everything.'

'Drink?'

'Yes.'

'Chocolate, coffee, tea, mineral, shake, synth-ale, soda..?'

'That! Soda!'

'Coke, Dr Pepper, Pepsi, Tag, Tango..?'

'Coke, by Xoanon!'

'Classic, clear, cherry, diet..?'

'Enough!' Leela leapt up and pressed the flat of her knife against the pale flesh of the waiter's neck. Kevin felt a warm, damp patch stinging its way across his crotch. 'Listen well, "Kall Me Kevin", for you prattle like a high priest of Xoanon caught at night in the children's corral. Bring me food and drink now or I will feast upon your flesh.'

'And I've been teaching my students that cannibalism is a myth.'

Leela turned to discover the source of this new voice and saw a woman walking towards her. She was in her late twenties and wore a sweat-rimmed hat, a short-lengthed, dust-coated leather jacket, torn denims and mud-encrusted calf-length boots. A canvas bag was slung over her right shoulder. Leela noticed that the hat all but covered a shock of red hair.

'I am not a cannibal, but I am willing to try,' retorted Leela.

'There's no need for the knife m'dear,' the woman beamed. 'I can see you're a stranger here. Allow me...' She ordered Leela a Ray Bunbury with mayonnaise, two side orders of fries and a Triple Edgar Rice Burger on Rye.

The woman introduced herself as Dr Ginger Corvette. 'But you can call me "Red" – everyone does. I hope you don't object to me helping out like that. I'm an anthropologist, so I know how difficult it can be adjusting to new cultures. I'm from New Guinea myself. My birth name is Con Ming-Zingibera. It means "Ginger". But tell me all about yourself.'

Kevin scuttled up to their table, deposited two trays of prepackaged food and quickly backed away. Corvette had ordered herself an Achocalypse Now – double-whipped chocolate-chip chocolate ice cream with a chocolate sauce on a bed of chocolate- coated wafers. Her tongue played across the smooth textures of the ice cream, then probed its cocoa heart of darkness. 'You may not be a cannibal, but you are tribal,' she said. Leela watched a drop of chocolate sauce dribble from Corvette's lips. 'Territorial,' the anthropologist continued. 'Some would say you are more feral than human.'

'I am a warrior of the Sevateem,' said Leela, certain she was being insulted. Corvette's manner was warm and welcoming, but there was something about the woman that she did not trust.

'So you said, but I don't recognize that name from Earth.' The anthropologist peered quizzically at the warrior.

'The Doctor says my people came from Earth long ago. He called my people the Survey Team.' Corvette considered this information. 'I am the Doctor's protector. The Doctor is a wise man, but he lives in his thoughts.'

'An ivory tower,' said Corvette.

'No, the TARDIS.'

'Where is your wise man now?'

Leela was unwilling to admit that had she lost the Doctor in the crowd. 'He confronts a race known as the small-minded bureaucrats. He challenges them to answer the riddle of the fish. Should they fail, he will defeat them by the wisdom of science and the magic art of paperwork. This is not the way of a warrior'

Suddenly whooping klaxons shattered the somnambulistic Musak of the mall.

'Mall alert,' said Corvette.

A man trailing a long, rainbow-coloured scarf dashed across the mall. A mechanical dog reversed behind him, haphazardly picking off mall police with its blaster.

'Doctor!' Leela leapt from the table. 'K-9!' Corvette followed. Leela looked for exit points and waved. 'Over here Doctor!'

Suddenly a shock wave spun her across the mall. The Mars Bar was engulfed in flames. A pall of smoke covered the area. The pursuing security guards faltered and then, as foam and sprinkler systems came into effect, began slipping and sliding across the marbled floor, turning tragedy into slapstick.

A rhinoceros chewed on an indifferent meal of straw. Captain Van der Meer held high the rhino's horn and a short whip; twin talismans testifying to his triumph over nature. Aristocratic spectators joined Van der Meer in the nearby safety of a stall. The courtesans were ambivalent. Their gaze wandered from the beast – black, still, inscrutable – to its captor – pale, anxious, inappropriately excited. The faces of the courtesans were masked, but still revealed smirks and knowing glances. Captor and captive. Both creatures were worthy of a moment's amusement.

Ares was amused by the urine-stained dirt and pungent dung, which had been rendered by Longhi, the painting's eighteenth-century artist, with the same botanical accuracy as had the rhinoceros and the aristocrats. By inextricable association, he followed the gaze of the gilded rhinoceros and looked up towards the moon Phobos and, on its surface, New Xanadu. Phobos was receding into the distance, hurtling along its seven-and-a-half hour orbit of Mars, but Ares could still see New Xanadu and its ivory parapets adorned with a sculptured bestiary of elephants, lions and shrivenzale.

Ares had designed the pleasure palace in consultation with the Last Martian itself. Their conflicting views had resulted in a collision of Bauhaus and Cecil B. de Mille across its staircases, bridges, galleries, swimming pools, menageries and arboreta. Ares felt that in this, as in so much else, his vision had been corrupted. He looked disconsolately at the red flocked wallpaper, heavy tapestries and encrusted paintings that adorned his office. Once he had happily displayed works of Lichtenstein – *Look Mickey*, *Whaam* and *The Melody Haunts My Reverie* – and covers of comic books, the pop art of mass production. But now his taste reflected a more ancient, decadent, European sensibility.

'*Longhi, tu che la mia musa sorella*,' he murmured. '*Chiami del tuo pennel che cerca il vero.*' Longhi, you summon my sibling muse. Your pen like mine is seeking truth. Ares circled a number in his ledger. The number was in red. Business was bad. Unless the company's creditflow improved, the next chapter in the history of Mars would be written in red ink, the blood of bankruptcy. The forthcoming meeting with the company's financial backers would be crucial.

A VDU icon indicated an incoming message. It was from New Xanadu. An anxious security officer was portraited on the screen. 'Mr Ares, sir. There's been an. . . incident.'

The cabin of the *Dejah Thoris* was illuminated only by a pocket TV. Leela brooded in a corner. In the flickering light, she used her knife to dig out small shards of glass which had lodged in her legs and arms. The Doctor and Corvette remained hunched over the TV set. Corvette extended a miniature satellite dish and attempted to improve its reception. Eventually an LED picture of a newsroom unscrambled itself on the screen. Other pictures followed.

'We made the news,' said Corvette. The anthropologist had guided the Doctor and his companions to the marina. The emergency services had been too busy tending to the victims of the explosion and the numerous secondary fires that had broken out in the mall to pay the travellers much attention. The *Dejah Thoris* had cast off under the cover of night and was now heading away from the city along the Grand Canal.

Leela, glancing up at the TV, recognized a smouldering shop front as the remains of the Mars Bar. The rubble was wrapped in blue and yellow striped ribbons which read: Police Line, Stop, Do Not Cross and Crime Scene. The restaurant's final moments were then replayed in slow motion. A portrait of a young Arab was superimposed over images of burning figures. 'I recognize that face,' said the Doctor. 'He was one of the demonstrators outside the Administry.' The Time Lord pulled the crumpled pamphlet from his pocket. 'He gave me this.'

'He's Arif Hilâl, a co-ordinator of Redpeace,' said Corvette. 'And, if the news is to be believed, the leader of a group of eco-terrorists called the Crimson Dawn.'

'In my experience, terrorists are usually more camera shy. Why would a group of ecologists start blowing up shopping malls?'

Corvette explained. 'Redpeace always opposed the terraforming of Mars. When they lost that battle, they extended their conservation campaign to establishing merchandising and land rights for the Ice Warriors. The difficulty is that Redpeace is dedicated to the democratic process, but Mars has been developed by private industry with almost no accountability to the governments on Earth.'

'So the Crimson Dawn are bringing them to account?'

'That's the theory. Although I sympathize with their aims, I don't support their means of achieving them. In any case, the Ice Warriors are now scattered throughout the galaxy and no-one is going to allow an aggressor species to occupy such a strategic position next to the home world of the Federation. The Ice Warriors have demonstrated their hostile intentions in the past.'

'You can't condemn an entire species for the actions of a few of its members.'

'Some of your best friends are Ice Warriors?' Corvette jibed. 'Anyway, their claim is untenable. Mars is owned by the Ares Corporation, and their President is a Martian. In fact, the Last Martian.'

'So the Last Martian is more than just a line of toys?'

'Oh yes. He was discovered near one of my digs. I was researching aboriginal Martian culture with a team of archaeologists in the Cydonia region. The creature was discovered in the permafrost as a small plankton. The cold had put it into suspended animation for nearly a billion years. The Ares Corporation oversaw its maturation into adulthood. When the creature was found to be sentient, it was elected as the company's President. A smart move.'

'Doctor! Look!' Leela was pointing agitatedly at the TV screen. 'You are on the telling vision. Its pictures are speaking lies.'

The screen showed images taken from surveillance cameras. A computer search had gathered together a sequence tracing the Doctor's movements: his arrival at the waterfront; his stroll through the city; his shopping trip; the incident at the Administry; his arrival at the mall; and his escape with his companions to the marina. The Doctor listened as a narrator's voice denounced him as a cold-blooded terrorist and cell leader for the Crimson Dawn. It went on to accuse him of masterminding the Mars Bar bombing and creating the red bloom algae. The pictures of him at the Administry for Environmental Affairs had been suitably adjusted, edited and dubbed to make it seem as if he was threatening further acts of terrorism unless his demands were met.

'I think we should pay Cydonia a visit,' said the Doctor grimly.

'But it's thousands of kilometres away,' protested Corvette.

'In my experience, thousands of kilometres away is a good place to be when one is accused of terrorism.'

'But the security forces will have sealed off all the canals to and from the city.'

'Oh, the *Dejah Thoris* has a few tricks up her hull, don't you old girl?' The Doctor patted the houseboat and grinned.

Minutes later, hydro foil jet engines lurched into life beneath the waves. The houseboat picked up speed and headed through the Eos Chasma complex.

Leela joined the Doctor at the boat's helm. 'Doctor we should leave Mars.'

'What? Just when I'm beginning to enjoy myself?' Once Leela had thought the Doctor was the mad god Xoanon, then she had believed he was a wise man dedicated to fighting evil.

Now she wondered if he was nothing but a child. The Time Lord seemed to read her thoughts. 'Leela, there's something terribly wrong here. Those algae were created to destroy an entire ecosystem. Someone is playing God and using Mars as a playpen. And we both know what happens to Gods.'

Ares stepped out of an airlock and into the Last Martian's private reception suite. Chlorine bit at his face. Underfoot, mouldering filter pads formed a putrescent mat which carpeted the poolside. Condensation clung to the windows, binding fungal growth to the glass. Obviously the Last Martian had cancelled the valet service. A pullulating mass broke the scummed surface of the pool and greeted Ares with outstretched tentacles.

'Poisoner! Assassin!' Tentacle tips whipped petulantly back and forth above Ares's head. He ducked, slipped and sprawled amidst the matted filter pads.

The Last Martian looked worse than ever. Spotlights set in the vaulted ceiling illuminated scabrous patches of small crustacea, possibly barnacles, clinging to its skin. It was predominantly burnt umber in colour, but with livid patches of red. Ares noticed that some of these patches were tentacle-picked wounds, self-inflicted by the Martian in its attempts to groom itself. The pain alone must surely be enough to drive the creature mad, thought Ares. He was reassured, however, to note the pale pink colour of the cephalopod's eye rings. Red would signal an attack.

'Marty, I can assure you that our security forces have the situation under control,' said Ares soothingly. 'The Crimson Dawn are under continual surveillance. Besides, the publicity will work in our favour in the long run. Redpeace are almost totally discredited.'

'Fool Paul,' pecked the Last Martian. 'Do you think I care about blatant publicists like the Crimson Dawn? No, I am talking about the real threat. Suicide squads of well-wishers, diplomats, servants.' A single tentacle flipped a boxed set of CD-Is into Ares's hands: *War of The Worlds* by H. G. Wells, directed by George Pal. Ares was none the wiser. The cephalopod coughed out an explanation, its beak punctuating its account with clicks and squawks.

'I watched this and it all made sense. Of kuck-kuck-course some of the details are wrong. Those absurd space ships. And the ridic-kuck-kuck-culous Martians look more like mushrooms. But the end is the same, and in the end I die. Don't you see what I am saying, Paul? My kuck-kuck-kind kuck-kuck-conquered them. They defeated us only by luck-kuck-kuck, by their bac-kuck-kuck-teria. That housemaid we employed. We trusted her. Her references seemed impec-kuck-kuck-cable. She charmed me with her smile, her eagerness to please, her skick-kuck-ill with the mantle skuck-kuck-raper. To think I allowed her to desc-kuck-kuck-ale me, while all the time she was plotting to kuck-kuck-ill me. She kuck-kuck-claimed she had a kuck-kuck-cold of kuck-kuck-course, but I knew. Oh yes. I lay in wait for her, and when she wasn't look-kuck-kuck-ing I kuck-kuck-cured her of her kuck-kuck-cold.'

'You killed the maid?' Ares was incredulous.

'The assassin Ares, the assassin.' The Last Martian became more agitated. 'Oh yes. I kuck-kuck-cured her kuck-kuck-cold in a kuck-kuck-chlorine bath. That kuck-kuck-killed her germs, her assassin's weapon.'

Ares felt sure that the Last Martian was having some kind of psychotic attack, but the future of the Ares Corporation depended on the creature's appearance at the forthcoming shareholders' meeting. The City was becoming suspicious. Rumours were already circulating on the stock exchange and in the society pages of the Inter-World Web that the Federation's most eccentric and wealthy recluse was dead; that he had in fact committed suicide and been replaced by one of his own inflatable Last Martian toys.

Ares tentatively raised the subject of the meeting.

'Are you mad Ares? Bring humans here?' The Last Martian's

eye rings darkened perceptibly.

'We can hold the meeting on board the *Aelita*.'

The Last Martian relaxed on hearing the name of his personal pleasure liner. He had designed the *Aelita* himself. It was the largest vessel of its kind in the Federation. One day, he thought, he would supervise its restoration. He knew it could float, despite the critics', engineers' and other nay-sayers' claims to the contrary.

'You will be safe in your chamber and still be able to greet the guests.' Ares decided to lay on a masquerade. That would be the best way to present the Last Martian to the shareholders. He reminded himself to order a mask for the creature. With luck it would cover some of the scar tissue. A cape would help too. Or maybe a body bag. Perhaps it was time to announce the miraculous discovery of the Last Martian's son.

Suddenly, in a comic, Tintin sees an oasis. He runs towards it, Snowy at his side. The oasis vanishes. A sign reads: *Danger – Mirage Ahead*. Later, sweeping up dust and dirt in the colonel's office, Tintin finds a label. The label reads: *Flor Fina. The Cigars of the Pharaoh*. Elsewhere, Mîkî leads a team of scientists to Mars and discovers that the Martians have captured the Pharaohs and forced them to build pyramids. Ramsîs rides to the rescue on rockets shaped like mummies.

Arif Hilâl thumbed the pages of the comics in his collection and returned them to their vacuum-sealed mylar bags. He had grown up reading these antiquated strips, which he had excavated from a forgotten trunk in his uncle's bazaar in SoHo. After the exploits of Tintin, he had quickly graduated to the political satire of cartoonists such as Ahmad Hijâzî and Sî Juhâ. From their critical perspective, he had recognized how modern Egypt came to be represented in terms of its ancient Pharaohnic past.

Hilâl heard a Camel-class Desertstormer arrive outside his tent. It belonged to Dr Sam Morgan.

'What's the vibe from H.G. Central, dude?' asked Hilâl, affecting the dress and argot of a late 20th-century cybergeek-homeboy-net- slacker.

Morgan, an archaeologist, wore a seen-it-all-before expression on his face. He regarded the young Redpeace co-ordinator appraisingly. Hilâl's head was shaved skin-close beneath his back-to-front baseball cap; his pinstriped chippies billowed in the wind; and his billy-can, climbing tackle and sextant were slung from his hips like six guns. The boy's a prat, thought Morgan, but at least his heart is in the right place.

'The Mars Bar has been attacked,' reported the archaeologist. 'They're also blaming the algae on the Crimson Dawn. And, oh yes, someone called the Doctor is your co-conspirator. A nasty piece of work, if the press are to be believed.'

'Bogus!' said Hilâl.

'My thoughts exactly.' Morgan picked up a comic. It was the 'Electrifying First Issue' of *Peter Cannon: Thunderbolt*. In the cover painting, ski-masked eco-terrorists stormed an airship over Nelson's column. The terrorists called themselves the Crimson Dawn. Ares and Hilâl shared the same taste in literature, thought Morgan. The Mike Collins artwork and storytelling were suitably dramatic, but the world's problems couldn't be solved by heroes in absurd costumes. 'We're not safe in the Tharsis Region, and the best defence is a good offence.'

'The Sphinx?' questioned Hilâl.

'Climb on board the Camel.' Morgan pulled a scarlet cape over his shoulders for additional protection against the cold of the Martian night. 'Next stop: Cydonia.'

'Slammin'!' yelled Hilâl.

Leela screamed. Her body spasmed as if impacted by a tremendous force. She clutched at the air and tried to prevent herself from being hurled across the deck.

Corvette watched from the cabin. 'Fascinating,' she observed. 'An ecstatic trance.'

Leela's face rippled. Finally she slumped into unconsciousness.

'The sacred Sevateem ritual of departure,' observed the Doctor. 'Mimicking the G-forces experienced by astronauts. It's intended to bring good luck for our journey.'

'She must be concerned for our safety,' opined Corvette.

'Leela isn't concerned,' said the Doctor. 'She's terrified.'

The *Dejah Thoris* had reached the Cydonia region and the limits of the canal system, and its passengers were now preparing to depart for the site where the Last Martian had been discovered. The trek would take them past two of the most impressive archaeological finds on Mars: the Valley of the Warriors – the ruins of an ancient Ice Warrior settlement – and the Great Pyramid.

'Have you ever seen the Pyramid?' asked Corvette.

'Not from the outside,' replied the Doctor enigmatically.

Leela had regained consciousness now, and rose unsteadily to her feet. Leaving K-9 to keep guard on board the *Dejah Thoris*, the three travellers then boarded a Camel Mark II transporter which had apparently been abandoned by the canal side. The Doctor took charge of the controls, fired the engine and sent the craft skimming towards the dried riverbeds, landlocked islands and ancient encrusted lakes of lava that lay to the west.

A sandstorm and four monolithic statues with faces elongated like the snouts of crocodiles welcomed the Doctor, Leela and Corvette to the Valley of the Warriors.

The transporter was being buffeted against the valley floor, and Corvette indicated they should stop and seek shelter in the ancient city. The Doctor brought the craft to a halt and they all climbed out.

Leela made for the nearest cover and found herself in a courtyard where she was confronted with what appeared to be a statue of two Ice Warriors locked in combat with each other. At first, she assumed it was a memorial erected to honour a great contest or battle, but when she saw similar statues in more domestic spaces she realized that what she was actually looking at were the ash- embalmed corpses of males, females and children driven mad by fear – or by something far worse.

'This place is evil, Doctor. The dead have been denied their proper place. Their spirits must surely walk among us.'

The Doctor ignored her. There was a time and a place for mysticism, and this wasn't it. 'An entire city held in suspension,' he mused. 'It's just like Pompeii. The pyramid must have been built on the site of a volcano. The eruption certainly caught the Ice Warriors by surprise. Perhaps they thought it was extinct.'

'As you can see, the Pharaohnic elements become more pronounced the closer the buildings are to the Pyramid,' said Corvette. 'The parallels with ancient Egypt excited great interest. That was why I was invited on the dig – my specialism is alien influences on ancient Earth cultures.'

'I see the pyramid has been left unopened,' the Doctor noted. 'Very sensible. But why was the dig abandoned?'

'Perhaps you could tell us all,' said a new voice.

The Doctor turned. The travellers were surrounded by robed figures carrying a motley collection of weapons – all of them trained on the Doctor. The Doctor recognized Arif Hilâl, grinned and raised his hands. 'We have met before, but haven't been formally introduced. I'm the Doctor, and you must be the Crimson Dawn.'

'According to the news, you are the leader of the Crimson Dawn,' said Hilâl.

'Weren't we all tarred with the same brush?' asked the Doctor. 'Besides, I think it's obvious that the Crimson Dawn doesn't really exist. I think the terrorist attacks are being staged by the Ares Corporation to discredit your attempts to repatriate the Ice Warriors. I also think the sooner you realize we are all on the same side, the sooner you will achieve your aims. Now why don't we talk, before Leela does something I will regret.'

Hilâl felt a sharp object pressed against his throat. Leela had spotted the group and crept up on them even as they had been surrounding the Doctor and Corvette. 'I'm prepared to die for my cause!' shouted Hilâl. Leela grinned and pressed the blunt base of the janis thorn harder against his skin.

Morgan indicated to Redpeace to put down their weapons. 'Since we are neither murderers nor terrorists we have no choice, Doctor. Let's talk.'

The base for Redpeace's operations was a hastily established encampment in the ruins of a temple, aligned in front of the gigantic claws of the Martian Sphinx.

'Ugly bastard isn't he?' said Morgan.

'Hey, don't diss the Sphinx, dude,' said Hilâl.

'We've confirmed that the Sphinx is four thousand years older than the rock strata in which it is claimed that the Last Martian plankton was found,' Morgan continued. 'The Ares Corporation must have closed the dig to prevent anyone discovering the truth. This evidence establishes the Ice Warriors as the oldest surviving indigenous species. It can only help our cause.'

'Perhaps.' The Doctor was unconvinced. He was more interested in deciphering a series of cryptograms carved into the walls of Redpeace's temple encampment. In the baleful light of the moons, he appeared to Corvette as a lector-priest, bringing together the powers of Hu, Sia and Heka to decode the divine order of the cosmos. 'Do any of you recognize this hieroglyph?' The Doctor asked.

'It's the symbol for Mars,' said Corvette.

'That's what I thought. Isn't there something missing, though?'

'There's only one moon. Deimos.'

'How do you explain that, Doctor?' asked Dr Morgan.

'I don't, but I've got a few ideas. I've been listening to your argument, and it seems to me that the Ares Corporation holds the solution to all your problems. I intend either to access their records or to meet this so-called Last Martian face to face. Preferably both.'

'But that's impossible!' said Morgan. 'The Ares Corporation and the Last Martian are based on the moons. The Corporation's core systems are accessible only from a few terminals, and the Last Martian is a recluse.'

'There is a way.' Corvette stepped from the shadows. 'The Ares Corporation has its annual shareholders meeting tomorrow on board the Last Martian's pleasure cruiser, the *Aelita*. The Corporation is in big financial trouble, and my guess is that the Last Martian will be pressed to attend.'

The *Aelita* loomed above the wrecked tugboats of the Utopia Marina, like a gigantic prop for an allegorical festival celebrating the emancipatory power of wealth and leisure. On board, the Doctor and K-9 sauntered through pools of angular light which threw the ship's forced-perspective corridors into sharp relief. Oblong cabins, suspended by powerful magnetic fields, blocked out the open spaces of the decks. These cabins, providing accommodation for land dwellers, were set amidst steel obelisks and aerodynamic columns of cones and spheres – totem poles of tomorrow. From their doorways stepped anthropomorphic frogs, jackals, cats, newts and a variety of insects.

The Doctor joined the masqueraders as they crowded towards the Exeter ballroom. Close behind him, K-9 conducted a low-level sensor sweep for a computer terminal linked to the Ares Corporation system core and located one in a cabin on the top deck. The Doctor was jostled by two women whose name badges identified them as Bastet and Sekhmet. Bastet, in the guise of a cat, saw K-9 and snarled playfully. The computer's drive system emitted a low growl before sending it lurching off through the jungle of legs in pursuit of its master.

The Doctor reached a sculptured perspex elevator and, with K-9 still at his side, began to ascend. In the distance, he heard an usher announcing the revellers as they arrived. They were all industrialists, but had used their money to buy themselves pasts in the form of aristocratic titles such as Lady Eleanor Rigby and Prince Ross Perot.

You wonder why you are in 19th century London. A sprite in the guise of a prostitute bustles over and greets you. You bluff your way past her, but she begins to scream for help. Whistles and running feet echo in your skull. You hear cries: 'Jack!'; 'It's the Ripper!'; 'Gawd 'elp us!' You notice that the Intrusion Countermeasures Electronics resemble London bobbies, but with the helmets of Ice Warriors. You realize that you are ripping up the guts of the computer system, but Whitechapel is within sight.

A hand clasps your shoulder, you turn and a gentleman's gentleman points you in the direction of a hunch-backed Tudor building. 'The Patent Office is in there, Master. Haste is suggested. I will protect you for as long as I can.' It is K-9.

You enter the Patent Office. Thickening layers of dust cover all but one of the filing cabinets. You rifle through parchments, photographs, yellowing envelopes. You realize that you are looking at the Last Martian's family album. More files on flora and fauna follow. A scuffle breaks out as police batter down the door. You are about to leap from a first-floor window when you see an oil painting of Mars. You touch Phobos and the computer gives up the secret of the sleepers within the moon. Satisfied with your investigations, you jump and rip through the roof of a waiting cab. K-9 reins the horses into action. You gallop towards realspace.

The Doctor hurried from Ares's office. He had hoped that the Corporation would be content to rely only its software to deal with intruders, but the sound of padding feet announced the arrival of hardware: two security guards. K-9 stunned them with a wide-angle force beam. The Doctor knew it was imperative that he left the ship, but after his raid on Ares's database he wanted to meet the Last Martian more than ever.

Paul Ares felt relaxed, happy, confident. A Prozac moment. He watched the passing masquerade. Everything was falling into place. This was to be the Last Martian's finest and most tragic hour. Mars's favourite son killed by cold-blooded terrorists as innocent shareholders look on. Ares could see the headlines now. A burly security officer dressed as a teddy bear walked discreetly over to him and whispered in his ear. The executive paled as he was told of the intruder. Ares thanked the officer, borrowed his pulse rifle and stalked towards the elevator.

The Last Martian swam in what appeared to be a gigantic light bulb. Beams from the spotlights set in the room's vaulted ceiling enmeshed the creature in a net of light. The light combined with the creature's chromatophores and iridocytes to create mottled areas of colour which slowly shifted position as its pigment-filled cytoelastic sacs expanded and contracted. The cephalopod held an absurdly small mask in front of its face. A cape was slung over its mantle for melodramatic effect.

The Doctor thought the scene was desperately kitsch. 'May I say how terribly impressed I am by your ship?' he said, trying to placate the agitated Martian. 'The grandeur of its design, the overreaching ambition. I'm reminded of the *Hindenberg*, the *Spruce Goose*, the *Titanic*. Did you design it yourself?'

The Last Martian seemed in a state of shock. Incapable of action, it spluttered an incoherent exclamation about human assassins.

'Well, first of all I am not human,' the Doctor reassured him, 'and secondly I am not here to harm you. Why are you afraid of humans?'

The creature's eyes glazed over and it began to intone a familiar litany.

'When our world began to die, we look-kuck-kuck-ed towards the other planets of the solar system. We kuck-kuck-oveted the Earth. It was a water world as our own had been. The logical solution was to kuck-kuck-colonize the planet. We built great machines: tripods, heat-rays, cylinders in which we travelled a-kuck-kuck-cross space. We thought we had left nothing to chance. To our vast, kuck-kuck-cool intellects, humanity was nothing more than transient bac-kuck-kuck-teria. We would cleanse the Earth of such infestation. We would bring reason and order to the world.'

'You were going to turn Earth into a sort of global science park!' the Doctor enthused.

'Exac-kuck-kuck-tly. But in the end, our colony was destroyed, wiped out by a virus, something as common as a cold. Only I survived, frozen as Mars cooled and the atmosphere thinned and the rivers evaporated. Now I am the Last Martian. Only *I* remember the glorious history of Mars.'

'Yes, I've read H.G. Wells,' said the Doctor

'A remar-kuck-kuck-able historian.'

'A writer of scientific romance. I'm afraid your story is just that. You're a fake, a fiction, a creature of écriture.' The Doctor heard the airlock open above him. A figure descended into the hold. He recognized the man from the database. 'Ah, the author himself. Have you come to deliver some final words, dot the i's and cross the t's, so to speak?'

'Ares! Ares!' squawked the Last Martian. 'This kuck-kuck-kuck-kuck-creature, kuck-kuck-kuck-kuck-claims I am living a lie. Kuck-kuck-kuck-kuck-kuck-kuck-kill him.'

'I will Marty, but not for that. My company staked everything on terraforming Mars. We couldn't just hand it over to the Ice Warriors. So my biotechnology division created our very own Martian. Something that would live up to everyone's expectations. A real crowd pleaser. But there were flaws in your genetic make-up. I see that now. We'll get it right next time. Your son, perhaps. Or daughter. The Ares Corporation likes to think of itself as an equal opportunities employer.'

'That's right Ares, shoot him, put him out of his misery,' the Doctor goaded sarcastically. 'He's just a wounded animal with delusions of grandeur.'

The bull octopus charged, its body pulsing with the multi-coloured hues of a Microsoft Satori screen saver. Its supporting equipment was wrenched from the walls and the glass bulb crashed against the Plexiglas hull of the ship, causing it to fracture. Water began to cascade into the room. Ares looked into the creature's eyes and backed away up the staircase. Waves swelled upwards. The octopus flayed the air with its tentacles, its beak pecking and squawking.

As Ares pulled his gun and opened fire, the Last Martian submerged itself in the water-filled chamber and released an obscuring stream of gelatinous black ink. Ares trembled. 'I didn't know he could do that. Did you know he could do that?' But the Doctor had already escaped through the airlock. Water surged unrestrained through the shattered Plexiglas hull, the ink spreading rapidly through it as it foamed towards the ceiling. The *Aelita* groaned as its substructure finally collapsed.

The Doctor looked back at the vessel from the *Dejah Thoris*'s inflatable life raft and was reminded of the sinking of the *Lusitania*. But the waters of the marina were shallow and the *Aelita* already rested near the bottom. There would be little loss of life.

A gale picked up and wailed its way along the valley, chasing clouds across the face of the moons. Members of Redpeace crouched on the deck of the *Dejah Thoris*, while inside the cabin the Doctor and his fellow conspirators huddled around the warmth of the houseboat's iron stove.

'The Last Martian was created by the Ares Corporation?' Corvette sounded incredulous.

'Yes,' replied the Doctor. 'A remarkable feat of genetic engineering, but hardly an aboriginal Martian.'

'And the algae. They framed us all,' said Morgan.

'I'm afraid so. The Crimson Dawn were nothing more than hired mercenaries in the employ of the Ares corporation. The red bloom algae, the explosion at the Mars Bar and all the other terrorist actions were just black ops designed to discredit Redpeace. Ares stopped at nothing to secure his company's claim to Mars. Not even the destruction of his own creation. Sometimes I wonder if the human race isn't a little *too* indomitable.'

'Chill out, Doctor dude,' enthused Hilâl. 'Now the Last Martian's blown, Mars belongs to the Ice Warriors. Most excellent!'

The Doctor's pupils became twin back holes swallowing the cabin's meagre light. Only Leela sensed his troubled thoughts.

Suddenly a muffled pinging noise echoed around the cabin.

'Doctor, that noise?'

The Doctor swept aside a dust-encrusted tapestry. The houseboat was bathed in the eerie luminescence of a Benchley Mark Five Fish Finder. The Doctor saw a large blur of light pulse across its screen. 'Something's moving towards us.'

'It can't be a shoal of fish,' said Corvette.

The Doctor stared at the indecipherable shape surging across the screen. Suddenly the cabin lurched violently to one side. On deck, the night was punctuated by a series of dull thuds and startled cries. Hilâl was the first to reach the cabin door. He just had time to see the fallen bodies of his comrades before his chest exploded into a blood-darkened ruin of flesh and bone. He fell back onto the stairs.

'But how?' Corvette asked in a stunned tone.

The *Deja Thoris* lurched again. Only Leela kept her balance. In the dark, wires of light sliced through the oak hull. A jet-boat bearing the logo of the Ares Corporation pulled up alongside. Paul Ares, armed with a particle rifle, stepped on board and into the cabin.

'Murderer!' exclaimed Morgan.

Ares smiled. 'You and your fellow travellers are wanted terrorists. I am merely executing my civic duty.'

Leela lunged at the executive and he fired his gun, slicing a furrow into her thigh. The laser heat cauterized the wound almost instantaneously. Leela fell to one side as Ares calmly took aim again. Corvette screamed. The boat pitched and yawed. Ares was gone.

Morgan, Leela and Corvette stared at the empty stairwell. 'I don't wish to seem ungrateful,' said the Doctor, 'but what happened to our guest?'

Leela considered her answer carefully. 'He vanished.'

Leela and the Doctor scrambled up on deck. In the dark, the Time Lord picked out an oil slick bubbling out of the depths of the canal.

'Something was here,' said Leela. 'Something alive.'

The Doctor stared out across the night-shaded canal, his breathing shallow. From inside the cabin, the Fish Finder sounded again. 'Leela, on the wall at the bottom of the stairs is a harpoon. Do you see it? Good. Bring it up on deck for me, would you? K-9, activate your sea water defences. When I say "Now", I want you to run an electrical current through the iron ribs of the hull.'

'Specifications, Master?'

'Oh, something along the lines of a small power station should do it. A current of one amp at 30,000 volts, say. 900 megawatts.'

'Master, I am unable to sustain such a current for longer than a second without completely draining my power supply. Subsequent damage to my neural nets may prove irreparable.'

'I'm sorry K-9. I hope this will be brief.'

'Understood, Master.'

Leela took up a position on the prow and hefted the harpoon experimentally in her right hand, shifting her body weight to give her the maximum possible leverage.

Suddenly Morgan screamed. Leela turned and saw that he was being lifted into the air by a fleshy tentacle which had wrapped itself around his torso and was slowly squeezing the breath from his body. She hurled the harpoon towards the waterline at what appeared to be its point of origin. The tentacle uncoiled itself from Morgan's waist, dropping him back to the deck.

The Doctor turned to K-9. 'Now, K-9!'

For a moment the night smelt of burning flesh. Then the tentacle slithered limply back beneath the waves.

From somewhere in the hold of the ship came the sound of splintering wood. The *Dejah Thoris* began taking on water. 'Shouldn't we head for the shore?' asked Corvette.

'No,' replied the Doctor. 'If the creature's still alive, the sound of the engine will attract it.'

'It was the Last Martian, wasn't it?' Corvette was visibly shaken.

'It must have followed the vibrations of Ares's jet-boat,' confirmed the Doctor. 'The question is, how did Ares find us?'

Morgan groaned in pain and the Doctor moved across to examine him. The man's torso was studded with crescent-shaped wounds left by the cephalopod's serrated limbs. He winced as the Doctor began bandaging his chest. 'A few cracked ribs, nothing to worry about,' the Time Lord reassured him.

'You mewl like a baby,' jeered Leela playfully. 'Warriors should wear their wounds with pride.' She pulled aside a leather thong and revealed a jagged scar just below her left breast. 'A Horda bite. The creature was dying, but it still clung to life.'

The Doctor welcomed the diversion from their perilous situation. He pulled open his shirt. 'What about this,' He pointed to his unblemished chest. 'Sarah Jane Smith. She broke my hearts.'

Leela noticed a row of thin diagonal lines scarring Corvette's right arm. They were too regular to be battle wounds. 'Are those the markings of your tribe?' she asked.

'They're glyph codes,' Corvette replied. 'From the *Orion VI.*'

'You were on the *Orion VI*?' asked Morgan. The doomed expedition had acquired a legendary status amongst academics of the Federation.

'They were tattooed on my arm by the Department of Employment,' Corvette continued. 'I was a victim of the last round of downsizing in the higher education sector. They contain my CV and a constantly updated record of my attempts to find work. Without it, I wouldn't have been entitled to apply for unemployment benefit.' Corvette rolled up her sleeve. The grey stain extended from her wrist to her elbow.

'My secret shame,' she laughed. 'There aren't many jobs an anthropologist can do. Eventually, I was sent on a community service programme to the outer planets. There were a hundred of us, mostly anthropologists, sociologists and cognitive psychologists. We were shunted off to Aridius as part of a covert operation to assess its suitability for entry into the Federation. They sent us on a Class Three Warpskip, the *Orion VI*, but I could see that it was in no condition to make the journey. When we got to Aridius, the engines blew. Only one life pod worked. We crowded in, but there were too many of us and we crashed in the Northern Mire. The first night, the Mire Beasts found us. We could hear their snuffling as they looked for weaknesses in the hull. There were plenty of those. We might as well have been wrapped in Alcan foil. Soon the screaming started. And I watched the class of 2420 being torn apart. A century ago they would have been members of an intellectual elite, now they were just so much dead meat. One hundred academics went into the Mire, only I came out. On the fourth day, just before we were rescued, my partner tried to push me in front of a Mire Beast so I would be eaten before him. It was then I realized that human beings were no better than the Mire Beasts. From that moment on, I stopped being prey and became a hunter.'

The Doctor considered the story, and asked, 'So after you were rescued, you sold out to the Ares Corporation?'

Corvette looked up sharply. How had she given herself away?

She said nothing. Instead, she reached inside her jacket and pulled out a stubby black cylinder.

'A particle bomb, how original,' sneered the Doctor. 'It was you who planted the bomb in the Mars Bar, wasn't it? And you who led Ares here. I saw the look in your eyes when he was about to kill us. It was our escape from the capital which first made me suspicious. It was far too easy. K-9 has been keeping you under surveillance since then. Haven't you K-9?'

'Affirmative, Master,' chirped the faithful computer.

'K-9 has also disarmed your bomb.'

Corvette quickly checked the bomb's read-outs, discovered that the Doctor was telling the truth and threw it angrily to one side.

'You're all fools. Give Mars back to the Ice Warriors? The greenies are nothing but monsters. I know. I've seen. On Aridius, Mars, Venus. . .' Corvette stared at the Time Lord. 'What are you?'

'Who am I?' the Doctor corrected her. 'Just a wanderer passing through, righting wrongs, doing good deeds, that sort of thing.'

'No. That's not it. As soon as the girl described you, I knew I had heard of you before. During my research, I gathered stories of a creature such as you: the Zonewalker, the Shadow-Thief, the Trickster of Time. The names and the myths changed from world to world, but I always suspected that there was a real, living creature behind them. A monster.'

'A monster?' The Doctor was incredulous. 'I think you've confused me with a Dalek, or a Krynoid, or yourself.'

'Your companions may be fooled by your performance, "Doctor", but myths allow me to see you with the eyes of time. You are a hollow man, an empty vessel. Without the lives and dreams of humanity to fill you, your existence would be without meaning. You are a black hole gorging on the light of the living, as soulless as a mere commodity. For the moment, you may be satisfied with exchanging the hopes of your companions for a future, but one day your insatiable desires could open up a chasm so wide that all the universe itself would be consumed. Well, your future ends here.'

The Doctor stared at her in astonishment. 'You know, I think you need a little lie down.' Then the Fish Finder began to scream. 'More red herrings?' the Doctor quipped.

The stern of the *Dejah Thoris* was suddenly catapulted out of the water. Its crew tumbled onto the deck. They were face to beak with the Last Martian. The creature had wrapped its tentacles along the length of the narrowboat and hauled itself on board.

'Good evening,' welcomed the Doctor. He pulled a crumpled paper bag from his pocket. 'Care for a jelly baby?'

'More! More! What happened next?'
Small figures pressed around Morgan to hear his tale. Some slithered up a nearby wall to get closer to the storyteller. Children are bloodthirsty little devils, he thought. But it was Resurrection Eve, and they had a right to be excited.

'Leela could see the Last Martian's limbs tearing the *Dejah Thoris* apart, plank by plank. She saturated her lungs with oxygen and dived into the canal. Beneath the water, she stared into the soulless eyes of the cephalopod. With a knife in one hand and a janis thorn in the other, she propelled herself into the heart of the creature's medusan locks. In front of her, Corvette lay dead, almost bitten in two by the monster's relentless razor beak. A tentacle wrapped itself around her leg, a second around her ribcage. Leela lashed out with her knife. The octopus's eye rings darkened to a livid purple. She was dragged towards the creature's beak. Then, the Last Martian convulsed. Its grip loosened. Leela plunged the janis thorn into its fleshy eye and the creature died in a plume of black vitreous humour. Later, as we all floundered in the water, the Doctor explained that the red bloom algae had attacked the monster's nervous system. The beast had died from the poison of the janis thorn and from the humblest things that Ares in his wisdom had put upon Mars.'

'And then? And then?' chorused the children.

'You know what happened next,' said Morgan. He had told this tale for twenty years, for twenty successive Resurrection Eves.

'Yes, Morgan, tell us more.' A cloaked figure stood silhouetted against the stars. The children's eyes widened. A few brave ones ran up to touch the hem of the cloak.

'I last saw the Doctor in the Utopia Planitia dockyards. He was rebuilding the mighty *Dejah Thoris*. Leela was there, and K-9 too. The plucky computer had floated ashore on a raft of wooden planks. I told the Doctor that an Adjudicator was being sent from Earth to settle the Ice Warriors' claim to Mars, but that it would be many decades before the scattered families and tribes could be found. It was then that the Doctor revealed the secret of Phobos. He had noticed that the moon was missing from the ancient hieroglyph in the Valley of the Warriors, and had followed up his lead when he entered the Ares Corporation's database. His suspicions were confirmed. Phobos was the generation starship that had first brought the Ice Warriors' prehistoric ancestors to Mars. And when the planet had begun to die, the Ice Warriors had tried to use it to escape. But its systems had been worn, it had failed to leave orbit and a million Ice Warriors were still trapped inside it in suspended animation. The Doctor had sent a signal to the ship. Soon the Ice Warriors would awaken. And the day they awoke was called Resurrection Day.'

The children cheered. And along the slopes of Olympus Mons, Ice Warriors turned to greet the dawn. As the curtain of night was drawn back, they applauded the planet as their own.

'And the Doctor?' the Ice Lord asked.

Morgan simply smiled and glanced towards the nearby canal – one of the vast network of irrigations channels that now encircled the whole of Mars. He liked to imagine that the Doctor was still out there somewhere, fishing from his houseboat.

Where the Heart is

By Andy Lane

'Perhaps we can move on to item five,' said Robert Walker, the rather chubby Deputy Parliamentary Permanent Secretary to the Minister for the Armed Services. He didn't even bother looking at the agenda in front of him. 'I believe it concerns the withdrawal of the UK from the protocols governing the United Nations Intelligence Taskforce.'

For a moment Brigadier Alastair Gordon Lethbridge-Stewart thought he'd misheard, but as the full import of Walker's words sank in he felt his fingers clench on his fountain pen. He forced himself to relax. That pen had been a present from Doris. 'With respect, sir,' he said, trying not to show his anger, 'I think you'll find that the agenda item actually refers to a discussion concerning the level of *funding* for UNIT. There's no mention of the UK pulling out of its commitments.'

'Commitments are all very well, Brigadier,' Walker said smoothly, 'but in a situation of reduced public expenditure, we have to make all the savings we can. I'm under pressure from the Treasury to cut an extra five billion pounds this year, and we've squeezed the Ministry of Defence, the Security Service and the Secret Intelligence Service until the pips squeak. The money has to come from somewhere, and, as I'm sure you'll agree, UNIT is a *very* expensive organization to run. The ground rent on those central London headquarters of yours alone is astronomical. UNIT, I'm afraid, is in the firing line.'

Lethbridge-Stewart glanced around the heavy table at the members of the Secret Vote Finance Committee: bland civil servants and choleric military officers with not an ounce of guts between them. Above them, faces of long-dead men stared down from the massive oil paintings that lined the walls, their faces glossy with varnish but just as unhelpful.

In the firing line? When was the last time they had looked down the business end of a Dalek gunstick? When was the last time they had watched a hole punched through a subordinate by a blast from an Auton's hand?

Switching his gaze back to Walker, he said: 'The UNIT protocols that bind member nations together to fight alien invasion were ratified in Geneva five years ago by the Home Secretary. No mechanism for withdrawal was provided for. Forgive me, sir, but the UK already puts less money into UNIT than does Luxembourg, and yet seventy-six per cent of the attempted alien invasions in the past five years have occurred in this country. Do I have to remind you' – he was aware that he was raising his voice but couldn't seem to hold back – 'of the three Nestene invasions? The attack on the Wenley Moor research facility? Surely you of all people remember the Sea Devils?'

There was a frown on Walker's podgy face, and Lethbridge-Stewart could tell that he wasn't getting through. Somewhere in the corridors of power, a decision had already been taken. It was too late.

'Let's not be melodramatic, Brigadier,' Walker said. 'HMG believe that–'

'Good God, man,' Lethbridge-Stewart snapped, 'haven't you even read my reports? Don't you know how many times your precious Treasury has come close to being razed to the ground by an invading alien army?' He was half-standing now, breathing fast, and he forced himself to relax. Through the half-open window, he could hear the muted growl of buses and the angry hoot of taxis in Whitehall. Nobody out there cared about the small, private battle going on in this oak-panelled conference room. Nobody out there even suspected how thin a line separated them from their worst nightmares.

Robert Walker doodled something on the pad before him. 'Nobody would argue about your stirling efforts in defending us all against the threat from space,' he said testily, 'but we are paying vast sums of money so that your men can sit around for months on end doing nothing, just on the off chance that little green men from Mars might turn up in Tooting.'

'We do take on other duties, sir,' the Brigadier said stiffly. 'UNIT was responsible for the safety of delegates at the First World Peace Conference, as well as the follow-up talks at Auderley House. Then there was the safe disposal of the Thunderbolt nerve gas missile – '

'And a fine hash you made of that,' murmured one of the other men around the table.

'– and we are currently investigating the disappearance of one of your own Ministerial colleagues.'

'Yes, yes, I know all that.' Walker tapped his finger on the table. 'I understand your position, Brigadier, but the plain unvarnished truth of the matter is that UNIT is just too expensive for us. Please convey to your masters in Geneva the message that the United Kingdom is proposing to redirect its finance to a more cost-effective area.'

'Might I ask,' the Brigadier said calmly, trying not to snap his pen in half, 'for the record, what this area might be?'

Walker nodded. 'Of course. We're examining the possibility that the Corps of Royal Marines could take on UNIT's occasional duties. From a financial point of view it makes perfect sense, and – let me be honest Brigadier – your record of liaison with the regular military hasn't been exactly wrinkle free, has it?'

Lethbridge-Stewart had to look away, towards one of the oil paintings, in case the fury in his eyes became visible to Walker. *His* record of liaison with the military? *His* masters in Geneva? For God's sake, he hadn't *asked* to be seconded from his regiment to UNIT: he'd been posted. Doris had warned him that this would happen, but he'd ignored her. 'Don't worry,' they had told him, 'it won't affect your long-term career.' His father was probably *in* one of those paintings on the wall. And his grandfather. And now, without any warning, he wasn't one of *us* any more.

'May I request a vote on the matter, sir?' he inquired tightly.

'No point.' Walker smiled. 'The decision has been already been taken.'

'You realize that I'll fight this?'

'Of course,' Walker replied. 'I've read enough of your reports to know *that* about you. Now, if we could move on to item six. . .'

As the white-coated receptionist flicked through his appointment book, the Doctor looked appreciatively around the hall of the country manor house. Very impressive. Very impressive indeed. Late sixteenth century at a guess, and very well preserved. He wished he could spend a few hours wandering down in the wine cellar, but he had a job to do.

He could feel his hackles rising at the thought. It was beneath his intellectual abilities to trace missing people, even if one of them happened to be a Minister. It wasn't his problem that UNIT had become a dumping ground for puzzling cases. He'd expressed this view in no uncertain terms to the Brigadier, but had been instructed in good old-fashioned British military vernacular to wind his neck in and find the missing people. Fired by anger, he had quickly discovered that all the missing people had the same telephone number in their address books – a number registered to an exclusive health clinic owned by one Doctor Dantalion. Naturally he'd rushed straight down here to the place in question. Once he'd cleared up this little mystery he would take great pleasure in rubbing the Brigadier's nose in it.

'I'm sorry sir,' the receptionist said from his oak desk. 'I can find no record of your appointment.' His face was as blank as his white coat. 'What did you say your name was again?'

'I'm the Doctor, of course.' He smiled benignly. 'And I don't have an appointment, I'm afraid.'

'The Doctor?' The receptionist's face remained impassive. 'Is this a professional consultation?'

'Acquaintance of mine recommended this place.' He rubbed a hand across the back of his neck. 'I drove down from London on the off chance.'

'Doctor Dantalion does not receive –' he glanced briefly at the Doctor's velvet jacket and ruffled shirt '– casual callers. This is a rather exclusive clinic. We cater only for those who can afford our fees.'

'And just how high are those fees?' the Doctor asked. There was something about the receptionist which made him suspicious. That uniform was just too perfectly pressed, that hair too well arranged. There was something about the man which wasn't quite... human. Hmm. Looked like there might be more to this case than met the eye. Perhaps it *was* a case for UNIT after all.

'If you need to ask what they are,' the receptionist riposted, 'then you can't afford them.'

'And if I were to offer. . . oh, let's say something in the region of ten thousand pounds for a consultation? Would Doctor Dantalion see me then?'

The receptionist hesitated for a moment, then said: 'Perhaps I could take some details before I bother the doctor.' He pulled a form out from a drawer and picked up a fountain pen. 'Name?'

'Smith: Doctor John Smith.'

The receptionist didn't bat an eyelid as he wrote it down. The Doctor smiled slightly. Most people would have commented on such an obviously fraudulent name.

'Occupation?' the man continued.

'Eccentric inventor,' the Doctor replied. That got written down as well.

'Next of kin?'

This was the key question. 'None,' he said. 'I have no living family.'

The pen hesitated over the form, but the man's expression still didn't change. 'I'll go and ask Doctor Dantalion whether she can see you now.' He placed the pen in its rest, got up and turned towards a large oak door set to one side of the hall. 'Please wait here.'

The Doctor, acting on a hunch, quickly picked up the pen, leaned forward and drew a line straight down between the receptionist's shoulder blades. The man didn't react at all as he walked away toward the door. The Doctor wasn't surprised to see the ink trickling slowly down his white coat. Whatever the garment was made of, it certainly wasn't cotton.

The Doctor briefly considered calling the Brigadier from the telephone on the desk, but that would have been tantamount to asking for help, and he wouldn't do that; not after what the Brigadier had said. No, this thing might be bigger than he had anticipated, but he'd see it through and present the solution, neatly wrapped, to the Brigadier that afternoon.

'Doctor Smith,' a voice said behind him. He pocketed the pen and turned to see a woman in an expensive mauve three-piece suit bearing down on him. 'I'm so pleased to meet a fellow member of the medical profession.'

'Yes, you probably are,' the Doctor replied. As he had anticipated, there was no sign of the receptionist. 'Doctor Dantalion?' He extended his hand.

'Indeed I am.' Dantalion glanced at his hand but didn't return the gesture. 'Would you like to come this way?' She gestured towards the door behind which the receptionist had vanished. The Doctor couldn't help noticing that her smile was fixed upon her face.

'After you,' the Doctor said, waving vaguely. Dantalion eyed him for a moment, then swung away, still smiling. The Doctor followed her towards the door, noticing with some satisfaction that there was a line of still-wet ink in the centre of her pastel jacket, right between her shoulder blades. That cleared up one mystery, at least. There was only one of them. No telling its race yet, but that should only take a few moments.

The door led into a room with bookshelf-lined walls and a curtained French window. The curtains were billowing slightly as the breeze caught them. Dantalion sat down behind a large oak desk which bore nothing but a blotter, a decanter and two glasses.

'Now, Doctor Smith,' she said, smiling her fixed smile, 'what can I do for you?'

'Well, for a start,' the Doctor said as he leaned back into a chair and crossed his legs, 'perhaps you would like to abandon that ridiculous disguise.'

Dantalion didn't react.

'Don't worry that your alien form might frighten me,' the Doctor continued. 'I can assure you, my dear, that I will have seen far worse in my time.'

Dantalion's smile finally flickered, along with the rest of her. The Doctor watched calmly as her form distorted and faded away, revealing a small alien with a face like an apricot pit and six spindly arms poking through gaps in a chitinous breast-plate. One eye was a limpid black pool, the other a metal sphere.

'How did you penetrate my elaborate masquerade?' the alien asked in a buzzing voice.

'Experience,' the Doctor said. 'And sheer intelligence.'

Dantalion's faced creased in what might have been some alien form of chagrin. At least, the Doctor thought, this was its *real* face, and not just a holographic projection.

You're a Birastrop, aren't you.' the Doctor continued. 'And a long way from home.'

Dantalion nodded. 'I am. And you are not of genus Homo sapiens either, despite your superficial demeanour. Your implant is undoubtedly superior to my own humble effort.' Its one real eye widened slightly. 'Could I interest you in a small libation, by the way? I have a supply of *juke* that I keep for -' it coughed, '- purely medicinal purposes.'

'I don't mind if I do,' the Doctor replied, noting in passing that the alien's phrasing had become considerably more flowery. As Dantalion poured a milky fluid from the decanter into the two glasses, the Doctor continued: 'Now that we've got the pleasantries out of the way, perhaps you would be so kind as to tell me where the five missing humans are and what exactly you're doing on this planet.'

Dantalion handed one of the glasses of *juke* to the Doctor, who took a brief sip. 'It's obviously pointless of me to dissemble,' it said. 'You're far too clever to be taken in by any of my histrionics or thespian posings.'

The Doctor brushed a speck of non-existent dust from the sleeve of his jacket. 'Oh, I don't know,' he said. 'No cleverer than any fair to middling genius.' He grinned disarmingly and tried to raise his glass to his lips again, but found that his hand was suddenly frozen to the chair.

'But fortunately not too clever to imbibe a concoction that causes instantaneous immobility in any living creature apart from Birastrops,' Dantalion added.

The Doctor tried to pull himself from his chair, but his muscles wouldn't obey. Words seethed in his mind, but his lips remained motionless, fixed in a fatuous grin. If only he had told somebody where he was going, but the Brigadier had been at a meeting and Jo had been in the canteen with Mike Yates and Sergeant Benton. He had been so pleased with himself at having figured out where the missing people had gone that he had rushed off without even leaving a note.

Dantalion leaned forward and gazed into the Doctor's eyes with interest. 'I look forward to cutting you up,' it said, 'as I cut up the other five.'

The Doctor brought all his concentration to bear on his right arm. If he could move that, then he might be able to disable Dantalion with a right hook. He could feel his hearts labouring as he strained, but there was no movement. Not even a twitch.

Just as Dantalion loomed over the Doctor's paralysed form, the curtains covering the French window billowed open and Jo Grant stepped into the room. She was holding a large automatic pistol which must have taken up most of the room in her handbag. She swung it round to cover Dantalion. The Doctor was too angry at himself to feel relieved.

'Don't move,' she said with only the slightest quaver in her voice. 'I've spent fifteen hours on the firing range this week, and I know how to use this thing.'

Had the Doctor been able to speak, he might have been tempted to point out that it had taken her fourteen of those hours actually to hit the target.

Brigadier Lethbridge-Stewart could hear the voices drifting along the corridor to his office. It sounded as if most of his senior staff were in the Doctor's laboratory, celebrating the capture of some alien creature or other the day before. At least they'd found out what had happened to that missing Minister, as well as the other four people. The Brigadier had been invited, but he didn't have the heart to attend, knowing that the folder would still be sitting on his desk when he returned.

He picked it up again: a pinkish-red cardboard folder with the word SECRET stamped top and bottom. There were four sheets of paper inside it: the minutes of the Secret Vote Finance Committee meeting chaired by Robert Walker. It had been delivered by special courier that morning. It was the death knell for UNIT, spelt out in typical civil service circumlocution.

There had to be something he could do. There had to be somebody who could help. England needed UNIT. *He* needed UNIT.

As he reached for the telephone, unsure who exactly he was going to ring, a voice intruded on his thoughts.

'I thought that you were coming to the party, old chap?' the Doctor said. He was leaning against the doorframe, a plastic cup in one hand.

'I have some paperwork to do,' the Brigadier said awkwardly. 'I'll be along in a while. Best start without me.'

'We already have,' the Doctor said.

The operator squawked from the receiver, and the Brigadier barked, 'Get me Chinn at the Home Office, secure line.'

'Chinn, eh?' the Doctor mused. 'Ghastly chap: thought we'd

heard the last of him after that Axon business.'

'Needs must when the devil drives, Doctor.' The line clicked several times as connections were made through the government secure network.

'Problems?' The Doctor pushed himself away from the wall and subsided into a chair.

Lethbridge-Stewart sighed and rubbed a hand across his eyes. 'The Government want to close UNIT down,' he said. 'Damn paper pushers and desk jockeys think that all we do is sit here on our arses and wait to be invaded. I'm fighting it, Doctor, but I'd –'

'You shouldn't let them push you around in these petty territorial squabbles you humans are so fond of,' the Doctor said dismissively. 'Stand up for yourself, man. Did you hear about our little success, by the way?'

'I don't think that it's quite that –'

'I managed to find out where those missing people had gone. Turned out that an alien being had disguised itself as a doctor in an exclusive clinic and was doing away with rich people who had no family. We found them stacked in plastic bags, disassembled down to the individual organs. Very neat, very professional. Can't for the life of me see why, yet, and the creature in question isn't talking. We're holding it down in the basement.' He rubbed his chin. 'Still can't work out how it did that disguise trick – Birastrops aren't natural shape shifters, you know.'

Someone on the other end of the telephone line said, 'Horatio Chinn's telephone, can I help you?'

'Hold please,' the Brigadier said, and turned to the Doctor. 'Look, Doctor, I –'

'Calls itself Dantalion, this creature' the Doctor continued. 'Must have been here a while – enough time to buy the manor house, learn to speak perfect if slightly Victorian English, masquerade as at least two different humans and write an advertisement in *The Times* to lure its victims in. It promised treatment for incurable conditions – typical charlatan trick. Anybody who replied was sent a questionnaire asking them about finance and next of kin. Those who had a lot of one and none of the other were invited to the clinic – the others were fobbed off with some excuse or another.'

'Doctor, I really should –'

'The creature obviously needed rich people so that it could maintain its expensive lifestyle. They paid in cash, of course, and didn't tell anyone where they were going. That was one of Dantalion's conditions, and it knew that desperate people would agree to anything.'

'Hello,' said the voice on the other end of the telephone line, 'this is Horatio Chinn's personal assistant. Can I *help* you?'

'Please Doctor, I'm on the –'

'Have to say,' the Doctor went on, talking over the top of the Brigadier's protests, 'that I admire its gall. And its taste in fine wines – quite an extensive little cellar it had.'

'Doctor, *please!*'

The Doctor look hurt. 'Sorry, old chap. Obviously a bad time. We'll save a bottle for you.' He got up, and looked at his almost empty cup. 'Well, perhaps half a bottle.'

As he left, the Brigadier turned his attention back to the telephone. 'This is Brigadier Lethbridge-Stewart of UNIT. I want to talk to Mr Chinn about a matter of some importance. . .'

Jo Grant flinched as the Brigadier strode into the crowded laboratory. He was so angry that even his moustache was bristling. His gaze flicked around the room and fixed on her, sitting on one of the Doctor's benches listening to one of Corporal Bell's dirty jokes.

'Miss Grant!' he barked.

Corporal Bell straightened to attention and backed out of the line of fire. Jo sprang to her feet. 'Yes sir,' she said, 'I mean, no sir. I mean –'

'Any more of that wine left?'

She nervously bent down, opened a door in the bench and retrieved the bottle that she had been hiding from the Doctor. 'Just the one, I'm afraid, sir.'

The Brigadier swiped a plastic cup from beside her, poured himself a generous measure and gulped it down in one.

'Bad day, sir?' Mike Yates said, smiling at Jo as he moved through the crowd towards them. He was holding a plate of food from the buffet.

'Appalling,' the Brigadier said. 'Government want to give UNIT's responsibilities to the Navy, go it alone and let Geneva handle the rest of the world. Empire building by Walker – and he must have pulled some favours to get it ratified so quickly. The word around the bazaars is that they've already appointed some hidebound rear-admiral to run the show. Name of Jonathan Zecca. Ever come across him?'

'No sir.' Mike's face had turned white. 'But sir, how can they justify –'

'Cost, Captain Yates. The great god profit. If we're going to fight this, we'll have to cut our expenditure significantly. I've been phoning round pulling favours, but there's no joy anywhere. Horatio Chinn's refusing to talk to me and Sir Reginald Styles is out of the country.' He glanced across the laboratory to where the tall, white-haired form of the Doctor was leaning casually against the TARDIS, regaling Sergeant Benton with some long, involved anecdote concerning his travels. Jo thought she caught the word 'Medusoids', but she couldn't be sure. 'Problem is,' Lethbridge-Stewart continued in a quieter voice, 'the Doctor's got so many official backs up in the past few years that we haven't many friends left. He made Walker look like a fool over that Sea Devil business, and Walker won't forget that in a hurry.' His brown eyes locked with Jo's. 'I even tried your uncle, Miss Grant. He was sympathetic, but apparently he's up for a knighthood –'

'And doesn't want to rock the boat?' Jo nodded. 'That's Uncle Bill, all right.' She frowned. 'But there must be *some-*

thing we can do.'

'Your uncle did suggest one thing,' the Brigadier added. 'He pointed out that the major cost of UNIT is our HQ.'

Jo gazed around the laboratory. 'What, *this* place?'

'Yes, this place. Despite appearances, central London property is highly expensive. He said that if we could find somewhere cheaper off our own bat then he could put a good word in for us with the PPS. The whole thing's funding-led.'

'But where can we find somewhere suitable for an organization like UNIT?' Jo protested. 'I mean, it's not as if we can pop into an estate agents and ask for a secret base hidden in a volcano, like in *You Only Live Twice*.'

'I appreciate the problem, don't worry,' the Brigadier said, smiling slightly. 'But nobody at the MoD or the Home Office is going to do it for us.' He sighed, and took the last vol-au-vent from Mike's plate. 'Thank you Captain Yates.'

'Sir..?'

'RHIP, Captain. Rank has its privileges. Anyway, don't let me bore you with all this politics. Tell me about this alien you've captured.'

'Not me sir – Jo here,' Mike began, gazing forlornly at the disappearing vol-au-vent. 'The Doctor had breezed in alone, as usual, and Jo had to go in and rescue him.'

'Good thing I saw him leave his laboratory and followed him,' Jo added. 'I *knew* he was up to something, just from the expression on his face. I don't know what he'd do without me.'

'Just the one alien, this time?' the Brigadier said. 'Makes a change.'

'Yes sir,' confirmed Yates. 'The interrogator arrived this morning from Geneva – he's with it now, down in the basement, but it refuses to talk. We've sent a tissue sample to Liz Shaw at Cambridge so that she can try to develop a truth serum, and the scene-of-incident team are going over the house inch by inch.'

'The Doctor said it killed the five victims.'

'Yes sir. Sliced them up, took them apart and put the bits into plastic bags, labelled in some alien lingo.'

Jo shuddered, remembering. 'It was horrible! There was this big stainless-steel table with straps on and a drain for the blood. And those bags! Ugh!'

Mike patted her arm sympathetically. 'The interrogator's working on the assumption that the alien was on a sort of reconnaissance mission for an invasion force – sussing out the opposition, so to speak. All radar stations are on full alert, but there's no sign of anything out there. Me, I think it was harvesting something from the bodies – an alien delicacy or something. We'll probably find that there's a bit missing from each one.'

'Yes, very fanciful, Captain,' Lethbridge-Stewart said. 'What's the Doctor's opinion?'

'Don't know, sir,' Mike said, blushing slightly. 'The Doc's been helping the interrogator, albeit reluctantly, but the creature won't give anything away.' Mike glanced across to where Benton was listening to the Doctor with a glassy expression on his face. 'Oddly enough, I think the Doctor quite likes it.'

Lethbridge-Stewart stared across at the Doctor for a few moments.

'He should make the most of it then,' he said. 'If the Royal Navy take control of anti-alien operations, the kid gloves will be off. I've seen how the Marines operate. They'll strap it to its own table and cut a piece of it off for every one of their questions it doesn't answer.'

As Jo walked down the stained concrete steps into the basement, the interrogator was packing up for the night. His briefcase was resting on a bench, and he was stuffing papers inside. He was a thin, balding man in a nondescript jacket and corduroy trousers – perfectly suited for the dank, cheerless area of UNIT's holding cells.

'I was just delivering some food to the guards, and I thought

I'd pop down,' she said as the electronic security door rolled shut at the top of the stairs. 'Any joy?'

The man shook his head. 'None,' he said with a faintly discernible accent. 'We are still no closer to the reasons why it killed those five people.'

'And cut them up,' Jo added.

The man nodded, and looked across the room. Jo followed his gaze to the sheet of armoured glass that separated them from Dantalion. The insect-like creature was squatting on the concrete floor, its multiple arms folded beneath it in a complex and uncomfortable-looking arrangement. As the interrogator packed his papers into his briefcase, Jo approached the armoured glass, arms folded defensively across her chest. She knew that she was safe, what with all those armed guards at the top of the stairs, but there was something about the holding cells that always made her feel like she was at a zoo, watching a tiger walk mindlessly up and down the same patch of ground. Dantalion looked so dejected: staring bleakly at the floor without acknowledging her existence. She almost felt sorry for it. When she had sneaked into the manor house through the French window and discovered the Doctor being held captive she had been terrified, but Dantalion had given up without a fight. She had kept the gun trained on it the whole time while they had waited for the Doctor to regain the use of his limbs and for the UNIT team to arrive, but it had made no threatening moves. The worst it had done was offer her a drink, which she had, of course, quickly refused.

'Is there anything I can get you?' she asked Dantalion through the glass. It didn't respond. 'Are you hungry?'

The creature didn't stir. Jo was about to leave it and rejoin the party when something caught her eye – a dark ragged line running down Dantalion's chest. She pressed her face up against the glass to take a closer look. Perhaps it was ill. Perhaps it was dead!

'Is it. . . is it all right?' she asked the interrogator.

'Just resting, I think,' he replied. He looked at his watch and glanced up at the video camera set into one corner of the room. A red LED beneath the lens indicated that it was active. 'This is Ferrand, coming out at nineteen fifteen and thirty seconds.' The door at the top of the stairs rolled open, and he nodded at Jo. 'Goodnight, mademoiselle.'

'Goodnight.' As the interrogator headed towards the stairs she called after him: 'There's still some food left upstairs at the party, if you want.'

'Thank you,' he said, 'but no. I have eaten British quiche before.'

She turned back to Dantalion. The meagre light from the overhead neon tubes didn't help, but Jo could swear that she could see *through* the rip, all the way across Dantalion's chest to the hard casing on the other side, as if the thing squatting there was just a shed skin, and the real Dantalion was. . .

'Stop! Stop!' she shouted at the interrogator. He turned an impassive face towards her, and she knew, she *knew* beyond any shadow of a doubt that it was Dantalion. 'Guards,' she yelled at the video camera, 'stop that man – he's an alien creature and he's trying to escape from the building!'

The interrogator ran up the stairs, but Jo launched herself after him. A beam of light flashed from the interrogator's face to the door, and Jo caught a confused glimpse of the three guards falling to the ground. She flung herself up the last few steps and clutched at Dantalion's trouser leg. Whatever it was that she touched wasn't ordinary material – it felt cold and hard beneath her fingers – but she maintained her grip and yanked hard. Dantalion stumbled and fell backward on top of her. Together they tumbled down the stairs. The edges dug sharply into her as the two of them fell, and all she could see were flashes of gritty concrete interspersed with darkness. There was a searing pain in her head, and sparks exploded across her eyes, vanishing into a red haze which gradually faded to black.

* * *

The Brigadier slammed the receiver down so hard that Mike
Yates could hear it out in the corridor. He popped his head around
the Brigadier's door.

'Problems, sir?'

'Must you keep asking me the same stupid question, Yates?'
the Brigadier barked.

'Sorry, sir.' Mike started to withdraw his head.

'No, my fault. Sorry Mike.' The Brigadier sounded tired and
discouraged.

Mike walked into the office. 'Is it this Navy business, sir?'

The Brigadier nodded. 'Yes. I've been to three separate meetings today – with the Chief of the Defence Staff, the Secretary
of State for Defence and the Home Secretary – and had a long
phone conversation with UNIT HQ in Geneva. Nothing. Lot of
flannel, lot of hot air, but in the end it's a forgeone conclusion.
We're being disbanded.'

'Split up, sir?'

'They want a new team. Starting from scratch. Don't even
want to keep the Doctor on.'

Mike smiled. 'As far as the Doctor's concerned, the only
thing worse than working for UNIT would be to find out that
they don't want him for its replacement. What about this plan
to find somewhere else as our HQ, sir?'

'Geneva say they can't afford to pay anything toward its
upkeep, and the Home Secretary is unwilling to make any money
available from this end. We're stuck – unless you know of anywhere suitable going for free.'

'Ah, no sir. I'm already renting out the spare room in my
flat.' Yates paused for moment. 'Not that I want to add to your
troubles, sir, but that alien prisoner tried to escape earlier on.
Miss Grant was quite badly hurt.'

'That's all we need!' the Brigadier snapped. He levered himself halfway out of his seat, then subsided again. 'Is she –'

'The medic's with her now. Says she'll be all right, but she
hasn't regained consciousness yet. We recaptured the alien.'

Lethbridge-Stewart nodded. 'Well, keep me informed. Can you handle things, Mike? I'm running short of time on this closure business.'

Yates nodded and saluted. As he left the office, he heard the Brigadier pick up the telephone again.

When Jo Grant awoke, it was in a bed in the UNIT infirmary. Her head throbbed and she could feel bruises all down her arms, chest and legs.

'How do you feel, Jo?' the Doctor asked, leaning over her. His eyes were full of concern.

'I feel like I used to be a woodpecker in another life,' she said, and smiled weakly. 'Will I live?'

'Yes, you're perfectly safe.' The Doctor frowned, and looked away. 'Thanks to Dantalion,' he added.

'What do you mean?' she asked. Her throat was dry, and she reached for the glass of water beside her bed.

'I mean that you gashed your forehead on the stairs. You might have bled to death, but Dantalion stopped and sealed the edges of the wound together somehow. Curious, really. It might have got away if it hadn't stopped. It had already stunned all the guards.'

Jo replaced the glass and reached up to touch her forehead. There was a scar, rough against the skin just above her right eye. 'What have they done with Dantalion now?' she asked.

'Back in the holding cell. We found the real interrogator ly-ing unconscious beneath the bench. Nobody knows for sure how Dantalion got out of the cell, or how it fooled the camera, but I think its artificial eye must hide some kind of a holo-graphic projector as well as a weapon. It mentioned something about implants when I confronted it in the manor house, but I was too confounded pleased with myself to notice.' He grim-aced. 'Odd race – never come across one so developed that can shed its skin at will.'

Jo thought for a moment, through the haze of pain. 'I don't

understand why Dantalion stopped and helped me when it saw I was injured. Why did it do that?'

'Because it was concerned, perhaps?' The Doctor shrugged.

'I'm grateful and all that, but I don't see any alien invader stopping to treat the sick.'

'No, you're right,' the Doctor said, thinking. 'An invader wouldn't, but a *doctor* would.' He slammed his right hand into his left palm. '*That's* what it's doing on Earth – not invading, or harvesting delicacies.'

Jo raised her hand to the wound again. 'That must be how Dantalion knew what treatment I needed. But what about those five people it killed?'

The Doctor frowned. 'If I wanted to practise medicine across the galaxy, I might start by finding out as much as I could about every race inhabiting it. Perhaps Dantalion is doing just that – collecting knowledge about the metabolisms of as many creatures as it can. That's what the missing people were – anatomical specimens. After all, Jo, it didn't kill the guards, did it? It just stunned them. And it didn't kill the interrogator, or you for that matter. It just wanted to get out.'

Jo rubbed her forehead. 'I wish it had found a less agressive way of doing it, though.'

The telephone rang on the Brigadier's desk. He grabbed for it before the echoes of the first ring had died away.

'Lethbridge-Stewart.'

'Ah, Brigadier,' a cold, clipped voice said. 'We haven't met. Zecca here, Rear-Admiral Zecca. Listen, I'm setting up our HQ here in Portsmouth. Need your files. Sending a truck up now to collect them.'

'But. . . but *sir*,' the Brigadier blathered, wrong-footed by the speed of events, 'I'm still. . . that is, there's paperwork to be done, agreements to be reached. After all, it's not as if – '

'This is war,' Zecca said, cutting across the Brigadier. 'I've pushed things through fast. Don't want the buggers sneaking

in while we're still arguing over who gets whose desk. I hear
you've already caught one of these alien chappies. Good work
– we'll be up in force to collect him tomorrow.'

'Sir, I really must – '

'Don't argue, Lethbridge-Stewart – you have your orders.
The decision's been taken, and what's more it's the *right* decision. I firmly believe that.'

'Wait one moment, sir. I really – '

The sound of the dialling tone stopped him. He held the receiver away from his head, stared at it disbelievingly for a moment, then slammed it down into the cradle as hard as he could.

The guards were actually *in* the holding cell now, and their
weapons were trained directly at Dantalion. Jo could see a contempt and horror in their faces which hadn't been there before.
The same thing had happened upstairs, when she and the Doctor had explained their theory to Mike Yates. Whereas at the
party Mike had talked about Dantalion almost with respect, now
he was disgusted.

'Yes,' the alien wheezed, 'you're perfectly and incontrovert-
ibly correct, of course.' Its metal eye had been covered with a
large surgical bandage, just in case it tried to use its holographic
powers again. 'I've been ensconced on your magnificent world
for some little time, accumulating erudition on the subject of
human biology. I'm certified to operate on most major galactic
races now, and I'm working my way through the minor ones.'

'But *why*,' the Doctor said from the other side of the armoured
glass. 'Why kill people? Couldn't you just read a book or two?'

'Would you perform an appendectomy based upon a book
you once read?' Dantalion asked. 'There's no substitute for practice. And besides, humans are woefully ignorant about the way
their own bodies function. I was thinking of penning a little
monograph for publication before I left.'

The Doctor shook his head in incomprehension. 'You killed
people to study the way that they're put together? That doesn't

make any sense.'

'That's the manner in which Birastrops acquire their qualifi-cations,' Dantalion said. 'I appreciate that humans have a dif-ferent morality about it, but that's not my concern.'

Jo couldn't believe what she was hearing. 'But killing is kill-ing,' she protested. 'I mean, it's wrong.'

'According to whom?' asked Dantalion.

Jo frowned. 'Everyone knows.'

'Everyone on Earth, perhaps. Please don't try to apply your own morality to other races. It's the worst sort of cultural impe-rialism.' Dantalion shook its head in a curiously human ges-ture. 'Let me attempt to elucidate in another way. On my planet the only way to learn surgery is to cut up other Birastrops while they're still alive – the old, the weak, the criminal. . . If *you* came to *my* planet and wanted to learn surgery, would you do it *our* way?'

Jo shuddered. 'No, of course not.'

Dantalion nodded. 'Then why expect me to come to *your* planet and do it *your* way?'

Jo opened her mouth to argue, but nothing came out. She felt like saying, *Because we're right and you're wrong*, but even she could see the flaws in that argument.

'Even if what you say is true,' the Doctor interrupted, 'why didn't you save us all a lot of trouble by telling us all this in the first place?'

Dantalion pointed towards the guards with one of its multi-ple sets of limbs. 'When your soldiers thought I was killing people for military reasons, preparing for an invasion, they treated me reasonably well,' he replied. 'When they realized that I was killing people for medical reasons, their opinions changed.' It shifted position slightly. 'Typical human stupidity – it's noble to kill if you're a soldier but degrading to kill if you're a healer. To be fair, in deference to your rather odd moral system, I chose only those people who had no relatives, and who had been diagnosed as being close to death.'

'And you took their money,' the Doctor pointed out.

'Where is the advantage in studying in poverty?' Dantalion replied, unfazed. 'This planet has much to recommend it. I'm a great fan of human victuals, beverages and standards of comfort.'

'Killing people who are going to die anyway is still murder,' Jo pointed out, 'and what if a cure came on the market for whatever was going to kill them?'

Dantalion shook its head. 'Their deaths might enable me to save hundreds of humans at some stage in the future,' it said. 'My race is immensely long-lived. I think you'll find I'll save more humans in that time than I've already killed.'

It sat there, looking smug. Jo knew that there was an argument that would blow everything it had said out of the water, but for the moment she couldn't think of it.

The Brigadier could hear the Doctor's raised voice all the way from his office. He glanced at his watch. Five seconds. . . four. . . three. . . two. . . one. . .

'This time you've gone too far, Lethbridge-Stewart!' the Doctor bellowed as he slammed the Brigadier's office door open, shivering the glass in its frame. 'My filing cabinets! My equipment! They've all gone!'

'Shipped down to Portsmouth for the Navy,' the Brigadier said wearily. 'I tried to warn you, Doctor, but you wouldn't listen. Just be glad I managed to stop them requisitioning the TARDIS.'

The Doctor opened his mouth to protest, but he suddenly seemed to catch sight of the bare walls that had once held maps and photographs of the Master. The room was empty now, apart from the chair, the desk and a framed photograph of Doris.

'So it's come to this,' the Doctor muttered disbelievingly, gazing round with his hands on his hips. 'Don't those dolts realize what they're doing? Without your knowledge and experience of alien attacks the Daleks will waltz right in. Or if not the Daleks, then any one of half a hundred other races.'

'Nonsense, man,' the Brigadier said tonelessly. 'This new fellow, Rear-Admiral Zecca, is a good chap. Knows his stuff. He's reading our files now: getting up to speed. I'm sure he'll do a better job than me.'

The Doctor was quiet for a few moments. 'Brigadier,' he said finally in a quiet voice, 'I know there have been times when we haven't quite seen eye to eye, but I have always had the utmost respect for your intelligence, your integrity and your humanity. I can't believe that anybody could do this job as well as you, let alone better.'

Lethbridge-Stewart cleared his throat and kept his eyes fixed on Doris's photograph until the prickle in his eyes subsided. 'Doctor, there's one more thing – Zecca will be arriving this afternoon to take the alien creature away for interrogation.'

'He *can't* – '

'He will. I have the orders here.' He tapped the pink folder. 'He's bringing an armed convoy. The Marines will get the truth out of the creature: one way or another.'

'But this is monstrous!' the Doctor exploded. 'Jo and I have talked to Dantalion. There's no invasion going on. Dantalion is doing what he believes to be right, but in the wrong way. Different moral code, that's all. All we have to do is ask him to leave the planet and he'll go.'

'God protect us from people doing what they firmly believe to be right,' the Brigadier muttered.

Rear-Admiral Jonathan Zecca watched as the white lines of the motorway slipped away beneath his staff car, counting down the distance to Portsmouth. The landscape to either side was hilly and green. The road was completely clear of traffic, as he had taken the precaution of ordering the police to close the motorway in a travelling box five miles on either side of the convoy. He was taking no chances with that... that *creature*. He felt his skin crawl at the thought of it. Horrible. Like a spider.

Like something he'd crush if he found it in the bath.

He couldn't wait to get it back to the compound. Let the men have a go at it. They knew how to extract information.

He wondered what colour its blood was.

The creature was strapped to a trolley in Guardian Six – a truck some twenty yards in front of Zecca's staff car. Apart from the driver, Zecca didn't have any men in Guardian Six, just in case he had to blow it up to stop the creature escaping. But he had a platoon of troops split between the four armoured personnel carriers – Guardians Two to Five – that were driving in a box around it.

A bridge flashed past. His eyes scanned the sky for signs of spacecraft attempting a rescue. That Doctor fellow had pooh-poohed the idea, but Zecca knew that if *he* was being held captive, his men would be in like a shot to get him out. Perhaps aliens were the same. Or perhaps, if the aliens were worried that the captured one might give away their invasion plans, they might try to kill it. Whatever happened, Zecca was ready. He'd requested air cover from the RAF, but they'd turned him down. Three weeks notice, they said. He'd have the hide of the group captain who'd told him that. When Zecca gave an order, he expected it to be obeyed. Still, he had anti-aircraft guns on the APCs, and RAF Fylingdales were primed to warn him if they detected any unusual air activity in his area.

He turned to the sergeant driving the car. 'ETA, Sergeant?'

'Fifteen minutes, sir.' The sergeant smiled. 'Traffic permitting, of course.'

Zecca allowed himself a brief smile. Humour was a valuable thing. It was what separated mankind from the animals.

And, of course, the aliens.

From her position in the TARDIS doorway, Jo could see the Doctor standing at the console, hands in his pockets. He sighed slightly, looking like a man who was trying to put off doing something unpleasant.

Jo looked back at the empty laboratory, then into the TARDIS again. The Doctor couldn't leave, but with UNIT closed down she wasn't sure where he could go. The TARDIS certainly wasn't in a position to take him anywhere. 'What's up, Doc?' she said, trying to sound cheerful.

'Don't be flippant, Jo,' he replied. 'I'm busy.'

'Busy doing what?' she asked. Her footsteps echoed as she walked towards him.

'Never you mind. Shouldn't you still be in bed?'

'The doctor discharged me. Apparently Dantalion did a very good job.' She ran a hand across her forehead. 'The scar's almost healed now, and there's no concussion.' She peered around his shoulder at the console. 'You're not expecting this thing actually to fly, are you? As far as I can see, it works only when you're not expecting it to.'

'That's the problem, Jo,' he said dejectedly. 'Despite all my best efforts, despite taking the console apart and putting it back together again, the old girl still works only when the Time Lords want it to. Every so often they like to loosen the leash a bit, just to remind me what I've been exiled from, but at the end of the day I'm just a back-seat driver.' His hands reached out hesitantly towards twin silvery nubs on the nearest facet of the console. 'I hate asking for help, but they owe me enough favours by now. Let's try calling in a debt or two. After all, the worst they can do is say no.'

He closed his eyes and began to mutter beneath his breath. The pearly light in the console room dimmed slightly, as if power were being rerouted elsewhere. After a few moments, he released the nubs and stepped back. There was a thin sheen of sweat on his face.

'What did you do?' Jo asked.

'I sent a message to the Time Lords, pointing out that I'd been a good little boy and done their dirty work for them on Uxarieus, Peladon and Solos without complaint – '

'Without *much* complaint,' Jo murmured.

'– and requesting two trips of a few miles and a few minutes each in return. After all,' he turned to her, and she was surprised at the bitterness on his face, 'it's not as if I'm asking for the moon.'

'And do you think they'll agree?'

'Without setting up a committee for a few hundred years to discuss the question?' He pursed his lips in frustration. 'I don't know, Jo. It's the only thing I can think of. They *have* to agree. I can't help the Brigadier in any other way.'

Jo was about to say something reassuring and meaningless when the doors silently swung shut behind her and the ever-present hum of the TARDIS deepened. 'Well,' she said brightly, 'it looks like you've got time off for good behaviour.'

They were thirty miles from Portsmouth when Rear Admiral Zecca spotted something odd. The truck carrying the alien creature, or what he could see of it between the armoured personnel carriers that surrounded it – was riding a lot lower than before on its suspension. It looked almost as if it was suddenly carrying a lot more weight.

'Sergeant, patch me through to the driver of Guardian Six.'

Without taking his eyes from the road, the driver tapped commands into the dashboard radio, then detached the handset and handed it to Zecca.

'Guardian Six, this is Guardian One. Do you copy? Over.'

'I copy, sir,' came the immediate response. 'Over.'

'Is anything wrong with your vehicle, over?'

'Funny you should ask, sir, but the truck's suddenly got sluggish. Thought the steering was playing up. Over.'

With thirty miles to go, Zecca wasn't going to let something as trivial as a mechanical fault stop him. 'Keep going, Guardian Six.'

'Understood sir. We shouldn't have – what the *hell*?'

'Guardian Six!' Zecca shouted into the handset, 'What's your status? Repeat, what's your status? Over.'

'Sorry sir.' The driver of the truck sounded a little shaken. 'There was this, like, flash of blue light from inside the truck. It's gone now, and my steering's back to normal. Bit weird, like. Over.'

Rear-Admiral Zecca suddenly felt as if something heavy was sitting on *his* suspension. 'Guardian One to all Guardians,' he barked. 'All stop. Repeat, all stop.'

The truck and the APCs all slewed to a halt. Within moments, Zecca's men had spilled out of the four APCs and formed a defensive circle around Guardian Six, guns at the ready. The anti-aircraft guns on the APCs were aimed outwards, covering the skies. Zecca strode up to the rear door of Guardian Six and inserted his special security keycard into the lock.

The door swung open.

The straps that had held the alien down were hanging loose, swaying slightly after the abrupt stop. The bench itself was empty.

'I presume,' the Doctor said as he gazed past the TARDIS and across the croquet lawn, 'that you will be leaving now.' Behind him, the bulk of the manor house shone a deep, tawny orange in the light of approaching sunset.

Jo wished that they would get on with it. She was cold, her head still ached, and she was acutely conscious that the Brigadier would take a dim view of their actions in kidnapping and then freeing an alien murderer. Once the Doctor got an idea into his head, however, there was no shifting it.

'That sounds more like an instruction than an inquiry,' Dantalion said from her side.

'You may take it that way, if you wish.' The Doctor shielded his eyes from the setting sun. 'This really is a most beautiful place. I admire your choice of domicile.'

Dantalion sighed. 'It was expensive, and I'll miss it. May I return one day?'

'I can't stop you,' the Doctor replied, 'but I would suggest that you leave it for a thousand years or so. Wait until humanity's moral sense and yours coincide more nearly.'

'Well, there are plenty of other races to learn about.' Dantalion's face twitched in what might have been a smile. 'I might sojourn with the Daleks for a while, find out what makes them tick.' It reached out with two of its right forelimbs and solemnly shook hands with the Doctor and, after a moment's hesitation on her part, with Jo. 'My spacecraft is in the greenhouse,' it said. 'Goodbye, and thank you for... for understanding.'

'One more thing,' the Doctor said.

'Isn't there always?' Dantalion said in resignation. 'What Herculean task do you wish me to perform before I go?'

The Doctor took a form out of his pocket. 'I'd be grateful if you would sign this.'

Dantalion took the form and quickly scanned it, then gazed up at the Doctor. 'As far as my atrophied legal facilities can determine, this complicated form transfers legal ownership of this entire estate to you.'

'I collect houses,' the Doctor said calmly. Removing a fountain pen from his pocket, he handed it to Dantalion. The alien gazed up at the Doctor for a few moments, then signed the form. The Doctor blew on the signature to dry it, and smiled. 'We'll make a doctor of you yet,' he said. 'This signature's almost illegible.'

Dantalion held the pen out toward the Doctor. 'You drive a hard bargain,' it complained.

'Please keep the pen,' the Doctor replied. 'After all, I took it from your desk in the hall when I first met you.'

Dantalion nodded, and walked off across the croquet lawn. As it vanished into the orange light of sunset, its grotesque, spindly shadow was cast back across the lawn and the facade of the house.

'We shouldn't have done that,' Jo said.

'We didn't have much choice,' the Doctor replied. The wind

ruffled his white hair, and his eyes were screwed up against the light. 'Dantalion could never have been brought to justice, not under British law, and the alternative was either to incarcerate it without trial or to execute it. I couldn't countenance either option. An unofficial deportation was the best thing.'

'But it killed people,' Jo said mulishly.

'According to Birastrop law and custom, it was within its rights to do so *if* it did it in the cause of medical understanding.' The Doctor gazed down fondly at Jo. 'I'm not saying that it was right, my dear, just that it had a point of view.' He patted her on the shoulder. 'And look on the bright side – the Navy have lost Dantalion within an hour of taking it into custody. What with that, and the promise of an empty manor house to use as his new rent-free headquarters, the Brigadier should be able to fight for UNIT's continued existence.'

Without a sound, a glowing, spiny shape rose above the trees, hovered for a moment, then rose into the air. Jo tracked it as it grew smaller and fainter. Within moments it was just a bright point of light, the first star of the evening. Shortly after that, it vanished.

'There's one thing you forgot,' Jo pointed out. 'I may have passed only O Level economics, but I did learn about capital gains tax.'

The Doctor frowned for a moment, then grinned. 'Oh, I'm sure the Brigadier can find that, out of all the salary he hasn't been paying me for the past three years,' he said cheerfully. 'Come on, Jo. Let's go and give him the good news!'

'Gentlemen, thank you for attending this extraordinary meeting of the Secret Vote Finance Committee,' Robert Walker said, his breath steaming slightly as he spoke. 'I must apologize, first for the short notice with which this meeting has been arranged and secondly for the lack of heating – a cost-saving measure recently implemented by the MoD, I'm afraid. . .'

As the Parliamentary Permanent Secretary wandered through

his opening remarks, Brigadier Alastair Gordon Lethbridge-
Stewart gazed around the oak-panelled room at the other members of the Committee. A few faces were missing, but they still
had a quorum. There were even a couple of observers sitting
behind Walker. Lethbridge-Stewart could have sworn that he
recognized one of them – a cherubic, balding man with twinkling blue eyes. As he tried to put a name to the face, the man
turned his head and smiled at him, then looked back at the chair-
man.

'So, if there are no amendments to the previous set of minutes, perhaps we can move on to the only agenda item.' Walker
paused, looking as if he was having to force the words out.
'The long-term future of UNIT. In the light of the recent Navy
fiasco, and given that UNIT have somehow managed to secure
themselves new premises at no cost, it has been *suggested*,'
Walker gave a sidelong glance to the balding man, 'that UNIT
be guaranteed funding for a period of not less than five years,
increasing annually by the rate of inflation. It has also been
suggested that the matter should be put to the vote this time. All
those in favour?'

Hands went up around the table, with the obvious exception
of Robert Walker. The balding man coughed discreetly, and
Walker slowly raised his hand to join the rest.

'Motion carried,' he continued. 'Details will be circulated
as soon as we have revised our budgetary figures. If there is no
other business..?' – he glanced around the table – '. . . then I
declare this meeting closed.'

Walker was first out of the door, closely followed by the rest
of the Committee. Busy men, the Brigadier reflected sourly as
he waited for the rush to die down. Probably on their way to
another meeting, having left one to come here. Some of them
looked as if they hadn't seen sunlight in years.

'He's been demoted, you know.'

Lethbridge-Stewart turned to find the cherubic man with the
bright blue eyes standing beside him. The man was small, but

radiated a sort of genial authority. 'Who?' Lethbridge-Stewart asked. 'Walker?'

'Rear-Admiral Zecca. Bit unfair if you ask me, but they didn't. How's young Jo getting on, by the by?'

A light suddenly dawned. 'Miss Grant? Fine, valued member of staff. Don't know what we'd do without her.'

'Seems to be enjoying herself. Can't say I'm sorry. Had my doubts when she asked to join you chaps, but I went along with it. Jo's always been my favourite niece.' He smiled. 'Well, tell the truth, she's my only niece. Have to spoil her. No choice.'

'I take it that I have you to thank for this meeting, sir?' the Brigadier said. 'I appreciate your help.'

'Sorry I was so discouraging on the phone,' the man said, 'but once you had got the house, and Zecca had lost the alien, I could start applying pressure to Walker. Been meaning to ask you, by the by. How'd you get such an amazing house for free? Who owns it?'

'You know,' the Brigadier murmured, 'I rather suspect that he does.'

The Trials Of Tara:

OR.
Would That It Were
The Comedie of
Count Grendel, The Mafter Of *Gracht*
With
The Life and Death of his
New Executioner

As it was Acted (with great Applaufe)
at the Privat houfe in BUCKINGHAM ROAD.

Written by PAUL CORNELL (Gent.)

Never Printed before.

LONDON
Printed for REBECCA LEVENE, and are to
be fold at her fhop at the fign of the *Virgin*
in Ladbroke Grove, 1653

Dramatis Personae

Oberon, King of the Fairies
Grendel, Count of Gracht
Augmentio, Prince of Thorvald
The Archimandrite, Prelate of Tara
The Doctor, of Gallifrey
Zadek, Swordmaster to Strella
Farrah, Swordsman to Strella
The Kandyman, Executioner to Grendel
Merrybone, a soldier
Claypole, a soldier
Guard
The Taran Beast
Strella, Queen of Tara
Titania, Queen of the Fairies
Bernice Summerfield, friend to the Doctor
Miranda, servant to Strella
Appolonia, leader of the Players
The Players
Two Servants
First Witch
Second Witch
Third Witch

Act I

Scene 1. A clearing in the woods.

Enter Merrybone and Claypole, two soldiers.

Merrybone: I'll tell you now, sir, that you may decide,
    While he is away on affairs of weight,
    Whether to take the shilling of the Count.

Claypole: But, fie, I have already ta'en it.

Merrybone: You mistake my meaning, take the purse and stay –

Claypole: As I am a yeoman and a soldier.

Merrybone: Or take it and run.

Claypole: With bolts in my back?
    I should look the model for an android
    The like of which the both of us create.

Merrybone: The rest of us may miss. I swear I shall.
    But hear the choice although your mind is made.
    Queen Strella rules o'er all of Tara,
    And her noble hand is twice fair –

Claypole: Twice fair?

Merrybone: Now four times fair. By fair I mean honest
    And also most beauteous, that's the second.
    And you did double her with your tongue...

Claypole: That's a rumour!

Merrybone: I meant mathematically.

But I doubt it not for honest she is
Also as in chaste, for her husband's dead.

Claypole: Dead? I heard Reynart had but long vanished?

Merrybone: Dead, vanished, fled, another silly
Definition. Like all those I have said.
But how are you defined, then, dear sir?
Be certain that you now are in service
To the royal pretender Count Grendel.
Who presses near to Castle Tara,
With surrounding mercenary army,
To keep the mind of good Queen Strella
On whom to place her whole heirless estate.
If she does it not willingly then short
Will she find herself compromised
As Grendel failed to manage once before.
What say you now? Is his a good shilling?

Claypole: It's as good as any general's fee.
And alms, not aims, are the thing for soldiers.

Merrybone: Arms and alms then, if not aims, except in
Aiming, as one does when sighting a back.

Claypole: Your definings will be the death of us.

Merrybone: I pray not. Let's join the company, straight.

Exit Claypole.

Hard it is, both hard in mind and hard in fact,
To enter in a Holmesian double act.

Exit.

Scene 2. Another clearing.

Enter the Three Witches.

First Witch: Since the days of plague did lay Tara waste
                And the first crude mechanicals appeared
                Never have the gates of power been so open.

Second Witch: So you say, but is this Grendel destined
                To take up mantle, throne and sceptre
                And all the supplements of kingship?

Third Witch: They say the death of his fair Lamia
               Has made him passing bitter, greater still,
               That he had an unhappy hand in't.

First Witch: Be that as it may – hush, I hear a step!

Enter Count Grendel

Grendel: Oh, but thou stars of Taran night reveal
           Thy plans and purpose for my villainy!
           They say the fates of men and princes
           Can be read in Thirteen Houses nightly.
           But all I see are distant suns, reached
           Only in stories imaginative.
           But hold, are these the three hags I seek?

First Witch: We are the three witches of Taran wood.

Second Witch: We speak the words of darkling prophecy.

Third Witch: We offer palliatives for power.

Grendel: You have the lotion that I did request?

First Witch: We have it.

Second Witch   You wish it.

Third Witch: Give us your boon.

Grendel: You have my solemn word of honour
   That should I gain the throne of Tara
   You will replace in my courtroom
   That ancient prelate Archimandrite
   And gain from him in worldly fashion
   As you triumph in astral power
   At this moment of sweet meeting.

First Witch: Done! Here is the bottle called Beshrewme.
   A drop of this in the ear of anyone.
   And since it's Taran, man or android,
   Will mimic the sweetest words of lovers
   False and closely persuasive.
   Those dosed will believe your own assertions
   At their natural selves' expense.

Grendel: Once I had no need of such offices.
   But thank you, weird sisters. I'll see you hence.
   The Taran stars and your provisions
   Leave nothing in my long-kept plans to chance.

Exeunt.

Scene 3. Another clearing, with TARDIS

Enter the Doctor and Bernice.

Doctor: This is the sweet and charming planet Tara.
   Home to android smiths. And nobles.

On which I own a field or two of land
Having earned it. In royal service.
My intent is to visit my old friend
Prince Reynart, and his princess bride Strella,
Who did resemble my friend Romana.

Bernice: Why is it that you had me change my dress
To that of such taped-down boyishness?
I had anticipated courtly frocks,
Not breeches and masculine moustaches.

Doctor: Yes, a marvellous hairy about-face.
This is a warmly feudal place, Bernice,
Where blood flows hot and nights are very long.
Better to avoid the stare of amorous ducs
Than risk their hard and hasty –

Bernice: Doctor, look, here what approaches?!

Doctor: Oh no, run! It is a Taran beast!
We'll meet elsewhere. Now flee with haste
You go West, me East!

Exeunt at different sides, pursued by Taran beast.

Scene 4. A room in the castle.

Enter Queen Strella and her maid, Miranda.

Strella: Oh Miranda, my heart does break with the
Shame and gross policy of this whole plan.
If I was not resolved that dear Reynart
Was long dead in some far Taran plateau
Then never would I stoop to bargain marriage.

Miranda: Yet dead he is, my lady and my friend.
And with him my dear Farrah, and his men.
You cannot mourn for him forever,
Nor can you allow the state of Tara
To perish for the want of your fair prince.
A king is required, for all ceremony.
So you, bereft of heir, must marry one
Or watch as vile civil war descends
To pitch son and father at the other's throat.
Or worse, there's –

Strella: Grendel. Always Grendel.
Your words are wise beyond your post, Miranda.
And this is why I have set in motion
A plot that shall carry us to safety
As Hector's boat did bob and hop him past
The maws of Scully and Charabdus.
I have sent out word that I desire suitors,
But that this is a suit most dangerous,
For I have in mind some tests true perilous,
That will test the princes' mettle.
And that those who seek but miss their target
May find themselves delivered
To the eternal everafter.

Miranda: Hah! And is not Grendel a famed coward?

Strella: Is the Archimandrite's hat not silly?

Miranda: Why then, be gay and deck the hall with spog!
You shall have a husband great or none.

Strella: That is my wish and to that end I have
Instructed all the castle
That any man who sets his foot inside

Shall be set on the quest for my hand.
Or be cut off. There and then. With axe.

Miranda: Ooh, you can be cruel Your Majesty.

Strella: Let them prove their manhoods with due vigour
Or lose them lightly, while we do snigger.
Come, there's much to do.

Exeunt.

Scene 5. The forest.

Enter Bernice.

Bernice: Terrific. Lost in forest depths
With my poor bosoms shut up like sardines
Or rather, not, since those fish live in sauce
And in this garb I'll see none of that.
It's usual to be so mistreated
By shorthouse Gallifreyan gits.
But hush, who comes, is it the beast back?

Enter Grendel.

Grendel: Fear not, good yeoman, it is I, the Count.
Grendel, that is, of Gracht, that good city
Where my serfs did play and jolly the day
Until my good and honest crown was torn
From me by the jealous Reynart,
My estate reduced to roaming nomad,
And me left to build my fortune again.

Bernice: This villain has the Doctor warned me of.

Grendel: Sorry, what say you? I did not catch it.

Bernice: I said only how now to good Grendel.

Grendel: Why how now to you, you foppish lad!
    I go to join my army of the wood,
    Who are all about assembled.
    We could offer a longshank rogue like you
    Good service. Tell me, what's thy name?

Bernice: It is Bertrand, and I serve no-one.

Grendel: Why then just share a draught with me good sir,
    This fine North Taran wine I carry.
    Can we not be comrades on the roadway?

Bernice: I think not sir, for have you not heard
    It is foolish to take drinks from strangers?

Grendel: Then I leave you with a warning.
    Those who are not of my company
    Will short find themselves sore sorry.

Exit Grendel.

Bernice: Mayhap, but now I'm sore glad he's gone.
    I'm sure that potion meant me ill.
    But soft, who else is in this forest?

Enter Oberon, King of the Fairies.

Oberon: Oh sadness! Oh pity! Oh my lost joy!

Bernice: Good clove-hoofed sir, what ails thy visage so?
    For monstrous as thy shape and face so is,

Thy bitter cries do tell of softer heart
And gentle sensibility.

Oberon: You are the first human that thought so.

Bernice: Some of my best friends are alien warriors.
You are quite sweet compared to them.

Oberon: That gladdens me slight. My pain is always.
I am Oberon, king of former might.
Whose realm encompass'd all those creatures
Made and consigned to the night.
Those lost and lonely metal strangers
Cast out from Taran host and home
Were often fantastical mechanicals,
Their novelty spent, their charm all gone.

Bernice: They think an android's just for Christmas.

Oberon: Indeed, their discards found me in the forest.
Soon we were a merry band of brothers.
But then came Grendel, and took my dear queen.
He holds her now, against my pledge of service.
I am loyal to the throne of Strella,
But my hand is oathed to Grendel,
And short shall I lead my kin in battle
To besiege yonder royal castle.

Bernice: Fear not, for I know a man to save you.
He has once beaten notorious Grendel,
And is a friend to those in power.
He shall raise their strength to aid you,
If you would but give direction
To aforementioned royal castle.

Oberon: Oh joyous day! Come, I'll take you hence.
　　　　　Your help may stop this rank impending prince.

────────────────

Act II

Scene 1. A room in the castle.

Enter the Doctor, held by a spear-carrier.

Doctor: I'm the Doctor, guard, unhand me!

Enter Swordmaster Zadek.

Zadek: Who is this minuscule intruder?

Guard: We found him on the castle drawbridge, master.

Doctor: Swordmaster Zadek! How is young Farrah?

Zadek: You mistake me sir, I know you not.

Doctor: My form has changed, that's true.
　　　　　And my gait. My voice. But not my memory.
　　　　　You and I helped save the state of Tara.
　　　　　Through a secret android of Prince Reynart.
　　　　　You knew that I was from the stars then,
　　　　　And you marvelled. But stellar men like me
　　　　　Can change their forms, their face and being.

Zadek: You are saying that you're the Doctor.
　　　　　Who did leave us ten years past now.

I see why you would ask of Farrah,
Who was with poor vanished Reynart.
But tell me this, if you are who you claim.
What great reward did Reynart give you
For your noble wit and assistance?

Doctor: Why, all the land from Freya's Furrow
To the brook that flows by the wall of Klat.
Including, if my mind serves me a'right,
The fair Pavilion of the Summer Winds,
Where some great actions of the battle
Were played out.

Zadek: Doctor, I believe it is you!

Doctor: I believe it too, but tell me quick,
What has become of dear good Reynart?

Zadek: Lost, all lost. He left on inspection
Of the farther settlements years past,
And never did return to us.
I shall tell you of all our problems,
But first let me warn you of your danger.
You are now engaged in a game
Of fast engagements.

Doctor: As in chess? Is that your meaning?

Zadek: In that both are concerned with mating.
You have set foot in the inner castle.
Thus you are committed to play a game.

Doctor: Oh, I'm often good at games. What's the prize?

Enter Queen Strella.

Strella: I am, Doctor.

Doctor:　　　　Oh, now, that's a puzzle.

Strella: I have heard all that passed between you.
　　　　You are a suitable suitor for me,
　　　　Though I wish we had met outside
　　　　The precincts of this castle.
　　　　For all men who venture into here
　　　　Must now hold their lives and manhoods dear.
　　　　You either play my game of a suit
　　　　Or leave in two pieces, thy suit a shroud.
　　　　It is good to see my loyal Doctor,
　　　　But, oh, thy sense of timing's rotten.

Zadek: Only my privates may pass here unscathed.

Doctor: Do not fear, my feeling is to try this sport.
　　　　If Taran King the Doctor is to be,
　　　　Then I shall serve until such duties
　　　　A better vessel them to do shall find.
　　　　As for thy hand, madam, I have no
　　　　Understanding of it. But I'll win it.
　　　　To stop those who would use it unkindly.

Strella: That is what I'd hoped you'd say, dear Doctor.
　　　　The game begins tomorrow noon at sharp.

Doctor: Sharp is right, just stick to cutting words.

Strella: Come, sly fellow, to hospitality.

Exeunt Doctor and Strella.

Zadek: It is well that he is with us now.

I did know of it at first report,
Of a blue box in the forest deep.
It may be sin to lure him into marriage
But sin is royal business for Zadek,
Who needs must be wolfish among sheep.

Exit.

Scene 2. Grendel's camp.

Enter Merrybone, Claypole and several soldiers.

Claypole: So what other words have you for us, sir?

Merrybone: I have no words but rabble and slothful
But that's because I am a sergeant
And very minded to the way of troops.
If you asked me in my closet now,
I would say that we are a pleasant force –

Claypole: That's exact, for peasants we most are.

Merrybone: Pleasant. It's well I used not pheasant,
Or you'd be comparing us to cocks.

Claypole: Why might you use pheasant?

Merrybone: That I might make the comparison first,
Our wit being proportioned to rank.
Armies are like pheasants since without
Their heads they can only run amok.

Claypole: Aye, my comparison would be bawdy
Beside that. But look now, here's our head.

Enter Grendel.

Merrybone: Count Coxcomb! I mean, Count Grendel!

Grendel: How now, good knaves? I have bought our victory.
    Behold, the lotion to smooth our passage.

Claypole: I will keep my bawdy tongue silent.

Grendel: The Three Witches did give it to me.

Claypole: And did he give it to them in turn?
    Truly, that potion must work wonders.

Grendel: Knave, dost thou narrate?

Claypole: No, I have a cold.

Grendel: This elixir, when dropped in't ear,
    Will cause the victim to believe my words.

Claypole: Mayhap he'll put it in the evening broth.

Grendel: Would you be the first test of it, fellow?

Claypole: No sir, I'll be silent, sir.

Grendel: Then let us have a merry contest
    The use of this potion to approve.
    Bring me the captured Titania
    Queen of the Fairies in her cage.

Exeunt Claypole and Merrybone.

Foolish Oberon loves his queen too much
That he'll give his state for her safety.
Unlike I, who cared so little for mine –
But these are not the words for soldiers.

Enter Claypole and Merrybone, with Titania in a cage.

Merrybone: Here is the Fairy Queen you ordered, sir.

Grendel: Ah, Titania, my most favoured guest.
            Your accommodation is sparse, true,
            But at least you can choose from several bars.

Titania: Oh, base, adulterated un-royal thing!
            What torment has your dark mind for me now?

Grendel: Merely, milady fairy, that I wish
            To gain the queen of midnight's ear.

He applies the potion to her ear.

            Now you will sleep. And when you do wake,
            The first sight that you see shall be your love.

Claypole: Oh, but that's villainy!

Grendel: Is it not?
            But you shall not profit by it, sirrah.
            Let it be known that no soldier lifts
            This cloth I now place over her cage.
            Some wandering beast may claim her heart
            But none so base as a mere yeoman.
            I would not have Oberon suffer that.

Merrybone: You are wise as you are worthy, sir.

Now, shall we – but look, in the sky, what's that?

Grendel: Some falling star, as signs the fate of kings.
Sirs, start your horses. We shall follow it.
Mayhap we'll know whose death it brings.

Exeunt.

Scene 3. A room in the castle.

Enter Bernice, secretly.

Bernice: All those guards and burly defences!
Since Oberon showed me the castle gate
I've strived to obtain secret access.
For when have guards ever followed stories
Told by such adventurers as us?
Now that I'm inside, thanks to that window,
I trust that on arrest I'll find the Queen
And may then reveal myself with safety.

Enter Strella and Miranda.

Strella: Who talks of revealing what before me?

Bernice: Oh, madam, I am called Bertrand,
That is my only revelation.
I am also a friend to the Doctor.
Has he arrived in your great castle?

Strella: Why, what shape or form of man is this?
Passing fair is he about the face,
With graceful stance and prowess of wit
Enough to penetrate a fortress.

Miranda: That is, methinks, the entire length of it.

Strella: What say you, maid?

Miranda: Yes, I say a maid.
         Have you been out of marriage too long?

Strella: Leave us, girl, I understand you not.

Miranda: This is a knot that I don't understand.

                        Exit Miranda.

Bernice: Will you kindly give me answer?

Strella: I shall answer you kindly in all things,
         For my eyes do alight lightly on you
         And find you pleasing, dear Bertrand.

Bernice: That's very kind, Your Majesty, but –

Strella: You knew the situation in this place
         Before arrival, did you not?

Bernice: Oh yes, a loyal subject told me.

Strella: Oh, I'm blessed, for I have found my hero!

Bernice: – ine.

Strella: In what?

Bernice: In a lot of trouble.
         Is the Doctor here or not, tell me?

Strella: I hesitate to say, for you both,
      Though friends, are on the same pathway set.

Bernice: Yes, we came together, and were parted.

Strella: Oh brave friends! Let me rejoin you short
      I hope that you love him as I do
      For friendship should not fall to sport.
      But I wish you, dear man, should win me,
      Even if the Doctor conquers nought.

Exeunt.

Scene 4. A clearing in the forest. With escape pod.

Enter Grendel, Merrybone, Claypole and soldiers.

Merrybone: I think that this is where the star fell.
      Ah, look, here it is, sleeping in the ground.

Grendel: Foolish sergeant. This is not a star.
      It is a vehicle for those who
      Travel amongst them. A stellar horse.
      Lamia and I did speculate
      Concerning such stuff, met two such travellers.
      Can we open it to see who's inside?

Merrybone: The mechanism is hardened with rust.
      No, it is not rust, but something sweet.
      I shall break it off. Holah! It opens!
      And what is this inside? A skeleton?

Claypole: No, but something that I know very well.
      This is the pyre of a dead android, sir.
      Those bones you gaze upon with dread are tin.

That skullish head is imprinted circuitry.
Alas, poor robot, I wish I'd known thee.

Merrybone: Mayhap that it is not too late for such.
Here are plans for reconstruction,
Smuggled in this being's cavities.
He did prepare for this consequence.

Claypole: Why then I can remake him new, Sir Count,
And use the only skill our class allows
Once more. You did like our last creation.
This is a passing powerful android.

Grendel: Let it be so done. This metal stranger
Shall increase my star-forged force by one.

Exeunt, with the skeleton.

Scene 5. A room in the castle.

Enter the Doctor and Bernice.

Doctor: So you now also are a suit, Bertrand?

Bernice: I am not he, do not so me address,
And if I had a dress then my suit
Would end at the point where ends this suit!

Doctor: A nice conjunction, but be assured,
That while you can, with mere embarrassment,
Reveal your gender and leave this place,
I am trapped into more deadly sport.
Still, no other challengers have arrived.
Perhaps I am the only man.

Enter Zadek and Augmentio.

Zadek: Allow me to introduce to you,
　　　His noble Lordship, one Augmentio.
　　　He is a Prince of far-off Thorvald,
　　　And shares your suit for good Queen Strella.

Doctor: Hello, I'm the Doctor, and this is my–

Bernice: Chum and good companion Bertrand.

Augmentio: I offer you both greeting, fellow braves.
　　　But advise you this place to leave in haste.
　　　For I intend to best you both at games,
　　　And thus prove my right to lovely Strella.

Bernice: For a prince you're not exactly charming.

Augmentio: But I'm full of vigour and boast
　　　An enormous codpiece full of passion.

Bernice: Take care lest your codpiece gets battered.

Zadek: I come also to present to you
　　　The first dispute you compete over.
　　　Bring on the casket of confusion.

Enter two servants, with casket.

　　　Each of you must in turn open it.
　　　The others I shall blindfold. Who's first?

Doctor: That's me. (*To Bernice*) Fear not, Bernice, I'll aid your attempt.

Enter Queen Strella and Miranda.

Strella: See how he inspects the box, Miranda.
        I can but hope he fails, though he's my friend.
        For I would see my dear Bertrand succeed.

Miranda: But dear Bertrand is –

Doctor: Alas! What's the trick?

Zadek: The sand runs fast before you, Doctor!

Doctor: There's no lock to pick, so it's these panels.
        Which one to bash or turn or tap into.
        That? No. That? No. This? No. What shall I do?

Miranda: His narration is for his friend's aid.

Strella: Be silent, good Doctor, for you do cheat.

Doctor: That is the thing I've most experience at.
        No more words. Time to reverse my fate!

  He flips the casket over, and opens the lid on which it sat.

Zadek: Well done, Doctor. Your wit has not faded.

Doctor: Oh, it's too simple for Augmentio.
        Let him keep his blindfold on to try.

Zadek: It is his turn now, but we'll unblind him.
        Even though his quality is such
        That he doubtless has no need of it.

  Augmentio looks at the casket, and turns it over.

Doctor: Apparently, you're correct in that.

Strella: Now let us see Bertrand chance his arm.

Miranda: That is all he has to chance, methinks.

Zadek: The sand is running on you Bertrand.

Bernice: Why, now, how did the Doctor do this?

Doctor: Look into my eyes and see the truth.

Zadek: Your majesty?

Strella: A look can do no harm.

    The Doctor wiggles his eyebrows at Bernice.

Bernice: Ah, so that's the trick of this puzzle.

    She turns the casket over.

Zadek: If that's a cheat it is a game worth losing
      To discover the code or language used.

Doctor: The language of a race from far away
      Who communicate by eyebrow.
      You cannot call it trickery now,
      Since you allowed its furtive use.

Strella: But why should you aid my dear Bertrand,
      Since your own life is against the wager?

Bernice: We are together in all matters.

Miranda: That will make a merry honeymoon.

Augmentio: This is but the first of many contests.
          You cannot team against me every time.
          Your double bridegroom need not irk you, Strella.
          Your hand, and thence your kingdom, all are mine.

                    Exit Augmentio.

Strella: Come all, and dine with me this evening.
        I fear there is reason in his rhyming.

                    Exeunt.

Act III

Scene 1. Grendel's camp.

*Enter Grendel, Merrybone, Claypole, Titania in her cage
                and diverse others.*

Grendel: Now tell me, good Claypole, of your progress.

Claypole: At your service, sir, I have erected
          A great vat of all the robot requires
          To form him and clothe him against the world
          As described in the notes we found on him.
          It is a noxious sticky substance
          That I have had to send out farways for.
          Sacks of southern Taran sugarbeet
          And the stolen sweets of many children.

Grendel: We now are stealing sweets from babies?
     Why, this is proverbially easy,
     Good yeoman android maker.
     I expect the results of your labour
     Will shake the heavens with its fierceness,
     But sweets?
     That is armour passing strange and soft.
     Is this another of Oberon's creatures,
     A discarded folly from the stars?
     What say you, Lady Titania?

Titania: I have closed my eyes now I have woken,
     For I know what you've upon me ordered.
     I would not glimpse the callow faces
     Of any of your bastard rabble.

Grendel: Nor would I have you abused so, lady.
     Hence the cloth around your prison.
     You cannot trust that I have done that
     Nor can you touch to check the fabric.
     But I know not that your eyes are closed,
     So, in a matter like Merrybone's wits,
     We both unseeing, uncertain, remain.

Merrybone: What's that noise?

Claypole: It is the vat, my creation lives!

         Exit Claypole.

Merrybone: I could dispute upon 'creation' sir.

Grendel: Do not, for I long for certainty.

     Enter Claypole, with the Kandyman.

Merrybone: Od's teeth! And were I to eat that lot
My teeth odd, and black, rather would be.

Claypole: Speak, my sticky, stocky, sweetheart speak!

Grendel: Yes, what are you, fudgy android thing?

Kandyman: We are such stuff as sweets are made on.
We are an executioner
And more, a sticky scientist grand
Whose skills are great with tasty torments.
I seek only to give good service
To some serious and stately master
With plans for hard and harsh dominion.

Claypole: I think you've come to the right place, good thing.

Grendel: Kneel, and I shall – what's thy name?

Kandyman: Kandyman.

Grendel: Then I knight thee, sweet Sir Kandyman
You're executioner to the Count
And cause of Grendel, reach exceeding all,
Whose plans, you'll cheer to hear, are near to fruit.

Merrybone: As he is also near to fruit, gone ripe.

Grendel: Thank you, Claypole, for such useful service.
Between this and your other android,
You two have contributed most surely
To the plan and purpose of Count Grendel.
Now, let us close about our planning be,
Two days brings marriage, and hence victory.

Exeunt Grendel, Merrybone, Claypole and the soldiers.

Kandyman: What strange folk these mortal Tarans be.
Yet their way with circuitry is fast.
It has been long since Terra Alpha,
And all the gay and merry plots there.
Here I am, with no good Gilbert handy
To make my way in a world that's new.
I must find some skulduggery short, or–

Titania: Hello? Who's there? I hear an android voice!

Kandyman: What's behind this dark obscuring cloth?

Titania: Oh, you did surprise me sir. Good sir.
Good sir with face and form so godlike.
Good sir with –

Kandyman: Wait, are you mad or blind?

Titania: I was blind sir, but now I do see.
I do see that, rightly, I do love thee.

Kandyman: This is very unexpected, lady.

Titania: For us both sir, but true, I do love thee.

Kandyman: Ah, but some agent has muddied your thoughts.
Follow me not, it's sad what change is wrought.

Exeunt.

Scene 2. A room in the castle.

Enter Zadek, Queen Strella, and the Archimandrite.

Strella: Your arrival always predicts joy,
   My dear and loyal Archimandrite.
   And this time even joy upon joy,
   For not only Taran-settling marriage,
   But marriage good and made from loving,
   Is in ferment upon your coming.

Archimandrite: That is news both great and glorious.
   Who is the lucky noble gentleman?

Zadek: We are not exactly sure at present.
   However, Her Majesty has high hopes.

   Enter the Doctor, Bernice and Augmentio.

Doctor: Archimandrite! You've not changed a jot.
   Nor has your taste in millinery.

Archimandrite: Doctor! I cannot say the same for you.

Zadek: How is it that you recognize his face?

Archimandrite: I am prelate of all Tara, Zadek.
   Nothing is secret to the high clergy.

Augmentio: How is it that he walks here without harm?

Archimandrite: As a gentleman of high church office,
   I am not officially a man.

Bernice: My problem is the exact opposite.

Archimandrite: Bearing in mind the gender dividing
   Order that surrounds this fair castle
   I have taken it upon myself

To bring with me some entertainment.
Enter, you womanly troupe of players!

Enter the female Players, led by Appolonia.

Strella: That was a thought most typically kind.
Have these thespian girls a play for us?

Appolonia: We have a large and seemly repertory.

Doctor: Then I have an idea, a game, a toy.
Let this be part of our great contest.
Myself, Bertrand, and Prince Augmentio,
Arrayed in female robes and courtly masks
Shall act out parts in tales familiar
And, in such careful acting, please or scold.

Bernice: Oh really?

Augmentio: This is sport sure trifling.
Bring on the part and have me learn it.

Strella: I cannot see a problem with this plan.
The man who has most skill with letters
Shall step a yard closer to my hand.
I'm certain, for example, good Bertrand
Will strut the stage a perfect acted girl.

Bernice: I can promise that, at least, Queen Strella.

Zadek: Come, let us prepare for the night's revels.

Exeunt Queen Strella, the Archimandrite, Bernice,
Augmentio, Zadek, and the Players.

Doctor: Fair Appolonia, I am a scribe
With some iambic past experience.
I have in mind some certain letters
That will reveal a close impostor.

Appolonia: An impostor, sir, who do you mean?
Is it one who walks close with the Queen?
My untutored eye distrusts Bertrand.

Doctor: But my eye sees that three dressed here are wrong.

Exeunt.

Scene 3. Outside the castle wall.

Enter the Kandyman.

Kandyman: My first mission as Grendel's chosen man
Is menial as would befit a serf.
I have but to approach this wall and say—

Enter Titania

Titania: Robot! Robot! Where art thou, robot?

Kandyman: I told you harshly not to follow me,
I find your countenance repulsive.
Why you do persist in this pursuit
Is vexing to all my circuitry.
It computeth not. You will make me
Look bad before my master Grendel.

Titania: Be not angry with me, dear robot.
I shall sit still here and listen to thee
Deliver thy message in blissful tongue

As befits so strong and sweet a man.

Kandyman: Very well. Not a sound from you, then.
Oh, thou man of Grendel in the castle!
Reveal thyself upon this password: mong!

Enter Bernice, above.

Bernice: Our fortunes seem to further advance not,
Despite the Doctor's usual secret plan.
I have been no aid to Oberon,
And wonder why, if Grendel plans a coup,
He is not here, in competition.
That's just as well, he seemed a drama queen.
But hark, what shape in yonder darkness calls?

Kandyman: Mong, I say unto thee again, mong!

Bernice: Mong yourself, whoever you may be.

Kandyman: I have the potion lately purchased
To help your subtle machinations
Within the bosom of Strella's household.

Bernice: Oh, well, that's all right then. Throw it here.
Tell me once more what this lotion does.

Kandyman: I am told it bends the will to one's words.
I have unfortunate example here.
One Queen Titania, former fairy.

Bernice: Titania's there? Oh, heaven forfend!
Can you not stay, to further help my cause?

Kandyman: No, I must return to our encampment.

Grendel's army lies in nearby waiting,
Ready for the night of Strella's wedding.
I shall see you next in bloody battle.

Titania: And adieu from me, friend of my friend.

Bernice: Friend of her friend? Then she's all potioned up.
This presages a soon and terrible end.

Exeunt.

Scene 4. A room in the castle.

Enter Queen Strella, the Archimandrite, and Zadek.

Strella: The test will hinge upon grace, character,
Timing, and remembrance of their lines.
I have copies of text here for us all.

Archimandrite: But these are all o'erwrit with scribble.

Zadek: That will be the Doctor's hand, I fancy.
It is spiderish enough to trap flies.

Strella: Hush now, here come the girlish players.

*Enter the Doctor, Bernice, Augmentio, Appolonia
and the Players, all as girls.*

Bernice: Thank God for that, my bosoms are at rest.
Now, Doctor, I told you of this bottle–

Doctor: Quiet. The play's beginning. Act your lines.

Archimandrite: I think that Bertrand's unconvincing.

Zadek: Aye, he seems a twee and awkward girl.
                One can but compare Appolonia,
                Who's fanciable fair and comely, phwoar!
                Oh, sorry, Your Majesty, I regret–

Strella: Worry not, Zadek. Not for nothing
                Are you known, I hear, as Swordmaster.
                I shall introduce you to yon actress
                Once play is over, but now it begins.

Appolonia: The Girl Players of Outer Traken
                Do present the Tragedy of Zob.
                Or, as it is known, Zob's Labours Lost.
                With Augmentio as the maiden Zob,
                Bertrand as Lady Mickeldiver,
                And the Doctor as Dame Fibbetjon.
                Our scene is a clearing in the woods.
                I shall be the woods, as round this castle.

Augmentio: Oh woe, woe, woe is me! I am pity
                In human person, awaiting merely
                The embrace of welcome, waited Death!

Zadek: He's good, I am moved beyond mere words.

Strella: Let us see how Bertrand interprets.

Bernice: But poor maid, what is the course of your
                predicament?
                Sorry. Cause. Cause of your predicament.
                Bloody iambic pentameter. I can't handle it at all.
                Doctor, I mean,
                Whatever your name is.
                Your turn.

Doctor: Your words are poetry perfected,
        Good courtly Lady Mickeldiver.
        Tell me Zob, of all the lands you've seen.

Augmentio: I have seen far Baloganinni
        And prepared pasta for Pastor Palaskar
        In Redlorryyellowlorry, Dorset.
        I have heard two of the one true threesome
        Talking treason in forefather's forest
        And three other kings saying fivefold things
        In nought ways that were honest. I – ack!

Strella: What possesses Augmentio, sudden?

Zadek: He is as still as a frozen statue.

Doctor: I think Augmentio's missed his cue,
        His gestures halt, his tongue is cold and dead.
        Let's put it down to cloying first night nerves.
        Or do you think the Prince has lost his head?

The Doctor pulls Augmentio's face off. He is an android.

        This were a prince of great mettle, indeed.
        His dialogue had a list of numbers,
        A standard android shutdown coding.
        To honesty bring, the play's still the thing.

Strella: Villainous robot, what were your orders?

Bernice: I have a potion to settle that.
        There, see what he says with that in his ear.

Augmentio: I am in service to Count Grendel,

A replica of poor, real, murdered, prince.
Who before his unhappy ending,
Did sign all his will over to Gracht.
I was to marry, then despatch you,
In the quiet of our marital bed,
Then self-kill, sent straight to oblivion,
In the deepest part of Taran lake.
My body would never have born witness
To my artificiality,
And Grendel would my state inherit,
In the sunlight of legality.

Zadek: Treasonous Grendel! Let us arrest him!

Strella: No, good Zadek. He has many men here
About this castle. They could assault us,
And Grendel would have all our estate,
And wait on our allies' compliance.

Archimandrite: Then what are we to do to save the state?

Doctor: I have an idea, from intelligence
That Bertrand brings of others in the wood.
Come, let this double-dealing android,
Double again, and for his queen do good.

Exeunt.

Scene 5. Grendel's Camp.

*Enter Grendel, Merrybone, Claypole, Kandyman, Titania
and soldiers.*

Grendel: What mean you that the robot's contact's lost?

Claypole: As I say sir, he vanished from the screen.

Grendel: Then he is destroyed or discovered.
          We must make haste to raise our army
          In one last desperate push for power.
          I shall lead them to this elusive crown
          That sways before me as a vision
          Or a snake that lightly strikes me down
          When I am closest to my royal fate.
          It struck, as I recall, old Lamia too.
          Though, with her art, she had no ambition,
          Beyond perfect science and marriage for love.
          Oh to be so free of lust for power.
          I fear that it will take a similar bite
          To still the urge that presses me along.

Kandyman: With the weapons I have provided,
           You may take the castle with no loss.

Titania: Oh, how clever, my darling sweetmeats.

Merrybone: I would that he gave her a gobstopper.

Claypole: I heard he had. That is why she says
           That his meat is sweet.

Merrybone: Hush your knavery.
           Someone approaches our encampment.

                    Enter Augmentio.

Grendel: What ho, my metallic mutineer!
          We'd thought you deactivated.
          Why have you returned to our circle so?
          Did you use the potion I got lately

To further your murderous mission?

Augmentio: Sir, I did. The wench, the Queen, is dead.
　　　　　She had the other suits beheaded,
　　　　　And married me, by Archimandrite's hand.
　　　　　Consumed in lust for my hard self was she,
　　　　　And in so consuming, was she consumed.

Grendel: And you did it in safety, that's well.
　　　　　But why have thou not taken to thy rest
　　　　　On't lake's muddy and decrepit bottom?

Augmentio: I wished to see again my master,
　　　　　And die an android knight of Grendel.

Grendel: Why, there's precedent for that.
　　　　　Here is my other android knight,
　　　　　Sir Kandyman, of Terra Alpha.

Kandyman: Greetings to my suicidal sir.

Augmentio: And who is this? Thy beauteous android bride?

Titania: I'm Titania, his love.

Kandyman: 　　　　　　　　No she's not.

Augmentio: But she is the former fairy queen,
　　　　　Held, I've long heard, in supernatural
　　　　　Suspension by Grendel's wily hand?

Kandyman: Yes, that's her.

Augmentio: 　　　　　　　My own bride I've butchered.
　　　　　May I steal from this living queen a kiss?

Kandyman: It is of no concern or weight to me.

Titania: If you will me so to do, then shall I.

Augmentio: Then listen to this softest word from me.
              Open your ear to my speech and be free.

Merrybone: What says he to her, can you hear it?

Claypole: It probably concerns her dental health.

Titania: Thank you sir, I am in your earnest debt.

Exit Titania.

Grendel: Where goes your gooey bride, Kandyman?

Kandyman: I do not know, I did not order this.

Grendel: What? Then she has been freed? After her!

Merrybone: Sir, if she is free, she has all the lore
              And trickery of fairy against us.
              It will be beyond us to find her
              In the heart of forest greenery.

Grendel: Aye, you curs, you're right. Why did you that, sir?

Augmentio: I used your potion against your own hand,
              And whispered to the lady to be free.
              The rest from me is silence. I offer
              Only the name of my current master.
              The Doctor has changed since last you saw him,
              But you have not done the same, Count Grendel.

Grendel: The Doctor?! Then die as he will, traitor!

He stabs Augmentio. He falls.

Kandyman: The Doctor? Could it be the same man?
    I shall enjoy this warfare you prescribe.

Grendel: Summon the whole of the army of Gracht.
    We march on the castle, swift and straight.
    My plans are on a tumultuous sea
    But we'll sail with the wind and make our fate.

Exeunt.

Act IV

Scene 1. A room in the castle.

*Enter Queen Strella, the Archimandrite,
the Doctor, Bernice, Zadek, Appolonia and the Players.*

Zadek: Your highness, the castle is besieged!
    On all sides come the armies of Grendel!

Bernice: I took a look from my balcony.
    You can't see out there but for archers.

Doctor: What's the strength of your garrison, Strella?

Strella: We are but thirty loyal guardsmen.

Doctor: But what of the android servants, chattels?

Zadek: There are two hundred of them, but they –

Doctor: Are quite equipped to fight, when I've altered
       Their ordinary circuits to defend
       The walls of this grand and ancient fortress
       If not attack the force of Gracht below.

Zadek: But that will not escape us from the siege.

Doctor: That will not. We wait upon our rescue.

        An explosion. Alarums and excursions.

Strella: They are at the gate! They have heavy bolts!

Zadek: So has the gate, the brigands will not pass.
       Miss Appolonia, please seek safety.

Appolonia: I think you'll find we're hardy performers.
       We'll take our place upon the wall and throw
       Whatever hard or dangerous articles
       You have to bombard soldiers below.

Bernice: Well said, female players. I too will help.

Zadek: And why should you not, Sirrah Bertrand?

Bernice: No reason. He is headed for a shock.

Doctor: Then let's all retire to our places,
       And stay the tide that seeks to wash amok.

               Exeunt.

Scene 2. A breach in the castle wall.

Enter Grendel, Merrybone, Claypole, the Kandyman and soldiers.

Grendel: On, on, you noble army of the Gracht!
　　　A single push into the castle
　　　And we'll at last have Tara's central throne.
　　　The breach is open and fast before us,
　　　So near it sings to me like victory.

Kandyman: Throw some more of my melted candy hence.
　　　Its poisonous solution kills the guards.

Merrybone: But look, they stand and resume the battle!

Enter the Doctor and Zadek, above.

Zadek: We shore up our walls with the android dead.

Doctor: I'm repairing them as fast as I can.

Zadek: Even so, the traitor's army presses on
　　　Towards the breach they've cast in the castle.
　　　I should lead my men out to meet them.

Doctor: No, wait at least until the odds even.
　　　Good strategy demands that you not leap
　　　And sacrifice your men in foolish ire.

Grendel: Zadek, you lapdog to the Taran court!
　　　Come out and meet me, if you have the nerve!

Zadek: Rather lapdog than cur, outcast mongrel,
　　　Despised in your own hearth as in Tara,

Scorned and mocked as heaven-hated traitor,
Shameless homeless loveless bastard Grendel!

Grendel: You have all the love, home and shame I need
Inside those proud defended portals.
My line is honest heir to all Tara
But you have made me villain with your words.
Your power allows your claim illegal
And thus I must resort to base misdeed
To reinstate my outcast family.
I, who never did kill beyond a duel
Until your house took my last hope from me
And I was forced to reassemble Gracht
From its scattered loyal men thrown about
The several false estates Reynart made
Of mine own dear dissolved homeland.
Your misdeeds visit back upon you now.

Doctor: Are his words the truth?

Zadek: I know not, truly.

Kandyman: We have all your castle surrounded.
Surrender, or we shall boil you out
Like and with the sweets of my cauldron.

Doctor: Is that the creature I think it is?

Zadek: They rush at us! The end of Tara's here!

Doctor: Hark, what is that distant bugle call?

Merrybone: Turn Count Grendel, turn the army now!
It is the warriors of fairy!

Enter Oberon and Titania, with Fairy Soldiers.

Battle is joined.

Oberon: Where is that felon Grendel, who did keep
    My fairy queen enshackled and thus
    Assumed my throne's support against his foes?

Enter Queen Strella, above.

Strella: The messages I heard were true, then?
    Oberon's great army comes to help!

Doctor: Queen, you put our cause at risk by coming–

*The Kandyman climbs above, and grabs Strella away,
wounding Zadek.*

Kandyman: This prize will ensure us the last assault.

Exeunt Kandyman and Strella.

Doctor: I must find the maid Appolonia,
    Or all my plan's for nought.

Exeunt, fighting.

Scene 3. The Battlefield.

Enter Queen Strella and the Kandyman.

Strella: What ill use do you hope for me, robot?

Kandyman: Your ransom is worth a kingdom entire,
    For dead, you leave no heirs or estate.

Enter Grendel, Merrybone, Claypole and the soldiers.

Claypole: Our army scatters, they flee without form!

Grendel: Stand close upon the Queen, she's our way out.
Good service you've performed there, Kandyman.

Merrybone: Sir, I heard your speech. What's a man of Gracht?

Grendel: Why, he's now a soldier in my army.

Claypole: But we are come from several lands and homes.

Grendel: There are those of you who once lived in Gracht.

Merrybone: Aye, but they are few and we are not –

Grendel: Silence, dog, you're the country I pay for!
Prepare, here come the opposing army!

Enter the Doctor, Bernice, Appolonia and the Players.

Kandyman: Doctor!

Doctor: Kandyman!

Grendel: Doctor?

Doctor: Count Grendel!

Appolonia: Count Grendel!

Appolonia pulls off her disguise. It is Reynart.

Grendel: Reynart!

*The Players pull off their disguises. They are Reynart's men,
led by Farrah.*

Farrah: Count Grendel!

Grendel: Farrah!

Strella: Reynart!

Reynart: My beloved!

Strella: Farrah!

Farrah: Your Highness!

Battle is joined.

Kandyman: Cease your struggle, Reynart of Tara,
Or I'll snap the neck of your beloved.

Doctor: Bernice, it's time to use those buckets.

Bernice: Sorry, Your Majesty, it's this or death.

*She throws the buckets over the Kandyman and
Queen Strella.*

Kandyman: What is this? I am feeling funny.

Doctor: It's rough red Taran wine.

Bernice: Very rough.

Kandyman: I am dying. But with my last strength –

Claypole: You'll do nothing to harm Her Majesty.

*He and Merrybone play with switches. The Kandyman
freezes.*

Kandyman: Oh, that this too sullied flesh does melt.
        I die, Count Grendel.

He dies.

Grendel: Gone, good android, gone.
        And similar gone shall I be now!

He exits at a run. The army surrenders.

Strella: Reynart, my love, and you flesh and blood?

Reynart: I am, dearest. My men and I were caught
        In a spell transfixing by three witches,
        And had remained so, through all of these years,
        Until most recent, when their temporal trap
        Did cease and allow us to escape,
        Which we did, killing the vile trinity.

Doctor: That sounds like my TARDIS's effect.

Reynart: We did return to the proud castle
        Only to hear of the ban on men.
        I surmised that you sought a husband,
        And steeled myself, if you were married
        To take my men back to the woodlands
        And live in whatever peace you'd forged.
        Hence the disguise, which was useful
        In the atmosphere of plot at Tara.
        Now let's find Grendel, and finish the snake.

Doctor: Leave him to me. He'll seek to match the score
  Upon a match that we did make before.

Exeunt, at different sides.

Scene 4. A cliff edge.

Enter Grendel and the Doctor, from different sides.

Grendel: So, Doctor, you return to frustrate me.

Doctor: You might be glad to see it's me who comes.
  They would have you crudely butchered.

Grendel: And what is your own alternative?

Doctor: I'll take you elsewhere in space to escape.

Grendel: You shall not. Tara is my homeland,
  And one day it will be my throne. *En garde!*

They fight.

Doctor: You're a stranger to real politics, Count.
  A troubled cynic, an idealist
  Who's been wrong a few too many times.

Grendel: What are you but that exactly, Doctor?
  The trouble is –

The Doctor casts Grendel's sword aside.

  You're a better swordsman.
  Adieu, I've lost this latest dance,
  Be grateful for your victory, Doctor,

I'll give you just this one more chance!

Exit Grendel, diving from clifftop.

Doctor: I salute thee, noble, homeless, Grendel.

Exit.

Scene 5. A room in the castle.

Enter King Reynart, Queen Strella, the Archimandrite, the Doctor, Bernice, Zadek, Farrah, Miranda, Merrybone and Claypole.

Strella: Good husband, I must confess it to thee,
            I did quite fancy noble Bertrand here.

Reynart: Bertrand? But the Doctor called you Bernice.

Bernice: And he was right sir, for I'm a woman.
            Don't worry o'er it, Strella, I'm flattered.

Miranda: I tried to tell her, she did not listen.

Zadek: I hope she forgets my professed
          Regard for Appolonia.
          That would wound me greater than my arm.

Reynart: The King and Queen of noble fairy,
            Given full kingdom over androids
            Both free and still made servant, have just left.
            Now then, Doctor, I did to you offer
            A boon for your great service to Tara.
            Riches? Marriage? Though not to Strella.

Doctor: I care little for any of that.
        My boon is this. Free these two men here
        And have them serve upon your council,
        For not only did they save Queen Strella
        But their class and faction must be heeded
        Should you wish to rule an honest Tara.
        The villain Grendel, vanished, can return,
        Only if you cast him discontent
        As a wolf may profit by discarded
        Bones, so he does feed on injustice.
        Perhaps you could also find a Gracht
        Who could represent that state at court
        Dissolved as it remains for now.
        I do surrender my own fiefdom,
        That a new Gracht may be established,
        Around that pretty old Pavilion,
        Where Grendel's life took its last turn.
        It will be memorial for him,
        In that it serves as Lamia's tombstone,
        And also it will sign departed
        Injustice, never more to return.

Claypole: That's a dispute worthy of Merrybone.

Merrybone: Hush, it means well for changeable villains
        Such as us.

Reynart: Very well, I appoint thee both my knights.
        Sir Merrybone and Sir Claypole of–
        I do not know thine origins, men.

Merrybone: Of Tara, sir.

Claypole: He's done defining, now.
        Tap him with your chopper afore he speaks.

Archimandrite: This day has become great for Tara.
>   Even the children have sweets for each mouth.
>   I shall now see a royal remarriage.
>   And, while that's on, mayhap there's another?
>   It will cost less in the price of spog.

Farrah: He means the two of us, Miranda.

Miranda: If you mean me, too, then we two agree.

>   *Exit King Reynart, Queen Strella, the Archimandrite, Zadek,
>   Farrah, Miranda, Merrybone and Claypole.*

Doctor: Let's leave, before they try to marry us.

Bernice: To each other, or are you still a suitor?

Doctor: My suit, Bernice, is not that of a dame.
>   And you're one to talk, you could now be king.

Bernice: King of Hearts, alas. Her suit's not the same.

Doctor: Well now that all's well, let's find the TARDIS
>   And set her for some distant heading.
>   By the Archimandrite's fashions,
>   I couldn't watch a Taran wedding.

>   *Exeunt.*

>   ***FINIS***

Housewarming

By David A McIntee

'Now that's what I call a country house!' commented Sarah Jane Smith admiringly as she locked her car boot and gazed up at the ramshackle yet imposing edifice in front of which she had parked. 'Are you sure you can manage these steps?' If it comes to carrying you, she added mentally, you'd better hope there are some fitter people than me in the investigating team...

'The dimensions of the risers are within the limits of my traction system, Mistress,' the squarely-caricatured mobile computer at her feet replied with confidence. She knew it wasn't really confidence, of course. K-9 was only a machine. But it did sound that way. Aunt Lavinia had always credited the family dogs with human attributes and emotions, but even she might have drawn the line at doing so with one that wasn't even organic. Then again, she hadn't had the sort of experience with such things that Sarah had. At any rate, K-9's assessment seemed correct, as his boxy body lifted off the ground with a whine of servos, leaving his traction system with almost a foot of clearance. By the time she caught up with him, his forward sprocket wheels were already raised and sliding onto the first of the flight of steps leading up to the porticoed front door.

The door opened and a casually dressed man with a militarily neat haircut came out to stand on the porch, eyebrows raised in astonishment at the sight of K-9. 'I don't believe it...'

'I did tell you about him at the reunion.' She let the man give her a friendly peck on the cheek. 'I bet you didn't believe me, did you?'

'You should have brought him with you,' Mike Yates said. 'You'd have had the Brigadier calling for armour-piercing biscuits.' He glanced around and saw that, apart from the robot dog, Sarah was alone. 'I half-expected Brendan to come as well.'

'It's too near exam time at Cambridge, so I'm afraid I'll have to do.'

'Is this the first time you've been on a psychical investigation?'

'Unless you count watching *Randall and Hopkirk*.'

By now they had entered the hallway. A long staircase led up to a U-shaped balcony from which doors opened onto the upper-storey rooms. The paintwork and wallpaper were dusty and faded, although the building seemed to have been quite well looked after. Sarah pointed to a cable which ran from a wall socket to a video camera mounted on a tripod at the end of the hall. 'Is the power still on, then? I thought you'd be using batteries.'

'The local council has been allowing groups to use the place as a sort of community centre. In fact, it was the members of a karate class who first reported... odd happenings here.'

'Odd?' Sarah didn't believe in ghosts as such, but weird alien energies of which man was not meant to know etcetera were quite another matter.

'Lights going on and off, music coming from empty rooms, all that sort of thing. One of these people even claimed to have been attacked by a poltergeist. Or maybe it was psionic science...'

'Why didn't you just call in UNIT? Or even Fox and Dana?'

'We have to find out if there's really anything to it first.' He opened the door to what must once have been the drawing room. Now it was just a bare area with several camp beds and a few rucksacks in it. A younger woman was setting up some sort of an oscilloscope, while another man was waiting with obvious impatience for a portable sandwich toaster to do its work. Mike performed the introductions. 'That's Shirley, on loan from the local university.' Shirley gave Sarah an absent-minded wave, concentrating on the apparatus before her. 'And that's Bob over there. He's been coming on these investigations for years.' Bob flashed Sarah an appreciative-looking smile. She returned it with a resigned one.

'This is your base?'

Mike nodded. 'We call it the ops room. All the video monitors will be set up in here. Shaun and Peter are off positioning the microphones and control objects now.' He looked around at the sound of footsteps approaching from the hall. 'Here comes our patron. I thought he wouldn't miss a chance to meet you.'

The newcomer was a tall, aristocratic man with aquiline features, a Vandyke beard, and a dark Italian-designed suit over a silk shirt and a cravat with a silver bird-of-prey tiepin. He walked swiftly over to Sarah, flashing a warm smile and extending a hand in welcome. 'Count Marius Castillo, at your service, as they used to say.' The Count adroitly shifted the position of his hand, bringing Sarah's up to kiss it gently. 'Charmed,' he smiled, releasing her hand. His proud expression softened into a somewhat self-deprecating half-smile. 'Far too old-fashioned, I know, but someone has to keep the old traditions alive, don't you think?'

'Thank heaven for old traditions,' Sarah laughed.

'Heaven? Oh, of course... I understand this is the first investigation you've covered, Ms Smith–' He frowned. 'Must I call you that? It sounds so... politically correct.'

'Just Sarah, then. And yes, I've never been ghostbusting before.'

'Then we must ensure that you see something interesting for you to write about, though I'm not sure that "ghostbusting" is a term I feel comfortable with.'

Sarah watched with cheery amusement as the Count bent down to check on Shirley's progress. Old-fashioned he might be, but at least he seemed to have chosen the *good* parts of the traditions to uphold. Somehow she doubted he'd be sending her to make the tea. 'He has that effect on everyone,' Mike said. 'Knows exactly how to start off on the right foot. Must be good breeding, I suppose.'

'There's no such thing.'

'My, my,' the Count said behind her, and she turned to see K-9 circling the room. The Count watched the robot dog closely for a moment, then moved towards him. K-9's ear-like antennae waggled furiously. 'What a fascinating device... Japanese?'

'Not exactly,' Sarah said carefully. 'It was given to me by an old friend – a scientist.'

'The Doctor?' Mike asked her.

'Who else?'

The Count looked K-9 over, grimacing at the designation on the right-hand side of his body.

'K-9? Very amusing,' he said sceptically.

'Affirmative, master,' K-9 agreed smugly.

Sarah raised an eyebrow in surprise. K-9 didn't take to just anybody like that. It seemed that Mike really was right about the Count's charm. The Count, for his own part, looked momentarily taken aback, but quickly recovered. 'Very friendly – I like him already.'

'I'm sorry if he startled you,' Sarah said, cursing herself inwardly. 'I should have warned you that he talks.'

'Think nothing of it, my dear; it's simply that I'm the sort of person who thinks of a computer as something on which to play games. If you'll excuse me, however, I must now fetch the last of the recording equipment from my car.'

'Do you need any help with it?' Mike asked.

'Thank you, but no; it's not heavy.' With a slight bow in Sarah's direction, the Count turned and left.

Mike looked at Sarah. 'You could maybe help *us*, though.'

K-9 whirred to a stop at the foot of the stairs. From somewhere inside his sturdy form there came the humming of servos ready to shift him into position to climb. 'That won't be necessary, K-9,' Sarah told him. 'Why don't you help Mike and Peter check their audio-visual equipment?'

The computer's sensor-filled head drooped in what Sarah

thought was an uncomfortably convincing kicked-puppy impression. That was the Doctor's sense of humour showing through, no doubt. 'Look, I just have to place some vases and things. It'll only take me a couple of minutes. Besides, ghosts don't come out until midnight.'

'Correlation of horological factors and parapsionic manifestations noted, mistress. The assertion, however, is –'

'I know! I was only joking. Anyway, in the time it would take you to get to the top, I'll have finished.'

'Affirmative, mistress. Ascent servo-mechanisms operate at only sixty per cent normal motive efficiency.'

'Exactly. You could give yourself a hernia – or whatever the mechanical equivalent is.' Sarah jogged up the steps, hefting a heavily laden plastic bag that Mike had handed her.

Mike gave K-9 a knowing look, although he had no idea whether or not the machine – damned if it wasn't difficult not to think of it as some sort of a living cartoon dog – would understand. K-9's ears – antennae, he reminded himself – swung around briefly, then Mike heard footsteps coming back down the stairs.

The lanky form of Peter hopped down to join them, almost miraculously managing not to trip on the cable that he was unravelling as he came. He stopped when he saw K-9. 'What on earth is that?'

Mike wished he had a good answer, but Sarah's explanations as to what made K-9 tick had been somewhat vague. She probably didn't really know either. Still, he had to say something. 'It's Sarah's dog, obviously.'

'Oh. I've heard of wire-haired terriers, but that's ridiculous!'

Mike laughed. 'It's some sort of a mobile computer, though why the designer made it look like a dog, I don't know.'

'The human ego requires a familiar reference point to aid in the adjustment to new concepts,' K-9 announced smugly. 'Animal forms are comforting to the majority of humans.'

Peter looked startled, then grinned. 'Nice voice synthesizer.

Sounds like that guy from *Beadle's About*. Computer, eh?' He bent down to address K-9 directly. 'You can obviously see and hear me, but can you record what your... sensors, register?'

'Affirmative. Audio and visual receptors can record and play back, as can infra-red and EM detectors.' As if to prove the point, the small screen-like holographic plate set into the left-hand side of K-9's body flashed into life.

'You can obviously see and hear me, but can you record what your... sensors, register?' a tiny three-dimensional duplicate of Peter asked clearly.

'You look a lot taller in real life,' Mike told Peter with a perfectly straight face.

Peter gave him a sour look before returning his attention to K-9. 'And you're mobile and fully self-contained?'

'Affirmative.'

'Interesting.' He turned to Mike. 'Do you think that Sarah would let us shanghai K-9 for a bit? If we got him to tour the house while recording, it would give us a good comparator for the static recorders. And he could probably get to an active location much quicker than we could, with all our gear to shift.'

'Probably. Why don't we go and ask her?'

K-9 shifted position slightly. 'Query: shanghai? Context eliminates possibility of reference to Chinese city.'

'Is he always like this?' Peter asked.

Bob watched through the drawing room windows as the Count passed by outside on his way to his black Mercedes. Lucky devil to have a car like that, he thought, as he retrieved some more sandwiches from the toaster and took one over to Shirley. 'The Count's probably got a hamper stuffed with foie gras and beluga caviare in that car of his, but this cheese and onion toastie will have to do for us.'

'Lucky us then. Have you ever tasted caviare? It's revolting.'

'You know what I mean. You'd think with all that money

he'd be living it up on the French Riviera or something.'

'You mean this sort of science isn't fun?'

Bob gave her a mock-pitying look. 'Science is fun. Sitting around draughty old houses isn't.'

Shirley straightened up from the oscilloscope now that she had got it tuned the way that she wanted, and took the warm sandwich. 'Well, whatever the reason, let's just be grateful he showed up when he did. The university would never have given us the expenses to cover all this equipment. Besides, the Count's been a big name in these circles for a little while now.'

'You've met him before, then?'

'No, but I've read his pieces in the journal of the SPR. How about you?'

'Same here. Odd, that; I can't think of anyone on the Committee who *has* met him before...'

'Who introduced him, then?'

'I'm not sure.' Bob frowned. This was very strange; the Count had certainly attended one of the Committee meetings, but where he had got his invite from... 'It doesn't matter, I suppose. Steven probably brought him along; he can't even remember his own name half the time! I sometimes think the only reason the Committee keeps him on is as proof of life after death.'

'That's cruel, you know.'

'You have to be cruel to be kind. Which reminds me...' He tugged a hip flask from inside his jacket. 'We can split this between us later on, if you're amenable.

'Since when haven't I been?'

Unusually for a house of this type, the conservatory was built atop the flat roof of what had once been a wash house, and the interior entrance was therefore on the first floor. Fenced in by the grey spars of its iron frame, Sarah had the uncomfortable feeling that she was standing inside a ghostly ribcage. The film of dust coating the panes of glass between the spars was as dry as the stretched membranes of dead skin across thin metal bones.

A few dead leaves lay scattered across the floor, though the slatted wooden shelves were swept clean. Taking a tall vase and a sachet of chalk dust from the plastic bag that Mike had given her, Sarah moved over to look out of the crusted glass. She had vaguely hoped to get a better view of the orchard grove on the little hill that she'd passed in her car, but darkness had already fallen too completely for that. Remembering her task, she looked around for a suitable spot upon which to position the vase and the chalk dust. Clearly the slatted shelves were no good, as the dust would fall straight through the gaps.

Spotting a low sink with a draining area beside it, Sarah put the vase down on the flat surface and, gently shaking a quantity of dust from the bag, drew around its base in a circle. This wasn't exactly what she'd imagined ghostbusting would be like, she reflected. Somehow, she'd expected to be either wandering around the house with a PKE-meter or sitting round a table holding hands with a group of shawl-wearing old ladies. Smiling to herself, she realized that she should have just asked K-9 if he could detect psychic vibrations.

Still, even if the ghost-hunting reality was very dry, there was always the Count. *Metropolitan*'s readers were invariably fascinated by tales of the rich and titled, so perhaps she could get some entertaining anecdotes out of him later, to run as a companion piece to the story on the investigation. Maybe the publicity would make up for K-9's having startled him.

Stepping back to admire her handiwork, she decided that the little circle of dust should certainly leave a trace if the vase was moved across the surface. Not that she could see the point, mind you; a hoaxer would simply lift the vase up to move it, and in all the films she'd ever seen, poltergeists either lifted or teleported objects. It was the team's investigation, though, and their rules. Shaking her head in amusement, she made her way back to the stairs.

A sorting and prioritizing subroutine picked out the distinctive

Doppler pattern of approaching footsteps from the multitude of ambient sounds in the immediate area. K-9 turned on the spot, antennae triangulating the direction of approach. The team's video camera, the operating frequency of which he had been comparing with that of his own recording systems, would have to wait.

Visual sensors caught the glint of metal, while heat detectors revealed a thermal image that was at the same time both familiar and yet different, causing a brief programming conflict. 'Master?'

'Electron-fusion nuclear battery. How quaint.' A smile flashed in the darkness. 'Time for you to be put to sleep, I think.'

The programming conflict cleared itself, settled by context. 'Warning, I am equipped for self-defence. Do not approach further.' K-9 started the charging cycle for the energy beam fitted under his sensor array.

A small but heavy looking black box appeared in the figure's hand. 'Go ahead, make my day, to coin a phrase.'

'Maassstttteeeeerrrrrr...'

Not even a mouse... It was closer to midsummer than the night before Christmas, but the house was silent and expectant nonetheless. The faint sounds of wood contracting and settling in the restful coolness after the heat of the day drifted through the shadowed hallways as the light of the sun gave way to that of the stars.

A few summer moths fluttered through the air, but their passage went unaccompanied by any sound. It was so silent, in fact, as the distant noise of traffic faded away outside, that one might even have been tempted to feel that time was standing still.

'... I, of course, had by far the better-trained mount, and easily outdistanced my closest rivals,' the Count was saying. 'None could catch up with me and, after the race, the Duke challenged me to hold the deciding contest in two sports cars, as he was

certain that I could hardly influence *them* with pieces of cake.'
Sarah could feel her smile becoming somewhat glassy. The
Count's stories were mildly amusing in their own way, but she
was much more interested in what had attracted him to these
nocturnal pursuits. 'I'm not boring you, I hope, Miss Smith?'

'What?' she shook her head sheepishly. 'Oh no, it's not that.
I was just wondering how you got interested in all this ghost
business.'

'One can hardly live for any period of time in one of Europe's historic buildings without at some point encountering
some of the... children of the night. The reason is a mystery, but
such challenges have always intrigued me.' He flashed a faint
smile. 'And once I have my mind set on something, I never
give up.'

'I'm sure the Duke would agree.'

'Of cou –' The small alarm clock that had been left beside
the sandwich maker started buzzing repetitively, and Shirley
reached out to switch it off. 'The witching hour. An appropriate
moment to check up on the control objects, I think.' The Count
rose, stretching his long legs and adjusting the hem of his jacket.
'We can all meet back here in ten minutes.'

Exchanging glances, the investigators shuffled out to the
stairs to begin their rounds. Mike turned to Sarah. 'We can take
the ground floor. I think I'll start with the kitchen.'

'Nothing ever changes does it? I fancy taking a look at the
ballroom, myself. I don't think I've ever been in a house with a
ballroom before. Palaces, yes, but never a house.'

'Well, be careful.'

'I thought these spooks never hurt anyone?'

'I meant watch you don't disturb any of the control objects.'

'Don't worry, I'll leave them untouched by human hands.'

Peter was kneeling by K-9 when Mike and Sarah emerged
into the hallway. 'Miss Smith,' he called, 'I think there's something wrong with your computer.'

Sarah was across to him like a shot, not even bothering to

try to tell herself that K-9 was only a machine and not a person. She had long since decided that if he had a personality then he must be a person, no matter what. It had been Aunt Lavinia, with typical acerbity, who had pointed out that there must be a lot of people around who wouldn't pass that test. Sarah had never been sure whether that was a funny or a worrying thing to say. 'I'd better fetch his leads from the car.'

'Jump leads, you mean?' asked Peter.

'Sometimes he can recharge from jump leads attached to his ears. Antennae, I mean,' she added a little sheepishly.

'Jump leads to the ears? The mains is still on, so I suppose I could try to rig up some sort of a transformer. Then we could just plug him in...'

It was a natural suggestion, Sarah supposed, but K-9 wasn't a toaster, and she wasn't really sure just how his power system worked. 'I don't know... You could electrocute yourself if you start mucking around in there.'

'Well, how do you usually recharge him?'

'Generally he does it himself. I did use a car battery charger once. It took a few hours, though.'

'That's okay then. I know how they work, so I'll just fix up a transformer and a few other bits and bobs and see if we can't get him up and running any quicker.'

Sarah still wasn't sure, but she didn't have a charger with her, and Peter seemed to know what he was talking about. 'All right, but start off on a low voltage just in case, and don't open him up – it could be dangerous.'

'Right you are.'

Sarah took a few steps away, then paused. She didn't like leaving K-9 in the hands of a stranger, but there didn't seem to be much of a choice – she was a journalist, not a cyberneticist. Keeping a concerned eye on him until the last possible moment, she climbed the main staircase.

The passageway leading up to the attic was narrow and cramped.

Since it was Shirley who had chosen to accompany him, however, Bob wasn't complaining. He almost cannoned into her as
she stopped abruptly at the top of the stairs. 'Something wrong?'

'I thought all the doors in here were supposed to be left open.'

'They are.' He didn't have to look to know that the attic
door must be locked – there would have been no point in her
asking, otherwise. She seemed surprised, but shrugged it off,
literally, and dug into one pocket for a set of the skeleton keys
that each member of the team had been given just in case of
such an eventuality. The Count had considered everything, Bob
thought admiringly.

Shirley unlocked the wooden door and pushed her way
through into the miniaturely vaulted attic. An exhalation of displaced air slipped almost imperceptibly past them, too weak
even to disturb the skeins of steel-coloured cobweb that formed
diaphanous awnings over the planked walkway laid across the
thick beams. Pyramids of boxes and cartons were sheathed in
dust so thick that it looked as if sheets had been tossed over
them. Maybe that was where the image of the old Casper type
of ghost came from, mused Bob, stepping cautiously onto the
planks. He tried to put to the back of his mind all the clichéd
haunted house movies he'd seen over the years, but recalled all
too well what happened to people who went into locked and
dusty attics. It was always: 'OK, Bob, we'll split up; you go
check up there.' Then it was: 'Sure, why not. I'm not afraid of
anything. Argh!' Followed, of course, by rip, squelch, thud and
occasionally splat. That was only fiction, thank God.

'Can you check if anything's disturbed the dust up there,
Bob?' He was glad Shirley had her back to him, as she wouldn't
have appreciated his gloomy grimace.

A couple of chairs were piled up in one corner, a rusting old
bedstead in front of them. Although brighter patches on the
faded walls betrayed the former locations of furniture, only a
cracked sink now remained. It dripped hollowly. Mike moved

over to it, irritated by the sound. These servants' quarters were gloomy enough without that. He reached out to turn the tap but found that it was rusted solid, although a small pool of water had collected at the bottom of the sink. As Mike watched in astonishment, with the hairs on the back of his neck prickling, a tiny droplet gathered itself together on the surface of the pool and fell upwards to the end of the tap.

He watched it happen twice more before his brain caught up with his eyes. What would the Doctor have made of this? Or the Brigadier, for that matter? You couldn't shoot a water droplet. He was tempted to beat a hasty retreat, but resisted the urge. This was, after all, exactly the sort of thing that he had come along hoping to see. Compared with plastic mannequins coming to life and dinosaurs appearing from and disappearing into thin air, this could almost be considered a mundane occurrence.

Experimentally, he stuck one hand between the sink and the mouth of the tap. The water tickled slightly as it leapt from the back of his hand up to the tap. Mike grinned. This was a pleasantly wondrous sort of weirdness.

He eventually had to force himself to turn away and continue with what he had first come to the room to do: to check on the waste-paper basket encircled with chalk. It was exactly where it had been left, the chalk circle undisturbed.

Leaving the room, albeit reluctantly, Mike decided to try the kitchen next. The control objects in there included several pots and plates – all marvellously breakable, if there was a typical poltergeist around. There was also a kitchen sink, of course, and it would be worth seeing if it was behaving in the same way as the one he had just found.

Shaun prowled the library nervously. A tune was running persistently through his head, but doing little to cheer him up. The shelves, that rose ceilingwards around the room's four walls, lacked the thick layers of leather-bound tomes that one would normally expect to find in a place such as this. The only books they bore, in fact, were a few manuals and pamphlets left behind by some of the community groups that had been using the house. He and his fellow team members had decided to leave them where they were, carefully marked to reveal any movement or change.

This was the sort of library where one half-expected to hear the gentle rustling of paper sliding on paper as insubstantial pages turned in an imperceptible breeze, or the persistent insect-like scritching of quill on parchment. Shaun shook his head, telling himself that if he wasn't careful he would soon start believing in all this supernatural nonsense. The self-admonition cheered him slightly; the lack of activity was, in any case, one more piece of evidence that it was all in the minds of gullible dreamers.

Humming the tune to himself, wondering where he had picked it up, he gave the pamphlets no more than a cursory glance. After all, there was no such thing as a ghost to be able to do anything to them, was there? Tossing aside a *Junior Woodchuck Guide* that he'd idly picked up – an action that would doubtless provoke interest and then annoyance from anyone else who checked later – he did a quick circuit of the room, knocking on the walls experimentally. There was no answer, although the sound of his knocking briefly drowned out that teasing music.

He froze, listening. Surely music in the imagination couldn't be drowned out? There it was again, insinuating itself through the walls like fungal damp. It sounded like a small ensemble of musicians, playing on woodwind and one violin. He decided that one of his colleagues must have brought along a radio, although strangely there now seemed to be the murmur of discreet conversation and the tinkle of cutlery and tableware mixed in with the music.

It seemed to be getting louder as he neared the wall opposite the big bay windows. A connecting door was positioned there, in a gap between two segments of shelving, and he pushed it open, psyching himself up to give whoever was playing the radio a good piece of his mind. The sound swelled and washed over him as he stepped through into a wide, open room. The place appeared totally deserted, and yet he could distinctly hear the individual instruments. The violin sounded as if it was only a couple of feet from his left ear, and a flute just ahead and to the right. In fact, it was as if he was standing right in the midst of the musicians.

With one last effort at rationalization, he looked down at the floor, hoping to find a radio sitting there. The sight that met his eyes was far from reassuring, however. Not only was there no sign of a radio, but the bare wooden floorboards were bouncing and writhing silently as if under the pressure of dozens of pairs of invisible dancing feet.

Sarah paused, listening as the music drifted faintly up to her. If she'd been anywhere else, she might have thought that she was going cuckoo; in a haunted house, though, this was exactly the kind of thing that one might expect to hear. She strained her ears, trying to work out which direction the music was coming from. It seemed oddly discordant, she reflected. The notes were tumbling down the corridor in disarray, although she could clearly pick out the sounds of flute and violin. Not wishing to complicate matters further with creaking floorboards, she stood perfectly still, regretting that K-9 wasn't around to give her the benefit of his sensor readings.

Suddenly a door slammed behind her, and she spun round, startled. Her widened eyes caught a glimpse of someone's back – Shaun's, she thought – hurtling round the corner out of sight. Presumably he had heard the music too, and perhaps seen something.

She didn't really relish the idea of coming across whatever had scared him like that, but firmly reminded herself that this was exactly the sort of story she'd come looking for. Besides, what mere thing-that-goes-bump-in-the-night could be more affecting than all the perils she'd encountered when she travelled with the Doctor?

Nervously, she followed the sounds towards the room from which Shaun had emerged.

So far, nothing had been disturbed in either the kitchen or the pantry, but the very thought of what those rooms were intended for had reminded Mike Yates that he hadn't eaten since breakfast. Certain that any ghosts could stand to wait for a few minutes, he returned along the corridor, weighing up the relative merits of a cheese and pickle sandwich and a mug of tomato soup. Meat dishes, of course, were something he wouldn't appreciate these days.

He turned into the main hall, and his leg had crashed through the floor up to his knee before he realized that K-9 was missing. So was the front door. Thick cobwebs and a quilting of dust shuddered smokily as he pulled his leg free from the rotted floorboard and looked around.

The main staircase had collapsed, and greasy patches of dampness stained the peeling walls.

'Are you all right, Mr Yates?'

Mike spun round. The Count was looking down at him with a raised eyebrow. Peter had stopped work on K-9 to glance over at them from his position near the front door. Mike quickly looked back to the stairs, and saw that they were now as solid as when he had climbed them earlier. 'I'm not sure,' he admitted. 'For a moment, everything looked different. The place was all run down, as if it hadn't been occupied for years.'

'Curious.' The Count hurried over and positioned himself where the passageway to the kitchen opened beside the stairs. He then slowly repeated Mike's steps into the hall. He shrugged. 'Whatever it was, it was evidently more partial to the blood of an Englishman.'

Inside the all-but empty library, Sarah found that she could hear the strange music much more clearly now. It seemed to be coming from beyond a narrow door set between two ranks of shelves. She crept forward and listened with an ear to the door, just in case. The music continued as before, but was now joined by the susurration of distant voices and the indistinct swishing sounds of movement. She wondered if the door was locked, half-hoping that it was. Clearly, however, there was something interesting going on in there, and she felt the old familiar urge to find out what. Occupational hazard, she thought, straightening up.

The screams started just as Sarah's hand touched the door knob. She froze, fighting down a wave of panic. Whoever was inside, it couldn't be any member of the group; it sounded like a crowd of people, the women screaming and the men muttering exclamations. She looked back to see if any of the others were around, but the hallway was empty. It seemed that she would have to go in alone. Steeling herself, she pushed open the door and went through.

No screams were audible inside the ballroom, but the strange, bizarrely disjointed music was louder than ever. Sarah was almost bowled over as a series of couples swept past her in a very odd waltz. The creased dinner suits and billowing gowns of the dancers were clearly Victorian, as was the formal attire worn by the small group of musicians playing their odd tune at the far end of the room. There was no sign of the dust and decay that characterized the rest of the house. The crystal and silver was all highly polished, and oil lamps cast a warm glow over the proceedings. It all seemed very luxurious, and the buffet arrayed on tables along one wall made her feel quite peckish. All the same, there was something distinctly odd about the scene, quite apart from the discordant hoots and crashes of the music and the fact that it was happening in this decrepit old ruin in the first place.

It took Sarah a moment to work out just what it was, but then she realized: the women in their sumptuous gowns were leading the men in the dance, rather than the other way around; their flowing hems folding and unfolding jerkily as they trailed across the floor. One couple almost bumped into her, the matronly lady shivering as if she felt a draught from somewhere. Sarah watched in fascination as the couple moved away, their footsteps only now audible and the lady apparently heedless of any chill.

It wasn't quite what she'd expected from a haunting. It wasn't scary as such; it was more like watching a play from the stage itself. No-one had taken any notice of her as yet, and she strongly suspected that they couldn't see her. Otherwise, these staid Victorians would surely have demanded to know who on earth this gatecrasher was.

Mike and the Count stood by the foot of the stairs and heaved at one of the floorboards, prizing it loose and throwing it clear. That was one point in the Count's favour as far as Mike was concerned: he wasn't afraid to get his hands dirty. It was an unusual enough trait to find in anyone these days. 'I'd watch out for your suit, if I were you,' he advised.

The Count wiped his hands on a silk handkerchief from his top pocket. 'Don't concern yourself, Mr Yates. I have many others. And the discoveries we may make tonight would be worth far more to me than any amount of mere attire.' Mike could quite believe this. The look of intensity in the Count's eyes as he gazed down into the dark pit that they had uncovered was as unshakeable as any expression of determined longing.

'I can't imagine what we might discover under a floorboard.'

'These here, perhaps.' The Count directed a small pocket torch downwards, and Mike noticed a number of iron, steel and even lead pipes curving away under the floor.

'They must come up from the boiler in the cellar.'

'Yes... Interesting that there should be so many under this particular spot.'

'How do you mean?' Mike hadn't been left this much in the dark by anyone since he had last seen the Doctor.

The Count didn't answer for a moment, and Mike began to feel that he was being deliberately ignored. Then the other man looked up, tearing his gaze away from the pipes. 'I very much doubt that you would understand, even were I to explain. Suffice it to remind you that metal and water are both admirable conductors – of many types of energy.'

'Do you hear music?'

The Count straightened, one eyebrow raised. 'Faintly. One of the others with a radio?'

'I don't know.' The sound was odd, disjointed somehow. 'It seems to be coming from upstairs.'

'If anyone has brought a radio into the house against my instructions, I will... Never mind.' The Count handed Mike a small tape recorder. 'Go upstairs and check. If someone has a radio, confiscate it – we can well do without the confusion. Otherwise, record whatever it is and then come back and fetch me.'

Turning away from Mike as if he was no longer there, the Count pulled a small grey box from his pocket and unfolded it like some fatter cousin of a cellular telephone. Mike felt a pang of concern at this; the device, which now began to emit a soft warbling sound, was exactly the sort of thing that the Doctor might have come up with. Then again, he'd seen technology from Japan in recent years that was more hi-tech, and weirder, than some of that brought along by UNIT's opponents in his days of yore. Sparing a last glance back at the Count as he proceeded to wave the grey box backwards and forwards over the metal pipes, Mike went off in search of the source of the music.

Bob jumped, a yelp choked off in his throat, as a hand fell on his shoulder.

'Well, it's as quiet as the proverbial grave up here,' Shirley said. Bob resisted the temptation to point out that he could almost have made such a comparison from experience. 'Did I startle you?'

'You could put it like that.'

'Sorry.' She opened the door through which they had entered the attic. A shaft of light spilled up from below. 'I'll make it up to you.'

'Is that a promise?'

Sarah slipped through the ballroom, noting curiously how the dancers seemed to shiver and look towards her, though not directly at her, whenever they approached. She had been polite enough to step aside for anyone on a direct collision course, although she wasn't sure if they would actually have bumped into her. They had a strangely insubstantial and two-dimensional look about them.

She thought several times about deliberately standing in someone's way and seeing what happened, but couldn't quite bring herself to do it. She would have done if the Doctor had told her it was safe, of course. But he wasn't here.

She spotted an old iron radiator on the opposite side of the room and, choosing this as a suitable landmark for which to aim, changed direction. As she traversed the floor, she noticed that the dancers were becoming more... well... solid. They were also slowing down, not as part of the dance but as if they were images on celluloid being projected at the wrong speed. The music was slowing too, rolling ominously across the floor like thunder. By this time, it would scarcely have surprised her to have seen Vincent Price arriving in a sheikh's costume with a red-hooded stranger close behind.

With less cause now to worry about collisions, Sarah was able to cross the room more quickly. She came to an abrupt halt, however, when she realized that everything had suddenly stopped. Not quite everything, she corrected herself. The music was still droning on in a single, impossibly prolonged note.

All movement had ceased, though, and the dancers were standing stock still, frozen into position.

Sarah closely scrutinized the nearest figure, waving a hand in front of the matronly woman's eyes in the vain hope of provoking a reaction. This was just too weird. Circling around, she took a few steps to the side, still heading in roughly the same direction. The musical note slowly changed tone and became a droning wail. The dancers started up again too, but this time moving forwards rather than backwards, albeit at an almost imperceptibly slow pace. Assailed by the unpleasant feeling that normality here would be a bad sign, Sarah darted around the last few couples. The music was playing quickly enough now for her to recognize it as a Strauss waltz, and she could even make out snippets of small talk about the situation in the Crimea. She had just started to wonder if this meant that she would soon become visible when the matronly woman pointed straight at her, eyes wide with horror.

Other figures turned, their faces paling with astonishment, and the women began to scream. Sarah retreated until she felt the cold metal of the radiator against her back. Then there was a sudden soundless white flash which left just a few stray notes of the waltz hanging in the air before they too faded into nothingness. Recovering her senses, Sarah realized that the ballroom was now silent and empty, the designated control object – a chair – standing undisturbed in its chalk-dust circle.

Sarah stood frozen for a moment, her mouth hanging open in astonishment. 'You'll catch flies,' a kindly voice told her from somewhere off to the left. Sarah jumped, but then relaxed as she saw that it was only Mike Yates.

Stiff fingers of blackness clawed their way across the faded wallpaper. Shaun backed away into a corner, driven only by his heels and palms, still too sober to dismiss the feeling that they were reaching out to grab him by the throat.

Doubtless the others would kick him off the project for hav-

ing brought his hip flask, but he would thank them for it. He'd
come here to listen to some night sounds and send up the true
believers, not to be assailed by strange music from empty rooms
and see the moon-cast shadows of the window spars dancing
around the walls even though the moon was as motionless as
ever up in the sky and there were no other lights outside.

The cold metal of a radiator scored into his side as he pushed
himself back as far as he could go. He drew his knees up in
front of him defensively, curling himself around the hip flask,
as the shadows swept back and forth, leaping across the wall as
if a whole night was being fast-forwarded and rewound over
and over again.

He focused his attention on the spars, half-hoping that he
would catch them unawares and see what was really going on,
half-hoping that he wouldn't. Either way, his attention was held
completely enough for him to be blissfully ignorant of the darker
patch of shadow that had gathered in the doorway and the gentle chuckle that briefly emanated from it.

The car was a grey and colourless mound under the bright moon,
its windscreen showing only a stretched reflection of the cratered
silver disc.

Gravel shifted underfoot, but too quietly for anyone to hear
– especially considering the rhythmic squeakings emerging from
the vehicle. Behind the enclosing glass of the window, a vaguely
human shape could be seen roiling on the back seat.

The gravel stilled, and a head shook with an amused tutting
noise. It seemed that providence had supplied a diversion here.

Peter finished wiring up a transformer to K-9's antennae and,
with a final flourish, switched it on. The robot's head rose
slightly and the twin, red-tinted lenses of his visual sensors lit
up with a faint glow. The effect lasted only a moment, however, and then the light winked out and the head drooped
floorwards once more.

Peter shook his head, puzzled, and reached into his toolkit, pulling out a different transformer and a handful of screws. Several of the screws slipped through his fingers and fell to the floor, but he was too engrossed in his work even to bother with a curse. It seemed as if putting more power into the computer only made it drain off even faster, he thought, as his hand swept idly across the floorboards. His train of thought was finally broken when he realized that he couldn't actually feel any of the errant screws. He shifted round irritably, pressing his head to the floor to take a look underneath K-9. He could just make out one of the screws, but became immediately distracted from it as he noticed a faint electrical purring sound which seemed to be coming not from K-9 but rather from somewhere beneath the floor.

Realizing that this might be the very thing that the team had come here to investigate, he lifted his camera and tape recorder from the chair upon which he had left them. A picture would show that arrogant Shirley that a university affiliation wasn't a prerequisite for being a good investigator. Listening at the floor again, he felt a faint chill as the purring continued, like a soft and very rapid beeping. It was definitely something under the floor. Maybe a cat had got in through a ventilation grille. If so, he should really let it out, and not risk the little mite starving to death in there.

The floorboards were quite short, but tightly packed. Taking a screwdriver to them, he levered up the end of one quite easily. He almost dropped it when the vibration of a soft footstep buzzed up through his knees. He turned with a gasp, his startled look dropping away sheepishly as he saw who it was. 'Oh, it's you. You scared me half to death there.'

'I never do things by halves.'

The ring of chalk dust around the chair was unbroken, exactly as it had been set. 'Strange that it all stopped when you hit the radiator.' Mike said.

'Maybe it's a sort of recording in the bricks,' Sarah suggested. 'Did you ever see that TV play, *The Stone Tape*?'

'Or metal, maybe?'

'Metal?'

'Well, the ballroom's above the boiler, and there are pipes leading directly up to the radiator. Maybe metal can conduct ghostly images like it conducts electricity?'

'Oh, come off it, Mike. If that was so, every house in Britain would be-' She stopped, her mouth frozen in a little 'O', as a hollow scream rose from elsewhere in the house and then gradually tailed off as if the culprit had forgotten what he was doing.

Mike raced for the door. 'That came from the front hall!'

Sarah followed close behind. 'K-9! If Peter's been mucking around with his insides he could have electrocuted himself.'

'Right.' Mike opened the door. 'You might want to stay here –'

'Not on your life, Mike Yates!' Sarah pushed past him into the library. Mike followed, a faint smile creasing his features.

Moving quickly but cautiously through the dimly lit rooms and around their carefully positioned control objects, the two friends made their way back to the landing. The Count was just ascending the top step, a flat black attaché case in hand.

'Ah, Mr Yates, Sarah.' The Count consulted his small grey box again. 'You saw something in the ballroom?'

'How did you know that?' Sarah asked.

'The pipes lead straight there. So, I was right, it does all relate to the heating system...' The Count put away the box and laid down his case, tugging out a notepad and pen. 'That gives us a reading of approximately point two on the Bocca scale,' he murmured, scribbling furiously.

Sarah chanced a quick look at the pad, but the squiggles of mathematical formulae could have been Sanskrit for all she knew. 'What on earth is that?'

'Merely a minor application of Minkowski's theorem of four-dimensional vectors.' The Count looked up. 'You seemed to be in rather a hurry. Don't let me detain you.'

'Didn't you hear that scream?' Mike asked.

'Just a small problem; nothing serious. Ah, perfect!' He put away the notebook. 'If you'll excuse me?' Lifting the attaché case, he turned and hurried back downstairs. Mike and Sarah exchanged a look of bemusement.

'We'd better check,' ventured Mike.

'You're right,' Sarah agreed. 'You know, I don't think he really registered that we were even here.'

'Yes, I got that feeling too. You know, it's funny, but in a way it reminded me of–'

'The Doctor! Yes, he could be like that sometimes.'

They descended the stairs together, keeping an eye out for any of the others.

'There's K-9,' gestured Sarah as they reached the hallway, 'but where did Peter go?'

'Into the ops room?' Mike hurried over to the door and peered inside. 'Just Shaun, asleep I think.'

'After that scream?'

'There's an empty hip flask too.'

'Oh.' Sarah knelt beside K-9. A transformer was lying next to him, the cables not yet plugged in. 'Peter hadn't finished the job, anyway.' She squinted more closely at the floor. There seemed to be some scratches around one of the floorboards. Her curiosity aroused, she tried to get a grip on it, noticing that it felt slightly raised. 'Mike, can you give me a hand with this?'

'Of course. The Count got me to help him take up one of the others as well,' he said, indicating the gap over by the stairs. 'What's so special about this one?'

'I don't know, but it's been moved, and recently.' She took hold of a screwdriver which had been lying amongst the cables. 'If I prize it up with this, you can grab it when it comes free.'

'Right.' He waited, hands open, as she levered the board up with the screwdriver. It popped free with a creak, and Mike pulled it aside, peering into the gap beneath. 'Good Lord!' he breathed. Sarah fought down her rising gorge at the sight of the tiny, moulded-putty-like corpse that they had uncovered. 'I never thought I'd see anything like this again after leaving UNIT.' He didn't look any better than she felt, Sarah noticed. He reached past her down into the gap, being careful to avoid touching the corpse, and lifted out a small silver spiral of metal with a flashing light at one end. There were a few buttons on it, and he pressed them experimentally. After a moment, the light stopped flashing. Almost immediately, K-9's lenses began to glow and his head rose slightly.

Sarah looked up at Mike. 'You know what did that to poor Peter?'

'The Doctor used to call it a tissue compression eliminator. The Master's favourite weapon.'

'Congratulations!' The Count's voice came from the cellar doorway under the stairs. They turned to look at the grinning figure there. 'You always were the intelligent one – meaning no offence to you, of course, Miss Smith. Our acquaintance in the Death Zone was all too brief, I'm afraid.'

'What are you doing here?' Mike's voice had suddenly taken on a hard and determined tone.

The Master looked offended. 'Now is that any way to greet an old friend?' He shook his head sadly. 'Young people today... When I first heard of the time breaks in this house, I realized at once that it was built on a time fissure. But the strength of the disturbances was too great to be entirely natural.' He tilted his head slightly. 'Do you know to whom this house belongs?'

'The local council, I think.' Sarah was still shocked, but experience told her that it was best to try to avoid letting it show.

'Actually, no. It is only leased to them. It is owned by our mutual friend, the Doctor.'

Sarah couldn't help but look surprised at that. The moment quickly passed, though, as she told herself that she might have guessed the Doctor would crop up in a situation as weird as this.

'Any time fissure can be stimulated by an external source,' the Master continued, 'and a TARDIS is a perfect example. In this case, the fissure is being stimulated by temporal spillage from a TARDIS's imminent arrival. Hence the temporary bubbles of other time zones that are breaking through. Artron energy is being conducted backwards in time along the metal and running water of the pipes in the heating system.

'The time fissure effect can have natural advantages, of course, such as increased sensitivity of a TARDIS's scanners. But more interesting are the dangers.' The Master grinned slowly. 'Thanks to your gallant efforts, and the readings I have taken of the location and strength of the time breaks, I have now calculated the precise moment of the TARDIS's arrival, and can stimulate the time fissure accordingly. When it does arrive, it will find itself trying to coexist with the energy released from the fissure–'

'Time ram?' Mike interrupted uncertainly.

'Ah, I gather that Miss Grant told you of our exploits in Atlantis. Yes, time ram indeed.'

'I hate to interrupt,' Sarah put in, doing just that, 'but what exactly will this time ram do?'

The Master sighed. 'Ever the curious student. Well, since you ask, nothing very much – on a cosmic scale. It's simply that the TARDIS, its occupants, this house and everything for, oh, roughly a mile and a half in every direction, will be completely erased from existence.' He lifted the tissue compression eliminator slightly. 'Speaking of which...'

'Now K-9!' yelled Sarah, diving headlong for the door to the ops room. She wasn't sure if he would be sufficiently recharged to respond, or even if he would actually understand what she meant, but her hopes were answered as she heard the familiar sound of his blaster extending from beneath his nose. A red flash briefly tinted the air, but the Master leapt agilely over the bannister onto the stairs and the energy beam merely scorched the wood.

K-9 started to trundle towards the foot of the stairs as the Master ran up them three at a time. 'K-9, no!' Sarah stepped cautiously out of the ops room, while Mike picked himself up off the floor. 'He must have some means of affecting the energy of this time fissure,' she went on. 'K-9, can you sense anything that might do that?'

K-9's antennae whirred slightly. 'Sensors detect an energy source of unknown type bearing zero-one-five mark three-four-seven. Probability that this energy is produced by alien technology, 99.74 per cent.'

'Can you deal with it?'

'Unknown until further data is acquired, mistress.'

K-9 really was like a child sometimes, she thought. 'Then go and find out!'

'Affirmative, mistress.' K-9 spun round on the spot and rolled off towards the cellar door.

Sarah stepped up onto a chair and began to tug at a pair of crossed swords displayed on the wall. 'And what do you think you're doing?' Mike asked.

'Surely you don't want to let the Master get away?' Sarah freed the swords and tossed one of them to Mike.

'He has the tissue compression eliminator,' Mike reminded her.

Sarah brandished her rapier. 'Well I've got this!' The prospect of becoming a tenant in one of her old dolls' houses didn't exactly appeal, but she had had just about as much as she could take. This was the nineties, for God's sake, and not the first time that she'd faced some alien killer. Besides, she'd fenced for the school team, what felt like a few lifetimes ago. Without waiting for Mike's reaction, she started up the stairs, silently hoping that the Master had already left the house and made his getaway. She didn't even want to contemplate what might have happened to the rest of the team – or to the real Count, if there ever was one.

K-9's hydraulics lowered his main body back onto his traction system as he came off the narrow stairway and settled onto the cellar floor. Triangulating briefly with his antennae, he locked onto the energy leakage that he'd detected and glided over to the squat and rusted boiler which sat within its nest of pipes.

An empty attaché case lay open on the floor, and a flat control panel covered in glowing lights was affixed to the centre of the boiler. A quick check through his internal database told K-9 that the device registered an 85 per cent match with a TARDIS's time vector filter. Reasoning that he had no means by which to prize it loose, and that decrypting the controls could exceed acceptable time parameters, he decided on a different course of action.

Extending his sensor probe from between his visual receptor lenses, he carried out a brief scan of the boiler and confirmed that it was non operational, so that there could be no danger from escaping steam. Focusing his energy beam to a narrower and hotter mode, he then started to cut around the time vector filter.

Mike crept nervously into the master bedroom, rapier held out in front of him. He felt sure that he had heard the Master come in here, but could see no sign of him in the dim light emanating from the single shaded bulb. Suddenly, just as Mike passed by, the door of a walk-in cupboard swung open and the Master lunged out. A flickering shadow alerted the former UNIT captain just in time, and he ducked under the sinanju strike that had been aimed at him. He turned on the balls of his feet, lashing out with the rapier. The Time Lord leapt back, a delighted look on his face. 'Just like old times, eh, Captain Yates?'

'Not really. This time I intend to put a stop to you – for good.'

'A duel? Are you challenging me to a duel?' The Master's eyes gleamed excitedly. 'Warrior to warrior? Two men enter, one man leaves? I never knew you had such a poetic soul.' He tugged a foil free from his ebony cane, bringing it up in a brief salute. '*En garde*, Captain.'

Mike lunged forward in a stabbing motion. The Master easily twisted the rapier aside, however, the tip of his foil flicking a button from his opponent's jacket. The Time Lord tutted softly. 'What a sorry effort you are without your guns. For your information, Captain, the rapier is a slashing weapon.'

'Like this, you mean?' Mike struck out at the Master's throat, quickly coming back for his midriff. The Master backed off, out of the room.

'That's more like it!' Their blades clashed tinnily in the corridor.

'Thanks for the advice.' Mike pressed home his attack, heartened by the fact that the Master was steadily retreating.

'Much as I dislike spoiling your concentration,' the Master said apologetically, 'there is something I believe you really ought to know.'

Mike risked another step forward, and the Master yielded the ground with an amused smile. 'And what's that?'

'I'm not really left-handed.' With a nimble flick of his fingers, the Master tossed the foil from his left hand to his right and immediately launched into a blindingly fast riposte. Struggling to keep his grip on the rapier as he parried the furious blows, Mike scuttled backwards along the corridor and tripped headlong through the door into the conservatory.

The square section of boiler to which the time vector filter was attached dropped onto the floor with a thud. K-9 reversed a few feet and adjusted his energy beam to a more standard setting. One shot blew the alien device to pieces in a shower of glowing filaments.

The Master slid gracefully into the conservatory, touching the point of his foil to Mike's adam's apple. 'A shame, really, we were having such fun.' Suddenly his eyes widened in surprise as another blade swept down from behind the door, neatly removing the tip of his own.

Sarah stepped out into view. 'I'm not left-handed either!'

'A *femme fatale*, eh?' Suddenly diving forward, the Master snatched up Mike's rapier and struck out. Sarah deflected the blow, but nevertheless gained the impression that she was lucky to do so. The Master leapt up onto the slatted bench, and Sarah nearly cut him off at the ankles. Steel and steel struck sparks as they circled each other warily.

'Why don't you just give up?' demanded Sarah. 'K-9 will already have destroyed whatever it was that you left down in the cellar.'

Keeping a wary eye on her, the Master pulled out the small grey box from his jacket pocket and scanned the readings. 'It seems you may be right, Miss Smith.' He glanced back at the conservatory's dusty panes, then pressed another button on the box. 'The best laid plans of mice and men gang aft aglee.'

Shirley squealed slightly as the twin beams of a pair of bright headlights knifed through the car window. She looked up and saw them sweep quickly across the front of the house as a black shape whipped through the darkness with a rush of displaced gravel. 'For a minute I thought it was the police.'

'It looked like the Count's car,' Bob muttered, trying to get his breathing back under control.

The Master nodded as a soft beep sounded from his grey box. 'It's been most pleasant renewing old acquaintances,' he said, smiling graciously to the bemused Sarah and Mike. Suddenly he reversed the sword in his hand and hurled it at Sarah overarm in the manner of a dagger. She flung herself to the floor, allowing the weapon to pass over her head and thud harmlessly into the doorframe beyond. At the same moment there came a loud crashing sound, and Sarah looked up just in time to see a shower of glittering glass follow the Master out into the night and disappear below floor level.

Picking themselves up, Sarah and Mike hurried over to the shattered wall of the conservatory and peered carefully out. Below, the sun roof of a large black Mercedes was just sliding closed. The car sped off down the driveway, fading into the darkness with a strange mechanical rising and falling sound.

K-9 ground to a halt at the conservatory entrance, antennae whirring. 'Has any injury been sustained, Mistress?'

'No, K-9, we're both fine.'

'How on earth are we going to explain all this?' Mike asked.

Sarah looked up at him with a wry smile. 'Very carefully, I should think!'

The Nine-Day Queen

By Matthew Jones

Amongst all the kings and queens of England, no rule was as brief or as tragic as that of Jane Grey, who was crowned in 1553 and whose reign lasted only nine days. This young woman has passed into history as the Nine-Day Queen, remembered more for this one sad fact than for any other aspect of her life.

EXERCISE: Read the following extract from Joan Stevenson's biography of Jane Grey, and then in groups of two or three try to imagine what life must have been like for this fifteen-year-old girl.

Extracted from *Journeys Through History: A Sourcebook for GCSE* (1985), prepared for the Associated Examination Board by Barbara Chesterton and Ian Martin.

'Barbara!'

The wolf sprang at the young woman, its jaws reaching for her throat.

Ian could only look on horrified as it leapt through the night air towards her. The world slid sickeningly into slow motion. For a moment the animal appeared to hang in the air, its teeth flashing in the moonlight, and then, from nowhere, an arrow thudded into its head and it crashed to the ground at her feet.

Whirling around to catch sight of the archer, Ian found himself staring up at a young woman on horseback. He backed away involuntarily, until he was at Barbara's side. Instinctively he wrapped his arms around her. He could feel her shaking violently in his embrace.

The archer was not alone. Four more riders emerged from the darkness to join the first. The tallest, a broad-shouldered man with a stern face and a full black beard, dismounted and walked over to where the wolf's corpse lay. Unsheathing a long knife, he cut through the creature's neck and freed its head, which he displayed to the others as if it were a trophy.

'See where the arrow has entered the beast. Through its eye! Can there be a finer huntress in all of Leicestershire? I say there cannot.'

The riders cheered. Only the young woman whose shot had felled the wolf seemed displeased. Rather than appearing flattered by the bearded man's comments, she seemed to be embarrassed by the attention they elicited.

'Uncle, please,' she begged, trying to dampen the celebratory atmosphere. 'The arrow found its target more through luck than skill. Leave the beast alone and let us return to the house.'

'Nonsense! I shall have the head mounted to mark the occasion. It will be hung in the Great Hall so that all will know of your skill.' He handed the beast's head to one of the other riders and finally turned his attention to Ian and Barbara. All trace of humour left his face and his voice took on the matter-of-fact air of someone used to dealing with inferiors. 'Now perhaps you will tell me who you are and what business you have in Bradgate? Trespassers are not welcome here and poachers are likely to lose their hands, if not their heads.'

Ian just stared open-mouthed at the man. Barbara was still in shock. Events had moved too quickly for the two schoolteachers. They were both speechless.

'Am I to take your silence to mean that you have no legitimate reason for your trespass?' A bored tone had crept into the bearded man's voice. He wiped his bloody knife on a rag and then looked from its glinting blade to the new arrivals. 'We have been troubled by poachers once too often this summer. I ought to finish the wolf's work for it, as a lesson to those who would steal from my relatives and good hosts, the Greys of Bradgate.'

'I think, perhaps, that I might be able to clear up this misunderstanding,' a new voice said.

The Doctor was standing by the headless corpse of the wolf, a lantern in one hand and his walking cane in the other. He prodded the wolf with his stick and then lifted the lantern to head height, where its light cast eerie shadows across his angular face.

'But first, I should like to know what has happened here. Is this slaughter your handiwork?'

From the look on the bearded man's face, it was clear that he wasn't used to being addressed in this way. 'Who the devil are you? How many peasants are abroad in Bradgate tonight?'

'I am the Doctor. These two people whom you have succeeded in frightening out of their wits are my travelling companions. Now, I asked you a question young man, and one that is considerably more important than your own. Perhaps you might have the good grace to answer it, hmm? Did you slay this creature?'

Such was the authority in the Doctor's voice that the bearded man found himself answering. 'The beast was killed by my niece,' he said, indicating the young woman who had sat silently throughout the whole exchange. 'You are directing your insolent questions to the Duke of Northumberland. A man whose patience is being most sorely tried.'

'No doubt you can manage to be patient a moment longer, my dear man.' The Doctor turned from the fuming duke and retrieved a thin cylindrical rod from his pocket. At the flick of a switch, a complex wire aerial extended from the device. The Doctor passed it over the wolf's body and then, apparently satisfied, pocketed the machine.

'The beast is quite dead,' the Duke of Northumberland said, joining the Doctor. 'The young lady is a master of the bow: there is no danger.'

'Just because it is dead, that does not necessarily mean that the danger has passed.'

The duke's eyes narrowed. 'I think I have indulged you long

enough, old man. You had better tell me your business or I shall have one of my men run you and your friends through.'

The Doctor pulled himself to his full height and turned on the duke, but before he could vent his impatience they were interrupted by the young archer.

'Why, surely it is Doctor Samuel Smythe. Sir, you are very late. We have been expecting you from Oxford for several days now. When we heard nothing, we dispatched a rider to the college to inquire of the fate of our new scholar. Did you meet with an accident?'

The duke stepped between his niece and the Doctor. 'You are to be this lady's teacher? Why did you not reveal your identity? And why has it taken you a fortnight to ride from Oxford to Leicester?'

The Doctor looked at the girl in puzzlement for a moment, but said nothing. He allowed himself to be led to where Ian and Barbara stood.

'Come,' the duke continued. 'We will arrange transport for you and your associates.'

Ian looked through the carriage window at the bleak landscape beyond. The moonlit countryside that rattled past the horse-drawn trap was wild and quite breathtaking. Their journey was taking them along the bottom of a low valley. Huge slabs of jagged granite lined the peaks of the hills, like the molars of an ogre's jaw. The view from the other side of the carriage was of a forest of tall deciduous trees that led down to a lake the colour of slate.

The duke had sent for transport to bring Bradgate's new tutor and his assistants to the house. Ian had taken an instant dislike to the brutish man and to the way in which he had delighted in embarrassing the girl who had dispatched the wolf.

Ian looked across to where Barbara sat staring quietly out of the window. He could tell from her expression that her thoughts were not on the view. The lines around her mouth looked deep and heavy in the silvery light, and her eyes were bloodshot. Ian knew that she must be on the brink of exhaustion. He wasn't far from it himself.

The last few hours had been a terrible ordeal for them all. It had started in the ship, when the fault locator had registered a series of minor systems failures. This in itself had not unduly worried Ian – despite the Doctor's protestations to the contrary, there was always something going wrong with his machine. A little later, Barbara had excused herself, complaining of a headache. Neither the Doctor nor Ian had made any connection between the trouble with the TARDIS and Barbara's ill health – at least not until Ian had woken up in his room to find himself being throttled by Barbara. The young woman had been laughing hysterically, speckles of foam gathering at the corners of her mouth, and it had taken all his strength to free himself from her grip.

Even before the Doctor had explained, Ian had instinctively known that the vicious intelligence that had glared through Barbara's eyes had not been her own. There had been more cruelty expressed in those few seconds than Barbara Wright was capable of in a lifetime. The image of Barbara's face screwed up into a triumphant sneer as she enthusiastically strangled the life out of him was one that would haunt him for many years to come.

The creature that had stared out of Barbara's eyes was, according to the Doctor, a Vrij. The old man had explained that he knew of it only from legend. Apparently its habitat was the strange dimension that the TARDIS passed through as it slipped between the years and worlds; a vortex of space and time, where the laws of physics as Ian knew and had taught them were without meaning. Once it had roamed the universe, creating chaos and disorder wherever it had struck, until finally it had been captured, stripped of its physical body and banished into the vortex where it could do no more harm. Or so it had been thought.

For countless years the creature must have remained a prisoner within the vortex. Then the Doctor's ship had appeared, spinning through the ether, a stepping stone between its dimension and normal space. It had used the opportunity to slip its chains, invading first the TARDIS and then Barbara's mind. Then it had dragged the Doctor's ship to Earth, where it had fled into the night seeking refuge in the first body it had encountered – the wolf.

Anxious to track the creature down, Barbara and Ian had found themselves ahead of the Doctor when the wolf had leapt out of the darkness at them. The creature had circled, snapping at them fiercely. Just before it had sprung at Barbara, Ian had looked into its wild eyes. They had seemed to be illuminated from within by a scarlet fire.

Unconsciously, Ian reached up and gingerly explored his bruised neck. He hoped with all his heart that the Vrij had died with the wolf. He never wanted to see those eyes again.

The silhouette of a large house filled the carriage window. Bradgate was a low, wide building, framed at either end by tall octagonal towers. Ian couldn't quite place the architecture. He thought it might be Tudor, but decided against asking Barbara's opinion when he looked across at her and saw that she was still shocked and distracted by the events of the night. The house seemed to be slumped between the two towers, and Ian thought that it looked almost as if it were sulking.

As the coach pulled up in front of the main entrance, the Doctor patted Ian on his knee. 'We must be away from here as quickly as possible. We don't want to risk being found out.'

'What about the creature?'

Pulling the tracking device from his pocket, the Doctor consulted its tiny control panel. 'My machine is reading no psychic disturbances in the area. Perhaps we have seen the last of it?'

'No,' Barbara said, and the anger in her voice shocked Ian. 'It's out there. I can feel it.'

* * *

'I should have thought that someone with your formidable skills would be out hunting with the others.' The Doctor was surprised to find his new student reading quietly in the library.

The young woman blushed. 'I am afraid that the events of yesterday evening have furnished you with a false impression of my character,' she apologized. 'I fear that I am no hunter. If the truth be known, I would have not a single regret if I were banned from hunting and riding for good.'

She closed her book, placed it on the arm of her chair and walked to the large window which looked out onto the estate. Outside, the duke and his men could be seen mounting their horses, preparing for another day's hunting. 'All their sport in the park is but a shadow of the pleasure I find in Plato.'

The Doctor picked up the copy of Plato's *Phaedo* that she had laid aside. He smiled approvingly as he noted that this edition was printed in the original Greek: the young lady was obviously a scholar of no small achievement. He reached into his coat pocket for his spectacles, but then suddenly realized that they would be more than a little anachronistic in this time period. Sighing quietly to himself, he left his glasses where they were and was forced to hold the book at arm's length in order to bring the tiny Greek letters into focus.

You are getting old, my dear Doctor, he thought to himself. He looked up to find the girl staring at him. In the light of day he realized that she was far younger than he had first thought, perhaps no more than sixteen. She wore her sandy-coloured hair scraped back from her face, which only made her serious expression more severe. She was a curious mixture of vulnerable child and scholarly adult. After spending so much time in the twentieth century, he had forgotten that childhood was a much shorter experience in the sixteenth.

'You are familiar with Plato, of course,' she said.

'Indeed I am, my dear child,' the Doctor replied, a mischievous grin spreading across his face. 'I once spent a few rather pleasant weeks in his company. Although he was a rather serious young man, as I remember.'

The young woman laughed a little hollowly. 'Plato lived and died many hundreds of years ago, Doctor – if you actually are a doctor – and I doubt very much that even you are that old. Please, if you are to be my teacher I would beg you to take me seriously, for no one else in this house ever does.'

The Doctor looked solemnly at the young girl and decided to end the charade. 'You know that I am not the Oxford scholar come to tutor you, don't you? You knew it last night when you saved me from the duke and his men.'

'What were you doing in Bradgate? You certainly don't look like a poacher.'

The Doctor was amused by the idea. 'No, no my dear, we are not poachers, although we are hunters of a kind. We are charged with a special and dangerous mission, which concerns a most terrible and fierce creature.'

'The wolf?'

'If only it were that simple. The creature that my friends and I were hunting does not belong in this land...'

The young lady looked puzzled. 'You mean it is from the continent?'

'Eh? Oh, yes, in a way. We brought it here by accident in my ship. It is my responsibility to return it to its natural habitat.'

She looked at the Doctor in alarm. 'And this creature is at large in Bradgate?'

'At first I thought so, but now I am not so sure. What I am sure of is that our quest will not be furthered by staying on here as your guests. Sooner or later our true identities will be discovered and that will only lead to trouble for us all. I wonder, would you help us to go quietly on our way?'

'What a strange man you are, Doctor. I'm really not sure what to make of you at all.' And then she smiled for the first time since they had met. 'I will help you, but I must make one condition.' The young woman paused, as if summoning the courage to speak. She took the copy of *Phaedo* from the Doctor's hands, and as she did so he noticed that there were dark bruises on her wrists. The young lady quickly tugged the sleeves of her dress down to cover the weals.

'Does the duke's harshness extend to his family as well as to strangers?' the Doctor asked.

His question clearly shocked the girl, who was unaccustomed to such directness. She pulled her arms to her sides and looked down. The Doctor realized that, despite her confident appearance, she was terrified.

'No. These bruises are the work of my father's hand. But it might as well have been the duke, so tightly does he have my father bound around his finger. They are forcing me to marry against my will. If I stay here I will be beaten until I yield, and I have nowhere to go. I will help you leave Bradgate. Tonight, if you wish it. But I must insist that you take me with you.'

'What?' the Doctor stammered, taken aback. 'My dear Lady...' he began, but at that moment they were interrupted by the arrival of a large middle-aged woman who strode confidently into the room.

'Ah, there you are, Jane,' she said, in a tone that suggested that she had been expecting to catch the young woman misbehaving. On noticing the Doctor, she looked him up and down, raising an eyebrow as she took in his frock coat and checked trousers.

'I had heard that your new tutor had arrived. Finally.'

The Doctor didn't miss the emphasis the woman placed on the last word. He straightened his back and hooked his fingers around his lapels. 'Good morning, madam,' he began. 'If you would allow me to explain...'

The woman continued to ignore him. 'Though you will hardly be needing a tutor once you are married, my dear.'

'I have told you, mother. I will not marry Guildford.'

Jane's mother pretended not to hear. 'Men do not like their women to be better educated than themselves; they hate to be bested at anything. It makes them feel small.'

'Then a kitchen maid with no schooling at all would tower over the duke's son. I tell you mother: I would rather die.'

The Doctor listened quietly to this exchange, absorbing the information. His hand rose to his mouth as it dawned on him exactly when and where the Vrij had brought them. How had he been so blind? He should have recognized the name of the estate when the duke mentioned it the previous night. In his hurry to track down the Vrij, he had given the TARDIS instruments only a cursory glance before hurrying out of the ship, noting just that they had come to England in the sixteenth century.

He looked at his 'student' in a new light. The girl who was standing before him arguing with her mother was Jane Grey. The Doctor was aware of the tragic hand that history would deal this innocent girl, destined to be exploited by political schemers for her tenuous link to the throne of England. And he was all too aware of the sacred laws that bound his hands, forbidding him to interfere in such an important historical moment. He could not possibly help Jane escape her destiny. To interfere with established history on such a scale would be inconceivable.

When Jane's mother had left the room and they were alone again, he tried to speak and was surprised to find that his throat had gone quite dry. How could he tell this ill-treated child that he could not help her?

He was distracted by a familiar sound emanating from his jacket pocket. The tracer was emitting a faint but steady tone. He coughed loudly, both to clear his throat and to cover the noise, and slipped his hand inside his coat to deactivate the device. On top of everything, the Vrij was still alive. Still alive, and on the move again.

'Are you all right, Doctor?' Jane asked. 'The colour has drained from your face.'

He pulled his handkerchief from his top pocket and breathed through it to calm himself. 'Yes my dear, do not worry about me.' He waved her attentions away with his handkerchief. 'Perhaps we ought to start your lesson. I don't wish to do anything to upset your mother further.'

Barbara eventually found the Doctor seated at a hastily constructed workbench in one of the unused stables. He was bent over a large, complicated-looking machine which seemed utterly out of place in its surroundings.

'Doctor, thank goodness.'

The Doctor leapt up from his chair and tried to cover the machine with some sacking. Then he realized that the newcomer was only Barbara, and sank back down and rubbed his chest. 'Please, don't do that to me, young woman.'

'Doctor, you must come quickly.'

'What is it? Can't you see I'm busy?'

'A rider has brought news to the house. The king is dying. The house is in pandemonium. Oh, Doctor, it's starting isn't it?'

The Doctor shrugged. 'I fail to see why I need to be...' He paused, suddenly realizing why Barbara had run to find him. 'Jane.'

Barbara nodded. 'There's already talk of bringing the wedding forward. The duke has demanded that it take place within three days. She's locked herself in her room.'

'The poor child,' the Doctor murmured, a deep frown cutting across his forehead. Barbara was surprised to see him turn back to his machine. She had expected more of a reaction than that.

'Aren't you going to do anything?'

'Do? There's nothing I can do, as well you should know. We mustn't interfere. It isn't our business. Jane Grey marries Guildford, son of the Duke of Northumberland. That is a historical fact. We can do nothing to change it.'

'You do know she doesn't want to marry him?'

'That is beside the point.'

'You could at least go and speak with her. That doesn't have to change history. You know how much she looks up to you.'

The Doctor busied himself with some of the components littered across the bench. 'I will speak with her later,' he said, in a tone that suggested that he didn't know what all the fuss was about. 'If my memory serves me correctly, we have a lesson scheduled for this afternoon. I shall see her then.'

Barbara wasn't convinced. In the few weeks since they had been at Bradgate, the Doctor and Lady Jane had developed a strong bond of friendship. It was clear that Jane hero-worshipped the Doctor, impressed by his insight and entertained by his stories. The Doctor, for his part, revelled in the flattering and uncritical attention. Jane was an exceptionally bright and engaging student and must have reminded him very much of Susan.

Barbara tried a different tack. 'How is your work going? Ian said that you were ready to test it.'

'Almost, Barbara, almost.'

She made one last attempt to engage him in conversation. 'Are you sure it's going to work? It doesn't look very impressive.'

The Doctor downed tools and wiped his hands on a rag. 'It doesn't matter what it looks like. I'm an engineer, not a sculptor.'

'But will it work?'

'Of course it will. It creates a time-space field – a miniature vortex, just like the one the ship travels through. If the Vrij is within range, it will be sucked into my dimensional trap like a genie into a bottle.' He tapped the machine proudly. 'Here, help me lift it into its case.'

The machine was heavy and unwieldy, but a snug fit in the travelling trunk that the Doctor had commandeered from the Greys. Barbara looked down at the large wooden chest. 'Well, we shouldn't have any problems dealing with the Vrij now that we have this machine of yours, Doctor,' she commented with a grin. 'As long as it doesn't take possession of anything that moves faster than a garden snail.'

The Doctor was not amused.

Barbara walked into the chapel on Ian's arm. As they stepped over the threshold, she caught his eye and they smiled at each other.

The little church was tucked away in a corner of the Grey estate. It was a simple building, clearly chosen as the site of the wedding for its convenience rather than for any aesthetic appeal.

Barbara could see the events that would inevitably lead to Jane Grey's execution unfolding before her like the pages of a textbook. Time travelling was like being strapped into a rollercoaster ride at Blackpool: history was as fixed and as certain as the tracks suspended in the sky, but this did nothing to make the journey itself any less terrifying.

She edged past a large, balding man to take her seat next to Ian and the Doctor at the back of the chapel. It had taken her most of the morning to strap herself into the folds of the gigantic dress that had been provided for her by Jane's parents. Tears had sprung into her eyes when one of Jane's servants had scraped her hair back into what she had been assured was the latest style.

Despite the dress and her new hairdo, Barbara felt distinctly out of place at the wedding. There were no more than thirty guests; the ceremony had been arranged in such haste that there had been no time to invite anyone from outside the county. Several of the faces were familiar to her from social functions at Bradgate. Jane's parents had made it quite clear that she, the Doctor and Ian were invited only to make the church appear better attended and the wedding preparations less rushed. Jane's mother had coldly informed them that they were not to show their faces at the wedding banquet in the Great Hall back at Bradgate.

The wedding was a sorrowful affair. Barbara had been surprised to learn that there were three couples marrying that morning. Despite the rushed preparations, it had been decided that not only was Jane to marry the duke's son, but her two sisters, Katherine and Anne, were also to take husbands. Like Jane's, her sisters' marriages had been arranged more for their political usefulness than for love.

Jane stood in front of the altar looking quietly defiant. Katherine sobbed unself-consciously throughout the ceremony. At times, the service was actually inaudible beneath her wails. Barbara had to fight back an urge to run up the aisle and comfort her. The poor girl was only twelve.

Katherine's husband-to-be was a lanky, uncomfortable-looking lord in his early thirties. He was the only one who appeared in the least perturbed by his new wife's distress; Katherine's father remained impassive throughout, and her mother actually looked proud.

Barbara buried her face in her hands. 'It's barbaric,' she whispered. This was a part of history not reported upon in the textbooks at Coal Hill School.

Looking up to find the Doctor staring at her, Barbara wondered if he understood what she felt. Or perhaps he was merely keeping an eye on her to make sure that she didn't interfere. For a moment he looked as though he was about to speak, but then he was distracted by a high-pitched chirruping noise. It came from the device he had used to track the Vrij.

A few of the wedding guests sitting close by looked around in alarm, the electronic sound completely unfamiliar to them. The fat, bald man seated next to Barbara turned to her, an anxious expression on his face. 'Is it an insect?' he asked, trying to make sense of a noise that was five hundred years out of place. 'I cannot bear insects at the best of times, and this one sounds so angry!'

'There's nothing to worry about. Really.' Barbara shot the Doctor a worried look. He was frantically stabbing at the buttons on the tiny control panel, trying without success to switch the alarm off. With a final cry of frustration he bashed the little device against the pew in front of him. The alarm instantly cut off.

'Thank heavens!' the fat man cried. 'The old man has crushed the devilish beast. Well done! You've saved me from a nasty sting.'

Barbara gestured for the large nobleman to be quiet, not wanting to attract further notice to the Doctor's intrusive device. However, the congregation's attention had already returned to the wedding ceremonies.

The message of the Doctor's machine was clear: the Vrij was at work in this very room. Barbara felt her stomach tense at the thought of it. She pitied the poor soul whose mind was now occupied by the creature.

She quickly realized why the incident had passed without much attention. There was an argument in progress at the front of the church: a much more interesting development than a panic over an insect. Jane was refusing to repeat the wedding vows, and her father was ordering her in an angry whisper to comply.

For a moment Barbara thought that the bishop conducting the service was going to have to call the whole thing off, but with a sudden inexplicable change of heart Jane lost her angry frown and began to utter her wedding script in a quiet, dull voice. It was as if someone had simply turned off her will.

As Jane submitted to the marriage, Barbara sensed the Vrij's presence growing in the room. She could feel the anger of the creature, although not inside her head as it had been in the TARDIS. This time it was outside of her, reverberating against her mind. Warm scarlet waves seemed to crash chaotically around the room. She grabbed hold of Ian's hand and gripped it tightly.

'Barbara, what's the matter?' Ian asked, as she sagged in her seat.

'Oh Ian,' she cried. 'It's here. I can feel it. It's here!'

Barbara staggered halfway out of the pew, straining to look

at Jane. For the briefest of moments she saw, or perhaps felt, a shadow fall across the girl, enveloping her like a shroud.

Ian tugged her back into her seat.

'It's Jane,' she cried. 'It's got Jane.'

The Doctor had not blamed her for his dismissal from Bradgate, but Barbara felt responsible all the same. After the wedding, he had tried to speak with Jane, but her parents had forbidden it. He had been coolly informed that Jane would no longer require a tutor now that she had gained the responsibilities of a wife. The Doctor had been given a small townhouse in Islington and a lump sum for his troubles, and then been told in no uncertain terms to leave. The travellers had been escorted from Bradgate without the chance either to retrieve the TARDIS or to see Jane.

The Islington that Barbara remembered had been a slightly dishevelled working-class area of London, made up of rows of council houses and blocks of red brick flats. In 1553, the parish of St Mary, Islington was little more than a collection of tiny houses scattered around a village green. London was still a few miles down the road.

The house was one of several owned by the Duke of Northumberland in Islington. It was clean and dry, probably a very desirable property for its day, but a far cry from her flat in London or from the TARDIS. It was a stone building with one large room downstairs and another above. The living room had a few chairs and stools to sit on and an imported rug covering the cold wooden floor. She shared the room above with Ian. The Doctor insisted on sleeping – if he did actually manage to sleep – on a chair by the fire downstairs.

Barbara was now making her way through the few stalls of the village market, her arms laden down with salted beef and vegetables. She stopped at a stall selling fruit, eventually buying some quince and mulberries, along with the more familiar apples. It would be a long time before oranges and bananas could be bought in Islington. She was getting used to life in the village, although she had to admit that she didn't much like it. Keeping a house was so much harder without electricity, running water and washing-up liquid.

She was relieved to be away from Bradgate and the vicious people who lived there, but what she really wanted to do was to climb aboard the TARDIS and just go. The Doctor had made it clear that he wouldn't think of leaving until he had dealt with the Vrij. And he was no closer to achieving that goal than when the ship had first materialized two months ago.

She stopped to rest for a moment; the handle of the basket she carried was digging into her hand, leaving a red mark across her fingers. Ahead of her, some villagers were gathered in a tight group. Intrigued, Barbara made her way to the edge of the little crowd to listen.

'Died last night,' she heard an old man assert. 'Consumption, they're saying, but it was really poison.'

A murmur of shock and disbelief passed through the gathering.

'Poison?' another questioned. 'Someone poisoned the king! King Edward's been ill for months; how do you know it was poison?'

'Seen the signs, didn't I,' the first speaker replied. 'Up Kentish Town, the Smith's daughter birthed a child wi' two heads and four feet. My cousin's friend helped deliver it. Screamed like the devil for an hour and then it died, it did.'

'You've been too long in the tavern.'

'It's not just me. They're saying it all over London.'

Barbara had heard enough. She collected her basket and hurried back to the house. She'd lost track of the dates since they had arrived in London, but if the king had died yesterday then it must be 7 July today. It was only a matter of days before the Duke of Northumberland would put Jane on the throne.

She met the Doctor on the doorstep of the house. He'd been out walking in London, listening for news. They went inside, where Ian was waiting for them, and she quickly recounted what she had heard.

The Doctor nodded gravely as she spoke. 'I've also heard of the death of the king. The city is full of people telling strange stories. I've heard of stillborn calves and children, and apparently Henry VIII's ghost has been seen walking the streets.'

'What on earth's going on? Is everyone going mad?' Ian asked.

The Doctor shook his head. 'It's the Vrij stirring itself, focusing its energy. Its presence creates... disturbances in people's minds.'

Remembering her own encounter with the creature, Barbara said: 'Then Jane will be in danger.'

The Doctor looked at her. 'You're sure you saw the creature within her? I still cannot believe that I could spend so much time with the girl and not be aware of some sign of it myself. I would know.'

'I did see something, Doctor, I'm sure of it. It was as if... as if someone had suddenly wrapped her up in a cloak.' Barbara tried to recall the exact details of what she had seen, but her memory remained hazy. 'I know that you don't want to think of Jane in danger, but I did see something around her, and I definitely felt the presence of the creature.'

Ian put a hand on the Doctor's shoulder. 'Are you sure that you are not letting your fondness for Jane cloud your judgment?'

Ian was slightly taken aback when the Doctor didn't angrily dismiss the idea out of hand. Instead, the old man shrugged. 'Perhaps I am, but I'm missing something, something obvious.' He tapped his fingers gently against his lip for a moment. 'When Barbara attacked you in the ship, did you see this cloak around her?'

Ian frowned. 'No, I don't think so.'

'There was nothing different about her at all?'

Ian glanced quickly at Barbara, who turned away, hugging her arms around herself. She didn't want to hear this.

'Not in that way, no,' Ian said after a moment.

'Perhaps the creature's presence around Jane indicates that she was attacked from without and not from within. Perhaps it was someone else who harboured the creature within him, unleashing it to force Jane to complete the marriage vows.'

Barbara had had enough of this speculation. 'It doesn't make sense, Doctor,' she said, exasperated. 'Jane would have married Guildford anyway, you said so yourself. Why would the Vrij try to force her to marry against her will?'

'Well, we won't find any answers here. With the Vrij on the move again, it is imperative that we get to Jane. It won't be easy, though. The streets of London are already filled with angry talk of the Duke of Northumberland and his plans to put Jane on the throne. As the key to those plans, Jane will be closely guarded.'

'Surely reaching her will be impossible,' protested Ian. 'Her parents won't let her out of their sight.'

The Doctor scoffed. 'Nothing is impossible, my dear boy.'

The royal barge drifted slowly down the Thames. From their position near the stern, the Doctor and his companions had a clear view of the crowds lining the banks of the river. Thousands of people had turned out to see Lady Jane Grey on her journey to the Tower of London, where she would be crowned Queen of England.

No-one cheered. No-one waved. No-one even moved. It was as if someone had placed a thousand statues along the riverbanks. The tension produced by so many people standing in total silence was palpable. It reminded Ian of the dramatic climax of a Western, where the Indians stand in their hundreds along the peak of an ochre-coloured cliff before descending upon the pioneers camped in a circle of wagons in the prairie below.

The stillness was broken only by the rhythmic splashing of the oars worked by the oarsmen in the galley beneath the deck.

Jane stood at the prow of the boat, dressed in green and gold. Earlier in the day she had struggled into chopines – built up shoes – intended to make her appear taller and more substantial. They didn't succeed. She looked awkward and vulnerable, like a stiltwalker in high winds.

'Why is everyone so quiet?' Ian whispered to the Doctor.

'Perhaps their silence is the only protest that they have.'

Barbara nodded in agreement. 'Most of the people support Mary. Despite her Catholicism, her claim to the throne has the greater legitimacy. Jane's is tenuous at best; she is really only about fourth in line.'

Several splashes sounded behind them. The entire royal entourage turned anxiously as one to look for the source of the noise, but it was only a few young boys taking the opportunity for an impromptu swim in the filthy water.

The time travellers had boarded the barge at its mooring point up river, but it had not been easy. Dressed in the clothes they had worn for Jane's wedding, they had first tried to bluff their way on board. Despite the Doctor's best efforts to convince the steward that he was the brother of the Duke of Nottingham who had somehow mislaid his invitation, they had failed. Barbara had eventually saved the day when she had been recognized by the bald man with the insect phobia next to whom she had sat at the wedding. On hearing that they had been denied permission to board, the bald nobleman had shouted at the crew, demanding that his three friends be seated with him. He had reassured Barbara that he would personally ensure that the chief steward was whipped for his impudence.

A shadow slid over the slow-moving barge. Ian looked up to see the light-grey walls of the Tower of London looming over them. The familiar outline of the building jogged memories from his days in London, before he had stepped into the Doctor's police box in Totter's Lane and his life had been turned upside down. He was reminded of one of the first occasions he had seen Barbara outside school. It had been during his first year at Coal Hill; he had helped her with a history trip she had organized at the end of the summer term. He hadn't enjoyed the tour. It had been an unexpectedly hot June, and a combination of the searing heat and a noisy party of school children who had spent most of the day getting lost, dripping ice lollies everywhere and screaming, had frayed both their tempers.

The barge passed through a low gateway which led into the Tower. Ian was relieved to be getting away from the silent and oppressive crowds.

'Traitors Gate,' he commented proudly as they passed under the arch, pleased to have remembered something from that dull tour all those years ago.

'No,' Barbara murmured, almost to herself. She looked to the front of the barge where Jane stood. 'At least,' she added after a moment's consideration, 'not yet.'

The ceremony had been a protracted affair and the Doctor was happy to be able to stretch his legs after sitting for so long. He desperately wanted to speak to Jane, having had no opportunity to do so since he had been so unceremoniously dismissed from service by her parents. Today, the duke had bustled the new queen from the coronation chamber as soon as the ceremony had ended.

Was the Vrij within her? He couldn't be sure. Barbara had said that she had sensed the creature around the girl at the wedding, but surely after all the time he had spent with her at Bradgate he would have known if she harboured the creature? Could Ian be right? Was he allowing his fondness for the girl to cloud his judgment?

Barbara brought him out of his musings. 'Well, do you have any idea how we get to Jane?'

'Hmm. Yes, indeed. I saw that terrible man drag her off into the Tower. No doubt beginning to issue the first of his demands. While I follow them, you must find Chesterton and go to the stateroom to collect the trunk with my equipment in it. All the coronation presents are being stored there until they can be displayed at the banquet. No doubt ours will be among them. We will need it, as I am sure that we will shortly be seeing the Vrij again.'

'It's a shame that your tracer is broken.'

'Indeed it is. Although, to be honest, my dear, I think I already know where the Vrij is now.'

'The duke? Well, I hope you are right.'

Leaving Barbara with her task, the Doctor slipped from the chamber and began his search for the new queen. He discovered Jane and the duke arguing in the Tower library. He listened at the door, where he could easily make out the duke's arrogant, angry voice.

'And I tell you,' the duke threatened, 'you will use your power to make my son king.'

'If you were as well versed in law as you are in threats,' Jane replied evenly, 'you would know that I have not the power to make kings. You will have to try your ugly words on Parliament, but I doubt that those fine men will entertain such an absurd suggestion for a moment. Guildford is an... is an ass!'

If the duke was upset by this insult to his family he didn't say so. 'Pah! It is Parliament who is the ass. It had not the courage nor the power to intervene in your ascension, and it will make no protest when you make my son king.'

At the door, the Doctor smiled with approval. The young queen was obviously not turning out to be the puppet that the duke had counted upon. Well good for her, the Doctor thought. Barbara would be proud!

The Doctor slipped the catch on the door and pushed it slightly open. From his restricted viewpoint he could see only Jane, who was standing her ground, her back to the door, facing the unseen duke. As the argument progressed, the duke's voice became increasingly loud and hard.

Surely the whole Tower must be able to hear him, the Doctor thought. It was almost as if his voice was being amplified.

There was loud slap and Jane cried out. Taking a firm grip on his cane, the Doctor threw open the door and charged into the room. Jane was lying on the floor, her arm raised to protect her face. The duke was standing over her, preparing to strike again.

'This must stop!' the Doctor barked. 'Leave her alone.'

The duke was only further enraged by the interruption. 'Out of my way, old man. You have no business here. This is between my daughter-in-law and me,' he sneered.

The Doctor helped the new queen to her feet. After steadying herself, Jane surprised the Doctor by agreeing with their adversary.

'This is my battle, Doctor. You more than anyone know that I am a most unwilling queen. But if Queen I am then I shall act as one. Stand aside. The duke is my enemy, not yours.'

'My dear, your words befit a queen, but you don't understand: the duke *is* my enemy, perhaps more mine than yours. You remember that when I first came to Bradgate I told you that my friends and I were hunting a creature? Well, that creature dwells within your uncle and he is under its influence.'

Striding over to where the duke stood quivering with rage, the Doctor prodded him in the chest with his stick. 'Sir, I grow weary of you and your petty concerns, and most particularly with your bullying of this young woman. I'll speak with the puppet no more.' When the Doctor spoke again, he was addressing the creature within the duke. 'You must listen to me. You have no business with this human or with this world. Your presence here could damage the very fabric of this reality. Already the events of history have been warped and bent out of shape, perhaps irrevocably. I must insist that you leave this world now.'

The duke stumbled as if he had been punched. He was bathed in a scarlet light, which quickly grew dense and opaque. The Doctor thought that he glimpsed the movement of wings within the mist, but he couldn't be sure. Despite the immediate and very real danger, the Doctor felt only relief that his instincts had been proved correct.

Trying to provoke the creature into showing itself had been a risk. The Doctor was confident that he could defend himself from any attempt to wrest control of his own mind, but he had no idea what other powers the creature might have. He could only hope that Barbara and Ian were on their way with the trunk that contained the trap that he had constructed.

Glancing at the open door of the library, he wondered how long it could take them simply to bring a box down two flights of stairs. Where were they?

The temperature in the room began to rise rapidly, and the Doctor felt his collar prickle with sweat. The red aura around the duke glowed brightly as if the creature was focusing its energy. The Doctor prepared himself for an assault, placing himself between Jane and the red cloud.

Come on Chesterton, he thought, as the energy in the room grew. You're cutting it a little fine. For an instant, the centre of the cloud burned with a fiery incandescence. Then a bolt of scarlet lightening flashed from its core, catching the Doctor full in the stomach. He shrieked in agony and dropped to the ground.

On one of the huge stairwells located at each corner of the Tower, Barbara and Ian heard the scream and paused in their efforts to carry the large trunk down the stairs.

'Ian, that sounded like...'

'The Doctor. Yes, I think it was.'

To make faster progress they started to drag the heavy box rather than to carry it. It dropped from stair to stair with a heavy thump, like the footsteps of some fairytale giant. The noise echoed through the stairwell. Ian wasn't surprised that, within a few moments, two Tower guards had appeared over the bannister of the floor above to investigate. The guards hurried down the stairs to where he and Barbara stood.

'Barbara, you run and help the Doctor, I'll hold them off.'

Barbara glanced from the approaching guards to Ian. 'OK, see you soon.' It was more a prayer than a farewell. Taking the stairs two at time, she slipped out of sight.

When Ian looked back, the two guards were almost upon him. He let go of the trunk and rested his hands on his hips, trying to muster all the authority he could.

'Ah, you've got here at last!' he said in his most aristocratic voice. 'I've got a job for you.'

Barbara ran into the library to find Queen Jane kneeling over the Doctor's prone form. Tears had smeared the young queen's make-up. She shook her head slowly in response to Barbara's unspoken question.

Barbara stifled an urge to run away. The Doctor couldn't be dead, he just couldn't! She forced herself to approach him.

'He has stopped breathing and his soul has left him,' Jane said in a quiet voice.

Slowly, conscious that she herself was close to hysteria, Barbara began to administer first aid. Her expertise was limited to what she had learnt from a one-day course as part of her teacher training some ten years earlier. She and her classmates had been taught by a retired army sergeant in the draughty gymnasium of the university. She remembered the embarrassment she had felt when her turn had come to give mouth-to-mouth resuscitation to the life-size doll. Today, the urgency of the situation overcame any such feelings she might have had.

The Doctor's chest rose dramatically in a parody of breathing as she forced air into his lungs, keeping her fingers pinched over his nose. In between breaths she could see Jane staring at her, a mixture of horror and awe on the young girl's face.

Jane screamed as the Doctor suddenly opened his eyes, sat up and, in attempting to speak, burst into a fit of coughing.

'What unholiness is this?' Jane exclaimed, backing away from the two travellers. 'He was dead. I felt for his heart. I know that he was quite dead.'

Pulling his handkerchief from his pocket, the Doctor dabbed at his mouth. He clambered to his feet, and turned to face Barbara. 'Did you blow the air back into my lungs?'

Barbara smiled. 'Yes. I learnt first aid when I was at college. I wasn't sure that I would remember it, it was so long ago. But it all came flooding back. Thank heavens it worked.'

The Doctor's face creased into a frown of incomprehension. 'Worked? Worked! Good heavens, woman, you almost killed me!'

'What?'

'My respiratory system is completely unlike your own. I would thank you in future to leave me well alone and keep your barbaric practices to yourself.'

'But Doctor, you were dying. You weren't even breathing.'

'Of course not. When the creature in the duke attacked me, I had to put myself into a restorative coma while this old body recovered from the shock of the assault.' He strode over to the door and checked the corridor outside. 'I see that your tardiness has given the duke the opportunity to escape.' He sighed, a little theatrically. 'This won't do at all. Now we shall have to track him down and deal with him and the Vrij all over again.'

'Well of all the ungrateful...' Barbara started and then stopped mid-flow as she remembered that she had left Ian alone facing two guards. She raced to the door, only to find herself face to face with the guards in question. The two burly men were carrying the Doctor's box of tricks carefully between them.

Ian appeared behind them. 'Where do you want it?' he asked.

Torches had been lit and placed at regular intervals around the village green. They must have been dipped in fat, as they sizzled and dripped flaming liquid onto the grass, filling the night sky with thick blue smoke. Barbara wrinkled her nose: they stank to high heaven, too.

The green was full of people. Men mostly. They sat on the

ground outside the taverns and around the hastily set up stalls, drinking strong dark ale and noisily enjoying themselves. Village business had been brought to a standstill by the crowds. One of the townsmen had had to arrange for the evening's London traffic of cattle, carts and coaches to be diverted through Battle Bridge, a smaller town which lay a few miles to the west.

Barbara surveyed the scene. 'There must be thousands here,' she breathed. After the duke had fled the Tower, he had disappeared without trace. They had spent several days searching London without success. It had taken a week before they had heard reports of an army being gathered in Kentish Town. They had spent most of the last afternoon riding up to the small town, which was in fact little more than a village.

Barbara was becoming a proficient rider by now, and they would have made the journey in a couple of hours if not for the Doctor: he tired quickly and needed to take frequent breaks from the jolting and jarring of the horse's gait. They had finally approached their destination as the sun was sinking. The road leading into the town centre had been busy and the traffic slow, so they had tethered the horses and continued on foot, Barbara and Ian carrying the Doctor's heavy trunk between them.

Taking stock of the masses around them, the Doctor slowly shook his head. 'Tens of thousands, I should think, and that may well turn out to be a conservative estimate.'

'And all willing to fight for Jane. It doesn't make any sense.'

'We must trace the differences and try to rectify them.'

'Working out what is different from history as I know it shouldn't be too hard. There shouldn't be all these people here, for a start. When the Duke of Northumberland tried to rally support for Jane, he wasn't at all successful. The majority of the people supported Mary, who is riding to London to press her claim to the throne – or at least she should be. According to history, the duke managed to raise an army of only six hundred to support Jane. That's one of the reasons why her reign was so short. By now, Mary should have gathered thirty thousand men to fight for her. Jane never stood a chance.'

Their discussion was interrupted as several drunken men pushed past them, heading for one of the local taverns which was already so full that its customers spilled out through its doors. The men shouted slogans in support of Jane and against Mary.

'Then why this change of heart?' the Doctor pondered, resting on his walking cane. He noticed Ian hurrying towards them from the crowd. 'Perhaps young Chesterton has news. Well, my boy,' he said, putting his arm around the breathless schoolteacher, 'has your reconnaissance proved useful?'

'Well, I found the duke. He's over on the other side of the green. They've set up a stage, and I think he's going to speak to his army.'

As if on cue, the duke's voice resounded across the centre of the village. Barbara was astonished. 'How can his voice be so loud? They don't have megaphones in the sixteenth century.'

'Of course they don't,' confirmed the Doctor. 'It is the creature inside him, projecting his voice.'

'Perhaps that's how he's been able to drum up support for Jane?' Ian suggested. 'With the Vrij inside him, he can be heard by many more people.'

Barbara shook her head. 'It's more than that, it must be.'

'Well, let's not stand around theorizing when we could go and see instead.' The Doctor indicated the direction from which Ian had come. They forced their way through the crowds until they could see the little stage and the duke stood upon it.

Barbara felt the now-familiar presence of the Vrij. As she watched the Duke of Northumberland, a powerful wave of emotion engulfed her. It spread up through her body like a rush of warm water, rising up her spine and setting her teeth on edge, making her feel a little nauseous. She heard the duke's voice, but could barely make out the words he was shouting. Fragments of speech reached her through the chaotic sensations that flooded her mind; she heard Jane's name, and something about

England and the threat the Catholics posed.

The crowd roared like a monster. Dizziness overcame Barbara, and she felt as if she were a few inches behind her eyes. She reached out to steady herself on Ian's arm. He was staring at the stage, the flickering light from the spitting torches reflecting in the tears that ran down his cheeks.

Suddenly she was transported back to the TARDIS, back to the moment when the Vrij had first entered her mind. It had crept into her head and started to whisper to her, to bring out feelings that she usually repressed. It had touched on her discontent, on her regrets; focused upon them and amplified them, projecting them out of all proportion.

She had found herself asking why she had ever settled for teaching in a comprehensive. Why had she given up studying after her degree? She should have gone for her doctorate: why hadn't she? She could be lecturing in a university now, researching history and not just trying to drum it into the heads of unwilling fourteen-year-olds. If it wasn't for her stupid job, stupid life, stupid Ian.

She had suddenly realized what an enormous fool Ian was. Everyone's favourite in the staffroom, good old reliable Chesterton. The type of chap who marked his essays the day he received them and actually looked forward to parents' evening. A walkover, that's what he was. He was spineless, he lacked ambition. Suddenly, she had known why she hated him: he was content with what he had; with Coal Hill School and with a pint in the local pub after coaching the boys' five-a-side on a Friday evening. He was pathetic.

She wanted more. There was so much to experience. She had been filled with the urge to hurt him. To really hurt him. And with the rewarding feeling of having finally taken control of her life, she had crept into his room, slipped her fingers around his throat and squeezed...

And then she felt the Doctor's arm around her, and she was back on the green in Kentish Town. She allowed herself to be led away from the scene.

By the time she recovered her wits, she was sitting by the fire in a tavern behind the stage. She could still hear the duke's voice and see the covered platform through the open door, but the tavern's stone walls muted the effect of the creature and slowly her head began to clear.

The Doctor pushed a mug into her hand. It contained a sweet drink which tasted strongly alcoholic, like a fortified wine. It made her lips tingle. Ian was sitting close by, cradling a mug in his own hands and gazing into the fire. Only the Doctor seemed to have been unaffected by the experience. He had now gone up to the bar to get a drink for himself.

She looked across at Ian. The Doctor had lent him his hanky and the young man was wiping his eyes on it. Barbara had never seen him cry before. He caught her looking at him and smiled, a little sheepishly. She wanted to say something reassuring to him, or maybe to herself. Something about the future. Their future. But the Doctor then returned from the bar with his mug of wine, and the moment was lost.

'This is it, isn't it?' Barbara asked, looking up at the Doctor. 'This is the moment when history could be changed irreversibly, when the Vrij could set events on a wholly new course.'

The Doctor nodded, looking tired. 'Yes, my dear, it is. If the duke's campaign continues in this way, then he could well crush Mary's army and...' – he let out a deep sigh – 'and then Jane would be queen in her place, reigning for rather longer than nine days.'

In all the time that she been in sixteenth-century England, Barbara had never considered the full implications of the changes that would result from the Vrij's influence. With the arrival of the Vrij, suddenly nothing was definite. The roller-coaster ride of history was no longer fixed on its rails. It was only now that she realized what a difficult battle this was for the Doctor to fight. In defeating the duke and his anachronistic army, the Doctor would be putting back in place the events that would lead inevitably to Jane's execution.

'Can we stop the Vrij?' she asked.

The Doctor considered this question for a moment. 'Perhaps. It would be an easier task if we knew more of its plans and its nature. It is quite unlike anything that I have encountered before.'

Barbara sensed the unspoken question in the Doctor's voice. 'I know that you've wanted to ask me about what happened to me in the ship, and to be honest I've been grateful that you've not. I haven't wanted to think about it. But out there just now, I relived it; it was as if I was back in the ship and it was happening all over again.' She paused, looking down into the depths of her drink. 'It's arrogance, Doctor. Somehow it gets hold of that part of you that thinks... that knows that you are better than everyone else. And it feeds it, and feeds on it.'

The Doctor reached over and touched her gently on the shoulder. 'Thank you', he said.

'I can't see how it will help us defeat the creature. I can't see how we will be able to defeat the Vrij at all. It's so... irresistible.'

'We shall see. Everything is possible. If we can operate my device close enough to the duke, then I think we should be able to trap the Vrij and return it to its home.'

'But can we get to the duke?'

The Doctor chuckled. 'That at least should prove quite easy. He's taken a room upstairs.'

The Doctor had easily picked the lock on the door to the duke's room, and now he and his fellow travellers were waiting there in hiding for the duke to return. The Doctor had positioned his trunk in the centre of the floor, his companions having retrieved it for him from the place where they had earlier concealed it close to the edge of town. The trap had been set to activate when it detected any movement in the room, and Ian and Barbara were under strict instructions to remain motionless in their respective hiding places. As long as the duke walked into the centre of the room after opening the door, the field of the vortex would pluck the creature out of him and trap it within the machinery in the trunk. Now all they had to do was wait.

Standing by the shuttered window, the Doctor could hear the noise of the army camped out on the green. Even if he managed to trap the Vrij, he still had the duke and his men to deal with. One thing at a time, he told himself. One thing at a time.

Footfalls sounded on the stairs and he heard the duke's voice demanding that some food and wine be brought up to his room. The Doctor held his breath. The handle turned, and through a crack in the curtains he saw the duke silhouetted in the doorway against the light from the hall.

A low electronic whine invaded the room as the Doctor's machine responded to the movement of the door and started to power up. The Doctor grimaced; in the stillness of the room, the noise was deafening.

'What's that?' The duke tilted his head, trying to identify the strange sound. 'Is someone there?'

He took a step into the room. Instantly the lid of the trunk snapped open and a cone of blue and purple light exploded from it, illuminating the room like an electrical storm. Wild kaleidoscopic shapes shimmered and swirled across the walls. The duke screamed and started to back out onto the landing in terror.

The Doctor watched, his heart sinking, as the vortex of light spiralled uselessly for a few moments before whipping itself back into the trunk with a crackle.

Ian leapt out from his hiding place behind the door and dragged the duke back into the room, landing a right-handed punch on his jaw. The duke should have been floored, but he only roared in anger and gripped his hands tightly around Ian's throat. Barbara quickly slipped out from under the bed and started to hammer her fists against the duke's back. Seeming hardly to notice this, the duke picked Ian up and threw him against the wall, where he collapsed unconscious in a heap.

'No!' Barbara yelled, and kicked the duke hard in the shins. The man yelped in pain and fell to his knees. Barbara ran to where Ian lay, but his head lolled limply in her hands. She turned to see the duke back on his feet and advancing purposefully towards her.

'Doctor! Help!' she screamed.

The Doctor stepped from behind the curtain. 'Enough!' he cried, in a voice that would have drowned out a sergeant major. 'Enough of this.' He raised his fists in front of him, but looked frail and spindly compared with his powerfully built opponent.

'You!' the duke shouted. 'I thought you were dead.' He dived at the Doctor and they hurtled across the room, flying through the curtains and smashing into the wooden shutters of the window. With a splintering sound, the shutters were torn from their hinges and the two men tumbled through the window and out into the night.

They landed in a heap on top of the canopy of the platform below. The Doctor gasped as the wind was knocked out of him. Summoning the last of his strength, he tried to drag himself to the edge of the canopy, hoping to swing his body over and escape. But he couldn't keep from sliding back into the well of material created by the combined weight of their bodies. He looked behind him and saw the duke's large hands reaching for his throat. He tried to push them away, but was no match for the possessed man.

His mind raced. He couldn't hope to defeat the duke physically. So use your brains, Doctor, he told himself. Use your knowledge.

'Are you so scared that you must hide within the body of a mere man,' he stammered, directing his words to the Vrij as the Duke clambered on top of him. 'What manner of creature are you to slope about in the shadow of another, hmm?'

The duke's eyes began to glow, burning red in the darkness. A few of the men on the green were hurrying towards the platform now, having been woken by the shouting and the sound of the shutters breaking.

The Doctor looked from them to the duke. 'Do you not dare to show yourself to me, an old man?'

The duke's hands closed around the Doctor's neck.

And then, from within the duke, there came a rustling noise, quiet at first but quickly growing in intensity. Something was coming. The duke's eyes, mouth and ears began to bleed scarlet light as the Vrij emerged from his body. It was a huge ethereal shadow, pouring out of its host and billowing up into the night.

The Doctor heard the sound of giant wings beating as slowly the formless shadow filled the sky above the green. He also heard the terrible sound of thousands of men screaming in fear for their lives. He couldn't take his eyes from the Vrij, but he was aware of the duke's army fleeing into the night.

A shudder rippled through the shadow as perhaps it realized that it had been tricked and its plans were ruined. It descended upon the Doctor, growing brighter as it reached down for him, preparing to strike. He felt the temperature around him rise as the centre of the creature began to burn fiercely. The Doctor closed his eyes and waited for the lightning blast.

There was a crackle of energy, and the Vrij let out a long agonized howl. The Doctor opened his eyes to see the creature bathed in blue and purple light, which played over its surface for a moment like wind on a sail. The Vrij shrieked once more and started to spiral downwards, eventually shrinking away to nothing.

The Doctor was suddenly alone in the darkness, which was relieved only by the purple, scarlet and blue splashes of colour that seemed to be burnt across his retina. He dragged his aching body to the edge of the canopy and eased himself over, lowering himself slowly down until he was hanging by his hands, his legs kicking out in the air. He was about to let himself drop when strong hands gripped his legs firmly. For a second he panicked and kicked out.

'It's all right, Doctor, it's me,' a woman's voice said.

'Barbara!' the Doctor breathed. He allowed himself to fall into her arms. She set him down on a hard wooden seat. It took him a moment to realize that he was sitting on his travelling trunk.

'Doctor?'

'Hmm?'

'If the Vrij is in the trunk, where is the duke?'

'I have no idea, my dear,' the Doctor murmured as he lay back on the trunk, trying to catch his breath. 'I have no idea.'

The trunk crackled beneath him.

The Doctor made a final survey of the house before joining Barbara and Ian at the front door. They had packed their few belongings into a sack, which Ian had slung over his back.

'Have you got everything?' the Doctor inquired, as he pulled his cape onto his shoulders.

His companions nodded.

'Good. Then we'd better be on our way.'

As he ushered them out of the doorway, Barbara paused and asked: 'What are you going to do with this place now, Doctor? I can't imagine an eternal wanderer like you ever having need of a fixed abode.'

The Doctor smiled, a little enigmatically. 'You shouldn't presume to know everything about me, young woman. This isn't the first house that I have ever owned, and I think it unlikely that it will be the last. Come along now.'

He locked the door behind them and the three friends walked across Islington Green to the stables where a carriage waited to take them to Leicester and the TARDIS.

'I still don't know what became of the duke, Doctor,' Ian said. 'Did he manage to get away, or was he killed when the Vrij was imprisoned?'

'Do you know my boy, I haven't the faintest idea. Perhaps

we should ask our resident historian. Barbara?'

'Well, if memory serves, he will be on his way to his house in Cambridge. He hides out in a hollow tree on his estate for a week, but one of his servants betrays him and, although he declares himself a Catholic, Mary has him executed for treason.'

Ian shrugged. 'It couldn't have happened to a nicer chap.'

The Doctor helped Barbara to climb into the carriage, slipping the TARDIS key into her hand as he did so.

'I will join you at the ship as soon as I can, my dear. Wait for me there. I have unfinished business in the city.'

'You're going to try to find Jane, aren't you?'

The Doctor nodded and set off without another word.

It was late when the Doctor finally managed to gain entry to the Council Chamber of the Tower of London. It had taken him longer than he had expected to reach his destination. The streets of the city had been filled with bonfires and processions in honour of the recent arrival of Mary, and the filthy roads had been packed with revellers.

He arrived just in time to see a bewildered Jane being guided from the throne.

'Come down from there, my child,' the Doctor heard her father tell her. 'That is no place for you.'

Jane climbed down to stand at her father's side. 'May I go home now?' she asked.

Her question was answered with a terrible silence. With great dignity, she removed the crown from her head.

'Take this crown of shame,' she instructed her father, 'it never did belong to me.'

The Doctor was about to announce his presence when soldiers loyal to Mary broke into the room and led Jane and her father away. After a moment, the old man slipped quietly from the room.

From her high vantage point in the Tower, Jane could only watch as the small black cart clattered out of the courtyard, beginning its morbid journey to Tower Hill. Jane knew that its sole and most unwilling passenger was her young husband, Guildford. It was a trip from which he would not return.

She found herself weeping silently for him as the carriage disappeared from view. She had never loved him, of course. Even on this darkest of days, the idea was so absurd that it brought a smile to her tear-streaked face. How had she described him in her rage? An ass? Be that as it may, the poor dumb creature didn't deserve the fate that awaited him on that bloody hill.

Turning away from the tiny window, she whispered a prayer for his mortal soul. They had become friends of a kind during the year or so of their imprisonment. Prisoners of the Tower were allowed a certain amount of freedom within its walls, and the two young inmates had taken to eating together in the evenings. Jane would then read to Guildford from the Bible and try and calm his fear. He would sit at her feet, his head resting against her knees like a faithful puppy. Sometimes she would stroke his hair as she read. She had been like a mother to him, despite the fact that he was four years her senior.

On this, their last day, he had asked to see her once more. Jane had refused, knowing that such a meeting would break the fortitude they would both need to face the ordeal that awaited them. Alone in her cell, she began to regret her decision.

The hours passed slowly, until at last the time of her execution finally arrived. Jane allowed herself to be led down from the Tower that had been her home for the last fifteen months and out into the courtyard where the scaffold stood, the wood dark against the brightness of the sky. Jane felt giddy at the sight of it. The distance between herself and the scaffold seemed to telescope until the executioner and his block were only dots on the horizon.

Jane kept her eyes upward, away from the crowd who milled

around her. After whispering a prayer, she began the long walk from the gateway of the Tower to the platform.

The history books report the event of Lady Jane Grey's execution in some detail. Like all royalty under sentence of death, she was permitted to address the crowd who had gathered in the courtyard of the Tower of London. She used the opportunity not to protest her innocence or to berate her successor who had sealed her fate. Instead she asked the crowd to join with her in prayer.

After she was blindfolded with a lace kerchief, she asked the executioner to dispatch her quickly. She then reached down for the block. In her blindness, however, she stumbled and missed it, her hands groping empty air. For a moment her composure crumpled, and Lady Jane Grey, who for the briefest time had been Queen of all England, was just a frightened girl, barely sixteen: lost, bewildered and terribly alone.

'Where is it?' she cried out. 'What shall I do?'

Several histories report that an elderly onlooker quickly mounted the platform and gently guided her hands to the block, before disappearing totally from the scene.

Jane, who was never to know the identity of the old man who had comforted her, then laid her head on the block and said: 'Lord, into thy hands I commend my spirit.'

And so she died.

The history books do not report the fate of the elderly onlooker.

Lonely Days

By Daniel Blythe

Survey Officer (Second Class) Sebastian Musgrove had got used to being the only human inhabitant of Monitoring Base XL-7.

He had the drones, of course. The pair of globe-shaped robots – one silver, one gold – bobbed on their little flames of propellant, bustling about the base on their never-ending tasks of maintenance. It sometimes amused Sebastian to watch them at work. He found it funny the way their spindly crab-pincer arms worked away, brandishing circuits or pulling out pasta-like tangles of wiring, while all the time they burbled and hummed to themselves like fussy old men.

He had precious little other entertainment. The tiny planet was too remote to get a clear signal from any of the galactic vid-channels, and the only audio he could pick up was hissy and agitated, throbbing as if straining to break free of the speakers.

Here, out on the fringes of the Magellanis system, there was rarely anything of note happening. Sebastian spent much of his time in the observation gallery, below the great spire of optriscopes and imagers in the Observatory itself. Every now and then he would be rewarded by the sight of a shooting star describing its white streak across the dark green sky. Sometimes the lights were too slow and erratic to be shooting stars and he wondered if he might have just seen the death throes of some alien vessel, its debris floating through space – a phantom of war.

If he got bored with observation, there was always the big dome that housed the green sea of the Conservatory. This was the location of a subsidiary project, the aim of which was to grow as wide a variety of plant life as was possible in the planet's soil – plant life that needed tending with a lightness of touch that the drones could not manage.

When the eight hours of greyish natural light were expended and darkness closed in around the Base, Sebastian would begin to shiver and feel all alone in the empty night. Tongues of blue dust would lick against the Plexiglas windows, the girders would creak like old wooden beams and the wind would sound like giants prowling around the Base and breathing into its ancient ventilation system.

Often, Sebastian fancied he could see the acres of green fronds in the Conservatory rippling as if touched by invisible hands. And if he peered out at the darkening dunes and ridges, he saw blue-black shadows on the land, like giant bruises, where no hollows had existed before.

At such times, he would go to the corner of his quarters, where he kept his favourite work of art.

It was a cold evening. Sebastian felt lonely and knew, by now, that he was being watched.

In search of reassurance, he gazed upon his treasure. Its beauty comforted him. A recess in the wall lit up in reddish gold, and there, in her red silk dress and gold earrings, stood the tall and slender image of Tarla McCail, looking as beautiful as the day she had died. The hologram could revolve on its own axis, blink and smile – but no more. For Sebastian, though, that was enough.

He saw himself reflected in the glass of her cubicle. Tired and drawn, his short black hair unkempt, his rodentish face in need of a shave. He scowled.

Sometimes, looking into the green pools of Tarla's eyes and listening to the wind rattling the Base, he wondered how being alone here for so long had not driven him completely mad.

'We didn't win, Doctor,' said Nyssa of Traken, her voice tinged with reproof.

'Hmm?' The Doctor, his blond fringe falling over his half-frame glasses, looked up from the TARDIS console. His companion was standing at the internal door, dressed in a regal costume of red velvet. Her youthful face was framed by brown curls and wore a slight frown as she held up a piece of red and white paper.

'I'm so terribly sorry, Nyssa,' said the Doctor, staring at a point just past her left ear as if trying to grab a past conversation from out of the ether while verbally treading water for as long as he dared. Nyssa put her hands on her hips and shook her head wearily. Realizing that he must have forgotten something, the Doctor lifted his hands from the console with a contrite expression. 'What... *exactly* didn't we win?'

Nyssa waved the ticket under his nose. 'This. The Intergalactic Lottery.'

'Ah.' The Doctor nodded, clasped his hands behind his back and looked thoughtfully at the floor. 'Well, Nyssa, it is gambling, you know. I was a little dubious about it at first – '

'I don't suppose,' she began impishly, with the hint of a smile, 'we could just pop ahead and –'

'Absolutely not!' cried the Doctor. 'Out of the question!' He leapt back to the console as if in feverish haste to take them to a different time zone. 'It would upset the delicate gambling balance of the continuum!' he added, removing his half-frames and waggling them at her like an alien talisman. The time rotor at the centre of the console began to rise and fall, and the Doctor stood back with a slightly breathless air of satisfaction.

'All right, Doctor,' said Nyssa with a shrug. 'I thought it would be an interesting experiment in the logistics of probability factors, that's all. I am – truly sorry if it upset you.'

'The structure of chance and fate is a very delicate filigree of strands, you know.' The Doctor's thoughts were still in full flow. 'I could no more cheat at the lottery than I could rescue Adric for you.'

There was an awkward silence, during which they avoided each other's gaze, and Nyssa settled herself into the basket chair in the corner of the room.

She was currently travelling alone with the Doctor for a short while. They still felt the loss of young Adric, killed in their battle against the Cybermen. And just recently their air stewardess companion Tegan had gone too, left behind at Heathrow Airport – the place she had been wanting to reach for the best part of a year. But something deep within Nyssa, a kind of intuition bestowed upon this last surviving child of the Union of Traken, told her that her friendship with the Earth girl was unfinished and that the three of them would be together again soon.

'Have you ever won anything, Doctor?' Nyssa asked idly, pretending to rummage through the open chest of old clothes beside her chair.

The Doctor looked up, gazing into the time rotor. He raised his eyebrows. 'Well. There was that time with Kublai Khan, of course, but that was more a case of getting something back.' He frowned. 'I did once win a small planet. But it was an awful place.'

Nyssa was unsure if she had heard right. 'A whole *planet*?'

'Well, yes... I had a few reckless moments in my last incarnation. It was in a game of poker with a rather arrogant Draconian – twenty-fifth-century Earth, I think. Anyway, this place turned out to be a bleak rock on the edge of the Magellanis system, so I gave it back to the Earth Colonies to develop. I still kept nominal ownership, so technically I could make an inspection visit every now and then...'

'But you never actually got around to it?' Nyssa ventured.

The Doctor pulled a face. 'For some reason, no. Maybe I was too busy saving the Universe from imminent destruction.'

'Well,' Nyssa said, 'why don't we go there now?'

The Doctor gave a boyish grin. 'I don't see why not. Nothing better to do, after all!'

* * *

It was growing darker. Sebastian Musgrove, chewing on an energy bar, passed Drone Gold in Service Corridor Seven. It had all six of its arms extruded and was polishing the metal walls.

'Keep up the good work,' he said, with a cheery wave, and the drone whirred in response.

Moving through into the observation gallery, Sebastian settled himself back in his padded swivel chair and activated all the screens.

'Right,' he said with a yawn. 'Let's see what's out there.'

The main lights gave a flicker and dimmed to a rusty orange.

Sebastian froze in alarm, then exhaled loudly, realizing this must be just another power dip. This was the first to happen after dusk, so it had taken him rather more by surprise than the previous ones.

He activated the internal comlink. 'Sebastian to Drone Silver.' There was silence. Sebastian sighed and drummed his fingers on the black curve of the console. 'Come on, come on, this is much more important than declogging the irrigators.'

A shrill bleep came from the speaker.

'At last. Drone Silver, do something about auxiliary power, will you?'

The robot bleeped once in response. Sebastian grunted and deactivated the comlink.

Outside, the wind was picking up speed. He could hear its remorseless pummelling of the rocks. He activated one of the land-level viewers and scanned 180 degrees – dark blue rock and sand and darkening green sky. Dull, as usual. But still faintly threatening.

Sebastian frowned. There was a cursor flashing on the panel immediately in front of him. It had been inactive for so long that he had almost forgotten what it meant.

His body went hot and cold. He felt a near-electric tingle of anticipation in his fingers, the way he always had when, as a

boy on Tenos Alpha, he had prepared to open his waiting
V-mail in the morning.

'A ship...' Sebastian breathed. '*Here...*'

He looked up, all around him, and there was a ragged grin
on his unshaven face. 'You've wanted this. It'll be *them* – whoever they are! Them!' He leapt to his feet, rubbing his hands in
delight, and scampered over to a wall locker, from which he
pulled his treasured bottle of Argolin brandy. 'Time for a change
around here,' muttered Sebastian to himself.

He poured himself a tiny amount into a glass – then he
weighed it up against the amount left in the bottle, shrugged,
and gulped straight from the bottle instead, wiping his mouth
on his sleeve. 'Your health!' he growled, and scurried down the
stairs to prepare for his visitors.

'Oh, dear,' said the Doctor. 'It seems they didn't do much with
the place.'

Nyssa, in a fur coat and a brown felt hat, both of which she
had found in the chest, decided she had to agree. It was cold,
for one thing, although the Doctor seemed comfortable enough
in his usual cricketing gear. It was also desolate.

She jumped up onto a boulder to take a look around. The
view was uninspiring. The TARDIS stood on top of a ridge of
blue rock overlooking a landscape of rolling blue sand dunes,
spindly plants and the occasional sad-looking pool of water.
The sky was a dull, metallic green and decidedly overcast. Cold
winds knifed her, and she shivered, huddling into the coat and
pulling the hat down over her ears. She recognized the all-per-
vading odour as some kind of sulphurous compound but, as the
Doctor had already established that it was not sufficiently concentrated to make the oxygen-rich atmosphere unbreathable,
she would have to put up with it.

The Doctor was pointing a torchlike device down the ridge.
'Energy source two kilometres to the south,' he said delight-
edly. 'Civilization, after all.' He offered Nyssa his hand to help

her down from the boulder. 'And where there's civilization, Nyssa, there's tea. Come on!'

Sebastian followed Drone Gold around agitatedly as it cleared up the visitor quarters – emptying ashtrays, tidying up bottles, wiping surfaces. 'Right,' Sebastian was saying. 'And there. And you've missed a bit, there.'

The lights cut out. Sebastian yelped. The only illumination, for a second or two, came from the green lights on Drone Gold's panel. Then reddish-purple emergency lights sprang up from concealment around the room.

Sebastian let out his breath. His heart was pounding furiously and he felt the hot-and-cold flush surge over him again.

'I can't take much more of this,' he snapped at Drone Gold. 'I need a drink.' He marched towards the door, then stepped suddenly back as he became aware that the doorway was occupied.

It was occupied by the hologram of Tarla.

He staggered back, clutching at the table for support, his throat coarse and dry. The holo-girl strode in, casting her blank gaze around as if looking for something. Her red hair, green eyes and marble-white skin all looked larger and brighter than life, fizzing with energy.

'This can't be happening,' Sebastian told himself. 'It's a motionless holo-unit, nothing more.'

Tarla stretched out a hand to him. Sebastian shrank away.

Drone Gold, bouncing unconcernedly on its flame jet, skimmed right through the phantom to continue its cleaning activities.

Sebastian had seen enough. He raced for the door, slamming his fist on the *close* control as he went.

He kept running until he reached the lounge on the other side of the Base, finally fetching up against the sofa, his ragged breath echoing around the room.

'I hope you don't mind,' said a polite voice from behind

him. 'There didn't seem to be anyone to let us in.'

Wild-eyed, Sebastian spun around.

Two people stood there – a tall, blond man in old-fashioned clothes and a girl with curly brown hair. For a few moments, he moved his mouth and wondered why nothing came out but a series of clicks and ragged breaths.

The man looked concerned. 'Is everything quite all right here, Mr –'

'M. . . Musgrove.' Sebastian was relieved to have recovered the power of speech. 'Se. . . Sebastian Musgrove.'

The man grabbed his hand and shook it warmly. 'Doctor John Smith – ah, on behalf of the Colonial Office. Just call me the Doctor.' Sebastian was aware of a long strip of identification cards being unfurled in front of him, like a conjuror's flags. Several of them bore images of faces entirely different from the Doctor's, he noticed, just as they were flipped away from him and back into the man's pocket. 'And this is my assistant, Nyssa.'

'Delighted to make your acquaintance,' said Sebastian weakly. 'I think you may have come at just the right time.'

The sky clanged and shimmered like a beaten gong. The sand seemed to lift itself from the darkness in jagged, glittering whorls, spinning skywards. Below, as if roused from slumber, pools of water bubbled and hissed, exuding noxious fumes.

Something was restless.

'These circuits seem in good order, Mr Musgrove.' The Doctor's muffled voice came from inside an inspection hatch.

'I know,' said Sebastian Musgrove. 'That's what I can't understand.'

Sebastian had relaxed now. The tea and biscuits he had given his guests seemed to have met with their approval and, furthermore, the Doctor had agreed to help him look into his mysterious power drains. He hadn't dared say anything about Tarla yet. He was secretly hoping he had imagined the whole thing.

The Doctor, assisted by the drones, had started work. He'd hung up his coat, rolled up his sleeves and was now lying on his back, his head and shoulders hidden beneath the hatch. Sebastian decided to leave him to it.

The girl Nyssa seemed friendly enough. He picked her out on a nearby monitor screen – standing in the observation gallery, looking out over the darkening landscape – and decided to take her some more tea.

Nyssa thanked him with a smile as he came in with the tray.

'Don't know why they keep me here,' Sebastian said, hovering just inside the doorway. 'I'm just a traffic beacon, really. We get no more than one or two ships passing through the spacelanes every few weeks.' He smiled nervously.

'That must be very dull for you, Mr Musgrove. How long have you been alone?' Nyssa sipped her tea.

Alone. How long. He had to answer. He could feel the roof of his mouth turning dry, aware that he had hesitated just a little too long.

'Since... my partner Tarla – working partner, I mean – left. That is, she had to go.' Sebastian was aware that his grip on the tray was weakening, and he was uncertain if he would be able to hold on to it for much longer.

There was a strange, pale light coming from the stairwell behind Nyssa.

'Solitude can weigh heavily on the heart and mind,' Nyssa observed sympathetically. 'I don't really have a family any more, so I'm glad to have the Doctor to travel with.' She frowned. 'Mr Musgrove – are you all right?'

Sebastian swallowed hard, wondering if Nyssa would turn towards the stairwell and see what he had seen there, behind the giant potted plants.

Silently, the shimmering figure of Tarla had appeared, watching them with hollow eyes.

* * *

'And now I need the linear tendency gauge, if you'd be so kind.'

The Doctor reached out for the penlike instrument, and felt it delivered smoothly into his palm. Drone Gold was certainly efficient, he thought, but where had its chum disappeared to all of a sudden? He supposed the drones must be constantly busy with one thing or another.

The Doctor prodded a panel of exposed circuitry with the gauge and watched the digital display flickering. 'Hmm... That's odd. Marked inconsistency...' He pushed himself back out into the room, causing Drone Gold to shoot upwards, clicking as if in reproof. The Doctor sat up suddenly. 'Did you hear that?' he exclaimed.

Drone Gold twirled its pincers and bleeped. It looked most apologetic.

'No,' said the Doctor 'Of course, you – '

The lights blazed orange, then dimmed to a low violet. A speaker on the far side of the room kicked into action, blasting out a bleating, repetitive alarm.

The Doctor made for the instrument banks. If he could isolate the power surge, maybe the problem could be solved.

The metal tray clanged to the floor.

Nyssa whirled around, looking to see what Sebastian was pointing at. There was nothing there.

At that moment, the lights dimmed and the alarm began its incessant blaring.

Drone Silver floated in, its thruster burning hotly and its arms twirling in mad agitation. It looked like a mechanized will-o'-the-wisp in the violet light and sounded like a mad macaw, chirping and squawking above the din of the alarm.

Sebastian, his hands clamped over his ears, sank slowly to his knees.

The Doctor burst breathlessly in and headed straight for the stairwell, pausing briefly to call over his shoulder.

'Nyssa?'

'Yes, Doctor?'

'Stay here, look after Sebastian. I'm going to the Conservatory!'

'No!' Sebastian, his face an unnatural white, had staggered to his feet and was holding out a hand to the Doctor like a drowning man. 'No, you mustn't...'

'And why not, hmm?' The Doctor opened his eyes in wide, feigned innocence. 'Ah! You're worried that I might really find the root of your problem for you!'

The alarm switched off suddenly, leaving an empty silence broken only by the rustling of the windswept sand against the exterior of the Base.

Neither the Doctor nor Nyssa saw where the gun had come from, but it had been drawn with remarkable speed. Sebastian staggered unsteadily across the observation gallery, levelling the weapon at the Doctor.

'You're staying. You can't go down there!' he commanded, his eyes bulging white and wide.

The Doctor sighed. Taking care to keep his hands in full view, he spoke in gentle tones. 'Now, come on, Sebastian. This isn't really very sensible, is it?'

'Don't go down there,' said Sebastian, his voice trembling. The purple shadows turned his face into something demonic.

With a raw smell of hot metal and burning gases, Drone Silver interposed itself between Sebastian and the Doctor, twittering loudly and rotating its small body. Sebastian began to shiver, the gun unsteady in his hand.

The gun fell. Nyssa, who had been watching from the sidelines, scooped it up and hurriedly handed it to the Doctor. He held it gingerly between his fingertips, as if he thought it might contaminate him, and raised his eyebrows ruefully.

'Not very adult, Sebastian.' He tossed the gun aside. 'Nyssa, look after him.'

Nyssa bent down to comfort the quivering figure. 'Be careful, Doctor.'

He gave her a brief, reassuring grin. 'That's my middle name,' he said, and hurried down the stairs.

The Conservatory seethed with moisture, brimmed with life. An air of expectancy hung over the place, almost as if it was waiting for something.

The giant transparent dome contained a series of platforms and mezzanines packed with multicoloured flora. Flowers shaped like bright scarlet bells bobbed over huge, serrated green leaves and sea-blue, cuplike plants with surfaces that shimmered like mercury. There were trees too, their knobbly branches reaching for the roof like titanic arms. Foliage stretched back in a verdant, mist-shrouded haze as far as the eye could see.

The Doctor, looking down from one of the uppermost platforms, frowned and brushed drops of perspiration from his eyes. 'Well, Doctor,' he murmured. 'If you can't stand the heat, get out of the greenhouse, I suppose.'

Wiping his forehead with his handkerchief, he turned a full circle and took in the sea of steaming foliage around him. He sniffed. An earthy, peaty smell, slightly acidic if he was not mistaken.

There was a metallic tang in the air, as well.

Very strange.

A sudden flash of movement caught his eye and he ran along the balcony, trying to get a better view through the twisted branches of the trees.

There. The plants on that far platform were shivering and flapping as if twisted by a minitornado. The whirlwind seemed to hop to the next platform, and then the next. A blue, thorny bush was ripped apart and the pieces scattered in the air, followed by a shower of deciduous green leaves.

The Doctor could taste the tingle in the air even more strongly now, sweet and sharp at the same time. The trees immediately in front of him began to shake, creaking and groaning like sails in the wind. Alarmed, he took a step backwards and began to rummage through his pockets for any useful device that might give him a clue as to what was happening. Before he could find anything, the whirlwind slipped under his feet and tipped him up, sending him crashing down onto soft, warm earth.

Arms and legs flailing, the Doctor went over and over, rolling in damp soil. Thorns and brambles snatched at him. With a thud, he reached the bottom of the artificial slope and lay there with the breath knocked out of him.

He lay still for some minutes. The sound was subsiding.

Eventually he sat up. He winced at a pain in his back but soon established that, save for a few bruises, he was unharmed.

'Well,' he said, brushing the earth from his cricketing coat, 'Barbara always told me how restful gardening was.' He sighed and began the difficult climb back up to the platform above, pausing now and again to apologize to the multihued species on which he had fallen, just in case any of them were intelligent. The Doctor liked to avoid giving offence.

Outside on the surface, a storm howled. Bubbling pools shone with an unearthly, spectral starlight. The twisted blue plants seemed to lift themselves out of the earth, as if straining to get a glimpse of the vulnerable little Base nestling in its hollow below.

A face appeared in one of the pools, like a reflection.

It was not a reflection, but a complete head, lifting itself seamlessly from the surface of the blue water. Eyes glowing, hair shimmering fire-red, it was the hologram of Tarla McCail. Her whole body emerged, smoothly and silently.

She stepped from the pool, mermaidlike, and stood, hands on hips, looking down at the Base.

A thin smile gradually formed on her blood-red lips.

Sebastian Musgrove sat on his own in his rest area.

Well, he thought, the Doctor wasn't giving much away. He'd come back from the Conservatory, brushing mud off his clothes, and said it would be better if they all got some rest until morning.

Sebastian had been only too happy to show them to the guest quarters. He was glad the Doctor and Nyssa still trusted him, even after he'd tried that stupid stunt with the gun. He still couldn't quite believe he'd done that. He needed them, after all, the Doctor and Nyssa. Oh, yes, he needed them.

He had made a promise.

'I don't trust Mr Musgrove, Doctor.'

Darkness seemed to lurk in the corners of the lounge. One of the shadows was that of the Doctor. He was pacing up and down, hands thrust deep in his pockets. He stopped when Nyssa spoke, turned to face her in the purple light and raised his eyebrows.

'Ah, well, trust is a very frail thing.' He frowned to himself for a moment, as if he had been looking for something rather deeper to say, then shrugged. 'For the record, Nyssa, neither do I.' He dropped into an armchair and sighed deeply.

'You're not going to tell him you've still got nominal ownership of this planet, then?'

'I think that would only complicate things.' The Doctor leaned forward, pressing his fingertips together. 'Besides, I'd like to know exactly *what* it is I own – and I think Mr Musgrove may know the answer to that one.'

Nyssa came to sit beside him. There was concern in her eyes, and she seemed to be having difficulty maintaining her usual inner serenity. 'This partner of his,' she said. 'I'm worried that he is withholding the truth about her.'

'Ah.' The Doctor nodded, opened his eyes wide. 'You're about to tell me,' he said, waggling his finger at her, 'that you think Tarla was murdered.' He leapt to his feet with a sudden burst of energy and gazed at a painting on the wall. It depicted a stylized vista of Pluto's icy wastes. 'That would be interesting,' he said in a far-off voice, 'very interesting. But possibly too easy... Now, Nyssa, I suggest you do your best to try to forget about the unpleasant surroundings and get some sleep.'

Nyssa gave him a knowing look. 'And I suppose you'll be doing the same yourself?'

'Don't be silly. I took a nap...' The Doctor paused to think for a moment. 'Well, definitely within the past week!' He smiled. 'The drones don't sleep either. Together, we're going to do some more circuit-testing, and a little unofficial investigation.'

Nothing stirred in the deepest levels of the Base. There was a low and gentle hum, indicating that the generators were running, but otherwise it was quiet and still.

Suddenly there came another sound: the gentle whine of a motor. A beam of blue light cut into the dimness, showing up the dust in the air. It was followed by a blue flame. Drone Gold bobbed into view, its searchlight rotating like the beam from a lighthouse. Then, behind the robot, the Doctor appeared, sniffing the air and patting the thick metal walls with his customary curiosity.

'You know, this is terribly good of you,' the Doctor said with a smile. 'I shouldn't imagine Sebastian has much time to check up on these things himself, and seeing as I'm something of an insomniac...'

The robot clicked and whistled softly.

'Yes, well...' The Doctor nodded sagely and rubbed his nose. 'That's more or less what I would have said. Now then, the main computer storage unit would be...'

Drone Gold whirled around and indicated, with a twist of one pincer, that the Doctor should follow.

'Right. Lead on, MacDrone.'

Hours passed.

With the morning came a softening of the land, as if an icy grip had melted into dew. The bubbling pools subsided, became flat and glossy once more, and the sulphurous clouds dispersed. The plants, the shadows of which had resembled hideous apparitions, were now just spindly, underfed foliage once more.

The sky remained leaden, anticipatory.

Nyssa awoke.

She pushed the durofoil coverlet off in irritation, yawned and levered herself up on one elbow. She had slept very badly.

'Doctor?' she said, rubbing her eyes as she focused on the tall, pale figure who stood at her window in the dawn light.

She realized, a second later, that it was not the Doctor.

The woman smiled at her. It was a smile of violent red, like blood on ice.

Nyssa gasped and suddenly felt as if all warmth had been drained from her face. She clutched at the edge of the bed and wondered whether to stand up and confront the intruder or to keep still and quiet.

In the blink of an eye, the woman was gone.

Nyssa swallowed hard and tried to ignore the pounding of her heart. It was getting light outside and there were no conveniently shadowy corners into which the figure could have ducked.

There had been numerous myths and legends on Traken, some of them – as on many other worlds – involving ethereal spirits. She shivered, and pulled the fur coat on over her thin top. As she swung her legs off the bed, she realized how tired she still was. Her eyes ached from the fitful sleep and her mouth tasted dry and salty.

So what had she seen?

Perhaps she had not been properly awake and had just imagined the shimmering phantom. She yawned and went off in search of the Doctor and breakfast.

Drone Silver had been busy. Now it hovered and twittered in the lounge, over three tables laden with bright silver trays of food – golden-brown croissants and toast, hard-boiled eggs, large pots of coffee and tea and glass jars of jam and marmalade.

Nyssa found the lounge strangely quiet and still, but at least the lighting had returned to a level that was restful without being ghostly dim. The curved Plexiglas windows once more revealed a soft, blue landscape of sand and rock.

She smiled nervously at Drone Silver, and the robot swivelled its head in response before jerking a claw at the array of breakfast.

'This is all very impressive,' said Nyssa, who had acquired a liking for the delicacies of Earth since travelling with the Doctor. She'd had toast and marmalade at Lord Cranleigh's, so she fell upon the familiar item with hungry relief. 'Where's the Doctor?' she asked between munches.

The answer came in the form of a succession of buzzes and bleeps.

Nyssa frowned and folded her arms behind her steaming mug of coffee. 'You must communicate with Mr Musgrove,' she supposed to herself. 'An intelligent drone... responds to intelligent ideas.' Her eyes lit up. 'I want you to bleep for yes and buzz for no. Is Mr Musgrove around?'

Drone Silver let out an obedient bleep.

Nyssa was delighted. She glanced over at the functional staircase leading up to the observation gallery. She couldn't see, but she supposed Sebastian must be up there on his first monitoring duties of the day. She took a gulp of coffee. 'And,' she said, 'apart from the Doctor and me, is Mr Musgrove the only sentient life form on this Base?'

That question seemed to perplex the drone. It bobbed on its hover jet, twittering like a nervous sparrow.

Nyssa raised her eyebrows and looked as stern as she could. 'I asked you a question,' she reminded the drone.

The answer came. It was a long, low buzz.

Nyssa felt herself go cold.

A shrill alarm, quite different from the one she'd heard before, kicked into action. It rang and rang, in short and urgent blasts.

Without any warning, feet clattered on the metal staircase from the observation gallery. Nyssa felt herself jump, but the newcomer was only Sebastian, dishevelled and wild-eyed.

'Make it stop!' he shouted at Drone Silver. 'Make it stop now!'

Obediently, the drone bobbed over to a control panel and twittered briefly. The noise shut off, leaving a harsh silence.

'What's happening?' Nyssa asked. 'Where's the Doctor?'

'We're under attack!' Sebastian snarled. Nyssa was alarmed at his manner. His face had become wolfish, infused with some kind of primal anger, and he was gripping the back of one of the armchairs so hard that his knuckles were a stark white. 'Don't you understand? That's what's been happening the whole time, since long before you came here!'

There was a noise like the scraping of metal, which seemed to shake the floor with its vibrations. Nyssa looked round fearfully, wondering what new terror this was, but Sebastian just laughed at her and pointed to the windows. They were being slowly covered by metal shutters, which were sliding down and blocking out the light from outside.

'Defence,' said Sebastian, with a brief flash of a smile. 'Automatic,' he added, making his way unsteadily to a wall locker and punching out a code on its keypad. 'Manual,' he concluded with a grin, taking out a large and heavy pistol and aiming it straight at her.

Nyssa felt her body begin to shake with fear, but suddenly Sebastian turned the gun around and tossed it across the room. Startled, she caught it fumblingly, aware that Sebastian had drawn another from the locker and was busy loading it.

'In an attack situation,' he said, his words clear but still high-pitched with nervousness, 'all civilian personnel will consider themselves under my command. You will follow orders at all times to defeat the enemy. Drone Silver, is that clear?'

Drone Silver let out a complex series of babbling bleeps.

'Good. Miss Nyssa, is that clear?' Sebastian raised his eyebrows at her.

She swallowed hard, her throat dry and constricted. The gun felt cold and alien in her hand. She felt comfortable neither with weapons nor with the idea of armed defence. But she knew Sebastian might possibly be unhinged enough to kill her if she disagreed with him.

'Right,' she said. 'Clear, Mr Musgrove.'

The lights dimmed to orange, as if something had suddenly sucked the power from the Base. Sebastian, sheened with perspiration, dropped to one knee and aimed his gun at the shuttered windows.

Nyssa suddenly realized there was a grating, dragging sound coming from the other side of the shutters.

And she wondered if Sebastian Musgrove might be not so mad after all.

With a spectacular whoosh of hydraulics, the inner door behind Nyssa flew open. She whirled around. The Doctor was framed in the doorway, his hands held out in front of him. He walked slowly into the room, Drone Gold bobbing along behind.

'Good morning, everyone,' said the Doctor. 'It appears we've done six impossible things before breakfast.'

'Get back,' muttered Sebastian.

Nyssa looked from Sebastian's firmly levelled gun to the Doctor, to the silent drones and then back to the Doctor again.

'*Get back*!' Sebastian screamed. 'I told you, I'm not going! I'll not be taken away!'

The scrabbling noises from outside began to increase in volume. Nyssa thought she felt vibrations in the floor again.

'Nyssa,' said the Doctor calmly, 'do you know, you were right about Mr Musgrove? He hasn't been telling us the truth. But I've just spent a few hours accessing some very interesting files with the aid of one of our friendly drones here. I know the truth now.' The Doctor spread his hands, raised his eyebrows. 'I know it, Sebastian. And I'm going to help.'

'You mean...' Nyssa backed away from Sebastian. 'He really did kill his partner?'

'He killed no-one.' The Doctor was still moving forward. 'You see, according to the Base computer, Sebastian's never had a partner here. Have you, Sebastian?'

Sebastian was shaking, retreating into the shelter of one of the tables. He looked, Nyssa thought, as if he wanted to retreat to a little world of his own making, to stay there for ever, never to have to come out.

'On the other hand,' continued the Doctor, 'there was a girl, back on Earth, called Tarla McCail. A girl Sebastian loved, who was killed by the Daleks.' The Doctor clasped his hands behind his back and lowered his voice, as if aware that he was speaking for Nyssa's benefit alone now. 'Sebastian built up a hologram from video images of her. It was something to keep him company. To stop him going mad here, cooped up all alone for days and nights on end without a survey ship, without another human being.'

Sebastian, his head in his hands, was whimpering.

The Doctor reached under Sebastian's table, into his world, and put a hand on his shoulder. 'It's all right,' he said.

'Doctor,' Nyssa whispered, 'I asked the drone if we were alone here.'

'Mmm. And it told you not, I imagine.' The Doctor stood up, his face resigned. 'There's something here, all right. It uses electrical power, I know that much. It's been causing power drains, playing havoc with the systems and doing some very strange things to Mr Musgrove's hologram.'

'Hologram... *That* was what I saw! This morning, I saw something in my room, like a ghost.'

'That may well have been it. But Sebastian's original was designed to be kept in one place, like a statue. It shouldn't function without a projector, you know.'

'So are we in danger?' Nyssa asked, feeling that she already knew the answer.

'Terrible danger,' sighed the Doctor, 'and all because of something I forgot when I first won this asteroid. Stay here.'

'Where are you –'

'Up!' he shouted, bounding up the stairs.

Beyond the observation gallery, there was only the Observatory itself. The Doctor found the metal ladder, pulled it down and began to climb, his breath sounding harsh and steely in the narrow shaft.

He emerged into a spacious, dimly lit dome. A narrow gallery ran around the edge, but otherwise it was dominated by a rocketlike cluster of instruments, towering above the Doctor. Jutting into the sky, ready to intercept the messages of the stars, the tubes, lenses and cables glittered and hummed like a beast cobbled together from the technologies of various different centuries. The Doctor sighed. He supposed that the colonies had to take what they could get, sometimes.

He could taste the metallic tingle in the air again, strangely sweet, like someone pressing a cold spoon of honey against his tongue.

He tilted his head back and called out. 'It's all right! I want only to talk!'

The light seemed to turn a shade dimmer and the shadows gathered themselves with a whispering, rushing sound.

Something started to cast reflections from the tower of glittering optics.

Nyssa glanced round. It had got darker again now, and Sebastian was weeping like a baby. A harsh wind blew, chilling her face and tugging at her hair. She shuddered.

Sebastian looked up, his face streaked with sweat and tears. 'No,' he murmured, 'not this time. Please. I told you they'd be

coming, didn't I? I said you could have them instead of me...
Please!'

Nyssa suddenly decided that she had no wish to be trapped
in the lounge with Sebastian Musgrove's madness and the unseen thing scraping and shuddering against the shutters outside.

'Where's the Doctor?' she cried to the drones. They quivered, bleeping to each other. Drone Gold began to bob towards
the stairs, gesturing with its pincers that Nyssa should follow.
She glanced back at Sebastian, then up at Drone Silver. 'Look
after him!' she commanded, and hurried up the stairs.

When they reached the observation gallery, Drone Gold indicated that she should ascend the metal ladder.

An unearthly light was spilling glutinously from the shaft.
Echoes, like cries from the heart of a pit of earth and iron,
throbbed down into her hands as she grasped the struts. Reso-
lute, she headed upwards. There was a ringing in her ears, a
metallic taste in her mouth and nostrils. She reached the top.

The Doctor was standing on a spindly gallery, raising his
hands as if to protect himself from the creature of dancing light
that crackled around the telescopes and instruments above.
Nyssa blinked. Sensations came at her in a confused rush. There
was a roaring, a sharp sweetness, a smell of hot metal, and a
bright glow from the surfaces of the optical devices. And then a
tendril of light reached out for the Doctor.

'No!' Nyssa, shocked, leapt forward and pushed the Doctor
out of the way. The crackling light hit the wall of the dome and
curved round, like a snake's head, looking for a new direction.

The Doctor, breathless with anger, struggled to sit up. 'Nyssa,
why on earth did you do that?'

'It was going to attack you!'

'It was going to do no such thing! I was about to enter into
communion with the *true* indigenous life form of this planet!'

Nyssa was perplexed. She shaded her eyes and tried to focus
on the roving tentacles of light. 'So, you mean –'

With a sudden stabbing motion, the tentacle plunged into Nyssa.

For a moment she was frightened as she felt herself being dragged upright, her arms pulled out by her sides, her head gently tilted back. And then a calmness spread through her limbs, as if she was floating in warm water.

She felt a voice lifting up from her, surging through her. The voice of an alien.

Sebastian, weak with terror, stumbled into the observation gallery. He shivered as he saw the slow light dripping down from the ladder shaft.

He felt a pang of conscience, telling him that what he had done hadn't been fair. During the past few months he had established that there was a life form on this planet, but the discovery had done nothing to lessen his despairing sense of loneliness. For Sebastian had become convinced that the creature, whatever it might be, was out to kill him.

He had begged and bargained for his life. The next space travellers to come here would be offered up in his place, he had promised. At least, that was what he thought he had promised, in those strange moments of communion with the invisible force. When it had taken on the form of his dead, beloved Tarla, that had been too much for him.

He wondered, now.

He wondered what the creature had really wanted.

He climbed the ladder, fighting against the light and the tangible electricity in the air. When he got to the top, he was chilled by what he saw. The Doctor, who was there beside him, lifted one finger to tell him to be silent.

The girl, Nyssa, was glowing in a pillar of whitish-blue light from which stray tendrils played over the Observatory dome, lighting it like strobes. Nyssa was speaking in a voice that was not her own.

'...*I am sorry for any distress I may have caused you. I am*

Telxzana, of the Pzorswihr. We are a dying race, and I am the very last. It is my body on which you stand, and upon which you have made your encampment.'

The Doctor's eyes opened wide and he leant forward, gripping the handrail. 'Ah... now it all becomes clear. This planet's single continent isn't a continent at all. It's you! The rocks, the plants, the water... they're all part of your... physical structure?'

'That is correct. We are – we were – electro-sensitive and silicon-based life forms. I have been attempting to communicate with you for some time. But I have been weak, and the ways I could find to attract your attention all seemed to cause disruption.'

The Doctor cleared his throat. 'Humans,' he said, spreading his hands, 'are very dependent on their electricity. You travel through it – I realized that when I monitored the flux patterns of the power failures – and that is as natural for you as it is for a human to breathe the air. You didn't realize you were causing power fluctuations?'

Nyssa's mouth opened again. *'I did not, until very recently. Then I tried to gather my energy in one place, to communicate with the human.'*

The Doctor nodded. 'The hologram.'

'My name's Sebastian,' said Sebastian, looking urgently from the Doctor to the incandescent creature. 'Sebastian, you remember! We had a deal!'

The Doctor lowered his voice and put an arm around Sebastian's shoulders to lead him to one side. 'I think you misunderstood the creature's intentions, Sebastian. It spared you because it never wanted to hurt you in the first place.'

'That is true. I wanted to warn you of my impending death.'

The Doctor looked up sharply. 'Ah,' he said. 'Yes. Now that was something I really should have known about.'

Nyssa felt wetness against her mouth. It was cool, fresh water, and her dry throat needed it.

She sipped gratefully as the room swam into focus. She was on a couch, she realized, and as details became less fuzzy in front of her sticky eyes, she saw the familiar surroundings of the Base lounge. The Doctor, his face full of concern, was leaning over her.

'Take it easy, Nyssa,' he said. 'Not too fast.'

Thirst consumed her. Sitting up, she grabbed the beaker from the Doctor's hand and gulped down the rest of the water, savouring the tingly freshness that it gave her mouth.

'Are you all right?' the Doctor asked.

Nyssa considered for a moment. 'Sore head,' she said, 'and I could drink another pint of water.' She looked the Doctor as steadily in the eye as she could. 'Doctor... how did you know that communing with that creature wouldn't be dangerous?'

'I didn't,' he said sternly. 'Nyssa, my constitution is considerably stronger than yours. That was why I had to do it alone. Unfortunately, you got in the way.' The Doctor gave her a grin. 'Still, no damage done.'

'And... the creature?'

'Telxzana is still here, although she won't be for long. That's what she was trying to tell us all along, you see. The storms, the tremors, the power failures... they're all linked to the death of the last of this planet's natural inhabitants.'

Nyssa put a hand to her head. There was a faint recollection of *a story, an ancient story... a tale of suffering, of death... and of the terrible pain of being the last of one's kind.*

She looked up at the Doctor. 'How long until she dies?'

'In human terms, about a year.' The Doctor shrugged. 'It would be wise to make sure that Mr Musgrove and the drones are shipped off this world before she disappears forever.'

The last...

Nyssa had sensed it like a lingering scent of home. Like the lost, distant face of her father.

The last of one's kind.

* * *

Sebastian Musgrove munched on a croissant.

On the monitors in front of him, two figures receded, heading for a distant ridge. He chuckled to himself as he wondered which part of the alien the ridge belonged to. Her shoulder? Her right eyelid?

He magnified the figures of the Doctor and Nyssa as much as he could, until he was able to make out the Doctor's panama hat and Nyssa's bob of curls.

He sighed. The next survey ship would be taking him out of here. Now that the alien knew this, the Doctor had assured him, he would not be bothered again.

Sebastian wasn't sure. Part of him had quite liked being bothered. Being communicated with. No-one had really communicated with him for a long time, not since that day he had got the beamed message that Tarla was dead.

There was one thing, at least, that the alien could give him until his departure. An illusion that she could preserve for him.

He leaned back on his chair and grinned at the slender hologram, who winked back.

'Drone Gold,' Sebastian shouted down the stairs, 'put the kettle on.'

'I remember,' said the Doctor as they trudged back up the rocky ridge that was not really a rocky ridge, through the blue sand that was not blue sand, back towards the TARDIS.

'What, Doctor?' Nyssa was deep in thoughts of her own.

'When I won this asteroid, the Draconian told me at the time that his people's seismic probes had detected instabilities. He thought it had not much more than a couple of orbits left.' The Time Lord pulled a face. 'He was quite gloating about it, as I recall. Always was one of those things I meant to follow up...' He turned round to look down at the Base, which now lay a good ten minutes below them.

Nyssa joined him. 'Well,' she said, 'are you glad that you satisfied your curiosity?'

'Oh, I think so. Mr Musgrove will be all right now, and I'll make sure the ship that picks him up is given a full explanation.' The Doctor sighed. 'It never does any harm to be reminded of perspective occasionally. To remember that there are still creatures in the Universe for whom we're just insignificant microbes...' He squatted down to cup a handful of sand. 'Take care, Telxzana,' he said softly, and let the sand fall as his gaze took in the vast, rugged horizon of her blue flesh.

Nyssa watched as he brushed the particles from his hands. The Doctor's face was strangely blank. He might have been thinking about the past, or the future. About his eternal wanderings, or about death.

'She'll die, and then they'll be extinct.' Nyssa's matter-of-fact tone concealed a multitude of inner thoughts.

'Yes.' The Doctor stood up. 'It's happening all over the Universe, you know. Old things dying, new things beginning. We can't prevent it.' He turned, jamming his hat on his head, and strode towards the TARDIS. 'Come on, Nyssa,' he said. 'Let's be off.'

She lingered a moment longer, the chilly, sulphurous wind buffeting her. A light drizzle was starting to fall, marking the sand with darkness.

Down there, in front of the Base, she saw someone waving in farewell. She lifted her own hand to wave back, although the Base was just too far away for her to be sure that it really was Sebastian. She thought – straining her eyes – that the figure seemed a little taller and more angular.

The Doctor was trudging on ahead, so Nyssa turned and hurried after him.

The rain started to spatter more heavily, and the first rumbles of thunder sounded.

People of the Trees

By Pam Baddeley

The bad feeling was back tonight but worse. Culbano's fur shivered as if a cold wind blew, though it was high summer. His large sensitive eyes swept the forested slope below for a sign of movement and his small black nostrils flared. An image came into his mind: the gaunt *urbarg* who had been outside the village two moons ago, who had stared up at the People as they made their way nimbly along their swaying bridges or sat outside their huts weaving or preparing food. Soon they had all felt the pressure of those eyes and fallen silent, waiting. But the *urbarg* had finally turned away as if satisfied to have got their attention. No-one had seen her since, but there were nervous over-the-shoulder glances now whenever anyone had to descend to ground level.

This was Culbano's second sleepless night. It was not the honour and responsibility of tending the shrine which kept him awake, for this was the third time he had served here. No, it was the thought of why the *urbarg* had trespassed on their land. None of the *urbargalim* had come here since the Doc-tor had taken the People under his protection. As a child, Culbano had shivered at stories of the evil *urbargalim* but been reassured to hear how the Doc-tor had turned the magic of the furless ones against them and saved the People.

Culbano's fur prickled again. The Doc-tor had left so long ago that the eldest elder who had set eyes on him as a baby, clinging to its mother's fur, had now passed to the Place of Beyond. Perhaps the Doc-tor's magical protection had faded? The voices of the Great Ones were a reassuring whisper at the back of Culbano's mind, yet he had to see them for himself. He turned and entered the hut, then bowed with hands crossed before him.

'Pardon your servant, Great Ones. Let me set my eyes upon you.'

His heart thudding in his ears, he straightened. The glimmer of light from the doorway showed enough to calm his fears. The three figures, each as tall as his arm was long, stood with their hands crossed over their chests; their dark wooden faces were placid and wise. He bowed once more.

'Pardon me again, Great Ones, for disturbing your meditation.'

He backed out of the hut onto the platform. How stupid he had been to think that the gods might have disappeared –

There was sudden agony below his shoulder blades, then Culbano was gone to the Place of Beyond.

Zusala looked down at the body for a moment, the gun hanging limply by her side. Praise the Maker that the stupid savage had finally gone into the hut. She had almost screamed with cramp when she had left the concealment of the bushes below and scrambled up the ramshackle ladder onto the platform. She glanced up at the lowering moons and realized that she had been waiting for half the night, forced to keep the same crouched position once she had seen that the savage was awake. She had known that the shrine was tended at all times – Aulian Thorolis had told her that much – but the creatures were not nocturnal, so why had this one been prowling?

She thrust the gun into her belt and swung the pack off her shoulder, then stepped over the body. She had better hurry. Aulian had assured her that this bunch had got careless: the special protection they enjoyed meant that they had not seen one of her kind for almost a century. But she remembered the history vids; the savages would kill anyone who tried to enter their shrine, even if it meant their own deaths.

The first idol almost slipped from her hands as she bent to pick it up. Maker! Thorolis had not warned her it would be so heavy. How was she going to lug three of these things all the way back to her aircar? As she stuffed the second one into her pack, the full extent of the problem became apparent. The pack was now filled to capacity, but Aulian had said that she would pay the rest of the fee only if all three idols were delivered. Cursing, Zusala fastened the pack and swung it onto her shoulders, then bent and took the third idol under one arm. Why did Aulian want these things, anyway? There were a few in museums, relics of tribes that had been wiped out when their presence became an inconvenience, but few people these days showed any interest in the primitives.

She swung herself carefully onto the ladder and began to make her one-handed descent. Sweat sprang onto her forehead as the pack dug painfully into her shoulders. She was really earning her money. Perhaps Aulian had some scheme which would be advanced by the disappearance of the idols? In that case, perhaps she could be persuaded to pay a little more than they had originally agreed..? Distracted by the thought, Zusala missed her grip on the next rung and toppled backwards. She grabbed wildly and grasped the strut of the ladder. It teetered, threatening to pitch itself over. The pack swung on her back and breath whistled between her teeth. Finally the ladder slammed back into place and she clung to it, heart racing, hardly aware of the thud below as the third idol hit the ground.

She made her way down the last few rungs carefully and turned to see where the idol had fallen. 'Maker!' It was in the middle of a ziajad bush, and she had no gloves. If she picked it out, she would have sore hands for days. She began to shrug herself out of the pack, meaning to wrap her shirt round her hands, but froze as she heard an ululating whistle in the distance. Instantly she reached for the gun at her belt, and moaned as her hand met with thin air. She must have lost it when she almost fell. The whistle was repeated and Zusala realized that the gentle breeze was blowing from behind her, taking her scent to the great catlike predator whose call she had recognized all too well. 'Maker take it!' Aulian would have to be satisfied with two of the idols. She pulled the pack onto her shoulders and turned to run, the heavy burden thudding against her back.

By the time she broke clear of the trees and stumbled across the scrub-covered ground beyond, her back had been pummelled into a bruised mess. Her breath stabbed her side and sweat ran down her body, soaking her shirt. She staggered to the aircar and pressed her palm to the plate on its side. The door slid up and she shrugged out of the pack, then threw it onto the passenger seat and climbed inside. The door closed behind her and the tinny voice of her aircar controller spoke. 'Engage preprogrammed course?'

'Yes! No. No, wait. Wait. Just a moment.' She rubbed her face with her hands. How could she go to Thorolis with only two of the idols? She had sensed a suppressed rage in the woman, beneath her icy control, a rage that seemed all too likely to explode given the right circumstances. 'Home. Home first. Retain preprogrammed course in databank.'

Safely home, Zusala winced as she climbed into a hot bath, then sank back with a sigh. Perhaps she should have gone straight to Aulian's house, and got it over with: it lay near the forest, after all. But she needed time to think. Her gaze strayed to the open door and the pack lying in the room beyond. Perhaps it would be better to sell the idols through her normal contacts, then abandon these rented rooms and lie low somewhere? Yes, that would be better than having to face Aulian.

Leela yawned and closed the reading primer with which she had been struggling for the past hour. The Doctor insisted on teaching her new skills, whether or not she could see a use for them. This one was starting to give her a headache. She looked up. The Doctor was still tinkering with the strange column that appeared to be the heart of the odd place she had learnt to call the TARDIS. There was no sign of K-9: the Doctor had sent him off hours ago to do something called cataloguing in a place called the library. Apparently, it was filled with more of these things called books. Privately, Leela was determined to keep well away from it.

The Doctor frowned and looked up, his gaze abstracted. As she watched, he shook his head as if trying to toss a misbehaved lock of hair away from his eyes. Leela looked round uneasily. The light hairs on her arms and the nape of her neck had begun to stir. She drew her knife and stood up, letting the primer fall to the floor. 'Doctor –'

'I know. Something...' The Doctor staggered back, putting his hands to his head, his eyes tightly closed. Alarmed, Leela stepped towards him.

'Doctor! What is it? Doctor!'

'It's... the People.' He opened his eyes and slowly lowered his hands. 'They... need me.'

'Doctor?' Leela sensed now that the presence within the TARDIS was not an evil one.

He turned his head towards her. 'The People... I'd forgotten them. It was so long ago.' He began pressing switches on the column. 'Too long. An assignment hearing might already have been called.'

'I don't understand –'

'I helped them before. Now they need me again.'

Aulian sat back in her chair, a satisfied smile passing briefly across her face before she remembered the need to keep an earnest, serious expression. Still, she could hardly restrain herself from laughing as she eyed the circle of self-important fools seated around the table. Everything was going to plan. She had made her case: this mysterious Doctor was surely dead after so many years, and no-one had come forward to test as heir. It was a fundamental belief of Dascarian society: land must not lie without custodian or it would wither. Soon, this particular piece of land would be offered to anyone with sufficient *verevan*, and who had more than she?

Her gaze went to the open window and the sprawling lawns beyond it with their clumps of stately hereash trees. The land that she sought to regain was more beautiful than this; she had seen it with her own eyes now, not just in old vids, although she could still scarcely believe it. She was the first Dascarian to have set foot there in almost a century. The last had been that thrice-damned fool, her great-grandfather, who had sold it to the Doctor. The only blot was the presence of those dirty, ver- min- ridden primitives, and she had already taken steps to get rid of them.

She was about to turn back to the room when a flashing light caught her attention. A blue box had suddenly appeared, by one of the distant trees, with a low groaning sound. She was still staring at the box in puzzlement when a voice jolted her.

'Gentlefemme Thorolis?'

'What? Oh, I beg pardon, Justiciar. The beauty of your grounds has me spellbound. It reminds me so strongly of what I have lost.'

'Indeed.' The kindly, sympathetic look on the old fool's face told Aulian that she had gauged her audience well. 'Perhaps not lost for ever, Gentlefemme. It seems evident that the Doc- tor has died without heir. He has made no provision for transfer of the land to any person with equal *verevan* and therefore –'

'Am I late?'

Aulian and the others turned. A tall man was standing in the doorway, hands in his pockets, a misshapen hat seated on top of his curly brown hair. And what was that colourful length of material trailing from his neck almost to the floor? Aulian frowned as the man stepped forward into the room, followed by the oddest looking creature she had ever seen. Something about the grace of its movements reminded Aulian strongly of the primitives, but then she saw that it had no fur, wore skins and – her heart jumped with shock – was a woman. Why should a Dascarian remind her of those accursed savages?

The skin-clad woman swept her gaze over the assembly. As those piercing blue eyes met hers, Aulian had the unsettling sensation of being weighed up and found distinctly wanting. A pulse began to beat in her temple.

'Late?' the Justiciar echoed.

'For the hearing? This is the hearing for the land assigned to the Doctor, isn't it?' The man beamed at them.

'Well, yes, er –'

'Good. What stage have the proceedings reached?'

'Well,' the Justiciar seemed completely thrown by this breach of etiquette. His clerk interceded.

'We had come to the conclusion that the Doctor had died without heir and left no candidate for transferral –'

'I think you're being rather premature, if you don't mind my saying so.' The man's voice was gentle but cut through the room. 'I am the Doctor.'

'Impossible!' Aulian could keep silent no longer. 'The records show the Doctor was an old man, white haired–'

'The original Doctor has had a number of heirs, all known by the same name.' The man shrugged. 'You might say it's a title.'

'I see.' The Justiciar had regained his tongue. 'Well, we can soon settle this.'

'The *verevan* test?' the Doctor asked.

His companion spoke for the first time. '*Verevan*? What is this test, Doctor? Is it like the test of the Horda?'

'How can you not know of *verevan*, young woman?' The Justiciar frowned. 'Are you a simpleton?'

The woman tensed. Aulian noticed that her hand had moved to the hilt of a knife at her waist, but she said nothing.

'I'll undertake the test,' the Doctor said. 'Now.'

'Very well. Will you ready a terminal, Topani?'

Aulian watched with clenched teeth as the tall stranger flopped into a chair before a nearby computer pedestal. The clerk tapped its upper surface.

'Topani, Justiciary.'

'Confirmed.' A field of shimmering blue light appeared above the pedestal and a face coalesced into existence. It was that of a woman of middle years with white hair fastened in a severe bun, her eyes pale blue and cold. The face stared out into the room, expressionless.

'*Verevan* examination of the putative heir of the man known as the Doctor, also known as the Doctor.' Topani spoke rapidly. 'Object, to establish custodianship of the area of land between the lakes of Dolamal and the present Thorolis estate. Designation is two zero four zero nine.'

'I – I mean, the Doctor – knew it as the Forest of Primitives, I believe.'

'That's the old name,' Topani confirmed. 'We tend to forget that the creatures are there these days.'

The Doctor gave him a penetrating look, but said nothing.

The face hanging in mid-air spoke. 'Place your hands on the terminal please.' The voice was like the face, colourless.

Aulian watched as the Doctor complied. The face broke apart into a shimmering field of colours which fluctuated so dizzily that she had to look away again. She realized that she was gripping the arms of her chair with a furious intensity, and forced her hands to relax. If the newcomer should establish the same level of *verevan* as his ancestor... She held her breath as the face reappeared.

'The heir of the Doctor, also known as the Doctor, has identical *verevan* for the area of land in question. There is some suggestion of a protective desire towards the semi-intelligent primitives found there.' The virtual persona paused, its face blank. There was a murmur around the table and a few raised eyebrows. The pronouncement came as no surprise to Aulian, however, as she had bribed Topani for a copy of the first Doctor's *verevan* record some months ago. She let out her breath convulsively and, as the Doctor's eyes met hers, let him read the hate there.

'Irrelevant,' the computer ruled. 'The *verevan* is identical to that of the original claimant. The claim is good.'

'Well,' the Justiciar frowned. 'Obviously you are a compassionate man to feel concern for those unfortunate creatures. But your *verevan* is the same as your forefather's. You have been judged a fitting custodian of the land.' He looked around the gathering, his expression softening as he saw Aulian.

Aulian set her lips in a bloodless line of fury. Let him keep his sympathy! Her *verevan* was for the land itself, not for those verminous savages. These fools were too blind to see it, even their computer. After all, it had been programmed by the likes of them. But the land would be hers yet.

'The Doctor's claim is proven,' the Justiciar pronounced. 'Let the record stand.'

'So noted,' said the bland face, which dissipated into blue light once more as Topani directed the terminal to close down.

The Doctor stood and approached Aulian's chair. She struggled to her feet on legs that felt like sacks of flour. She would go now; she would not speak to him.

'You must be... the granddaughter of Eliat?'

'Great-granddaughter.' The words forced themselves from her lips and opened a pathway for others, despite her resolve. 'That fool had no business selling the land to your ancestor, even if he was destitute! I have money enough and more – I'll give you a fair price for its return.'

The Doctor shook his head. 'I can't do that. The first Doctor gave his word to the People of the Trees, to ensure the safety of their homeland.'

'People of the – ' Aulian laughed bitterly. 'Is that what those vermin call themselves?'

'How many of them are left outside that area?' The man's blue eyes stared into hers. Again, Aulian had the sense of being weighed up and assessed.

'Too many!' Aulian hurried to the door.

Outside, the fresh air cooled the burning of her skin. She ran to her aircar and directed it to take her home. Zusala had to be there. Now everything depended on it!

Zusala's breathing was ragged as she ran. The primitive, his back scored with the burn of her laser, stalked her, a wickedly sharp bone knife in his long delicate fingers. She rounded a corner, panting for breath. A dark face reared up to cut off her escape, and hands reached out for her with a loud creak of tortured wood. A scream burst from her lips–

And fell away, against the walls of her small, dingy room.

'Maker.' Zusala groaned and rolled over, the bedsheet sliding off onto the floor. Daylight was gleaming palely through the threadbare covering which hung over the window. She sat up and rubbed her bleary eyes, then blinked. Two dark faces were watching her with deadly patience. This time, Zusala's scream was long and loud.

'Hello? Anybody here?'

The Doctor's voice fell into the silence of the trees. Leela eyed the wooden platforms visible through the fluttering leaves overhead. Her nostrils flared. 'Something is here, Doctor. Watching us.'

'The People, I should think. Of course, they wouldn't recognize me but...'

Leela slowly turned her head, gazing round at the grey boles of the trees. A chill stole up the back of her neck. She could tell that the Doctor's mind was still on their encounter with the woman in the large white house, the woman whose hatred and fury Leela had been able almost to taste. Her concerns, however, were more immediate.

She spun, knife in hand, and batted away a dart with a clunk of bone against metal. It flew off into the bushes. A spear then flashed toward them. Leela threw herself forward on top of the Doctor.

'Ouch! Can't you just say duck next time?'

Leela had had enough of this. 'People of the Trees! Is this
how you show your friendship for the Doctor?'

There was silence, broken only by the rustling of leaves in
the breeze. The Doctor cautiously raised his head, setting his
hat back into place. Leela crouched beside him, one hand out
for balance, the other holding her knife in readiness. She spun
at a soft footfall.

A short, grey-furred biped stood at the edge of the clearing,
watching them with large dark eyes. Small dark nostrils quivered in a short muzzle.

'Hello!' The Doctor unfolded himself from the ground.
'Don't be afraid. We mean you no harm.'

'You are not the Doc-tor,' the biped cried. 'Our foremothers
and fathers said he had white hair, like an elder!'

'I am.' He spread his hands. 'Let me prove it to you.'

'The Doctor is a Time Lord,' Leela spoke carefully. 'He –
changes.' She glanced at him, unsure if she had got that right.

'When I was here before, your elders were led by Soldea
and Eliash. They had a son, Yidor, and two daughters, Faron
and Wellomora. Wellomora had a daughter, Palamon-'

'Palamon was my ancestor!' The fur on the biped's arms
and chest bristled in excitement, or terror. 'How could you know
that?'

'He *is* the Doc-tor!' Another biped jumped out from concealment, this one white-furred. 'The *urbargalim* don't know
our names. We're just creatures to them, just things! It has to be
him.'

A crowd of bipeds burst from the trees and swung down
ladders and vines. Leela tensed, then sheathed her knife as she
realized they meant no harm. She set her teeth, though, as they
swarmed around, patting her and the Doctor and all talking at
once. At first glance they all seemed alike, but then Leela saw
that there were variations: some were taller than the others,
coming right up to her shoulder, and some had lighter fur like
the second one she had seen. None wore clothes, but all except

the youngest had a belt at their waist to carry a pouch woven from bark and either a bone knife or a short cylinder which Leela recognized as a blowpipe.

After a few minutes, one of the white-furred bipeds managed to assert some order. The crowd drew back a little and quietened.

'I am Caramir, an elder of this village and a member of the Council of Villages. Doc-tor, the Great Ones have sent you to us. We asked them to help, if they could still hear us. Now I thank them with all my strength.' The voice was lighter than those of the other bipeds who had spoken: this was a female, Leela realized. 'Forgive us that we did not know you at first. Or your companion.' The elder looked uncertainly at Leela.

'This is my friend, Leela. She is not a Dascarian,' the Doc-tor explained.

'Ah.' Caramir bowed. 'Please, honour my home.'

A little bemused, Leela followed the elder up a wooden ladder which was held together with some kind of vine. She glanced back to see the Doctor having a little trouble with his scarf, and grinned.

They reached a wide platform, about seven metres from the ground, where a number of the People lay stiffly on thin pads of what looked like woven leaves. Their eyes stared blankly upwards.

'What is wrong with them?' Leela asked. The Doctor bent over the stricken bipeds, examining them.

'They're catatonic,' he said. 'Possibly suffering from severe shock.' He straightened, looking questioningly at the elder.

'With the Great Ones, we are a whole branch,' Caramir said, her large eyes solemn. 'Without them, we are splinters. These are splinters.' She led the Doctor and Leela up another ladder to a smaller platform, fenced by a guard rail, with a hut built against the bole of the great tree. Leela noticed a bridge of vines and wooden slats fastened to the guard rail, spanning the gap to another tree.

'How many are affected?' the Doctor asked softly.

Caramir paused in the doorway of the hut. 'A hand and a half in this village, the same in other villages. Many hands altogether.' She sighed. 'The voices of the Great Ones were always faint with them. Now only one of the three still dwells with us, they hear them no longer.'

A second white-furred biped darted across the bridge to join them. The newcomer was similar in build to Caramir but had a short, stiff mane of hair along the neck. 'This is Dorakir, my mate,' Caramir explained. The male bowed, then followed them into the hut. The interior was dim, lit only by the gentle glow of a clay firepot and the light from the open door.

'Shall you sit?'

The Doctor folded himself onto one of the woven mats on the floor and Leela copied him.

Dorakir spoke. 'You had three companions before, Doc-tor. At least, so our stories say. We have handed them down from that time, so that we remember how you used the *urbargalim*'s own magic against them.'

Now Leela was on surer ground. 'There is no magic, only science. The Doctor has taught me this.'

Caramir and Dorakir looked questioningly at the Doctor. 'The Dascarian who owned this land needed money and I was able to buy it from him because of their law of *verevan*,' he explained.

The elders still looked puzzled, so Leela tried to help; the Doctor had explained *verevan* to her as they had walked to the forest. 'They believe they have a bond with the land. Even if they have riches' – she hesitated over this concept, knowing little more about it than did these small furred ones – 'they have to prove the strength of their... love... for it.' She looked at the Doctor, hoping for encouragement. 'The Doctor had a strong wish to protect you. That seemed to their machines to be a desire to protect the land. They don't understand why he...' She trailed off awkwardly, not knowing how to say it. The Doctor came to her rescue.

'They don't really think of you as being on an equal footing with themselves,' he said gently. 'So, in their eyes, I couldn't possibly have been motivated by a desire to protect you. They assumed that I must have a powerful desire to protect the land, and so they had to allow the sale.'

Caramir nodded. 'You used their magic against them, Doctor. Now we need you to help us again.'

The Doctor sat forward, an intent expression on his face. Leela felt the hairs on her arms tingle.

'Two moons ago,' explained Dorakir, 'an *urbarg* female appeared outside our village. It was the first time any of them had entered our land since you were here before, Doc-tor. She stared at us, then left. We turned to stone under the spell of her eyes, so we did not see where she went. But when we stirred at last and followed her trail, it led to the forest edge. Beyond that, we could not go. Then, last night, one of the tenders of the shrine was murdered.' Dorakir hunched forward, his hands clenched together. 'Our grandson, Culbano.' The Doctor and Leela listened as the elder told them of the burn on Culbano's back – evidence that the *urbargalim* had done this with their sorcery. The Doctor frowned when Dorakir spoke of the theft of the two idols.

'The third of the Great Ones lay in a ziajad bush,' Caramir said, taking up the tale. 'The shrine is well-guarded now, but we are destroyed anyway without all the Great Ones. Our life is in them; not just the life of this village but that of all the villages in our land. If we cannot recover them, we will all become splinters. All lie down without speech, without thought. Soon we will all go to the Place of Beyond.'

'But that's what she wants!' Leela turned to the Doctor. 'The woman with the face of hate, Doctor.'

'Yes, she did seem rather upset,' the Doctor said mildly. 'Dorakir, Caramir, the Dascarians can't drive you off your land. I have proved my claim to it and they have a strong code about property. They can't come in, either, if they're not invited – well, not without breaking their own law. They were about to declare me dead and the land forfeit, so perhaps that's why they've become a little bolder of late. But if they trespass here now, I can have them imprisoned.' He frowned. 'Aulian Thorolis must have forced that hearing, Leela. You're right. If anyone has the People's gods, it's her.' He stood abruptly. 'Could we see the shrine?'

Leela and the elders got to their feet. 'Let me conduct you,' Caramir said. She met Dorakir's gaze.

'I shall stay to tell the People,' he confirmed.

Caramir led the Doctor and Leela outside and onto the bridge Leela had noticed earlier. The elder skipped across without even touching the rails. The Doctor went next, then Leela followed, her stomach starting to see-saw as the bridge swayed. She clenched her teeth. She was a warrior of the Sevateem; she could do what the little furred one did so easily. But the bridge jolted as the Doctor stepped off onto the next platform and she had to grab quickly for the rails to steady herself. Finally she reached the platform, hoping the Doctor had not seen her stumble.

'The People are arboreal, Leela. They run across these bridges as soon as they can walk.'

'Ar– arboreal?' Leela followed him onto the next bridge more carefully.

'Tree-dwelling. That's why they have large forward-set eyes and long, grasping fingers and toes.'

Leela set her mouth. The Doctor was always trying to educate her. And he had seen her stumble; that much was obvious. They reached another platform, from which ladders headed both upward and groundward.

'This is the boundary of our village,' Caramir explained. 'We could go by the tree path but...' She eyed them both, checking their feet. 'We shall go the ground way,' she said, and swung herself onto the downward ladder. Leela followed quickly. As soon as both she and the Doctor had reached the ground, Caramir set off at a swift jog-trotting pace. They hurried after her.

'Come on Leela, this is good exercise!' the Doctor said cheerily. 'The People don't like being on the ground, so she's actually honouring us twice over.'

'Doctor, will they all become like those others we saw? Just lying there?'

'They're psychologically dependent on their gods – and maybe something more. I didn't manage to get to the bottom of it when I was here before. These voices...' The Doctor fell silent as he became lost in thought.

'Hmm.' The Doctor crouched, studying the ground beneath the platform. Leela had disappeared for the moment, scouting the area. 'Looks as if whoever stole your gods almost fell. There are two deep indentations by this side of the ladder where it shifted. That must be why they dropped the other Great One.' He straightened. 'The ziajad bush must have been quite a disincentive, but if they wanted to be sure of destroying you they had to take all your gods. I wonder why they didn't try to retrieve it?'

Caramir pointed. 'We found fresh caejel dung over there.'

'Ah!' The Doctor's eyes widened. 'I can see how the prospect of becoming a very big pussycat's dinner might have frightened them off.'

Caramir tilted her head to one side. 'You are not much like the stories say, Doc-tor. Could our ancestors have had such poor memories?'

'No, I don't think so. Where did you say the tracks led?'

'This way.' Caramir led him down the slope and showed him the print of a shod foot in the leaf litter under the trees. 'We followed them to the edge of our land. The prints of a female *urbarg*, we think, but not the same as those of the first who came here. Smaller.'

'And did that first trail lead in the same direction?'

'Yes. Both led towards a large *urbargalim* living place just beyond the forest.'

The Doctor suddenly remembered the clerk's reference to the 'present Thorolis estate' at the assignment hearing. 'Hmm. I looked older in those days.'

Caramir was initially confused by the *non sequitur*, but then realized what he meant. 'Older?' She gazed up at him.

'Your ancestors weren't mistaken, Caramir. As Leela said, I've changed since then. Three times, in fact.'

'You are a remarkable person, Doc-tor. Almost – almost like one of the Great Ones.'

'No.' The Doctor laid a hand gently on her arm. 'Never think that, Caramir. It's just the way of my... people.'

She nodded. 'As you say. I believe the Great Ones brought you here to give us the peace that we have enjoyed all these many years.' She sighed. 'If they are willing to return to us now, I pray your magic will restore it for as many more.'

Leela rejoined them. 'There are no fresh prints, Caramir. The murderer has not returned for the third god. Let us follow her trail now, while it can still be read.'

'Hmm.' The Doctor gazed up at the treetops. 'The People are protected by Dascarian law, Leela. I think I'd better try that first.'

Leela looked unconvinced. 'If we wait longer, it will be much harder to follow her tracks.'

Caramir broke in. 'The *urbargalim* living place beyond the forest: perhaps that is where the murderer came from? One of our People can guide you there.'

The Doctor shook his head. 'It won't be safe for any of your People to leave the area, Caramir.'

'If they show me where the trail heads,' insisted Leela, 'I can follow it alone. This may be a way to get proof.'

'All right,' the Doctor conceded. 'But don't tackle Aulian on your own. She probably has anti-intruder devices. If you see anything, report back to Caramir. I'm going back to the Justiciary Department.'

He could see from Leela's expression that her first impulse was to remind him that she was a warrior and scorned danger. But she had learned that lesson. 'I will be careful. Good hunting, Doctor.'

'Sorry.' The man shook his head. 'They're too distinctive.'

'Distinctive?' Zusala waved a hand at the figures on the table beside her. 'That's the whole point!'

The fence was standing with his back against the door. He had retreated there when Zusala had pulled the idols from her pack. 'Put them away. Now.' His gaze darted nervously towards the wooden figures and away again.

Exasperated, Zusala folded her arms. He was the third fence she had approached, having met with equally vehement rejections from the first two. 'I don't understand,' she said. 'A collector would pay plenty. Why are these any different from your normal merchandise; after all, your whole business is illegal!'

'I supply discriminating customers with special items,' the man said, stubbornness setting his jaw. 'They prefer to avoid petty restrictions, that's all.' He licked his lips, his gaze straying to the idols again. 'Besides, the primitives are a protected species. I know how you must have got these. I remember the history –'

'Yes, I saw those vids too,' Zusala snapped, covering for a momentary qualm. She had killed only one of them, not the whole tribe. 'I stole them while they were asleep, if that makes you feel any better. Look, everyone knows the law is only lip service. If you were caught, you'd probably get just a reprimand.'

He shook his head. 'Put them away, now.'

'It isn't that, is it?' Zusala looked from him to the idols and back again. 'You're frightened of these things, aren't you? All of you are.'

'Just get them out of here –'

'Why? For Maker's sake, why?'

'Because of what happened before, that's why! In the old days, when whole tribes of the primitives were exterminated. Those idols, those things...' He waved a finger wildly at them. 'No-one who touches those things lives for long!'

'Rubbish! What about the ones in museums –'

'Yes, museums! In glass cases. But what happened to the people who put them there, eh?' His face was flushed and beaded with sweat. 'Maker, just look at them watching us! Put them back in that pack – now!'

Shaking her head in exasperation, Zusala stuffed the idols back into her pack and left the shop. Outside, she hurried away to try another fence, the bundle bumping against her back with a monotony that became more unbearable with every step. She had to get rid of them!

Caramir regarded the row of limp bodies before her with growing sadness. They totalled two hands and three fingers now. There were too many for one platform to hold, and mats had been laid out for them in another tree. She had taken her turn at dribbling water past their lips, but how long could they live without food? She raised her head as distant whistles echoed amongst the trees again; the People of the neighbouring village speaking in the succinct, far-carrying language used to send news between communities. They told of further casualties in their own village and passed on similar messages from others.

Caramir sighed. At first, only those who had never heard the voices well had fallen away, but the strength of the People was in their wholeness. With this splintering of the tree, cohesion was being lost and even those who had previously heard well were now losing their awareness of the Great Ones. The greater the number of People who succumbed, the worse the problem grew. Eventually, even the strongest such as Caramir herself would be stricken.

'Oh, help us, Doc-tor, help us,' she whispered. She was an elder and knew that she must be strong for the People. To show despair would weaken them. She felt a hand on her shoulder and turned to see Dorakir.

'He will save us, Caramir. He can defeat the *urbargalim* magic.'

Caramir nodded. She did not speak the thought in her heart: that this might be a test of the People's faith, and one they might be unable to meet.

Leela squatted, studying the signs. The trail ended in a wide patch of scorched and flattened grass. What could have happened? Did the Dascarians have machines that flew? It was the only explanation. She stood and looked back at the forest, frowning as she thought she saw a movement between herself and the trees. She watched intently for a few moments longer, but all was still.

Turning away, she studied the bushes and clumps of trees that dotted the grassland around her. As the People had said, a house stood in the distance. It might not be Aulian's lair but, after the frustration of the lost trail, Leela needed some other challenge for her skills. Besides, she had learned that those who used machines could come to depend on them rather than on their own bodies. Perhaps the killer had flown to the house, rather than carry the idols any further? With that thought to encourage her, she set off towards it.

'I don't understand this interest in the primitives. It does you credit as a man of feeling, of course, but – '

'They are people, like you and me,' the Doctor snapped, his anger getting the better of him. He reined it in immediately, realizing that was not the way to persuade the old man. 'Doesn't it bother you that Aulian must be' – he sought the right words – 'severely disturbed, to say the least, if she's done this?'

'If. But where's the proof? Someone stole some idols. Tracks led off in the direction of her house. That's not much to go on, is it?' The Justiciar rose from his desk and paced to the window, where he stood looking out. 'Really, Doctor, I think you've been away from ordinary civilised people for too long. You must be aware of the history of the Thorolis family, given the role of your ancestor. I'm old enough to remember Aulian's grandfather, Lavick, and his sister. To have heard my parents discuss it. Their marriages, their children's lives, were blighted by it. Land-seller. It's the worst insult in the Dascarian language. Surely you haven't forgotten that? That stain has followed the family ever since.'

'That doesn't excuse what she's doing –'

'Her parents were cousins, the children of Lavick and his sister. Logical, I suppose, since no-one else would have married them. Even when her parents succeeded in starting an electronics business, certain people wouldn't deal with them. The disgrace was two generations old and yet still people whispered it behind their hands. Land-seller.' He shook his head. 'Aulian is the last of that line. I see a woman who has had a life of misery, despite the wealth she has built. Now she has failed in her dream of restoring her family's honour.'

'Justiciar –'

The old man was not to be interrupted. 'Did you hear how she acquired the place where she lives now; the estate which used to belong to the Cromadils? She had the best *verevan* of all those who applied to buy it. Why? Because it overlooked her family's former estate. That's how much the land means to her. And now you tell me she's some common criminal!'

The Doctor's frustration was nearing fever pitch. He had made insufficient allowance for the Dascarian mindset: all decency proceeded from the love of land. It followed that those with *verevan* were model citizens. 'How did the Cromadil land become vacant in the first place?'

'Oh, a most unlucky family. Over the years, a series of accidents–' The Justiciar broke off and turned to confront the Doctor, a shocked expression on his face. 'What are you implying? How could Aulian have been responsible? They were all accidents! If you're going to make wild accusations, I'll have to ask you to leave.'

'Justiciar,' the Doctor said, raising his hands. 'Of course not. No.' He realized anew how hampered he was in having to conceal the fact that Aulian's attack on the People was a direct assault on his own *verevan* qualification. 'Aulian wants the land back. Her logical first step is to get rid of the People – she detests them. No-one else has the motive to exterminate them.'

'Motive? Whether she exterminates the primitives or not, she won't affect your claim. I don't understand you, Doctor. Why this obsessive dislike of the poor woman? Surely your possession of her land is enough? Now, if you'll excuse me, I have a tribunal to attend.' He crossed to his desk and pressed a switch. 'Topani, see the Doctor out.'

Caramir bent over a still figure, holding his hand, squeezing it gently in an attempt to gain a response. 'Dorakir,' she murmured. 'Listen to the voices. They are with you.' Her mate lay unmoving, staring blankly upwards. She bowed her head on his chest.

After a while, she straightened and gently released his hand from hers.

'Elder, what do we do?' The figure of one of the People was silhouetted in the doorway, fear and despair clear in his voice.

Caramir went to him and pressed her hand on his shoulder in reassurance. 'We ask the Great Ones for their help, just as we asked them to return the Doc-tor to us. They heard us then, they will hear us now.' She hoped she sounded more sure than she felt.

'But we were more then. Many hands have fallen into this sleep and are lost to us. Your own mate –'

'We ask. If we are worthy, they will hear. Return to your home.' Caramir headed for the bridge. 'I am going to the shrine. Be calm.'

As she made her way along the tree path, she could hear

whistles rising in the distance, telling of the progressive loss of individuals from the People's bond. Her fur bristled as if a cold wind blew. Could this be the end of the People?

At the shrine, she found the guards slumped against the wall of the building, eyes vacant. She entered the hut and fell on her knees before the remaining god.

'Hear my prayer, Great One. If we have offended, forgive us. Forgive.'

It seemed that she remained kneeling, her head bowed, for a long time, crying out the word 'forgive' with her voice and her mind. Then, slowly, a feeling of comfort stole over her. There was only a faint whisper at the back of her mind now, and she could make out no distinct voice. But, despite that, she suddenly knew what she must do: she must go to meet the Doctor. She rose swiftly and bowed, then left the hut and headed off in the direction she had shown him. Perhaps he would have the answer.

Zusala set down her battered aircar by the trade entrance of Thorolis's house, aware that the woman would not want her to be seen by any other visitors. She climbed out and bent to pick up the heavy pack. Maker! She would be glad to get rid of these things. Even if Thorolis refused to pay the rest of her fee because of her bungling, that no longer seemed important. The nervousness shown by the fences she had visited must have been contagious, although she recalled that her growing unease about the idols had started even before that. She was convinced that she had left them in the pack when she had dropped, exhausted, into bed last night. Yet they had been standing right by the bed when she had woken from a horrible dream. The shock had made her forget the details of the nightmare, but it had left her with a sense of unease which had grown worse with every passing hour as she had hauled the things from one fruitless rendezvous to another, encountering edginess or outright hostility. Aulian could have them with pleasure.

As she approached the door, she was greeted by the voice of the household custodian and asked to state her business. 'Zusala,' she said nervously. 'I have a special delivery for Gentlefemme Thorolis.' After a moment, the door slid open and she went inside.

A dark form was outlined against a bright light. Zusala halted and called out nervously, 'Gentlefemme, is that you?' Behind her, the door slid shut with a startlingly loud click.

'Who do you think?' The voice was clipped but recognizably Aulian's. All the same, Zusala wished she could see the other woman's face. 'You took your time! Have you brought them?'

'Yes, but I – I had a little trouble.' Zusala fumbled with the fastenings on the pack. 'I had to get away quickly – a caejel was on my scent.'

'But you got them all.' It was a statement rather than a question.

Zusala looked up. In her growing dread of the idols, she had almost forgotten her reason for trying to sell them. She licked her dry lips. 'Gentlefemme, the idols were heavy. One fell into a ziajad bush. I would have got it, but the caejel was too near...' She trailed off, her heart thudding heavily.

'You shouldn't have left it behind. Didn't you understand me, Zusala? I said all of them.' The figure was drawing nearer, but Zusala could see only the glitter of Aulian's eyes.

She swallowed. 'I had to get away from the caejel. I'll go back if you like –'

'Now that they are alerted and have a whole band standing guard? No, I don't require that, Zusala. But you shall have what you deserve.'

'Thank you, Gentlefemme –' The words were cut off as a scarlet beam stabbed out and took Zusala in the chest. She flew back and thudded against the wall, then slid down, her head lolling.

Leela drew her knife as a faint rustle reached her ears. Someone had followed her, using the available cover with consummate skill. Now Leela withdrew further into a grove of trees near the house and waited.

Suddenly she turned and stabbed, but quickly drew back her hand as she saw grey fur and large startled eyes. The creature recoiled.

'No, it's all right,' Leela hissed. 'Do not run, Person of the Trees. I thought you an enemy.' She frowned; it was still not easy to tell the People apart, but she thought she recognized this one as the young male who had guided her to the boundary of the forest. 'You are – Woltias?'

The biped nodded. 'Yes. I wanted to get closer before I spoke. The *urbargalim* have ways of listening and seeing.'

Leela sheathed her knife. 'The Doctor said they might. Why did you follow?'

'I was a friend of Culbano – the one who was murdered.'

Leela nodded, approving. 'Let us go closer to the house. The one who killed your friend flew away in a machine, but might have come here afterwards. If luck is with us, perhaps you shall have your revenge.'

'If the Great Ones are returned, that will be reward enough. But...' Woltias hesitated. 'Yes, it would be good to bring his murderer to justice.'

They crept through the trees. Soon, they reached the far side of the grove and peered through the leaves. The house was much closer than before, but they would have to cross stretches of open ground to reach it, with only scattered clumps of bushes as cover. Leela froze as she became aware of a distant whine.

'Something comes!'

'I know,' whispered Woltias. 'We hear that noise sometimes when we are near the forest edge. Once I saw the flying thing that makes it.'

Leela nodded. 'We must watch and learn what we can.'

Soon a machine flew overhead and circled the house, disappearing behind it. The sound ceased, replaced by the twittering of insects and the soft rustling of leaves fluttering in the breeze. Leela beckoned to the young biped and they moved at a crouched run, heading for the nearest cover. When they reached it, Leela looked carefully around. There were no signs of watchers, but she had a prickling sensation at the base of her skull.

'We must circle the house,' she whispered, pointing.

They moved stealthily from one clump of bushes to the next and soon reached the rear of the house. They were still some distance away, but could see two flying machines grounded on a low platform next to a door. They had only just taken cover amongst some bushes when the door slid open. Leela's mouth tightened as she saw Aulian emerge, dragging something wrapped in dark material. Even at this distance, she knew a dead body when she saw one. Aulian opened a hatch at the rear of one of the flying machines and hauled the body inside, then returned to the house. She came back with a smaller bundle which she threw in beside the body, then closed the hatch and stepped towards the front of the machine. Annoyed, Leela realized she was going to escape. The smaller bundle must contain the gods!

A silver globe flew around the side of the house and halted in front of Aulian. Leela saw the woman speaking to it, but she was too far away to distinguish the words. Then the globe shot away and Aulian climbed into the flying machine.

'We have to tell the Doctor,' Leela whispered. She turned to Woltias, just in time to see a red ray stab out of the air above them and strike him in the chest. The young biped fell back into the bushes. Leela was reaching for her knife when a flash of green suddenly filled her eyes...

'Doc-tor.'

'Hmm? Caramir, I didn't expect you to be waiting.'

'I had a...' She hesitated. 'The voices of the Great Ones are less clear to me now, Doc-tor, but I felt that they wanted me to come here and wait for you.'

'Things are no better, then?' They began to walk back to the village.

'No, much worse. News from other villages has reached us; it is the same there too. If the Great Ones do not return to us soon...' She sighed. 'What of your mission, Doc-tor? Did you see the *urbarg* you sought?'

'Yes. I'm afraid though that... well, it's bad news there as well. He wouldn't believe that Aulian was behind the theft of your gods.'

Caramir shook her head. 'The *urbargalim* do not know jus-tice, Doc-tor. Or, if they do, they give it only to each other. It was only to be expected. But I thank you for your effort.' She halted suddenly and looked back.

The Doctor frowned, listening. A mechanical hum could be heard, faint at first but steadily growing louder. Caramir tugged his sleeve and darted behind a tree, but the Doctor stood his ground as a silver globe swung into view and approached. He recognized the device as it halted and hovered before him: a sophisticated version of the 'roving eye' – a mobile extension of the household guardian of any wealthy Dascarian. There was a sinking sensation somewhere below his two hearts as he real-ized why it must be here.

'What do you have to say to me, Aulian?'

The tinny metal voice answered. 'Your physiognomy con-forms to that of the individual known as the Doctor. Voice scan confirms ID. Message from my patron. If you wish your friend back alive, bring the third idol. This unit will guide you to the location.'

'She's got Leela?'

'Failure to comply will mean the woman's death.'

Caramir crept out from behind the tree. 'If you desire the third Great One, Doc-tor, you may have her.'

'I can't ask you to give up the only remaining –'

'We are as dead with one as with none,' Caramir said calmly. 'If it will save the life of your friend, let it be so.'

The Doctor turned to the machine. 'I have to fetch it.'

'Permitted. Do not delay. This unit awaits your compliance.'

The Doctor hurried back through the trees with Caramir. When at length they reached the shrine, he gently took the idol under his arm. 'Thank you, Caramir.'

'Take care, Doc-tor. The *urbargalim* are treacherous.'

He nodded and strode off. Caramir watched him go, then pursed her lips and gave a rising sequence of whistles. Soon, the sound was taken up, far off among the trees, as the signal was passed to the next village. Caramir sat down to wait for the People to come.

Cold stone struck chill against the bare skin of Leela's arm. Cautiously she opened her eyes a little. She could see a dusty, litter-strewn floor and a grey, cracked wall with crates piled against it.

'You look uncomfortable like that.'

Leela sprang to her feet, her knife fitting smoothly into her hand. The fool had overlooked her weapon! Determination burned in her eyes as she advanced –

And flung up her arm as she was assailed by a brilliant flash of green light. She staggered back, the knife slipping from her numbed hand, then halted, blinking. When her vision cleared, she could see Aulian, smiling.

'If you hadn't rushed forward like that, I could have warned you.'

'What – what was that?' Cautiously, Leela bent to pick up her knife, keeping her attention on the other woman.

'A forcefield – if you understand what I mean?'

Leela nodded slowly. It was invisible, but not unlike the black wall she remembered from her own planet. There were tall stands spaced out in a diagonal line before her; these must be the things which made the wall. She looked around. She was standing in one corner of a large room which stretched away into grey distance between stout pillars. Cool light shone in strips along the ceiling. A battered table was placed nearby and on it stood two wooden figures, their faces calm and wise. Leela had the odd sensation that they were awaiting some expected event. A few paces from the table stood a gleaming metal pedestal like the one she had seen in the place of law. Above it was an image of tangled trees with sunlight filtering through the leaves. The sight made her realize that the room had no windows. Somehow she sensed they were underground.

'We're in my family's old home – or what's left of it,' Aulian explained. 'The cellar.'

'Where is Woltias?'

'Who?'

'The Person of the Trees – the grey one who was with me.'

'Oh, that.' Aulian was watching the image above the pedestal. Leela remembered the red ray which had come from the sky. One of the flying silver globes must have done it.

'You killed him!'

'Don't be so sentimental.' The image changed as she spoke, to show another area of the forest. It drew Leela's gaze, and suddenly she realized whom Aulian was expecting. The picture dissolved to be replaced by the face of an attractive young man.

'The mobile is coming into scanner range now, Gentlefemme.'

'Good. Give me the visual again.'

The young man's face transformed into a view of the trees. A glinting silver object bobbed forward, then a branch swayed, pushed aside by a hand. The Doctor appeared, carrying something under one arm. Leela clenched the hilt of her knife.

'Your friend has brought your ransom.' Aulian crossed to the table. 'Not much to look at are they? Perhaps you need all three to be brought together to get the full effect.' She chuckled and turned back to the computer. 'Admit him.' Leela did not like the look of her smile.

The trees rustled as the People climbed among their branches. Grey figures swung down to the ground and gathered below the shrine to leave room for new arrivals. Waiting for them to assemble, Caramir listened to the whispers that lurked beneath thought. The voices of the gods had always been strong with her – even when two of them had been taken far away, she had not lost them altogether. Now she sensed that all three were together again, and much closer.

At last she judged that most of those from the nearest villages had arrived. She spoke in the whistling tongue that carried so well among the trees. 'Called you here to help Doc-tor. The Great Ones surely wish him well, even if we have angered them.' A tense silence received the notes. 'Only you of the nearest villages can help. Others too far to reach here in time. Fix your thoughts on the Great Ones, beseech them to help Doc-tor.' She fell silent, but around her she sensed the concentration against the soft rustling of the leaves and the stealthy footfalls of the last stragglers. The Doctor was in physical contact with the third Great One; already she could feel that on some deep level he was entering rapport with the People. She closed her eyes and joined her efforts to theirs.

Leela watched with frustration as the metal panel slid shut behind the Doctor. He must realize this was a trap, yet his stance showed only a calm wariness. 'Well, I have to congratulate you on fixing things up around here, Aulian. But don't you think you should go home?'

'This is my home, Doctor, although your family has allowed it to fall into ruin. I merely repaired a few essentials. My cursed ancestor gambled away the money yours paid him for the land, just as he squandered the family fortune. But some good came of it. We were forced into electronics for a living.' She gestured to the equipment beside her. 'I have rebuilt our fortunes, but I started out as a technician.'

'Yes, you've installed some impressive new gadgets. But it

still isn't your home, Aulian.'

'It will be, soon enough. I see you've brought the third idol.'

'Hmm? Oh, yes, this.' He glanced down at the object tucked under his arm as if noticing it for the first time. 'Yes, the People kindly lent it to me.' He looked up. Only a widening of his eyes told Leela that he had seen the gun in Aulian's hand.

'Put it down with the others.'

'I'd like you to release Leela first.'

'Put it down.'

The Doctor shrugged, then crossed to the table and set the figure carefully down beside the others. It seemed to Leela that the three dark faces had fixed their gaze on Aulian. Of course, they were only carvings, but she felt she would not want their gaze upon *her*. There was a peculiar feeling in the room, or perhaps it was just the effect of being so close to the forcefield. She stepped back into the corner, but the feeling persisted.

'Stand clear, Doctor,' instructed Aulian.

The Doctor remained by the table, frowning. 'If you're going to do what I think you're –'

'All right, Doctor, stay there if you want to be fried too. It's all the same to me.'

'Because you have to dispose of the witnesses?'

'Only if you force me to.' Leela tensed as she saw Aulian's knuckles clench whitely on the gun. 'Otherwise, I'll pull a few strings to arrange another *verevan* test for you. Since your so-called *verevan* depends on the primitives, and since they won't survive without their precious gods, the Justiciary will assign the land to me.'

'Aulian, think what you're doing. The People are individuals just like you, intelligent beings.'

Leela shifted uneasily as the hairs on the nape of her neck and her arms prickled into life. There was another danger here, something more than the pointing gun. The Doctor's head moved a fraction and she saw his eyes scan the room: he sensed it too. Could that fool Aulian feel nothing?

Aulian's heart beat faster, her pulse filling her throat so that she could hardly breathe. Only her habitual control kept her from revealing her nervousness to the fool standing in front of her. Perhaps not such a fool, if he had realized that she was going to get rid of him and his friend. What were two more deaths, when she had killed so many?

Her gaze drifted to the three idols lined up in a row on the table. Lifeless bits of wood. Not much to look at. But if those vermin believed that they would die without them, that was good enough. It was strange, though, the way their faces almost appeared to have an intelligence. Just a silly fancy –

Her arm suddenly jerked involuntarily. The Doctor stepped forward, but froze again as she pointed the gun back in his direction. 'Don't move!' Her breath was becoming steadily faster and shallower.

'I thought that was what you wanted me to do?'

Aulian steadied her arm with her other hand. Shoot him, that was all she had to do. The room suddenly dipped sideways. She shook her head, refusing to give way to the giddiness. Around her, it seemed that the light had grown a little dimmer. She thought that she heard a faint rustling of leaves, or was it voices?

The Doctor took another step forward. Aulian raised the gun, but her thumb slipped off the trigger button. 'Stay where you are!' She retreated, trying to find the trigger again. It was so dark in here now, and the whispering was getting louder, though the words were unclear. She must shoot him. But first she had to shut out that mumble of voices. Her hands rose to cover her ears, but still the voices came, louder, louder, all jumbled together, talking over each other. She let out a gasp of pain and terror. 'No.' Then she screamed. 'No–o–o!'

The Doctor darted towards her. Leela stepped forward involuntarily, then halted, remembering the barrier. She saw Aulian suddenly snatch her hands down, fumble with the gun and –

There was a blinding flash and a howl, abruptly cut off. Leela was propelled backward and fell heavily. After a moment, she found herself sitting on the floor, the wall at her back. She tried to open her eyes, but her vision swam. 'Doctor! Doctor, are you all right? I – I can't...' Fear gripped her. She remembered their fight against the Rutans. Had she escaped blindness then, only to suffer it now?

'I'm all right, Leela.' The Doctor sounded weary, subdued. Leela rubbed her eyes, conscious of moisture on her face. 'No, don't, you'll only make them worse.' There were footsteps, then she felt a touch on her face. She flinched, but quickly realized that the Doctor was simply wiping away her tears with a cloth. 'You seem to be making a habit of this. Just blink a little. That's it. You'll be all right.'

Relieved, Leela found that she could see him crouching over her, though a red light overlaid his features. 'What happened?'

'She fired as I knocked her down. The beam struck the forcefield and reflected straight back.'

Leela's eyes widened. She remembered the mirror that the Doctor had used to destroy the machine of the Tesh. At least her vision had cleared now, but there was a strange burning smell in the room and the air was wreathed with smoke. 'Doctor, are you on fire?'

'Hmm? Oh.' He brushed the right-hand side of his head. A plume of fine, dry dust drifted away; the remains of some crisped curls. 'I was travelling faster than she was. The beam caught her, vaporized her. And the blowback shorted out the field and most of the circuitry, though luckily it held just long enough to protect you.'

'Protect?' Leela rubbed the back of her head, then climbed to her feet and bent to pick up her knife. 'The gods are safe, Doctor?'

'Yes. The question is...' He crossed to the computer pedestal, which now displayed no image, and pulled off a plate in its side. 'Can we get out of here?'

Leela watched anxiously as the Doctor rummaged about inside the pedestal. She did not relish the prospect of dying trapped in this windowless box. The only hopeful sign was that the overhead lighting still worked.

'Ah, that should –' There was a sudden grating sound and the door panel began to move. It slid open a short way, but then became stuck. 'Oh well, you're a slim girl, aren't you?'

Relieved, Leela headed for the opening, but the Doctor's voice halted her. 'Haven't you forgotten something? I can't carry all three of them myself.'

The land of the People was behind them now and the TARDIS in view ahead, waiting for them in the shade of a tree. Leela frowned. 'The People's gods,' she began. 'Are they –' She hesitated, trying to find a suitable substitute for the word that had first come to her. 'Are they a thing of strange science?'

The Doctor halted by the door and reached into his pocket. 'The People have an emotional bond, between individuals and villages,' he said slowly. 'Perhaps so many years of treating their gods with reverence...' He fitted the key into the door and pursed his lips. 'I wondered about that last time I was here, but I could hardly carve off a piece of one of them and analyse it. That mystery will just have to wait... for another time.' Leela returned his smile and followed him into the TARDIS.

Caramir nodded to the young female kneeling before the shrine and went inside, bowing to the Great Ones. They had been restored with full ceremony to their rightful place. Once again they lived here in peace, as they had done for generation after generation, the wood of their physical forms becoming darker with each loving polish at the season of hereash blossom. All was as it should be, yet something had changed: her understanding. All her life, Caramir had known the soft rustle at the back of her mind as the voices of the Great Ones. Now she realized that it was the combined essence of the thoughts of her

People, heard only through their bond with their gods.

Caramir had believed the Great Ones angry, but perhaps this had been a test of the People's strength. The dwelling places of the Great Ones were made of hereash, the sacred wood, cut only when they indicated that their old forms were worn and needed replacing. There was a strange word which had seeped from the Doctor's mind during his rapport with the People: *catalyst*. Caramir wasn't sure why but she associated it with the physical forms of the Great Ones: the forms that focused the People's love for each other, their bond. That bond had been tested, and the People had been equal to the test.

Caramir bowed to the gods and left the shrine, turning her face to the sunshine. 'Bless you, Doc-tor.'

Timeshare

By Vanessa Bishop

'Just look at this!'

'Mm?'

'Well, you could at least look!'

'What's wrong with it?' The Doctor peered closer. 'Or perhaps I should ask, what is it?'

'You should know – you left it there!'

'I give up. Tell me.'

'It's a sandwich.'

'Of course! I knew all along really. What's in it?'

Taking a deep breath, Peri briefly wafted the squidgy contents of her hand beneath her nostrils. 'It's foul, Doctor – almost putrefied.'

'Where did you find it?'

'In your coat pocket.'

'Ah.'

He'd lost interest again. Strangulation was too good for him when he was in one of these moods. He'd be vague...

'Sandwich pocket, did you say?'

...uninterested...

'Look, not now, Peri – I'm busy.'

...and as arrogant as ever...

'What are you doing going through my coat pockets anyway?' Raising his voice over the hum of the TARDIS, he snapped shut the book that had totally possessed his soul for the last hour and glared at the dark-haired girl standing defiantly opposite him.

'You asked me to,' she pouted. 'You asked for a pen from your coat pocket. So being the kind, obliging person I always am, I searched this multicoloured monstrosity inside out. I even searched all these too,' she added, pointing to three other coats which hung on the hatstand in the corner.

Hand outstretched, the Doctor waited impatiently. 'Well?'

'No pen.'

'No pen? What d'you mean, no pen?' Pushing her aside, he scooped up the coat and began rummaging ferociously through the folds of material. 'No pen? No pen, indeed!'

Peri looked on, shaking her head at his increasing agitation. 'I told you – it isn't there. I found a piece of screwed-up paper, a spoon, a sandwich, this little fellow...' She picked up a small teddy bear from the chair onto which the contents of the pockets had been tipped. 'Cute bear, Doctor.'

'Yes, all right, thank you.' The Doctor waved at her to be quiet. In an attempt to look busy and change the subject, he wiggled his fingers demonstratively over the pile of objects, eventually homing in like the arm of a crane to pluck one out. 'My bicycle clip. I wondered where that had got to.'

Peri stifled a laugh. 'You on a bike? Are you serious?'

Indignantly, he continued to twist the clip round in his fingers. 'I shall ignore that last remark.'

Perhaps she was a little rude to him at times, and she knew it was somewhat childish, but his ample size and distinct aversion to exercise never failed to amuse her. Leaning over the chair, she plucked out a piece of crumpled blue notepaper which, when unfolded, produced a neat square onto which something had been messily scribbled. She proceeded to read aloud: 'FIRST WEEK OF NOVEMBER – 0262 by 04 by 05.'

'Let me see that.'

'It was in that green velvet jacket on the stand.'

Seconds later, the Doctor was himself studying the cryptic message: 'First week of November... First week of November...' Over and over he mouthed the words, trying to make himself remember what they meant. 'Ahh, yes, maybe...'

'What? D'you know what it means?'

'Maybe... yes... no.' He shook his head resignedly. 'But these coordinates seem familiar somehow...'

'Oh, is that what they are?'

'Of course that's what they are,' came the sigh in response.

'Well...' – Peri hated it when he corrected her, this ability he had to make her feel about two inches tall – 'if you're so sure, why don't you try them out?' He stared at her. 'Obvious, I would have thought,' she finished.

'I was just about to do so. Now – hold that and read the numbers out clearly.'

Peri did so, one by one, trying to ignore that annoying, crowded feeling as the Doctor peered over her shoulder.

'Zero five,' she concluded. 'That's the last one, Doctor, so you can stop looking now.'

'I was not looking,' he protested. 'And that...' he tapped the paper with his forefinger '...is not a five.'

'Yes it is! Can't you see?'

'I'm a little myopic in the left.'

'And mule-headed in the right!'

'That, my dear Peri, is a six, not a five.'

'Rubbish! The writing's appalling I know, but that's definitely a 5. I'd bet... well, I'd bet a lot of money on it.'

'Then you'd be a very poor young lady.' The Doctor threw her one of his twinkling 'I'm right' expressions and set the final coordinate... as a six.

Heaving back his shoulders, the Doctor took in a lungful of air.

'Ah! That wonderful English aroma, Peri. Taste it! There's nothing quite like it.'

Peri ran her hand along the top of an elaborately fashioned wrought-iron gate, disturbing the rainwater that had settled upon it. She shook her hand dry.

'Typically English, I suppose,' she said.

A hearty pat on the back threw her forward. 'Come on, Peri – a bit of rain never hurt anyone. Unless you're Dr Foster. And as I am not he, and we are in North Devon, not Gloucester,

there's very little to worry about.' His chest thrust out majesti-
cally, he stood upright, surveying the scene before him. '1929...'

'If the readings are right,' put in Peri dubiously. His exces-
sive confidence was certainly not shared by her.

'A lot happened in 1929 you know, Peri.'

'Such as?'

'Ooh... there was...'

'Yes?'

'Well, it was a very important time for...'

Arms folded, she eyed him with amusement. 'There was,'
she started, 'the Wall Street Crash, the St Valentine's Day Mas-
sacre...'

Suddenly he frowned. 'Exactly! Don't you know anything?'

'Who lives in the house?'

Scrabbling in his pocket, the Doctor pulled out the gradually decaying piece of paper that had brought them here. 'I wish
I could remember.' Lifting back his head, he concentrated on
the house. A typical, two-storey country house – quite pleasant
really, if one happened to like that sort of thing.

'Did you arrange to meet anyone here? An appointment, or
tea – something like that?' Making any sort of suggestion,
thought Peri, was better than standing around in the damp looking vague, like some people. Running her fingers around the
metal swirls of the gate, she stood waiting for a response. It
eventually came in unexpected form.

'Ding dong!'

She shook her head. 'Sorry? I don't understand...'

'Look!' The Doctor thrust a finger reflexively towards the
gate. 'H.O.P. Now, that rings a bell!' Even by twisting her head
sideways, Peri was unable to get the Doctor's gist until, eventually, he flung open the gate. Viewed from the front, three initials could be seen fashioned within it. 'H.O.P.! See?'

'My bells are dead quiet,' sighed his companion, exasperated by the non-logical track his mind appeared to be follow-

ing. 'So? What does it stand for, Doctor?'

'It'll come. Don't bombard me with questions while I'm thinking! Come on!' He marched off towards what appeared to be the front door.

Peri followed behind, breaking into a run at intervals to keep up. As the Doctor stopped abruptly outside the door, she crashed into him and was rewarded with a 'face'. 'If you can stand up straight,' he began haughtily, 'we'll continue. Observe.' He pointed to the polished brass door-knocker within which appeared, once again, the initials H.O.P.

'Here Open Please!' joked Peri brightly. No response. After what seemed like an age of muttering and cursing to himself, the Doctor suddenly seemed to come alive with excitement.

'Holiday Opportunity Promotions! That's it! This, my dear Peri, is an H.O.P. property! Now there's a name to conjure with!' Before Peri had time to ask her inevitable question, the Doctor had produced three ping-pong balls and briefly illustrated his comment. When there was a mystery without evident danger, the Doctor would attack it with a childlike excitement.

'You've dropped one!'

'I beg your pardon? Oh!' He retrieved the escaped ball.

Peri asked her question: 'Who are these H.O.P. guys?'

'These "H.O.P guys" ' – he threw her a disgusted sideways look to express his feelings at her choice of phraseology – 'are what you would call timeshare operators.'

'Timeshare?' Peri was surprised. 'So this house is a timeshare?'

'Indeed. Although, seeing as we're in 1929, holiday home might be more apt.'

'But I thought...' She carried on thinking to herself, fully aware that the Doctor wasn't listening, preferring to mutter to himself whilst nosing through the letterbox.

'Strange – I hadn't realized that any of these were still operational. As far as I was aware, the Time Lords had closed them all down.'

'The Time Lords? Doctor... what are you doing?'

He had his hand firmly jammed in the letterbox. 'Just checking in case there was a key.' The hand, now removed, glowed a
raw shade of red.

Peri looked the building up and down. 'It's funny, Doctor,
but I always thought that timeshares were villas on the Algarve
or the Costa del Sol, something more glamorous than this. My
aunt had an apartment in Corfu...'

'Ah, but this, Peri, is no ordinary timeshare!' The Doctor's
theatrical announcement made her wonder whether it was safe
to question him further or better to give up now whilst the going was good. However, curiosity and all that. The Doctor was
fingering the blue notepaper again. 'The next problem, my dear
Watson, is how to get ourselves inside.'

'Try knocking?' suggested Peri, wondering if perhaps she
had missed something. 'There's a doorbell too – look.' It was
getting cold and she pulled her long, bottle-green coat tighter
around her. 'I'd like to know why we've landed here in the first
place. I mean, who lives in a house like this?'

The Doctor raised a finger in the air and eyed her playfully.
He appeared to be enjoying this little game. 'Let's look at the
evidence. The coordinates. The words "FIRST WEEK OF
NOVEMBER". And the familiar initials "H.O.P.". What does
that tell you?'

'Not a lot,' came the mumbled reply.

'Engage your brain! Perhaps someone's trying to tell me
something!'

'Well have you ever bought a timeshare property, Doctor?'

'I? Buy a timeshare?' The indignation of his expression
grew until she hurriedly retracted the suggestion. 'I would
never be so gullible, so imprudent, so... oxlike! Buy a timeshare
indeed! Me?' He leaned across to his shivering companion
and smiled a smile befitting a maiden aunt. 'Nevertheless, don't

you think, considering the evidence, that it might just be possible that I myself possess the key to this house?'

Peri shrugged. 'I suppose.'

'Then there's not a lot of point knocking on the door, is there, because I won't be in!' Peri delved into her coat pockets, retrieving a pair of woolly mittens. She felt a tap on her shoulder. 'Peri? What has twelve feet and eight hundred pairs of shoes?' Her face was as blank as it was cold. '*Me*!'

'What?'

'I do!' He nudged her in a jokey fashion. 'The key will be where I keep all my keys – in my shoes... probably.'

He was doing it again, maddening her to the point of screaming until she lost the ability to do so. 'But you've got hundreds of pairs of shoes, Doctor! You've just said so.'

'Then the sooner you start looking, the sooner we'll get inside and you can stop your teeth chattering in that irritating manner!'

The TARDIS door slammed shut, sending several birds fluttering nervously out of the surrounding trees. Across the dewy grass, her boots growing damper and her footsteps heavier, marched Peri, firmly gripping two bulging carrier bags and muttering darkly to herself. The contents of all manner of shoes had been uptipped into the bags after individual consideration had proved too time-consuming. Ahead of her, whistling merrily, strolled the firmly fleshed figure at whom her mutterings were directed.

'All right back there, Peri?' the Doctor hollered cheerfully.

'Oh, fine... just fine!' she called back, face like thunder. 'You just carry on.'

'Good!' Moments later, a loud curse of frustration caused him to glance casually back again. 'Problems?'

'Wretched handle's broken!' snapped Peri, scrabbling to restore the spillage to the flimsy plastic bag. 'Am I sick of keys!

And your boot cupboard stinks! Haven't you ever heard of odour eaters?'

'Hah!' scoffed the Doctor. 'My feet do not smell! It must have been a touch of damp or something.'

'Well, you ought to get and undamp it then, cos that was two hours of pure cheese. Here.' Joining him once again at the front door, she handed him the broken bag of keys. 'Though I don't know what kind of door you'd open with this,' she continued, fishing into the other bag and pulling out a glistening crystal about the size of a golf ball.

Snatching it, the Doctor held it up as though examining it. 'That is a most important key on the planet Zircona,' he mused, trying to sound authoritative. 'But of no use here. Next.' An exceptionally large jailer's key was offered and, again, discarded. 'Next.'

Big keys, small keys, some as big as your head – all were tried, but all to no avail. A rubber-duck shaped key which looked for all the world like a common or garden rubber duck was brought out. 'Now that's not what it seems, you know, Peri,' he said, and it was hastily put away again.

The words 'gonna be here all night' flashed regularly through Peri's mind until, at last, that glorious sight greeted them – a key with the letters H.O.P. imprinted upon it. 'Aha! At last!' grinned the Doctor as he triumphantly jammed the key into the lock. The door opened.

They found themselves in a small lobby.

'At least it's warm in here,' said Peri, stamping her feet on the mat. 'Wow!' She surveyed the decorative gilt wallpaper and mahogany panelling. 'Nice place you've got here, Doctor.'

The Doctor screwed up his face and tipped his head a little to one side.

'Hmm. Not really to my taste.'

'Yes – it is rather elegant, isn't it?'

'Charming! I invite you into my house and all I get is abuse!'

'Nice wallpaper, nice carpet, nice lampshade...' Peri continued.

'Never liked that word "nice". Too obligatory, too meaningless.'

'Nice mirror. Hey, you've got a gas meter too. I once jammed up my grandma's gas meter by putting a button into it...'

'Only to be expected,' smiled the Doctor, 'from you.' His smile soon disappeared as Peri displaced some of her weight onto his toe. He winced a little and, with his hands, swivelled her head towards the meter. 'Anyway, it's not a gas meter. It's something else... in disguise!'

Folding her arms, Peri continued mischievously: 'Oh I see. So it's really a Rembrandt...'

'No...'

'...or a cuckoo clock...'

'Not exactly, no.'

'...but whatever it is or isn't, it's pretending not to be.'

'Mmm...'

'Okay – so what is it then?'

The Doctor now looked a little confused himself. Scratching his mop of sandy hair, he sought for an explanation. He let out a little gasp, followed by a considered 'Mmm' and finally, a short, precise cough. Then...

'Tick tock boiiiing!' He pointed to the meter. 'Makes a good sound when you turn the dial.' Still Peri waited. 'It's a time meter. A meter. For time. You see, Peri, an H.O.P. timeshare property exists in many different time periods, all at the same time.'

'No ordinary timeshare right?' She nodded slowly. So far so good.

'Right. Take this lobby, for example. How many people can you see?'

'Is this a trick question?' asked Peri.

'Just answer!'

'OK – just the two of us, I guess.'

'Indeed. But this lobby is probably full of people, all occupying the same space but in different time periods. We're in the year 1929 and, so it seems, alone in it.'

'Got it. I think. Sounds a pretty neat idea, if a little creepy!'

'Neat? Neat? Hmm. The Time Lords didn't think it was neat.' He looked up from fiddling with a patch of loose wallpaper. 'No, they weren't impressed at all.'

'You mentioned something about them closing these places down?'

'Did I? Yes, well they did. Or so I thought. Can't have people messing around with time.'

'You do.'

'That's different. I'm a professional. No, these people...'

'These H.O.P. guys...'

'Yes, these H.O.P. guys,' he continued, 'as you insist on calling them, had agents selling timeshare properties in all time periods. But instead of selling weeks and keeping them booked with each passing year as is, I believe, the normal practice on this planet, they would sell all weeks and keep them booked in all years, but all at the same time. They gained quite a reputation as time racketeers, you know.'

'Where'd they get the houses from?' asked Peri.

'Anywhere. The company would simply buy up appropriate properties and convert them into timeshares using their own technology and time travel know-how. Then along comes the agent, who seeks out an interested party, sells them a timeshare and leaves with his pockets full of money. Pity I didn't think of it myself, actually.'

'Sounds to me like the Time Lords were jealous! Did the company make a lot of money?'

'Make a lot of money? They were sitting on a gold mine! They would bank the money paid in each time period and then pick it up a week later, with accumulated interest, three hundred years down the timeline!'

Peri let out a whistle. 'Some interest! But if the Time Lords were so anti the whole idea, how come you've got a timeshare?'

'There's your riddle of the Sphinx, Peri. I just don't know.'

He picked at the wallpaper again. 'Poor. Very poor. Have I made some semblance of sense to you?'

'For you, Doctor, that was almost straightforward.'

'Yes, it was, wasn't it?'

'What happens if you die?'

'Are you being theological or do you mean, what happens to your timeshare?'

'Yes... I mean, the last one.'

The Doctor loomed closer to his cowering assistant in headmasterly fashion. 'Then speak properly, in correct sentences! Make yourself clear! Inheritance, my dear girl, inheritance. People can leave their properties to family, friends, dogs' and cats' homes, whatever. Then the inheritors have to continue making maintenance payments.' She was looking blank again. 'Maintenance,' he repeated, looking fatigued. 'For this sort of thing,' he added, pointing once more at the wallpaper.

'Look, this lobby is very charming and all that, but I'd like to see the rest of the house, if that's OK.' Stepping forward, she placed a hand on the round, brass doorhandle.

'*Stop*!' The Doctor was rigidly poised, pointing to the doorhandle with all the flexibility of a wooden signpost. 'It won't open.'

'I haven't tried it yet!' objected Peri.

'It won't! It can't! We-haven't-put-the-money-in-the-meter!' he sang boisterously, to the tune of something which sounded vaguely music-hall-esque.

He really was enjoying this far too much, thought Peri; letting out the rules of the game one by one. 'Sure, I forgot. We have to pay for the lighting and stuff, don't we?' she said.

'Ah! That's exactly the impression they want to give. But...'

'Let me guess. It's something else... in disguise!'

'Yes!' The Doctor clasped his hands together in childlike delight. 'That's it! You think you're paying for the amenities when in fact, what you're actually paying for is the use of your seven days' worth of time in the house... as long as you're registered, of course. Registration was always very strictly controlled, you know, Peri. The company might have been criminal, but they certainly weren't irresponsible. Imagine the opportunities for error, with the timelines so fully booked up. It wouldn't have been in their interests to make a blunder with all that money at stake.'

'So, are you registered, Doctor?' Peri waited for the realisation and the long, drawn-out 'Aahh' but, surprisingly, they didn't come. Instead, he began digging into his pocket jovially.

'Of course I'm registered! I must be. Remember the evidence. The note that popped us down here. And I recognized the H.O.P. initials. Oh, and why would I have a key if I wasn't supposed to be here?'

'Heaven only knows.'

'Here we are!' He waved some large bronze coins at her as if about to perform a trick. Having consulted a small notice which indicated the required amount, he placed them in the slot of the meter. 'In they go. You'd better leave this to me, Peri. Considering your past record, you might jam it up. And I'll ignore that,' he added as he caught the reflection of her poked-out tongue in the glass of the lobby door. 'Right, there we are.' He twisted the doorhandle with successful results. 'Well, come on then. And don't forget those carrier bags.'

What a pleasant surprise. It was warm, comfortable and, in keeping with the decor observed in the lobby, tasteful. The gaudy orange sofa and luminous green drapes which, in Peri's imagination, would have dominated this house had it belonged solely to the Doctor, were fortunately nowhere to be found. Instead, the large, open hall was furnished in rich browns and warm spicy shades. A polished wooden staircase reached down to the middle, and Peri's eyes followed it back up to a landing, of which little more could be seen than a door and several pictures. She smiled, unbuttoned her coat and mentally earmarked an armchair as hers.

'Now, what's that, I wonder?' mused the Doctor.

Two large strides saw him bent over a small table, on which was placed an open book. 'Ah – the signing-in book. Interesting.'

Peri peered round the side of the table. A large hand shot out in front of her, almost socking her in the face. 'Pen!' it demanded. 'Quickly! Pen! Pen!'

'I already told you – I don't have a pen!' She glanced at the table. 'Try the penholder!'

'What? Oh...' Grabbing the pen, the Doctor continued to pore over the book. 'Look at this, Peri – the date.'

She leaned forward to see that the book had been left open between the last week of October and the first week of November. 'First week of November,' she mused. 'At least that bit ties up.'

Together they continued to absorb the page. Apparently, the first week of November had been taken consistently from 1900 by a Mr Woodruff. Tracing his scribbled signature down the page, year by year, eventually revealed something far more interesting. Mr Woodruff's last week spent at the property had been in 1920. Underneath his final signature, Peri slowly read the words...

'*Bequeathed to the Doctor – 1920.*'

The Doctor shook his head as if trying to shake water from his ears. 'Well, upon my sword!' he announced. '"Bequeathed to the Doctor,"' he repeated, trying to make some sense of the words. 'Bequeathed by whom, I wonder?'

'Did you know this Mr Woodruff?' asked Peri.

'Never even heard of the fellow. How very strange.'

Peri was reading again. 'Well, it doesn't look as if you've been here before.' She ran her finger down the eight blank boxes alongside the dates that followed the mysterious bequest. 'Hold on.' Squeezed in, almost unnoticed, at the bottom, was the final box of the page... 1929. 'I thought we were in 1929.'

The Doctor glared at her. 'We *are* in 1929.' He followed Peri's finger to where it rested. 'Ah.' Beside the date – 1929 – were signed two words: *The Doctor*.

'Well?' asked Peri. 'Are we here already? Are you here already? Or are we in a totally different time from the one you said?'

'Hold on a minute! That's not my handwriting!' The Doctor looked up triumphantly and then, prodding the page in time with every syllable, reiterated emphatically: 'That-is-not-my-hand-wri-ting!'

'Should have guessed.' Peri took another look. 'It's actually legible.'

'Another mystery!' The Doctor stood upright again. 'Pettifogger, Peri!'

'Eh?'

The Doctor circled her, throwing his arms up in the air at every new word that came to mind. 'Bamboozler! Hoodwinker! Defrauder! Imposter!' He faltered and his voice trailed off to a whisper. 'Peri! There's a man at the top of the stairs!'

Quickly composing herself, Peri turned and raised her hand uncertainly in an attempt at a wave. 'H- hi.'

'May I enquire what you're doing here?' The onlooker seemed almost as wary as Peri herself, although his drawn, grey complexion probably contributed to this. A man in his late forties who wore navy blue pyjamas beneath a dressing-gown of burgundy paisley was a man, thought the Doctor, to be reasoned with. After all, no man could be unreasonable in carpet slippers.

'Now, whom might I be addressing?' enquired the Doctor.

'Shouldn't I be asking that of you, sir?'

'I...' began the Doctor. Peri sighed. He always enjoyed this bit far too much. 'I am known as the Doctor. Oh, and this is Peri, of course,' he added. 'And, if I'm not mistaken, this is my week.'

'Ah.' The gent's face appeared to drain a shade greyer than before, and Peri feared he might actually pass out. 'Oh dear. I'm awfully sorry. I think I'd better come down.' Smoothing his thinning auburn hair across his forehead, he grasped hold of the bannister and began a steady descent.

'Can you manage?' asked Peri, concerned at his haggard appearance.

The man waved a hand. 'Yes... thank you. I'm fine – just a trifle stiff after being confined to bed for so long.'

'Well, OK – if you're sure.'

'Your accent – are you...'

'American,' Peri confirmed.

'I have a cousin who's American.'

'Oh, I am sorry!' commiserated the Doctor.

On reaching the bottom stair, the man breathed a sigh of relief. 'Thank you for being so terribly patient. Now, I fear I owe you an explanation, and another apology.' He led them through an archway into a large drawing room and seated himself in one of the armchairs. The Doctor took the one that Peri had wanted, leaving her to perch meekly on the edge of the sofa. 'We're the tenants from the last week of October, you see.'

'We?' questioned the Doctor.

'My sister Milly – Camilla, that is – and myself, of course.'

'And you are?' persisted the Doctor.

'So sorry, I'm not quite myself at the moment. Godfrey Richardson's the name. We've been coming here for simply ages, Milly and I, but this year I went down with damned bronchitis. Odd really – she was always the weaker child. I said we shouldn't come, but Milly insisted – it would give me the chance to convalesce, she said. So in the end I thought, hang it all, and agreed.'

'But you're still here,' noted the Doctor.

Rubbing his forehead in obvious embarrassment, Godfrey continued: 'Yes. Well, we got to the end of our week, and Milly thought I still looked a touch peaky. Have to say she was right, you know.'

'So you decided you'd stay on another week?' suggested the Doctor.

'Milly looked in the signing-in book, and it did rather seem as if you'd never turned up for your week. So she suggested staying on.'

'Good old Milly!' beamed the Doctor, chirpily but with a hint of sarcasm.

Peri hissed at him under her breath to be quiet. Had he no sensitivity?

'Well, it's true that I've never used the week before.'

'We did come here only out of curiosity,' said Peri, firmly.

The Doctor ignored her, preferring instead to gaze stubbornly around the room. 'Mmm. Well, of course you must stay, my dear fellow. We wouldn't dream of asking you to leave in your present condition. Would we, Peri?'

'I wouldn't, no.'

Godfrey looked greatly relieved. 'That really is awfully kind of you both. Milly will want to thank you too. She's out at the moment – gone to visit friends in the area.'

'Yes, I can't wait to meet the enterprising Miss Milly.' Sinking deeper into his armchair, the Doctor smiled contentedly. All he needed now was a mug of cocoa and some brandy schnapps, and he'd feel almost at home. Whatever at home was. 'I take it that it was she who forged my signature in the signing-in book?'

Godfrey nodded, but suddenly leaned forward as though he had remembered something vitally important. 'We did put the money in the meter, though. An extra week's worth. It was only right, after all. I hope you don't think us both dreadful bounders, sir?'

'Not at all, not at all.' The Doctor hurriedly waved away the anxious question, although it had obviously worried him. He rose from his armchair for an impromptu wander around the room, taking a sudden, accentuated interest in its every nook and cranny. Peri felt unsettled by his strange behaviour.

'Doctor?' He was standing to the left of the centre curtain now, peering cautiously behind it. 'What's the problem?' Peri joined him to the right.

'They've put a week's money in the meter!' he whispered.

'So?'

'We've *also* put a week's money in the meter!' His head had almost completely disappeared behind the drape.

'So?'

'Then we've overcharged it, jamming fourteen days into the span of one week!'

'Everything all right?' Godfrey was clearly becoming a little nervous at all the whispering. Simultaneously, the Doctor and Peri's heads bobbed back into view, both wearing clownish smiles.

'Sure! Just admiring the pile. Aren't we, Doctor?'

'Mmm? Oh... yes! And the braiding – it's very... uh... nice."

Their heads sprang instantly back behind the curtain.

'I thought you didn't like the word "nice"?'

'Peri!'

'Sorry. Does this mean we've sort of, like, messed up time or something major like that?'

'Not necessarily, no. Everything seems fine at the moment. But it might be wise if we stayed around for a little longer, just to make sure.'

'Great!' Peri's enthusiastic whoop was the first thing Godfrey had heard for some time with any clarity.

'Mr Richardson?' The Doctor resumed his seat with a hefty bounce. 'We've decided to stay on for a few days.'

It was only when the grandfather clock chimed seven times that they realised how long they had been talking. Godfrey, it seemed, could almost match the Doctor's talent for talking the hind legs off any animal foolish enough to possess them. Culture was like alcohol to this Doctor – one good conversation and he was drunk on it. Peri had managed to sneak in the occasional 'Great!' and 'That's nice' but little more. The two men had talked about everything from food and literature to music and the theatre. At a quarter past six, the Doctor had disclosed his top-secret pasta recipe, which placed particular emphasis on the use of Tabasco sauce, salted peanuts and sausage meat. Come half past six, they were well into the Bronte Sisters – particularly, it seemed, Charlotte, who had of course written that great classic...

'*Wuthering Heights*!' proclaimed the Doctor, at a volume which shook the furniture. 'One of her best. Tragic! I sometimes see myself as something of a Heathcliffe... Wasn't Charlotte the first one to die?'

'Indeed, she may have been,' Godfrey was becoming quite excited now, 'but she most definitely didn't write *Wuthering Heights*!'

The Doctor, reddening, appeared to be on the verge of erupting fiercely in a cry of 'Rubbish!'

'Actually, that's true, Doctor,' put in Peri tentatively. 'Emily wrote *Wuthering Heights*.'

Although his expression suggested that he might utter the word 'Rubbish!' for the rest of the evening, the Doctor merely let out a sort of disbelieving 'Mmm' noise and changed the subject.

By a quarter to seven, he was in his element again, extolling the virtues of Flanders and Swann through his own rendition of one of their, in his opinion, best numbers. Standing with one foot on the carpet and the other planted firmly on a small coffee table, he threw back his arms and began to sing:

'*Mud! Mud! Glorious mud! Nothing quite like it for cooling the blood!*'

Godfrey, of course, hadn't a clue who Flanders and Swann were, but nevertheless sat smiling politely, whilst Peri cringed from behind a cushion.

And so seven o'clock had arrived, just as Godfrey was filling the Doctor in on the various attractions at the local theatre. One particular George Bernard Shaw play had evidently appealed, as the Doctor had fallen quiet for more than five seconds. Almost before Godfrey had finished talking, he had grabbed Peri by the arm in excitement.

'Come along, Peri! Culture beckons! Here's your opportunity to see real actors in the flesh!'

'Thrilling!' replied Peri, pulling on her coat. 'But I have been to the theatre before, you know.'

Godfrey appeared amused at her obvious lack of enthusiasm. 'It really is terribly good,' he encouraged. 'Milly and I have seen it twice already.'

'Think of all the tram rides, Peri!' The Doctor's eyes had the glint of an excited two-year-old's. 'We could go up and down all night, if you like!'

There was nothing anyone could do when he was like this, thought Peri, apart from humour him. 'Okay. But I'm not going to the theatre with you wearing that... that coat!'

Horrified, the Doctor looked at himself in a full-length, gilt-edged mirror in which he had been trying to catch glimpses of himself all evening.

The Doctor protested, Peri argued and Godfrey wouldn't be drawn – although he mentioned that he had a red velvet smoking jacket, if that was of any help.

'Thank you, sir, but velvet jackets I have a-plenty!'

'Does yours have anything in the pockets?' Peri asked Godfrey.

'No.'

'Then he'll wear yours!'

'Capital! What size are you, Doctor?'

'Jumbo,' said Peri, and was rewarded with a heavy frown.

'I suppose I could try it on,' muttered the Doctor, sulkily. 'But don't think you're having it all your own way, miss, because I'm sitting by the window on the tram! In fact, I'm sitting on top!'

'But it's raining!' cried Peri.

The Doctor smiled one of those worrying smiles of his. 'Then you'll get wet!'

Godfrey approached the grandfather clock. His gaunt reflection stared back at him. Distorted by the curvature in the glass, it damned the hands that appeared never to move. And yet they had eaten the last hour, albeit painfully slowly. The Doctor and Peri would be back soon. He prayed that they would.

At ten past eleven, he heard the key turn in the lock and voices in the lobby.

He heard Peri's voice first: 'Well, you shouldn't have moved your arms so much if you knew it was tight!'

Then an exasperated reply from the Doctor: 'Not move my arms? How can one possibly go out for the evening without moving one's arms?'

'Well, you didn't have to go and split it!'

'I didn't mean to go and split it – it's too tight! It's your fault for making me wear it in the first place.'

Opening the lobby door, the two travellers crashed through together, but stopped quite still at Godfrey's expression. 'Godfrey?' questioned the Doctor, stepping forward. 'What's the matter, old bean?'

'It's Milly.' Godfrey had intended to be terribly British about it, but he began fumbling with the sash of his dressing gown and all was forgotten. The words came tumbling out. 'Oh, Doctor, she's wretchedly ill. She's babbling, having hallucinations. She says she's seen a ghost, here, in her room – she's obviously fevered, poor dear. I really don't know what to do, but I thought that you, being a doctor...'

'Good man.' Peeling off the velvet jacket, the Doctor placed it on the sofa, revealing a large tear in the black silk lining. 'Ah, Godfrey – bit of an accident...'

'Don't worry – it's not important. Will you come and see

Milly now?'

'Of course.'

Together they ascended the staircase into the darkness of the landing.

Milly sat bolt upright in bed, her face drained in the dim light, her smooth white complexion exaggerated by a sleek bob of short black hair which fell just below the ears. She gave the impression of being some years younger than her brother – at least ten, thought Peri. A moan filled the empty room. Milly flung her head violently from side to side until pure exhaustion forced her to stop. For a few moments, she fell silent. Godfrey bit his lip in an effort to contain his obvious distress.

'Is it brain fever, Doctor? I've never seen her like this before.'

'She appears to be in a severe state of shock.' The Doctor lifted the woman's head from her propped-up pillow and directed her gaze towards his. 'Milly?' He spoke softly but clearly. 'I'm the Doctor. Can you tell me what's upsetting you?'

'Milly? It's me – Godfrey.' Her brother edged closer to the bed, but stumbled suddenly backwards as Milly flung herself forward to face him.

'Just there... where you are standing.' Her voice wavered as she spoke.

'What did you see, Milly? Tell me.' The Doctor spoke urgently, grabbing her by the shoulder. 'What did you see?'

'A spirit,' she cried, 'come to take me away!' Her eyelids closed and she sank backwards into the battered pillow.

As Peri helped Godfrey make his sister comfortable and rearrange the twisted bedcovers, the Doctor paced the room silently. What he had heard had made him restless, and it was partly to ease his conscience that he subsequently volunteered to sit with Milly throughout the night.

'Get some rest, both of you,' he ordered, resisting Godfrey's protestations that surely it should be he who remained. 'I promise to wake you if there's any change.'

A knock. Loud and repetitive. It rapped on Peri's door with all
the delicacy of a rampant wildebeest. It was unmistakable.

'Peri? Are you awake?'

'No.'

'Come on. Milly's seen another one of her spirits.' The Doctor's voice trailed off as he headed back down the landing.

He had at least interrupted her dream, reflected Peri. It had
been of the sort which would have had Freud throwing in the
towel. Something to do with a Harley-Davidson and riding pil-
lion with a giant frog.

Dragging back the bedcovers and rearranging her twisted
satin pyjamas, which she had insisted on retrieving from the
TARDIS, she pulled herself out of bed. Getting up wasn't one
of Peri's stronger points. Facing a long, narrow mirror, she ruffled her hair and fought once more with her 'peachy jim-jams,'
as she called them. A flicker of reflected movement suddenly
caught her eye. She stared closer into the glass and then behind
her.

Nothing.

She returned to the mirror.

Nothing.

She closed her eyes, then snapped them open again to the
sight of a tall man, in nightshirt and nightcap, carrying a candle.

Her cry activated the house into urgent motion and, within
seconds, both Godfrey and the Doctor stood at her door. The
man in the nightcap had since vanished, but Peri's wide-eyed
expression and firmly voiced insistence of what she had seen
was proof enough – if any was needed – for the Doctor. Bid-
ding Godfrey to return to his sister, the Time Lord placed a
comforting arm around Peri's shoulders.

'Chin up, Peri. Look.' He pointed to the far corner. 'There's
another one.'

There, in the gloom, sat an old woman, knitting and smiling a toothless smile to herself. She existed but a few moments, then the room swallowed her up, taking with her the monotonous clack of the wooden needles. 'A stitch in time, Peri.' The Doctor addressed his companion, but he was really talking to himself.

'I saw a man! A man with a nightcap... and a candle! A man...'

'Like that?' concluded the Doctor. The man's return was greeted with a nod of recognition from Peri, who looked on as he proceeded to blow out his candle and climb into the bed that she had vacated only minutes before. There he faded into nothingness.

The Doctor looked unusually sombre. 'It's as I feared, Peri. By overcharging the time meter, it appears that I have upset the timeline.'

'Is that what's making all the ghosts appear?'

'Oh, they're not ghosts, Peri – not strictly speaking. They are all very much alive, believing themselves to be in their own present. You see, each of them has, at a certain point in history, occupied this timeshare during the first and second weeks of November.'

'And now they're sharing the wrong time... right?'

'Exactly.'

'So what do we do?'

'It's a tricky one, Peri.'

The Doctor shook his head and adopted a series of twisted facial expressions which conveyed to his companion the thought that she was now up a certain creek... with a Time Lord who had lost his paddle.

Side by side, the Doctor and Peri sat on the last stair but one, looking out across the hall. Peri had remarked that it was rather like watching some bizarre play taking place all over the house, before she had briefly retired to change out of her peachy jimjams into her previous attire. This had been done at the Doctor's request – he had been feeling decidedly overdressed.

Peri squeezed closer to the Doctor, allowing a small child to pass by. It was a boy, dressed in a sailor suit. 'Elspeth!' he called, as he galloped up the stairs two at a time. 'It's your turn! Are you ready?'

A small, blonde girl frothing with ringlets and lace, was seated on a wooden tray, ready to descend the stairs. 'Yes! Start counting... now!' Crashing down the stairs, she arrived at the bottom just as the boy shouted 'Eleven!' and the Doctor and Peri hurriedly vacated their seat. Subsequently, both children disappeared.

'Can they see us, Doctor?' asked Peri, stepping onto the spot where the boy had previously been standing.

The Doctor shook his head. 'They don't appear to... although, having said that, they might well do... oh, how do I know!'

'Touchy!'

Peri left her friend, the bear with a sore head, to himself. Her attention was captured by two very refined-looking gentlemen involved in a game of backgammon in the far corner of the drawing room. She guessed that they were Edwardian (although she couldn't be exactly sure) by the way their collars were turned up in that funny pooked style. Both had evidently begun the game in full evening dress, but as it had continued, various items had been removed – jackets draped around the backs of chairs, bow-ties arranged neatly on top. As Peri watched, waistcoat buttons were being undone while unfavourable comments were made on the level of heat in the room. The men resumed their game, and a final move was made by one player to the exclamation of 'Jolly good show!' by the other. At which they both disappeared.

The quick, sharp slam of a door drew Peri's attention to the lobby entrance, by which stood the Doctor, trying desperately to evade a man in a great coat who was stamping up and down and breathing laboriously.

The Doctor, considering himself to be totally in the way, dodged behind a tall bookcase and watched as the man placed a long hunting rifle against the wall, removed his gloves and began to rub his hands together furiously.

'Great heavens, that's a cold frost out there!' breathed the man, unfastening a brown tweed deerstalker dusted with snow. 'It's been a good five or six years since it was as cold as this! 1896, one fellow said today, and I don't believe he was far wrong. Too cold for shooting rabbits! Now, what I need is a large glass of port, a warm fire and a hearty...' Whatever he was going to say faded away with him and his rifle, but the Doctor offered 'meal' and thought it to be correct.

The Doctor stepped out from his hiding place straight into a short, bustling young woman wearing a long black dress, white frilled apron and matching cap. A parlour maid, thought Peri, as she crossed the bottom of the stairs with split-second timing to avoid the persistently suicidal Elspeth.

The Doctor stood aside to let the maid pass and continue with her frenzy of polishing.

As she dusted a table, the girl muttered to herself in a rich, Cockney accent: 'Yes Mrs Prendergast, no Mrs Prendergast, three bags full Mrs Prendergast.' To the Doctor's surprise, the girl then stood up straight and addressed him directly. 'Ooh!' she screeched. ''ello, my luvver!' The Doctor spun around but, to his horror, found that she was addressing him. 'D'you know what I'd say to that old bat if I had the bottle?'

His head still reeling from the word 'luvver', he found himself unable to reply. Instead, he remained open-mouthed.

'I'd say.' The girl let out a mischievous giggle. ' "You can stick it where the sun don't shine, Mrs Prendergast!" What d'ya think of that, then?' The Doctor didn't get a chance to tell her, for she vanished in a wave of giggles.

'Well, she could certainly see you!'

'Yes, Peri, I think we must conclude that she could.'

Hearing the clatter of the tray again, Peri decided to abandon the stairwell completely. At the stroke of three o'clock, Elspeth crashed to the floor, the backgammon game returned to its winning move and it was once again affirmed by the hunting man – as Peri had privately termed him – that it was 'too cold for shooting rabbits!'

From a far door, a rotund, whiskered vision blustered loudly into the hallway. He headed off across the polished floor, straight into the path of the Doctor, who sidestepped him only at the last moment. He had the appearance of a retired army general who had spent his latter years doing little more than eating and drinking and supplementing it with more of the same. His waistcoat buttons fought to keep his stomach from view and his ill-fitting dinner jacket displayed a row of swaying medals. Across the hall he pounded, stopping at the bottom of the stairs, right next to the Doctor, who had singularly failed to shake him off. Pulling out a large, white handkerchief, the general blew his nose in traditional trumpet style and then proceeded to roar at the top of his voice the most peculiar of requests, before he too disappeared.

'Melon?' questioned the Doctor. 'What on Earth does he want with a melon?'

Peri felt a tap on her shoulder and turned around to see the maid, who had momentarily stopped her polishing.

'What's up with ol' luvver?' she whispered, gesturing towards the Doctor. 'Face like a wet weekend!'

'He's confused.'

The maid turned back to her dusting. 'I should say. Probably 'ad a run-in with Mrs Prendergast. I can symp'fise with that. Yes Mrs Prendergast, no Mrs Prendergast, three bags full Mrs Prendergast...'

And so it went on. As the large man with the melon deficiency emerged from the unfamiliar door for a second time, Peri became curious and decided to take a look at the room beyond.

The long table surrounded by high-backed chairs indicated that she stood in the dining room. It was empty when Peri entered, but was almost instantly transformed into a babbling dinner party, at the head of which sat the large, whiskered man. Around the table sat a host of gents in dinner suits and ladies in elaborate finery. Silken gowns were matched with evening gloves and sparkling jewellery. The conversation seemed, on the whole, to be about 'Gladstone and the rest of the blasted Whigs!' This was peppered with the occasional comment on how the British 'should have given those damned Boers a good hiding at Majuba Hill' from the melon man (another of Peri's labels). The various threads of discussion continued, with loud cries of 'hear, hear!' echoing from the men and polite noises of agreement emitting from the women, until the melon man began a loud protestation relating to the fact that his guests had yet to be served their melon. Eventually he stood up and marched to the door, passing Peri as he did so.

'Are you the new maid?' he demanded. 'What's happened to the melon?' Peri had no time even to think of an answer before he grabbed the doorhandle and waved her aside. 'Too slow! I'll do it myself. Consider yourself dismissed!'

What a charmer, thought Peri, as she watched him thunder across the hallway and over to the stairs, from which the Doctor was sensibly absent, to bark his command.

Over and over, round and round, the scenes were performed before Peri's eyes. The Doctor appeared in the archway of the drawing room and beckoned her impatiently to join him. And so she began her journey. Avoiding the duster, dodging around the melon man, escaping the tea tray, eluding the rifle held by the hunter. Through curses of 'Prendergast!' and cries about the cold, past counting, games and orders for fruit. She negotiated a dizzying cycle of words and images.

'Look at them, Peri, look at them! Continuously replaying themselves. Sometimes the scenes are shorter, sometimes longer.'

They turned into the drawing room, towards the backgammon players.

'Excuse me,' said one. 'Aren't you Louise's cousin Matilda?'

'No... I- I'm Peri.'

'No, not you – your friend.'

'No I most certainly am not!' replied the Doctor, indignantly. But the two men had gone.

Briefly the Doctor and Peri were alone in the room. Then there was a woman singing, whilst another played the piano. Seconds later, a boy chased a puppy through an obstacle course of furniture.

'I'd say,' ventured the Doctor, 'that we're as much guests in their timestreams as they are in 1929.' He started to pace, up and down the length of the sofa, swerving to avoid the boy and dog at regular intervals. 'I'm in a quandary, Peri. A mistake has been made...'

'By you.'

'Yes, all right, by me! No need to rub it in! A mistake has been made,' he repeated, emphasising the next two words sarcastically, 'by me, and now time is trying to readjust itself–'

'What was that?'

'What was what?' The Doctor turned and saw nothing. These continual petty interruptions were beginning to aggravate him.

'Well, it's gone now, but it was kind of weird – not like the others.'

'Kind of weird? Kind of weird? What, pray, does that mean?' His tone did not encourage Peri to continue, but she thought it would probably end up the worse for her if she didn't.

'Weird. Like a human face, but with... warts or something. Look – there it is again! Did you see it?' But again, the Doctor's eyes had been elsewhere. 'It was similar to the first time – but sort of different as well.'

The Doctor raised his eyes to the ceiling and then buried his head in his hands. 'Why must you be so confusing? What-do-you-mean?' He spoke in sharp, staccato tones and, by doing so, produced results.

'OK. They both looked like the same person, but with different clothes, and... they both had warts, or abrasions, or something. There it is again. By the window.'

The image was not as strong as those of its fellow apparitions, who busied themselves with playlets, and it was indeed unusual, thought the Doctor, who waited to witness the suited figure a second time.

His concentration was broken by a familiar voice – Godfrey.

Peri felt an immediate rush of guilt. 'I'd completely forgotten about Godfrey!'

'Don't persecute yourself, Peri.' The Doctor moved towards the staircase. 'So had I.'

'How many chimes?' asked the Doctor.

Peri was counting along. 'Eight,' she said, as the last one echoed away. 'Morning already.'

An ambulance had left a few minutes earlier. Young Elspeth had been remarkably compliant and the hunting man had seemingly missed his cue as the Doctor and an exhausted Godfrey had helped Milly descend into the hall. Wrapped in a variety of coats and shawls, which had evaded Godfrey's hurried packing, she had been bundled into the waiting vehicle.

'She's definitely not up to snuff, Doctor,' Godfrey had said.

'And neither are you, Godfrey. This is for the best. I'm sure you'll both make a splendid recovery.' The Doctor had beamed an expression of encouragment and given Godfrey a series of sympathetic pats on the shoulder. He had stopped this friendly gesture on realising that it was only aggravating the man's cough, and had then offered him a humbug – unintentionally covered in fluff – to rectify it, before helping him into the ambulance to join his sister.

Godfrey had been not unduly perturbed by all the activity in the house. He had, as a child, seen what he had termed a ghost, and this, reflected the Doctor, had probably left him quite open-minded on the subject.

'D'you know, Peri.' The Doctor reached for the handle of the lobby door. 'I think that things have quietened down somewhat.' He pushed the door open onto a whirling cacophony, an escalating storm of sound and imagery.

'On the other hand...' she added.

'Oh no!'

'What?'

From the other side of the hall, approaching at terrifying speed, came a dreaded apparition. It stopped inches from its target.

'Where you bin to, my luvver, ay?'

The Doctor quickly pulled the door to again, throwing an exasperated look at Peri.

'Well, we can't stay out here all day!' she said.

'No!' came a shrill voice from the other side of the door. 'I ain't got time for games, luvver! I got me dusting to do!'

'Stuck between a rock and a hard place!' muttered the Doctor. He opened the door and faced the excitable maid with another of his beaming smiles: 'Hello!'

''ello to you, luvver!' She winked. He coughed as a cover, for the maid had a unique knack of rendering him speechless. 'That's a nasty cough you've got there, luvver. Want me to 'ave a look at your chest for you?'

To the Doctor's great relief, she suddenly spotted a rogue cobweb nearby and zoomed off to attend to it, muttering something about 'the dust in this house!'

Peri tugged at the Doctor's arm. 'Look – that's a new one.' She pointed to a man at the head of the stairs who, despite his agile appearance, was, she guessed, at least sixty years old. Well-dressed, he carried a shotgun with him as he ran. Before reaching the middle stair, he had disappeared.

Almost immediately, he was back upon the landing and entering the bedroom previously occupied by Godfrey. The Doctor and Peri exchanged a startled look as they heard the discharging of a barrel. The man retreated from the room and tore down the stairs in apparent panic, before again disappearing.

'What was all that about?' asked Peri.

'I think we should take a look.'

Steadily they climbed the stairs, keeping to the left so as not to disturb the man when he next began his flurried descent down the right – and also to evade the ongoing descent of Elspeth.

Once again, they heard the gunshot.

The Doctor and Peri reached the bedroom just as the gunshot rang out for a third time. They stood quickly aside to avoid the escapee, then pushed open the door and entered the room.

Peri walked across the drawing room to where the Doctor sat, musing, in her adopted armchair. She gave up and chose another.

'He's gone now,' she began.

'Who's gone?'

'The man with the gun. He's not on the stairs any more.'

'Oh, he'll be back, Peri – you'll see.'

The Doctor was as fascinated by what he had seen as Peri was sickened. 'Not what you'd expect to find in a country house, mm?'

'No, it was horrible.' She spoke with a tone of disgust that the Doctor found faintly amusing.

Bouncing up from his armchair, he administered a jokey punch to her upper arm. 'Where's your pluck, Peri?' he teased, and sauntered over to the window.

'It was an alien, right?'

'Right!' he remarked. 'But how did it get there? What happened to it afterwards? I mean, it would have to be removed. You can't go carting alien bodies around the countryside without at least somebody noticing – even if this is North Devon!'

Rising from her armchair, Peri joined him. 'Well, someone

must have moved it 'cos it's not there now. Now now, I mean.'

'By that grammatical nonsense I take it you mean 1929?'

Peri thought of the way it had lain there on the bed, crippled and miserable. She had found it difficult to read straight away. The body, clothed in folds of dark green herringbone tweed, had twisted unnaturally within its confines. The Doctor had macabrely called it 'An alien with a passion for fashion!' and she had scolded him for it. It had smelt sweet, like delphiniums, she thought. Its skin had been rough, wart-like and glistened like oil, but despite this there had been something humanoid about it that went beyond its simple bipedal structure.

The Doctor broke into her thoughts. 'Judging by that fellow's clothes, it can't have been that long ago.'

'What fellow?'

'The one with the gun! Aren't you listening? It can't have taken place that long ago, as his clothes were fairly modern.'

A loud slam of the lobby door caused Peri to turn, but it was only yet another indication of yet another arrival by the hunting man. 'Doctor!' she began as the Time Lord settled himself, unaware, into the armchair that she had just unwisely vacated. 'That's my chair!' Her protest was drowned out by the habitual cry for a melon which echoed from the stairs. A new one followed immediately after it.

'Godfrey!' came a woman's voice. 'I'm bringing you up some hot lemon!' It was Milly. Up the staircase she hurried, tray in hand, whistling merrily.

Peri and the Doctor crossed to the bottom of the stairs and watched as she knocked on Godfrey's bedroom door. Then she abruptly vanished.

'Doctor, this is getting crazy!'

'Thank you for stating the blindingly obvious!' He responded at top volume to avoid an interruption.

'Should have given those damned Boers a good hiding...' interjected a voice.

'Does that mean she's...'

'No – not necessarily, Peri. It's simply that the disturbance of the timeline is escalating.'

'1896, one fellow said today,' sprang a voice from the lobby, 'and I don't believe he was far wrong.'

'Will we appear?'

'I hope not – that would cause all manner of problems...'

'Elspeth! It's your turn! Are you ready?'

'Are you listening, Peri?'

'Ssh... What was that?'

'What was what?'

Brrrriing!

'That!' she said. Then, in disbelief, 'It's the doorbell!'

It rang again.

'What a time to call!' cried the Doctor, hands on hips like an agitated housewife in the middle of a major baking assignment.

'Who is it?'

'How do I know?' The Doctor sighed. 'Who d'you think I am – Madame Zolga?'

Another brisk ring.

'Do something, Doctor!' wailed Peri.

'Well, I can hardly invite them in for tea and scones, can I?'

'Perhaps they'll go away.'

Brrrriing!

The general stormed across the hallway for the hundredth time.

'You go, Peri. Say that whatever it is, we don't want any.'

'Where's my melon?'

'Oh, do shut up, man!' erupted the Doctor. 'I've had just about enough of you!'

Another ring.

'Got it!'

'What?'

Flinging open the lobby door, the Doctor launched his plan

into action: 'Go away! I'm washing my hair!'

Another ring, this time longer. The Doctor pursed his lips firmly together. This persistent caller was beginning to get under his skin.

'That's it!' He snapped open the letterbox and bellowed through: 'I'm in the shower! All right?'

'Let me in please, Doctor.' The voice on the other side of the door had a weary tone. Firm, but weary.

'Whatever it is, it can't be that important...' He stopped, suddenly aware that he had been addressed by name.

'I've come to read the meter,' continued the voice.

'Oh no!' The Doctor rose to his feet, feeling first hot and flushed, then cold and drained. He swallowed hard and opened the door.

The man who stepped inside had a face and manner that perfectly matched his voice. His deeply lined forehead made him appear constantly worried, and he would at intervals run a hand aimlessly down his right cheek, ruffling his lips as it went. His thick grey hair peeped out from beneath a peaked cap and he wore a pair of navy blue overalls – which he thought to be historically correct – with a brown satchel bag.

At the sight of the Doctor, his face visibly deflated.

With the lobby door and the chaos beyond it shut firmly behind her, Peri smiled the sweetest smile she could muster. 'The meter's just here. I'm sure there won't be any problem with it.'

'Don't bother, Peri,' sighed the Doctor. 'He's one of them.'

'One of who?' Peri looked confused.

'A Time Lord, come to stick his nose in and no doubt to give me a long and hypocritical lecture on what I should and shouldn't do!'

'I knew it would be you.' The Time Lord, old in his twelfth body and nearing retirement, gestured to Peri. 'I knew it would be him. I could feel it in my bones. I said, "It'll be him." I told them, "I can feel it in my bones." I said to them, "If it's him, there'll be trouble," I said.'

Shaking his head, he began to tut-tut under his breath. 'I told them, I said, "I can deal with the velveteen gentleman. I liked him. Or that nice young man with the vegetable. But if it's him," I said...'

'Well, I'm very sorry to disappoint you!' retorted the Doctor.

Walking past the meter and Peri, the Time Lord opened the lobby door.

'Oh, look at this mess.' He addressed Peri once more. 'I told them it'd be a mess if he was involved. I said, "It'll be a mess," but they wouldn't have it. I didn't want to come. I told them, "I don't want to go." But here I am, though what good it'll do I don't know.'

The Doctor had folded his arms patiently. 'Is there a point to your visit or have you come just to send us both to sleep?'

The Time Lord sighed. 'We've been watching all this, you know.' Glancing around the hall, he ran his hand down his cheek again and shook his head firmly. 'I said it would be a mess. "It'll be a mess," I said. I could see it coming, of course, that you'd mess up the timeline. I told them you would. Now, of course, things haven't turned out at all as intended...'

'Intended?' Now it was the Doctor's turn to be firm. 'What do you mean by "intended"?'

'You should have listened to this young lady, Doctor – at least she can read.'

'What do you mean?' Peri noted the Doctor's confusion with amusement.

'The note, Doctor. The note in your pocket. You're supposed to be in 1920, putting a stop to this timeshare malarkey once and for all. And that's where you would have been' – he rolled his eyes – 'if you hadn't misread the coordinates. That last number was a five, not a six.'

'Misread the co-ordinates? Misread them?' The Doctor assumed his most arrogant poise. 'They were impossible to read to start with! With such appalling handwriting, is it any wonder I misread them?'

'Your companion didn't.'

'She's American – it doesn't count.' The Doctor tried desperately to shift the emphasis of the conversation. 'And what exactly do you mean by "putting a stop to this timeshare malarkey"? Putting me to good use again, mm?'

'Ooh, he's getting stroppy! I told them. "He'll get stroppy," I said.' The lines on the Time Lord's forehead were almost joining up now. 'Oh, I knew it wouldn't be easy with you. You always were a difficult child!'

'I was a model child!' protested the Doctor.

'What exactly was supposed to happen in 1920?' put in Peri.

'Well dear, in 1920, the ownership of the first week of November in this timeshare property was passed over to the Doctor – to him – by the Time Lords – that's us.' He gave a small laugh. 'I wouldn't have advised it, but there you go.'

'That makes sense with the signing-in book!' cried Peri.

'Oh, does it? Good.' The Time Lord gave a little cough and continued. 'That was done after the death of the week's previous owner, known on Earth as Mr Woodruff. In reality, Mr Woodruff – an adopted name – had been exiled to this planet by his own people.'

'I know the feeling,' muttered the Doctor sarcastically.

The Time Lord found some small amusement in the irony, and told Peri that it was quite common practice with regard to the Earth. The planet was simply teeming with exiles. They were particularly numerous in Radstock, and made up almost the entire population of Luxembourg.

'Now, where was I?'

'Mr Woodruff,' offered Peri.

'Oh yes. Thank you, dear. This Mr Woodruff came from a

vampiric race, and to enable himself to continue living on Earth, he had to absorb the energy of young humans. Not a nice thing to do, I know, but there you are. Of course, this timeshare was an ideal way for him to do it, with the privacy and all that. Every year, he would use the body of a certain young man who regularly took the previous week, and would then use the first week of November to adjust. Is he listening?'

'Of course I'm listening!' snapped the Doctor. 'There you are, Peri – that explains your "kind of weird" warty apparition.'

The elderly Time Lord glanced over at the stairs. 'I told them it'd be a right to-do coming here. "It'll be a right to-do," I said, "going there." There'll be an accident with that girl on the tray before long, but what can you do?'

Peri reassured him that the child had been making her descent down the stairs for six hours and hadn't yet come to any harm, while the Doctor requested that they should at least stick to the subject in hand.

'Mmm.' The Time Lord scratched his neck agitatedly. 'Anyway, in 1920, this young fellow didn't turn up for his usual week – dose of flu or something. Instead, his place was taken by his elderly aunt. Mr Woodruff was therefore forced to use this older body. Unfortunately, the poor woman died at the moment of absorption. This caused Mr Woodruff to revert somewhat to his natural form, producing the unfortunate creature that I believe you both saw upstairs.' He waited for their nods of acknowledgement. 'The chap over there who keeps running up and down in that exhausting manner' – he pointed towards the man with the rifle, who was currently acting out his scene for them – 'was the then owner of the second week of November, who made the gruesome discovery on arriving for his week's stay.'

'So who moved Mr. Woodruff's body?' The Doctor waited for an answer, but the lengthy silence was all the answer he needed. 'Oh, I see. I get it. Muggins here was supposed to do it! Had it all arranged, did you?'

'As a matter of fact, yes,' declared the Time Lord. 'You were supposed to return to 1920, remove the alien body and close down this last remaining H.O.P. timeshare. I told them that would be tricky. I said, "That'll be tricky." '

'But I didn't.'

'What?'

'Remove the body.'

'Well, no... not as yet.'

'Manipulated again!' cried the Doctor. 'Can't you lot do anything for yourselves?'

'You know the rules, Doctor – a strict policy of non-interference. You've always been the exception to the rule. A trouble-maker, I'd call you, and I said so, out loud. "He's a trouble-maker, that one," I said. "Not like that nice young man..." '

'With the vegetable,' finished the Doctor. 'Would you prefer me if I fetched a marrow from the kitchen?'

'What did I say?' gasped the Time Lord. 'Well, I did try to tell them, but what can you do?'

'Hypocrites, the lot of you!' cried the Doctor anarchically.

Turning to leave, the Time Lord spoke to Peri: 'Do sort it out, dear – they're in one hell of a hullabaloo up there.' He cocked his cap at her. 'Cheerio.' And with those parting words of encouragement, he left.

The Doctor had splayed himself on the drawing room carpet with all the style of a rag doll dropped from a great height. Legs in front of him, coat-tails behind, his head drooped over a pile of – as it appeared to his approaching companion – multi-coloured spaghetti. The ghostly puppy now took wide berths of him after an episode of excited yelping during which it had tangled itself helplessly amongst the wiring.

'Doctor?' Peri crouched beside him and placed a plate in an

available space on the floor. 'Brought you a sandwich.'

'Sandwich bandwich!' The cry came from the depths of the Doctor's stomach. 'Can't you see I'm busy? When would I possibly have time to eat a sandwich?' The curly head sprang up. 'What flavour?'

'Peanut butter, lettuce and potato chip flavour.' There followed a long silence. It was his favourite. Would he resist? With the speed of a snake devouring its prey, a hand emerged, grabbed the offering and rammed it whole into the waiting mouth. Peri winced at the sight: 'You're gross!'

'Possibly. Now go away.'

She ignored him. 'Are you onto something?'

'Could be.' He broke into a sudden burst of song: '*England swings like a pendulum do*... Time, Peri, is an enigma.'

Peri got up to leave. She did this whenever the Doctor felt tuneful.

'Look, what's the problem that we're trying to solve?' asked the Doctor.

'We're trying to get time back on course... right?'

'Right. Now, it's quite impossible for me to retrieve the extra seven days by removing my money from the meter. That is simply not an issue. But what if I can devise a method of using up time at twice the normal rate, and thus set the weeks in this house back on course?' His eyes twinkled, and Peri realised that this was the bit where she was supposed to tell him he was brilliant.

'You're brilliant, Doctor!'

He sniffed the air proudly. 'I know.'

'So? Can you do it?'

'I, my dear Peri, can do anything, if I set my mind to it.' With the vigour of Jack Horner, he delved into the clutter. 'This,' he announced, 'is the gauge.'

'From the time meter?'

'Precisely.'

'But isn't it dangerous to take it apart like that, Doctor?'

'Most of it's still ticking innocently away out there. And these,' he continued, waggling various wires, 'are some of its innards. Time giblets, if you like. Except these are going back inside! And this...' This is it, thought Peri. 'This is an override!'

'Jolly good show!' cheered the backgammon player, and it couldn't have been better timed.

'I'm going to adapt the meter so that it operates at double its regular speed.'

'A twenty-four hour day using up forty-eight hours?'

The Doctor slapped her on the back. 'You've got it! And by the end of the week, I'll have condensed fourteen days into seven!'

'But you won't have. Fourteen into seven doesn't go.'

'As long as the meter thinks everything is running correctly, time will realign itself. Rather like a watch, really. You can adjust it to read any time and the watch itself will believe it. It doesn't have to be the correct time, does it?'

'Nearly finished?'

'I'm getting there. Another ten minutes or so.' He looked wistfully at the empty plate. 'But a little more pabulum would undoubtedly speed up the process.' She looked at him blankly, and he sighed loudly: 'Edibles? Munchies? Food!'

'Oh, right! If you wanted another sandwich, why didn't you just say so?'

This was to be just the start of many refills, many curses and much more mess.

This was the seventh time that they had rounded this corner, past that same shop with the tobacco advert and along towards the park. Seven times. On a tram. On the upper deck. And Peri was cold.

'Doctor, are we ever going to get off?' I mean, they're great, trams, she thought, but there is such a thing as overkill.

'Just once more round the block, Peri! It doesn't start until six. And this is our last day.' 'It' was a film. The Doctor gripped onto the seat in front of him, and Peri swore that he imagined he was driving. 'Go on – another ten minutes or so.'

She remembered the last time he'd said that, five days ago, amidst a pile of time meter components. Another ten minutes or so had turned into an hour, and then into many hours. There had come a point when she had doubted they would ever be able to get the timeline back to normal (and a similar thought had passed through the Doctor's head, she felt sure, although he would never admit to it). But he had done it. The newly adapted meter, with its override clumsily attached to its side with Christmas gift tape, had been reinstalled. Then had come the worst bit – the waiting. She remembered that well. The hours of nothingness, the overwhelming sensation that they had failed and the Doctor's increasing paranoia regarding the whereabouts of the maid. Then there had come that magical moment when he had said...

'She's gone!'

'Who's gone?'

'Milly! That's five minutes now since she last appeared – I've been timing her.'

Peri was pleased for him, but... 'Isn't it taking rather a long time?' She had made him sigh. She seemed to do that rather a lot, some days.

'We are talking about readjusting the timeline here, not changing a light bulb!'

He had been right, there, of course. Over the next few days, the apparitions had gradually diminished. The lobby door had slammed no more, the furniture had remained undusted and so on, until only the children playing on the stairs had remained. Finally, silently, they too had gone. All had become strangely quiet once more.

Then the house had seemed rather empty. The Doctor had explained that they should remain until the end of their week, allowing him to disconnect the time meter at the precise moment his override allowed it to catch up with itself. So Peri had occupied herself with various activities, including several renditions of *Chopsticks* on the piano, while the Doctor had always stayed around to keep her company, asleep in one corner of a room or another.

On one such occasion, she had looked up from her repetitive keyboard tinkering to see that he had disappeared from her favourite armchair. She had eventually found him in the kitchen, rifling through the biscuit tin. 'Hi! Where'd you go to?'

His reply had been casual. 'Nowhere exciting. Only 1920.'

'1920?'

'What a parrot you're becoming, Peri! Yes, 1920! I've removed Mr Woodruff's body, disposed of it discreetly, and now I'm back. Happy?'

'What happens to the house next?' was all she had managed to say.

The Doctor's response had been apathetic. 'Who knows? It won't be a timeshare any more, though, that's for certain. Now, how about a film at the Picture Palace and another ride on that tram... Oh!' He had slammed down the tin lid. 'Where are all the Custard Creams?'

And Peri had apologized.

Again, the familiar sight of the shop with the tobacco advert confronted Peri, and finally she decided that enough was enough.

'That's it, Doctor. I'm getting off. I'm starting to get tramsick!'

Despite a loud, blustering protest from the Doctor about wanting to make it to ten, they got off and walked the short distance to the Picture Palace.

Outside the cinema, they were greeted by a large black-and-white image of Mickey Mouse.

'*Steamboat Willie*!' The Doctor rubbed his hands together

gleefully. 'Can you restrain your excitement?'

Peri peered closely at the poster. 'Well, you're going to have to restrain yours. You've got the time wrong.'

'Never!' He peered at the same spot, and then to a note he had made earlier for confirmation, only to see that the programme had, in fact, begun at...

'Five o'clock, not six! Doctor, you can't even read your own writing!'

'I can! It was you who said six, not me! Of course that's a five – how could you have been so... so...' He began to pout, taking in the full extent of his loss. 'Now I've missed *Steamboat Willie*!'

He turned and headed off back to the tram stop, and Peri knew he would make it to ten... just to compensate.

Question Mark Pyjamas

By Robert Perry and Mike Tucker

> What is House and what is Home,
> Where with freedom thou hast room,
> And may'st to all tyrants say,
> This you cannot take away?
>
> Joseph Beaumont

'This is crud, Professor. Let's go.'

Ace kicked at the ground, sending a shower of grit into the air.

'Oh, give it a chance, Ace.' The Doctor sounded irritable.

Ace knew when he was on the defensive. Covering up for a bad decision. 'But it's a rock.'

It was. A rock. A lousy asteroid in the middle of nowhere. Stone and dust, breathable atmosphere but nothing there to breathe it. Nothing except them. The Doctor, Benny, Ace.

Even Benny looked vaguely disappointed. She had grown excited when the Doctor had revealed exactly where this asteroid was, a little-explored quarter of the galaxy that had on occasions yielded some spectacular archaeological results. She trudged up the grey slope on which the TARDIS had materialized. Ace was right. Ace was always complaining, but this time she was right. It was a depressing hole. The sky was like lead, like an Earth sky before heavy rain. Except that here there was no prospect of rain. The sky was as dead as the ground.

She stopped. Over the ridge the view was just the grey same, except... Surely not...

'Doctor!'

Benny broke into a run, down the other side of the slope,

kicking up dust as she went. She stopped, breathless, outside the structure, her hands on her knees, her head next to the wall. It was the real thing. Dark green stone, narrow, gently curving blocks piercing upwards from the ground like the blades of Samurai swords. A Martian dwelling-house.

'Remarkable.' Drawing up next to his companion the Doctor leaned forward on his umbrella. 'What do you think it's doing here?'

'I don't know,' Benny replied. 'There's no evidence of Martian settlement in this part of the galaxy. They never came near here.'

'I know. Odd, isn't it?'

'The building is genuine, Doctor. It's not a fake. And yet...'

'The setting...'

'Of course! It's all wrong! No Martian house would ever be plonked down in a dust bowl. The setting would be highly ordered... decorative...'

'Great. A wigwam.' Mooching up slowly, Ace kicked a stone at the wall of the building. No-one was listening to her. Benny was trying to open the door. The Doctor was suggesting she knock first. Ace was bored.

'It's locked,' said Benny.

'Hmm. Nobody home. Well I suggest we find somebody before we walk into a locked dwelling-house. We wouldn't want to disturb a sleeping Ice Warrior.'

The Doctor turned on his heel in the dust and strode around the side of the building.

'There!' said the Doctor, pointing to something on the horizon. It was too far to make out any detail. He fished an old pair of opera glasses from the pocket of his baggy, off-white jacket and raised them to his eyes. 'Curiouser and curiouser.' He passed the glasses to Benny.

'I don't recognize that, Doctor. Definitely not Martian.'

'Argolin,' the Doctor stated, already walking towards it. Benny set off after him at a trot.

Ace watched them go. Nobody had offered her the glasses. Taking her time, trying to register her contempt with every slow movement, she followed her companions.

By the time she reached them, other buildings had appeared over the horizon; three of them, each as different from the other as this Argolin cloche – as the Doctor had called it – was from the previous Martian thing. It reminded her of an awful trip they'd been on from school.

'This is just like that place in Wales, where they have all the old buildings. Farmhouses, old churches, that sort of thing. Saint...'

'Of course! Ace, you're a genius. Don't you see, Benny, she's absolutely right. This is some kind of an exhibition. I believe the expression on twentieth-century Earth is...' He paused, searching for the words. '... A theme park. Yes, a theme park.'

'Please Keep off the Grass.'

Ace spun round in an instant, her hand instinctively reaching for her belt. She had no gun.

'Please Keep off the Grass,' the electronic voice whirred again, crackling with politeness and servility.

Standing – or rather hovering – about four feet off the ground in front of the travellers was something vaguely resembling a rugby ball, upright, on its end. It was a bit bigger, a bit squatter, and made of metal, with vents and scanners, grilles and a bright red push-button arranged so that the first impression Ace got, and one that it would prove surprisingly hard to shake, was of a face. A cute, smiling face. It was a rugby ball with a face.

The thing bobbed slightly in front of them.

'Please Keep off the Grass.'

What grass? There was no grass, only dust and rock.

The thing floated nearer. If it is possible to float purposefully, that's what it did.

'I rather think it's trying to shepherd us,' the Doctor almost whispered. 'Shall we see where it wants us to go?'

He started to walk away from the floating, fussing robot and the others followed.

Their escort bobbed from side to side like a squat sheepdog.

'Please Keep to the Designated Path.' It swung in a wide arc to the Doctor's left. He turned. His companions turned.

'It hasn't got much in the way of conversation, Professor. Shall I press its button?'

'Don't touch anything, Ace.' Sometimes the Doctor suspected she did this sort of thing deliberately. The only time she ever called him Professor nowadays when she was trying to annoy him. 'Let's just be patient for a change, shall we?'

They must have walked for about twenty minutes. Still no path, still no grass, just the same polite instructions every time one of them transgressed this invisible highway code. They passed many more buildings – a Gond hut, a benefit office from Inter Minor – bizarre clashes of style and technology from a hundred worlds that had never heard of one another. Ace was getting bored again. This *was* bloody Wales.

And then she stopped dead in her tracks.

'Doctor...'

They had just rounded a steep outcrop of rock. There, nestling in a huge, shallow, natural bowl between hills was a house she knew. A house they all knew; the Doctor better than any of them.

It was his house. His house from Earth. England. Kent.

'This is *my* house!' he declared, his voice brusque with indignation. Digging the tip of his umbrella into the ground, he swung in the direction of the dark stone walls, the gables, the eaves he knew so well.

'This Exhibit is Closed at Present.'

The guide robot was hovering directly in front of him. The Doctor stepped smartly to one side. The robot moved with him.

'This Exhibit is Closed at Present.'

He stepped the other way. The robot moved with him.

'Please Keep to the Designated Path.'

'Please Keep to the Designated Path.'

A second electronic voice took up the refrain. Another robot was floating towards them, and a third. The three clustered around the travellers, ushering them earnestly forward.

Now it was the Doctor's turn to sulk.

'Without so much as a by-your-leave...' he muttered.

They trudged on in silence. Benny was getting tired now. Her shoes were full of stones, her clothes dusty. And she had a headache. Beside her the Doctor walked, head down, staring furiously at the ground. On the other side of him Ace stomped and scowled.

'Why not Relax with a Hot Drink or Even a Meal in our Visitors' Centre?'

'Why not Visit our Gift Shop?'

In front of them was a long, low dome. It was pink. Coloured lights ascended columns at either side of a pair of glass doors, and then descended again.

Suddenly the doors flew open.

'Ladies, ladies... and gentleman... Welcome! Welcome to the Ararax XIV Heritage Centre. Buildings shipped stone by stone, block by block, rivet by rivet, module by module from the four corners of the galaxy! The largest – and newest – heritage centre in three quadrants!'

The figure bounced towards them. A large, beaming, avuncular face (almost human, just a little redder), nodded and danced on the top of a rotund body resplendent in dark pinstripe. Two fat hands reached out for them.

'Heritage Centre...' The Doctor nodded slowly. 'Not a theme park, then.'

'Oh, goodness me, no sir. Allow me to introduce myself. Garpol's the name. I am the owner and manager. This is my assistant, Mr Blint.'

A much smaller, much paler figure appeared from somewhere around the back of their large host, looking even sillier in dark pinstripe.

'Of course, we're not actually open yet,' the figure announced, breathlessly. 'We don't open for another month. There's still so much to do. The replicas of all the species, for one thing...'

'Not open? Nonsense!' Garpol threw his arms wide. 'You are our first customers. Free, of course. The facilities are a little... incomplete...' He leaned forward, conspiratorially. 'To be perfectly honest it's lucky you didn't come last week. We only had the atmosphere fitted a few days ago.' He shook his hands, dismissing the thought. 'No matter, no matter. I'm sure that none of this need mar your enjoyment of our fine exhibits. Come in, come in!'

He backed under the pink dome, all the time beckoning. Casting a weary glance from Ace to Benny, the Doctor trudged up to the glass doors. The two women followed.

Slipping between them, Blint scurried up to the Doctor, a clipboard in one hand, a pen in the other.

'Can I ask you a few questions? How did you get to hear of the Ararax XIV Heritage Centre? Was it (a) through an advertisement on telecast; (b) through one of our brochures; or (c) by word of mouth?'

'(d)!' snapped the Doctor, swinging the door closed in the little man's face.

To one side of the entrance a map of the galaxy showing the original locations of the exhibits curved elegantly away into what was obviously the restaurant, whilst on the other side the foyer opened out into a wide area where telebooks, holocards and sticks of sugar-free rock swivelled on metal display racks. Garpol turned to face them and pulled a slip of paper from his jacket.

'I should like to present you with our special family pass which entitles you to visit all the exhibits and contains a voucher that may be exchanged for one free child's meal in our spacious cafeteria. Is she yours?'

A chubby hand pinched Ace's cheek. She tensed. This creep was about five seconds away from a broken arm.

'Charming child. We do love families here. There is just one thing I ask. When you are visiting the exhibits, please keep off the grass. It's only just been laid, you know.'

'What grass?' The creep had withdrawn his hand just in time. 'There's no grass out there.'

The anxious head of Blint suddenly appeared around the far side of his employer. 'Er, there's been a slight problem with the grass, Mr Garpol.'

'Problem...' The fat man's voice had suddenly acquired a deeper tone.

'The contractors have said they can't now fit it for at least a month.'

'A month!' The fat hand was now raised, clamped into a fist. 'But we open in a month!' As if suddenly remembering himself, Garpol returned his hand to his ample belly. His face turned from a snarl into a dripping smile. 'A few teething troubles, you know. Nothing more. Now don't tell me... Terran? We have a couple of Terran exhibits which might be of interest to you.'

'Yes.' The Doctor was running out of patience. 'One of them interests me a very great deal. Terran dwelling, large, nineteenth-century English.'

'Ah yes. Exhibit Nineteen. I know it well.'

'So do I, Mr Garpol. So do I. You see, I happen to own it.'

Garpol let out a slow, polite laugh, as if at a joke he didn't quite understand.

'No, no. I can assure you, I own it. I own everything on Ararax XIV. I bought the whole asteroid, you see. Freehold. Everything on it is therefore mine.'

'And may I ask how that particular house came to be on this particular lump of rock?'

'Oh dear. Let me explain, my dear fellow.' Garpol was speak-

ing slowly now. An air of distaste, or at least of disappoint-
ment, had begun to creep into his voice. This wasn't the sort of
customer they wanted to attract at all. The man obviously had
no appreciation of where he was. 'This is a Heritage Centre.
We take buildings and monuments from all sorts of civiliza-
tions, not just Terran, and we bring them here for people to
visit. There's nothing to worry about, I can assure you. I suppose seeing a house from your own world must have come as a
bit of a shock to you, eh...?'

'First, I happen to be Gallifreyan.'

'Ah, yes. Gallifrey. I've heard of that. Now let me guess...
Ireland?'

'Secondly,' the Doctor interrupted, 'you appear not to be
listening to me. I happen to own a piece of property, which I
had assumed was sitting exactly where I had left it: namely,
Earth.' The Doctor jabbed the elegantly curving galactic map
hard with his umbrella. 'I now find to my surprise that the said
piece of property, which I own, has been moved without my
consent to here,' – he jabbed at the map again – 'where it has
been dropped in a... a dust bowl! I should like to know why.'

Garpol's eyes narrowed, then bulged. Then narrowed again.
His mouth flickered between half-smile and hard slit. He was
digesting what this Terran had to say, and attempting to assimi-
late it into his own plans. The possibilities were tantalizing.
Was he in his right mind, this funny little creature? Did he really own the house? Right species. Then again, did it matter?
He clearly thought the house was his own. How much better
than overpriced, unconvincing replicants?

'Then of course you must go to your house,' Garpol sim-
pered. His fat hands grew red as he rubbed them together vig-
orously. 'You must live there. Consider Ararax your home. You
will be very happy here. And lots and lots of people will come
and visit you.' For a moment Garpol had a faraway look in his
eyes. 'A real Terran family.' Beaming at Ace, he reached out
and tousled her hair.

That was it. The fat creep had gone too far. She grabbed. She pivoted. Four hundred pounds of bone and blubber crashed to the polished floor.

'Oh dear, oh dear!' Blint fluttered around his master like a fly at a whale carcass. 'Guide, please! Guide, please! Emergency code three!'

With a dull hum two floating robots bobbed around the corner.

'Don't just stand there, Blint!' bellowed Garpol, trying to haul himself to his feet. 'Get your gun out, man! Shoot them!'

His hand shaking, Blint drew from his belt a hand-blaster, which somehow contrived to look friendly in the same manner that the robots did. Awkwardly, shaking, he shifted the aim of the weapon from one to another of the companions.

Benny snorted. 'You should be careful with that. You might take your foot off.'

'Stupid,' Ace snarled at the terrified midget. 'Very, very stupid.'

She launched herself through the air. Blint fired wildly, shattering the elegant cosmic map into a thousand viciously pointed shards.

With a sudden whine one of the smiling robots cannoned into the flying girl. There was a crackle of power, and Ace bounced off the wall and into a rack of authentic poly-porcelain reproductions of Martian dwelling-houses, Argolin cloches, Draconian temples. . .

The last thing she heard before she blacked out was Garpol's rasping order:

'Take them to Exhibit Nineteen!'

'Ace...! Ace...!'

She jack-knifed upward, fists clenched. Wood panelling swam into view. And books. Books looming over her. This was the sprawling study in the Doctor's house. She was stretched out on the leather *chaise longue*, Benny staring down at her.

'What happened? Where's Metal Mickey?'

'The robot had some kind of electric charge passing though its casing. You took quite a shock.'

Ace sprang to her feet. 'I'm fine. What are we going to do?'

'Not a lot at the moment, Ace.' The Doctor slipped in through the door of the study. 'It's getting dark. And our host has surrounded the house with his little friends.'

'So we're just going to sit here?' She slumped back into the *chaise longue*.

'Oh, no, no.' The fruity tones of Garpol suddenly swam around the room. Ace was instantly on her feet again.

'Do forgive me for interrupting you, but it's dinner time.' Garpol's voice boomed from concealed speakers. Somewhere a tinny, out of tune gong was sounding.

'Dinner time? You are mad aren't you?'

'Young lady, regular meal times are very important. You want to grow up big and strong, don't you?'

Ace shook her head in amazement. There was no point trying to reason with him.

'If you would care to step into the kitchen... Blint has prepared something rather special to welcome you, though don't expect this sort of treatment every day. From tomorrow on, you're on your own.'

The idea of food didn't sound half-bad to Benny. Anything was better than sitting around in here. She looked hopefully towards the Doctor.

He smiled. 'Come along then. This might be rather nice. The house likes to keep a good larder. It never knows who might drop by.'

With a wink he led them from the room of oak and books.

That was the thing about this house: it was almost too perfect. Benny could see why Garpol had acquired it. Logs roared on the massive, black kitchen range, and game and ham hung from the rafters. On the far wall a clock ticked hollowly. It was annoying Benny.

The Doctor wiped his mouth with his napkin and leaned back in his chair. 'Excellent. My compliments to the chef.'

'Thank you, Doctor.' Garpol's voice seemed to come from everywhere at once.

More than the clock, more than the creak of the Doctor's chair, the crackling of the fire, the almost-too-real old-worldness of the place, that voice set Benny's nerves on edge.

'I shall pass them on.'

'I see you've cleaned up in here a bit, too,' said the Doctor, his head back, talking into the middle distance.

'Why, yes. I do particularly like this room. So much cosier than the dining room, don't you think?'

'What are we going to do, Doctor?' Benny had had enough. The Doctor had talked rubbish through the meal, mindless banter, as if they really were sitting down to a family supper in a Victorian house in Kent. Ace had sulked and gnawed savagely at a chicken wing. The Doctor had chastised her for her table manners.

'Do? How about a nice cup of tea? Always nice to have tea to round off a meal.'

'I mean do to get out of here. To find out what this is all about.'

'As for what is going on...' The Doctor's face was suddenly serious. 'I would have thought that was obvious. Our friend Mr Garpol has been stealing properties from all over the galaxy and bringing them here.'

'Why stealing?' asked Ace, more to be difficult than anything else. 'Maybe he bought them?'

'This house has been transported here against its will. I can feel it.'

'You talk about this place as if it was alive.' Benny shuddered. She was an archaeologist. She was trained to deal with dead places.

'Is it haunted?' Ace piped up.

'All houses are haunted in some way, Ace. All places. Things happen, people come and go, places remember.'

'Doctor, how are we going to get out of here?'

'We're not, Benny. This is my house, and I'm not moving. It's pointless, anyway, whilst our all-seeing, all-hearing host wants us to stay.'

'Very sensible, Doctor.' Garpol again. 'I can see you're not the simpleton I first took you for.'

'How are we doing so far?'

'The eating of the meal was excellent, Doctor, although I must say your daughter's table manners leave something to be desired. I feel sure it is not the custom on Earth for young ladies to eat with their feet on the table.'

'Yes, you're right. Take your feet down, Ace.'

Ace swore and let her feet fall heavily to the floor.

'Don't you think it's a little past the young lady's bedtime, Doctor?'

'Bedtime!' That was the last straw. 'Now listen to me, fatso. Meet me outside, just you, without your floating friends, and I'll show you who's a young lady!'

'We can still use replicants, you know.' Garpol's voice was petulant. 'And you know what that means...'

'Come on, Ace,' Benny cut in. 'It doesn't usually take this much persuading to get you into bed.'

'Up yours!'

'Don't you dare speak to your mother like that!' Garpol sounded horrified. 'If I'd spoken to my mother like that...'

Ace's jaw dropped. Her mother!

It was Benny who found her voice first as the implications of Garpol's assumption hit her. 'If you think I'm old enough to –'

'Ace, Benny, calm down.' The Doctor's voice was soothing, but the look on his face was urgent. They both knew that look. This was serious.

'Doctor...' Garpol's voice was trembling with barely controlled fury. 'Put the girl to bed!'

The Doctor let out a leaden breath. 'Ace, go to your room. First door on the left at the top of the stairs.'

Flashing him an angry look, Ace got up and headed for the door.

'I'll come up and read you a story,' he called after her.

Ace had to bite her lip.

She felt a complete prat.

Lying there, blankets up to her chin, striped pyjamas, a teddy bear clutched in one hand.

She had been on the verge of marching back down the stairs and demanding a different room. The walls were covered with cartoon ducks. The paintwork was baby pink. Why the hell did the Doctor have a room in his house done out like a nursery anyway?

And now here he was sitting on the edge of the bed reading to her. The book was *The Lion, the Witch and the Wardrobe*. She remembered it from school. The Doctor had begun, in his lilting tones, to tell the story of a girl, just like her, who went to live in a house just like this one. She wasn't happy there, until she noticed an ornament sitting on the mantelpiece. A magic ornament. The girl took it and used it to pass through a blue door into a magical kingdom.

The Doctor's storytelling voice was hypnotic, and it was a long while before Ace realized that this wasn't *The Lion, the Witch and the Wardrobe* at all. She was about to say something when the Doctor snapped the book shut.

'That's enough for tonight, Ace. It's been a busy day. You must be tired.'

'You must be mad if you think I'm going to sleep...'

'You must be tired, Ace.'

The bastard wouldn't dare. He wouldn't...Already she could feel her eyes closing.

* * *

Benny slumped into the sofa's deep cushions and tried to relax. The Doctor's behaviour was irritating her. No plan, nothing. He had insisted upon going upstairs to read his daughter a bed-time story, assuring Garpol that it was an inviolable Earth tra-dition. Garpol had replied that he would look it up. His voice had returned some minutes later, chortling and sniggering, tell-ing the Doctor to go ahead. It had made Benny feel quite queasy.

In front of Benny yet another real fire raged. The lounge. Baby grand piano (although the only thing she had ever heard the Doctor play was the spoons), an elaborate painting on the wall, eighteenth-century if it was genuine, in a frame so gar-ishly baroque it had to be the real thing. The heavy ornamenta-tion of the room dwarfed the television set in the corner.

The TV was on. She hadn't switched it on. It had just been jabbering at her from the moment she had entered the room. News. One of those endless twentieth-century wars. Tanks fir-ing on peasants in the hills.

'It's good to see you making yourself comfortable, my dear. Such a nice family home.'

Was there nowhere they were free of Garpol's presence?

'Shall we see what's on the other channel?'

Suddenly the tanks and peasants were gone. Suddenly there was a tall man with a prominent, pointed chin and an uncon-vincing hair-piece coaxing and cajoling four overweight, laugh-ing members of the public who were each trying to make some-thing out of dough. They were racing against the clock. They were mostly covered in dough. It never failed to amaze Benny what had passed for entertainment in the centuries before she was born.

'Ah, here you are, Benny,' said the Doctor poking his head around the door.

'A very nice story, Doctor.' Garpol's voice oozed with pride at his latest acquisitions. 'Oh, we are going to have fun here. The public will love you.'

'Look, can't you leave us to spend our... family evening...' –

Benny tried to infuse the words with the contempt she felt – 'in peace?'

'So, Mr Garpol,' said the Doctor, smacking his hands together in anticipation. 'What's the plan for this evening?'

'Oh, your charming wife and I were just watching a little twentieth-century television, Doctor.'

The picture in the corner of the room changed again. A snooker match.

'I have thousands of hours of recordings, Doctor. I find it fascinating the way all human desires, all human needs, are satisfied through that little box.'

'Oh yes,' replied the Doctor, sinking into the sofa, 'it's a marvellous machine. Do you have any *Blind Date*?'

They had watched Cilla, Jeremy, Professor X, Bill Grundy and the Sex Pistols and the 1966 World Cup Final. Benny felt her head starting to spin. The Doctor seemed to be enjoying it all; she would have preferred to spend a bit more time studying each of the snippets of history that Garpol paraded before them. Not this late at night, though. At last, quite involuntarily, she yawned. The Doctor jumped to his feet. 'Come, Mr Garpol, more TV!'

'I think your wife might have watched enough television for one night, Doctor. I think it might be time to proceed with the next part of our programme.' Benny could have sworn the disembodied voice paused for dramatic effect. 'Bed!'

The Doctor shuffled into the room from the *en suite* bathroom. Already in the huge four-poster bed, Benny had to stifle a laugh. Pale blue pyjamas, festooned with red question marks.

'Your own nightwear is hardly edifying, you know,' the Doctor sniped.

It was true. She had been appalled on lifting the pillow to see a pink negligée. By the side of the bed were a pair of pink, fluffy mules.

'Well,' Benny said coyly, 'are you coming to bed?'

An unreadable look on his face, the Time Lord slipped under the covers. As Benny reached across and switched off the light, he whispered, 'Be gentle with me...'

The Mickey Mouse alarm clock managed to announce that morning is the best part of the day twice before it was shattered under a single blow from a child's cricket bat. Ace had never liked mornings. She hadn't liked them in Perivale, she hadn't liked them on Iceworld. Somehow the mornings on board the TARDIS had always seemed like lie-ins, even when she had been dragged from her bed to join the Doctor and Benny on yet another wild-goose chase. Something to do with the ship's relative time, no doubt.

She grimaced. Somehow, being here, being in a house again, being part of a family, albeit Garpol's idea of a family, was bringing old ghosts to the surface, and she didn't like it.

She hauled herself from the bed, her feet curling on the cold wooden floor, and hurled the cricket bat into the toy chest where she had found it. Cat-like, she sniffed the air. From somewhere downstairs, breakfast smells were drifting. They could wait. For the moment all she wanted was a long, hot bath to restore her humanity.

She padded down the hallway and into the bathroom, remembering the last time she had been in the Doctor's house – that business with the boy in the barrel. An age ago.

She turned the taps on and stripped off her pyjamas. She stood for a moment in front of the mirror, looking at herself. The teenage girl from Perivale was long gone. In her place stood a battle-scarred woman, old before her time. For a second Ace wondered what her life might have been like without the intervention of Fenric and the Doctor. A normal life, the life of a London teenager. Then her mother's face swam before her eyes and the thought was gone.

She slipped into the bath, luxuriating in the old-fashioned

sensations. The sonic showers in the TARDIS were no match for this. As she relaxed, she remembered the Doctor's story from the previous night – the ornament on the mantelpiece. What was the cunning old bastard up to?

Downstairs, Benny was not in good shape. She sipped her third coffee of the morning and desperately tried to shake the sleep from her eyes. It had not been a good night. The Doctor had been in bed barely five minutes – five minutes during which he had done nothing but twitch and fidget – before he had leapt to his feet again and paced endlessly around the room, muttering to himself in Gallifreyan. Benny's temper had eventually snapped and she'd told him to stop pacing and come back to bed. The Doctor had duly complied and had immediately fallen into a deep, comalike sleep.

For the rest of the night she had had to put up with the Doctor's constant, and loud snoring. There had been only one point when he had stopped: just as Benny had been on the verge of nodding off, he had suddenly sat bolt upright and shouted, 'But, Brigadier, the Autons are disguised as traffic cones!' Then he had fallen sound asleep again.

Benny had spent the rest of the night awaiting another outburst. It hadn't come, but by the time she eventually got to sleep it had been three in the morning. Four hours later the Doctor had leapt from the bed and vanished downstairs. Benny had tried to get back to sleep, but without success, and had eventually resigned herself to breakfast at what she considered to be the most ungodly hour imaginable. She had now been up for four hours.

She looked up as Ace entered the dining room. The younger woman seemed fresh and invigorated.

'You look very perky.'

Ace grinned. 'A night on my own, what do you expect?'

Benny snorted and returned to her coffee. Ace reached for the pot and poured herself a cup. 'So, do you have anything to tell me?'

Benny looked her in the eye. 'No!'

Ace returned her gaze with wide-eyed innocence. 'Only asking! Where is the Doctor, anyway?'

As if on cue he appeared in the doorway of the kitchen, a frying pan in each hand, a Snoopy apron around his waist. 'Kippers or bacon?'

Ace turned. 'Both!'

'A-ha! A breakfast connoisseur!'

He smiled that unique smile of his and vanished back into the kitchen, reappearing a few seconds later with a plate piled high. The butter from the kippers mingled with the yolks of the eggs; the toast vied for position with the fried bread. Everything that could be eaten for breakfast was on this plate.

He set it down in front of Ace and, sitting himself down, began to smother a single piece of toast with an inordinate amount of marmalade. Benny groaned as Ace tucked into a breakfast that most people would consider inedible. Both of them seemed remarkably calm considering their predicament, and Benny suddenly felt distant from her two companions, the experiences that they had been through before her arrival suddenly very prominent in her thoughts.

Both women watched the Doctor as he proceeded to get marmalade all over his fingers, waiting for him to begin outlining his plan of action, a plan that they both knew he must have. Ace opened her mouth to speak, but the Doctor raised a finger to his lips, sucked the marmalade from it, then solemnly elevated it like a conductor's baton.

On cue, Garpol's fruity tones boomed around the room. 'Good morning, my lovelies! I'm so glad to see you all at breakfast. It's nice that families start the day together.'

The Doctor waved cheerily at nothing in particular. 'Good morning, Mr Garpol. What can we do for you?'

'I'm just letting you know your daily routine. You might as well get used to it now, before we start letting the public in.'

'And what did you have in mind? Long rambling walks in the country? Outings to the seaside? A daily trip around the asteroid by hot air balloon perhaps?'

Garpol chortled theatrically. 'Nothing so wide-ranging, Doctor. I've been doing my research into twentieth-century family life, you see. Ideally I would have liked to have had you washing your car all morning, but I'm afraid that Blint has been woefully inefficient in procuring a motor vehicle for me. He's not very good with anything mechanical, you know. Still, we've come up with a suitable alternative. You shall cut the grass! We've even managed to find an original twentieth-century lawn mower. A Metatraxi that I know thought that it was a weapon, and had it hanging on the wall in his clan hive.'

Ace stopped eating. 'How's the Doctor going to cut the grass when there isn't any grass yet, bog-brain?'

Irritation crept into Garpol's voice. 'He can go through the motions can't he? I've told you, the grass will be here at the end of the month.' He sighed. 'Oh Doctor, I don't envy you having to bring up this impetuous child. Or you Bernice. May I call you Bernice?'

Benny smiled sweetly. 'Certainly. Only my friends call me Benny. What did you have in mind for me today?'

Garpol clapped his hands with glee. 'Oh my dear, all manner of things. Washing up, hoovering, I get quite giddy with the possibilities. You have no idea how well the videos are going to sell!'

Benny bristled. 'If you think for one minute. . .'

The Doctor abandoned his toast and bustled to her side. 'Ah, ah, Benny, one moment.' He looked up. 'And what about Ace?'

'She will join you in the garden, Doctor. You can keep an eye on her whilst she plays.'

The Doctor straightened. 'Good, that's got that sorted out. It looks a little chilly out, Ace. I think you'd better get your jacket.'

Ace made as if to reply, then caught the look in the Doctor's eye. She grinned. 'OK, Dad.' She pushed the debris of her breakfast to the centre of the table and bounded out of the room, heading for the lounge where she had left her combat jacket the previous evening.

The Doctor strolled over to the back door and opened it. He turned to Benny. 'See you later dear. Have something nice ready for lunch.'

The door shut just as one of Benny's pink, furry mules bounced off the frame.

Ace slipped into the lounge, eyes scanning for hidden cameras. She glanced over at the mantelpiece. There was the ornament that the Doctor had mentioned in his bedtime story. A snow-storm. She frowned as she picked it up. Inside was a representation of the Doctor's house. She shook it, watching the snow swirl and settle. How the hell was this going to help? On a wild impulse she rubbed it with her sleeve. Nothing. No genie. No three wishes. No bloody good at all.

'He's really losing his marbles this time.'

She snatched her jacket off the sofa and headed for the front door. She was unsurprised to find several of Garpol's robots lurking at the end of the path. As she walked around the house she could see an unbroken line of them, at five-foot intervals, all around the grounds. Garpol certainly wasn't taking any chances.

She found the Doctor, with his shirt sleeves rolled up, push-ing an antique lawn mower up and down the dusty surface of the asteroid, small stones flying up around his head, a grey cloud slowly settling in his path.

'You really have no idea quite how incredibly stupid you look.'

The Doctor looked hurt. 'Don't be like that Ace, just go and play nicely.' He fixed her with those twinkling grey eyes of his. 'You did get your toys didn't you?'

'Of course. I'm a good girl.' Her voice dropped. 'Though I don't see what bloody good it's going to do.'

The Doctor tapped his nose and Ace sighed. She wasn't going to get any more out of him for the moment. He actually seemed to be enjoying himself. 'Where do you want me to go and "play",then?'

He waved his hand towards the end of the garden. 'Why don't you get your bike out of the shed?'

Ace looked. A reasonably sized shed stood in the shelter of the wall. She turned back to the Doctor but he was off again, halfway across the garden, pointlessly mowing the grit.

She picked up a hefty chunk of rock and threw it at one of the robots, smiling with satisfaction at the metallic thunk that resulted. Some of her frustration vented, she crossed to the shed and tried the door.

The lock was stiff with disuse and the door creaked alarmingly. Ace stepped into the gloom, the smell of compost filling her nostrils. The shed was a mass of flower pots, tools and boxes. She had to admire Garpol. When he said that he had moved everything, he meant everything.

Suddenly something caught her eye. Above her. To her left. A blur of orange. Horns and a taut body. Eyes, and teeth in a grinning mouth. She whirled, a garden fork in her hand in seconds, stabbing at her attacker. There was a soft pop, and the hiss of escaping air. Ace mentally kicked herself. She hurled the fork, and the swiftly deflating space hopper, to the floor. She was too jumpy. Where the hell was this bike?

She pushed a pile of boxes to one side. A low shape, covered with a tarpaulin, stood before her. She pulled at a corner of the sheeting. It slid to the floor like a stage curtain, revealing the most beautiful bike that Ace had ever seen.

A huge smile spread across her face.

'Wicked!'

The Doctor smiled as he heard a low rumble from the far end of the garden. The rumble became a throaty roar and Ace, high on the back of a vintage Harley-Davidson, exploded from the shed in a spray of flower pots and timber. She swung the bike round and gave the Doctor a triumphant wave, then gunned the engine, wheelied through the garden gate and set off across the asteroid's surface.

The astonished robots stood stock still for several seconds. Queries were sent. Orders sent back. With an agitated, metallic chittering, several of them set off in pursuit of Ace, whilst the others closed ranks, camera eyes all firmly centred on the Doctor.

Whistling happily to himself, the Doctor retrieved his jacket from the wall where he had left it and strolled back to the house.

Benny's day had got no better. Since the Doctor and Ace had left, Garpol had proceeded to tell her how famous she was going to be. The videos, the books. He had even tried to entertain her with the idea of a road show. The Doctor, Benny and Ace, the wonders of the modern world. The twentieth-century Earth family. Her already frayed temper had eventually snapped and, using all the twentieth-century expletives that she could muster, she'd told Garpol what he could do with his road show. His voice had faded, shouting to Blint about censorship and video classification.

With nothing better to do, she'd begun to put away the disaster area that had been breakfast. It was then that she'd heard the commotion from outside. She was on the verge of going out, when the door opened and the Doctor stepped into the kitchen, shaking the dust from his shoes. She looked at him quizzically.

'Do I gather that you've found a way to severely piss off our host?'

The Doctor smiled. 'Ace is merely playing on her bike.'

'A bike that just happens to make a noise like the royal beast of Peladon!' Her professional curiosity suddenly took over. 'Just out of interest, what is it?'

'A Harley-Davidson. I bought it several regenerations ago. I always used to like my gadgets.'

Benny shook her head. 'Boys will be boys. I gather that a plan is now underway then?'

Before the Doctor could answer, the door crashed open and a barely restrained Garpol thundered in, with Blint lurking in the shadow of his bulk.

'Doctor! Will you please explain to me just what you think you are doing!'

The Doctor turned, his face a picture of abject apology. 'Mr Garpol. What can I say? It seems that nothing I do can temper the girl's capacity for mischief. You know what teenagers are like.'

Garpol was almost purple with rage. 'No I do not! But I'm beginning to learn!'

He held up the deflated remains of the space hopper. 'Look what she's done! Have you any idea how difficult that will be to replace? Have you?'

He slumped onto a chair, shaking his head in disbelief. Blint patted him on the shoulder. 'Never mind Mr Garpol. I'll get onto our suppliers at once. I'm sure that I'll be able to find a replacement for you.' He paused, then added, 'At not too great a cost.'

Garpol looked up, his expression driving all flippancy from the Doctor's face.

'Hear this, Doctor: if that girl damages one more item in my collection I shall not hesitate to have her filleted and fed to my Stigorax, is that clear?'

The Doctor said nothing, just watched as Garpol pulled his bulk from the chair and turned to the door, ushering Blint out in front of him. 'You are confined to the house until further notice.'

The door slammed.

Benny turned to the Doctor and let out all her pent-up breath in a rush. 'Remind me never to spill red wine on his carpets. What do we do now?'

'How about finding something nice for lunch?'

Benny was incredulous. 'What?'

'Well it is nearly midday. I'll lay the table.'

He trotted out of the room, leaving a speechless Benny staring at the sad, deflated face of a punctured space hopper.

Ace's hair streamed out behind her. She could have whooped with delight. After all the angst that they had been through recently, culminating in that business with the Monk, this was something different. This was what she had joined the Doctor for in the first place. This was fun!

She glanced in the mirror. Behind her, barely visible in the dust of her wake, the pursuing robots were specks. She would be at the TARDIS long before they were even close.

Above her, stars were beginning to show through the clouds with an intensity that would never have been possible on Earth – certainly not in the middle of the day – and the absurdity of the situation struck her. Laughing out loud she pulled back hard on the throttle, and the bike surged forward.

Benny watched as the Doctor bustled around the kitchen. He looked utterly at home. Understandable really; it was his house. She wondered what the Doctor's home – his real home, back on Gallifrey – must have been like. He never talked much about his past, or about his family. He occasionally made reference to a granddaughter, but the implications of that always made Benny feel uncomfortable.

He whirled round, a basin full of potatoes in his hand, catching Benny's eye. She looked away hurriedly, scared that he might ask her what she was thinking. Or, worse still, that he already knew what she was thinking.

'Are you going to help with lunch or not?' he asked.

She snatched the bowl from him. 'Since Ace left, all you've done is lay the table and put a roast in the oven! Is that all we're going to do, eat?'

'No! I thought that we'd get a nice bottle of wine as well.

Hurry up and peel those potatoes and you can come down to the cellar and help me choose one.' He turned away.

Benny was about to hurl one of the potatoes at the back of his head, then the thought of what the Doctor's wine cellar might be like filled her imagination. Lunch was beginning to sound like a good proposition after all.

Ace pulled the bike to a sudden stop, the back wheel skidding round, sending clouds of dust into the star-filled sky.

'Shit!'

The TARDIS was gone. The only indication that it had ever been there at all was a perfectly square patch of flattened dust.

Ace's heart sank. Whatever the Doctor's plan was, it had been going well up until now. She glanced round. The robots were nearly on her. If she was going to escape she had to go now. She stopped. Go where? That moment's hesitation was enough. Suddenly there were robots all around her, hemming her in. She braced herself as the robot nudged against her.

'Please Keep off the Grass'

No shock. No indication that it was going to harm her at all.

'Please Keep to the Designated Path.'

The robot shepherded her towards a vague track in the dust. The circle of robots parted as she wheeled the bike onto it. As soon as she was on the rough pathway, the robots began to disperse. Ace smiled. That stupid git Garpol hadn't changed their programme. They were still operating under their old orders – keeping people off the grass and on the designated paths. And if they were still programmed to help visitors...

'Oi! Tin head!' The nearest robot spun, and drifted slowly back to her. 'Where would a girl go to see a police box around here?'

'Please Consult a Guide Book for a Listing of All Exhibits.'

'I haven't got a guide book, you metallic moron.'

'All Curator Robots are Stocked with Guide Books. If Your Particular Robot is out of Stock, Please Contact the Ticket Office.'

Ace studied the squat metallic shape in front of her. 'All curator robots are stocked with guide books, are they?' She peered at it more closely. This one had a name. A badge with *Hi, I'm Baz, How Can I Help?* hung next to the red button. The button... She pressed it.

With a satisfying whirr of machinery, a glossy, laminated sheet slid out of a slot in the robot's casing and into Ace's hand. It was a map of all the exhibits in Garpol's exhibition. Ace scanned it for any indication as to where he might have put a police box. She smiled. The Doctor's plan might work yet.

'OK, Baz, take me to Trafalgar Square.'

Benny was in seventh heaven. After she had peeled what seemed like an endless supply of potatoes, the Doctor had led her through the house to a door under the stairs. Unlocking it with a great key from his pocket, he had led her down into the Stygian gloom.

There had been a moment of panic when she had suddenly lost her grip on the Doctor's hand, but seconds later there had been the click of a light switch and Benny's archaeological taste buds had gone into spasm.

The Doctor's wine cellar was huge. Not only huge, but full! The first bottle that she had lifted out had dated back as far as the Crusades. Every rack that she had examined had been simply packed with drinkable history. Earth had come off best of all, with wines from every conceivable century represented in the collection; but in the few minutes that she had been here she had also discovered an entire rack devoted to the wines of Ribos, another to the Champagnes of Manussa and a shelf stacked high with every single brand of Ogron ale.

She picked up a bottle and examined it more closely. 'For a man who doesn't drink much, you've got bloody good taste!'

The Doctor smiled. 'I entertain a lot. Come on.' He gestured to a barrel-lined corridor. 'Lets see how Ace is doing.'

Before Benny could question him, he had vanished into the gloom. Benny followed, clinging onto the bottle as if it was a child and promising herself that when all this was over she would spend some time down here. About a year.

'What!' Behind his huge imitation mahogany desk, Garpol's four-hundred-pound frame was shaking with rage. 'And those stupid machines are showing her the way?'

Blint was shuffling through the sheaf of papers attached to his clipboard. It was what he always did when he was nervous, which was most of the time. 'It . . . it's what they're pro-grammed to do, Mr Garpol.

'You must stop them, Blint!'

'It's not that easy, Mr Garpol. There are procedures. We can't just reprogram the guide robots. We have to call an accredited service engineer. Otherwise we lose our warranty.'

'I've had enough of this, Blint.' Garpol's hand slammed down on the authentically grained desktop. 'We shall use the Group Five Security Robots.'

Pale as he already was, Blint seemed to turn several shades paler. 'But . . . but . . . they're not tested yet, Mr Garpol. They're not even unpacked.'

'Then this will be the perfect opportunity to test them.'

Ace's admiration for Garpol went up by several million points. There, in front of her, sitting incongruously in the middle of a crater, was Nelson's Column. Not just the column, but the li-ons, the fountains and, to one side, a police box.

She patted her attendant robot on the head. 'Thanks, Baz, this is where I want to be.'

The robot chirruped, happily. 'Glad to be of Service. Please Keep to the Designated Paths.' With that it floated off.

Ace revved the engine, and set off towards the waiting TARDIS. As she approached, she eyed a small, incongruous bit of technology that she had noticed affixed to the handlebars. A single switch marked *Doors*. She pressed it. In front of her the doors of the TARDIS swung open and, with a squeal of tyres, Ace steered the Harley straight through the void and into the console room.

She dismounted, parking the bike next to the hat stand. She liked the look of the bike in the TARDIS. She would have to talk to the Doctor about keeping it.

Now then. She fumbled in her pocket and removed the snow-storm, then circled the console, scanning the lively surface. There. An indentation. An indentation into which the base of the snowstorm would fit perfectly. An indentation which hadn't been there before. Ace scowled. Typical. The TARDIS was as bad as the Doctor.

She reached out and placed the ornament into the space. It was immediately snatched from her grasp, locking tight onto the surface of the console. The room began to grow dim, and the familiar hum of the instruments dropped in pitch alarm-ingly.

'Oh shit!'

Ace scrabbled desperately at the snowstorm, trying to re-trieve it from the panel, but the console seemed to draw it into itself. Her fingers slipped uselessly on the glass dome. The snow began to swirl furiously, an inner light illuminating the orna-ment. The room itself continued to get darker, until the only source of light came from the dancing, flickering snowstorm.

Ace tucked herself into a corner and waited.

Benny and the Doctor had been walking for a long time. Much longer in fact than should have been possible in the cellar. Bar-rels lined the walls. Benny had given up trying to memorize the contents. She tapped the Doctor on the shoulder.

'Is it my imagination or is this house not quite as it seems?'

The Doctor smiled. 'You should know by now that nothing is ever quite as it seems.'

'So, am I right in assuming that this house is, in fact, another

TARDIS?'

The Doctor stopped dead. 'Good grief, no! I couldn't possibly own more than one. They get terribly jealous, you know. Lets just say that the house may have picked up a few tricks over the years. Come on, I think we're nearly there.'

He set off down another aisle. Benny looked around her. The barrels had slowly petered out, to be replaced by a circular motif that was very familiar. Very familiar indeed.

'It's back to plan A,' Garpol had said. 'Replicants, Mr Blint. Dispatch the Group Five Security Robots to eliminate the Terrans.' Then he had had a thought. 'No, on second thoughts, I'll do it myself. I want to see this. You may accompany me.'

Now Garpol was sincerely wishing that he was somewhere else. This was the first time that he had set eyes on the Group Five Security Robots; they had arrived only a day or two before, and had still been in their carrying crates. He had been impressed as they had glided out of their packaged darkness. They had looked as if they meant business. No hint of a helpful, smiling face in the arrangement of their various parts; no shiny red button or guide-book-dispensing slot; and definitely no badge saying *Hi, I'm Baz*. They were squatter and heavier than the guide robots, and each had what was obviously a high-calibre gun fitted to the front. Even the low droning sound that they made as they flew seemed designed to impress and intimidate. He had rubbed his hands with malicious glee as he had pictured the robots closing in on those wretched humans.

The only trouble was, they didn't work. They kept bumping into each other, firing high-velocity shells at random over the horizon. They had already blown apart the Pavilion of the Summer Winds from Tara. By the time they reached Exhibit Nineteen, the Doctor's house, Garpol was resigned to the inevitable. He had hoped to preserve the exhibit – fine example of the period as it was – and merely watch its occupants die slowly. This was clearly not an option now. Very well, let the robots have their head. The house must go along with its owner.

It was directly in front of them. Garpol had changed his customary pinstripe for something of a more military cut – a dull khaki, brass buttons, what looked like gold scrubbing brushes on the shoulders and length upon length of lanyard trailing beneath his fat arms. Blint was buried in something equally gaudy. Garpol threw his hand forward in a vaguely military motion and the convoy – the general, his lieutenant and a cohort of floating, droning metal – proceeded downhill towards their target.

They got about ten yards.

Suddenly it was chaos. A savage wind was howling around them, cold and vicious. It snatched off Garpol's hat. It almost blew Blint off his feet. A savage wind and, carried on it, a thick blanket of swirling, driving snow. Snow; something never before seen in the Ararax system. The wind sent the security robots cannoning into one another like skittles; the snow blinded them, clogged up their guidance systems, causing them to spin like tops. One fired a projectile. It hit another. The resulting explosion destroyed two more.

Garpol was barking out orders, his voice lost in the gale. Blint was chasing the flying sheaves of paper that the wind had snatched from his clipboard and sent dancing across the asteroid's grey surface. The robots waltzed in chaos.

Lost in the shadows of the dim TARDIS control room, the door that led into the guts of the ship silently opened. Ace leapt to her feet, cursing herself for allowing her mind to wander.

'It's all right, Ace. It's only us.'

The Doctor and Benny emerged from the twilit corridor. Benny had a faraway look in her eyes. Cradled in her arms was a dusty, dark red wine bottle.

'Very well done, Ace.' The Doctor clapped her hand between his and shook it heartily.

'What exactly did I do?'

'Created a dimensionally transcendental corridor between

the service levels of the TARDIS and the wine cellar in the house. Simple really.' He peered at the raging snowstorm. 'It does tend to disturb the atmosphere a bit though.' He reached across the hexagonal console and pressed hard on the glass dome. It sprang up and out from amongst the controls. 'There we are,' he said. 'Popomatic.' The hum of the control room rose again to its normal pitch. The room was once more brightly lit. He pocketed the little ornament. 'That should stop anyone following us. Now...' He flicked through a familiar sequence of switches. The time rotor at the centre of the console began to rise and fall.

The storm ended just as quickly and inexplicably as it had begun. The wind, the snow, all seemed to vanish. Garpol looked around him. Blint was still scrabbling around for his errant papers. Only three robots remained. The others had either crashed into each other or blown themselves up. No matter; three would be enough.

'Forward!' the fat commander shouted. He began the fatal march on the house, with the three robots moving in an erratic line behind him.

Blint, buried in paper, brought up the rear, forlornly murmuring, 'My schedule...'

Those humans would rue the... Garpol stopped. That sound. It resembled his own digestive system after a particularly heavy meal. For a moment his hands clutched at his gut, until he realized that the noise was actually coming from the house. The air in front of them seemed to shimmer; there was a hint of a flashing white light; the sound ended with a sudden dull clunk.

The house was gone. In its place stood a rectangular blue box.

'Not bad, if I do say so myself. Quite a tricky landing.'

The Doctor tapped at a button and the TARDIS view screen glowed into life. Red, going on purple, the image that filled the screen was that of the globular cheeks and popping eyes of their former host. He looked about to explode.

A second tap, and the screen went dead.

'Hmm. We don't really want to look at that before we eat.' The Doctor's hands were a blur on the console. The time rotor started moving again. 'Right... Home!'

'Doctor?' Benny was hovering at his shoulder. Ace, uninterested, was squatting in front of the bike, her hands already covered in oil.

'I've materialized around the house, Benny. Now we're going to put it back where it belongs. Have you never heard the expression, "Wherever I lay my house, that's my home"?'

'Uh...' Benny hadn't.

'No? How about "Home is where the house is"?'

'Doctor, what about all those other buildings? What about that pair of crooks?'

'Ah yes. Remind me to send a message to the Braxiatel Heritage Trust. I'm on the Board of Governors, you know. Irving can sort this mess out. What our friend Mr Garpol is doing is quite illegal. The trust will prosecute him and return all the buildings to their proper places. They're very hot on this sort of thing.'

He turned to the crouched figure of Ace. 'Ace, don't make a mess in here. And wash your hands before lunch, will you?'

'Lunch?' Benny was surprised. Mealtimes in the TARDIS were usually sporadic affairs.

'I think it should be ready by now, don't you? Come along, Ace.'

The Doctor disappeared back through the door into the ship's interior. Benny followed, smiling to herself, her fingers tapping lightly on the wine bottle she still carried. Excellent; she would have a chance to sample this superb vintage in a proper setting. Grumbling and rubbing her filthy hands on her trousers, Ace followed.

* * *

It always amazed his companions how the Doctor knew his way around the ship. To Ace and Benny, the corridors seemed endless and virtually identical. This was a relatively short journey. The Doctor stopped at a small door set unobtrusively on a corner. Probably a cupboard, Ace thought. A wardrobe or something. The door swung open at the Doctor's gentle push. The light coming through it was wrong, somehow. Too bright. Too... real.

It was daylight. A gentle breeze. The sound of faraway birds. An English country garden.

'I was right,' said Ace, more or less to herself. 'It was a wardrobe. Magic!'

In front of them sat the house. Around it, immaculately laid out, were lawns, flowerbeds and conifers cut into tall, elegant cones. Their feet crunched on washed gravel as they walked towards the front door.

The Doctor stopped, suddenly alert. He sniffed at something on the air. A look of barely controlled panic crossed his face. 'No,' he muttered. 'Oh no!'

His feet began to beat on the gravel as he ran forward, clutching his battered hat to his head. 'The roast..!' he bellowed as he flung himself through the door.

Ace looked at Benny, Benny looked at Ace. A smile flickered between them.

'Miss Summerfield,' said Ace, extending her arm to her friend, 'shall we go in to dinner?